FORCE
OF ATTRACTION

D.D. Ayres

St. Martin's Paperbacks

This is a work of fiction. All of the characters, organizations, and events portrayed in this novel are either products of the author's imagination or are used fictitiously.

FORCE OF ATTRACTION

For information address St. Martin's Press, 175 Fifth Avenue, New York, NY 10010.

ISBN: 978-1-250-04218-7

Printed in the United States of America

St. Martin's Paperbacks edition / April 2015

St. Martin's Paperbacks are published by St. Martin's Press, 175 Fifth Avenue, New York, NY 10010.

10 9 8 7 6 5 4 3 2 1

My husband, Chris, who lives with a writer and still maintains I'm a good deal.

ACKNOWLEDGMENTS

Happy to spotlight those who help make this K-9 series work. I couldn't do it nearly as well without you.

My K-9 law enforcement expert for the entire series, Brad Thompson, a true dog man. He's a twenty-nine-year veteran police officer, former senior handler and instructor/trainer of the FWPD K9 Unit, now investigator with the Fort Worth Police Department. The things I got right I owe to him. The things I got wrong are all on me, or a bit of literary license. Great instructor. Nice guy.

Let me add, the Dog Agility competition as a backdrop for puppy drug mules is purely my imagination at work. Terrific people and wonderful animals participate.

Scott Silverii, Chief of Police of Thibodaux, LA. A veteran law enforcement officer of twenty-plus years, he spent sixteen years in SOG's undercover narcotics task force and SWAT. A PhD, Scott wrote *A Darker Shade of Blue* about SOG culture. Our conversations helped me shape the real-life consequences of a law enforcement agent going undercover, and how and why some never come back. Now he's writing fiction, too. Best of luck.

Richard and Kimberly Wilson of "Peace Bouviers" who own Marko, the dog my fictional Hugo is fashioned after. Their friends, Lee and Dave Young, Ron and Cora Wilkinson, Erica and C.J. Westmoreland, Ana Rodriquez and family, who invited me to a Bouvier Day in the Park. Erica, your photography rocks.

My editor Rose Hilliard. She sees no obstacles, only opportunities to make it better.

My daughter Theresa, who helps me plot when I'm stuck and reads for me.

My daughter-in-law Kimberly, who designed my website.

As always, my agent Denise Marcil. You're the best!

PROLOGUE

Scott Lucca fumbled in his pocket, looking for change for the pay phone as the twang of a guitar solo wailed through the hazy bar. He was a little buzzed. When liquor got between his head and his heart, he made stupid decisions. That's why he didn't drink to excess anymore. But this was a special occasion. At least he had the presence of mind not to use his cell phone.

He thrust the coins into the pay phone slot and stabbed her number into the keypad.

One ring. *Two. Three.* It was not quite four A.M., East Coast time. Was she out? Out with someone else? *Five.*

"Yes?" It was her. One syllable, and he was cradling the phone a little tighter.

A foolish smile tugged his mouth. "Hey. I was just . . . thinking." He hadn't thought past the need to hear her voice.

"Who is this?"

He leaned his head against the wall. Who was he? Good question. "I—sorry. Wrong number."

"Scott?"

He halted the receiver halfway to its cradle. Two years since they last spoke, and she still remembered the sound of his voice. That had to count for something. But he had nothing else to offer her.

Gritting his teeth, he completed the hang-up.

"Hey there, handsome. You wanna dance with me?"

He turned toward the voice. A young woman in a cowboy hat and not much else stood beside him with a sly smile.

He smiled back but shook his head. "You deserve better than what's on my mind."

"Depends on what that is."

He gave her a slow grin. "My wife."

Her mouth twisted down. "Your loss."

"No doubt about it. You have a good evening."

Scott made his way back to his table without further incident. He was a long way from home, on his way back from drug interdiction training in west Texas. Instead of hightailing it back to D.C., he'd decided to take the scenic route, trading the expediency of interstates for country roads that led through one declining weed-choked Southern town after another. For the most part the drive was boring, and that was the purpose. He needed to think. About his life. Past. Future. Hell, everything!

A thousand miles later, he'd come to no conclusions other than that thinking was overrated.

On the other hand, he still understood physical needs. It was late. He was hungry. That's when he'd passed this roadside inn with a flashing neon sign, promising beer and music. They probably also sold food.

A quick scan of the customers had revealed they were locals, a few still dressed in their uniforms from the chicken plucking plant he'd passed driving in. The air was pungent, thick with the natural humidity of a Southern July night and the heat of bodies packed close together.

He had meant only to stop for a burger. But halfway through his meal, a man with a guitar had stepped up to the lone mike at one end of the room to offer up his version of Al Greene's "Love and Happiness." It was the song they'd chosen for the first dance at their wedding reception.

He'd heard it probably a hundred times since but it never clutched and clawed at him like this rendition. That's when he remembered. Today should have been their fourth anniversary.

It had been a dumb move but he couldn't help himself. He closed his eyes to let his mind drift back to a time when the mere sight of Nicole Jamieson made his skin catch fire and his dick so hard he had to pause in his stride.

After a few seconds he could almost feel his bride in his arms again. He saw in his mind's eye her lopsided smile of happiness that trembled with the audacity of what they'd just done. Above it all was that look of trust in her wide green gaze.

Her eyes on him. That's all it took. He'd known from that first glance. She did, too. The force of attraction was undeniable. Insoluble. Magnetic. Meant to be.

Maybe that was because she'd kissed him before they had even exchanged a word. In answer to that kiss, he'd dragged her out on the dance floor and hauled her in against him to do a slow grind that left the other patrons of the D.C. law enforcement hangout feeling like maybe they should go home and give the couple some privacy.

Their sixty-day courtship contained every idiotic love cliché in overdrive.

When it went to hell, the explosion had left craters in more lives than their own.

A hailstorm of darker memories had struck him so hard Scott had had to open his eyes to keep from drifting away to the ugly place that he had fought too long and too hard to come back from.

When the song was over, he'd bought a beer, to celebrate his return to the human condition. And then another. Suddenly, making that phone call hadn't seemed like the sorry-ass loser idea it was.

Why the hell did I just let her go?

Scott stared at his empty plate as if it were a Ouija board. Two years later he still didn't have the answer. What he did know was that he didn't deserve Nikki. No surprise there. From that very first night, in the back of his mind, he had known it was just a matter of time before she realized that, too. He had never been able to live up to anyone's expectations, not his family's nor even his own. He simply wished on everything holy that Nikki had discovered that truth about him another way. She deserved so much better than the way it went down.

Scott winced. Nikki not only left him, she had left the D.C. police force. That was a real shock. She was good, had great instincts, and a way with the public he'd never had. She'd have quickly climbed the ranks, if she hadn't wrecked her career by running from him.

So when he'd learned, purely by accident a few months ago, that she had become a Montgomery County, Maryland, police K-9 officer, he'd done a little digging until he came up with an address and phone number for her. He'd told himself he'd never use either. He just needed to know where she was. Just that. Until he could make amends.

Now he'd gone and stirred up a hornet's nest by calling her.

Scott.

That's all it took, the sound of his name in her voice. The longing had flooded back, nearly bending him double with regret and desire. Things he could—should—do nothing about. Not that that was going to stop him. He owed her. Some things he couldn't change. Other things he was going to try to make up for.

He reached for the fresh beer the bar girl set before him and tried to empty it in a single swallow. It was like swallowing glass. He'd made that call to prove something. He'd learned something else. Something that presented a real danger to his plans.

He was still in love with her.

An hour later, as he crossed the parking lot with the intention of sleeping off the beer in his truck, Scott felt the sudden tingle of approaching danger without even a visual cue.

It came as the distinctive sound of approaching Harleys, identified before seeing the bikes. The pipes were ugly. Loud and percussive, they announced riders whose most gentle thought about the general populace was that they would all go deaf. These were one-percenters.

From one second to the next, Scott went from slightly buzzed to stone-cold sober. Because he knew his life might depend on it.

As a pair of bikers came roaring up the two-lane blacktop out of the darkness, Scott did a quick mental survey of his situation. A pancake holster holding a SIG P239 fit snug in the small of his back. A .38 was strapped above an ankle. A sheathed Ka-Bar strapped to the other. Enough, maybe.

This wasn't his first encounter with bikers on this trip. That's why he was armed with more than a handgun. A cop knew there was always the chance that some criminal out there somewhere would recognize him, and maybe held a grudge. Paranoia was a good state of mind for a cop. It was crucial for a former undercover narc. Tonight he was dressed as a civilian and would act as one, unless provoked to do otherwise.

He didn't make direct eye contact as they rolled to a stop, blocking his way just for the hell of it, but his adrenaline kicked up a notch. Always before they had kept their distance. His peripheral vision gave him the general outline of biker gear, complete with insignias of a gang he knew all too well from his bad old days.

"This shithole serve decent burgers?" The big overly muscled one of the two bikers had a voice as tender as boot leather.

Scott shrugged. "If you like grease and dill pickles."

"What about the waitresses? Any got tits worth lookin' at?"

Scott smiled slightly. "One."

Alert to any sudden movement, Scott waited out the beat of silence as they dismounted. When they moved to walk around him, one on either side, he sidestepped, giving them enough room to walk past him together. They didn't force the issue.

The bigger man was five feet past when he paused and looked back. "You're a cop."

Scott's gaze corrected to direct confrontation. The challenger was a stranger but he knew the other one. Impossible not to remember a man so skinny his skin seemed shrink-wrapped to his skeletal frame. This man regarded him with a squint-eyed stare. Scott met and held it.

Three years ago he'd gone undercover to infiltrate a chapter of the Pagans, operating out of D.C. He had looked much different back then, a skinhead with a steroid-enhanced body. Nearly a year off the juice, his once-bulked-up physicality had been slimmed by thirty pounds to a taut, lean-muscled physique. His hair had grown in and his once bristling beard was shaved to a smooth cheek. No casual glance should have pegged him for his alter ego, who had been arrested in a bust that went sideways two years ago.

Yet, his gut told him he'd been made. Nothing to do but tough it out.

The skinny man stepped forward. "What the fuck you starin' at?"

Scott braced himself, all cop in his expression and stance. "I was wondering the same thing. I don't know who you think I am, but you're mistaken. I have no beef with you."

The bulkier partner shook his head. "What the fuck are you dicking around with him for? I'm hungry."

His partner glared. "He reminds me of someone."

"The pretty boy about to piss himself?" The bigger man snorted. "What? He a former bitch of yours from lockup?"

The skinny man swung around on his friend. "Shut the fuck up!"

The larger man didn't answer but just swung a meaty fist that landed hard on his companion's jaw.

Scott took the moment to put more distance between himself and them, though he remained facing them. He'd seen many a fight between friends in the biker world end in near death. Or, they could just as easily turn on him.

His gut tightened as he went through in his mind what his next three moves should be. He might get wet but he had an advantage they weren't aware of.

At that moment several patrons exited the establishment, spilling light, music, and laughter onto the parking lot.

The two bikers scuffled a bit more and then laughed, slapped each other on the back, and turned toward the restaurant.

Scott waited until they had entered before sucking in a breath of relief. It was short-lived. Now that he could think past the next thirty seconds, his brain supplied the details he hadn't had time to deal with.

The skinny guy called himself Dos Equis because of his fondness for using a knife to carve double *X*s in his victims. From the West Coast, he'd said. Once he'd attached

himself to the group Scott had infiltrated, the gang short-
ened it to X.

What the hell was he doing in Georgia? Last he heard,
X was serving a five-year prison term.

Scott made his way with a deliberate stride toward his
vehicle and in one continuous motion climbed in. He was
immediately accosted.

A four-year-old chocolate Lab named Izzy had launched
herself through the door of her cage in back and landed in
his lap. His K-9 partner, and secret weapon. There was a
button on his belt that would have freed her from her cage
if she'd been needed.

She was shivering beneath her shiny coat and he understood immediately that she had not only been watching the
scenario taking place in the parking lot, she had sensed
his own anxiety and was responding in kind. She was
trained as a drug dog, not an attack dog, but he knew she
would have come to his aid.

He pulled her in close to his body though he was shed-
ding pheromones, adding to the excitement even though the
moment of danger seemed past. K-9 partners for the past
year, he and Izzy worked drug enforcement for the DEA.

"Good girl, Izzy." He stroked her firmly to calm her.
"Gute Hund."

During all this, his gaze never left the front door of the
restaurant. When Izzy was sufficiently calm, he ordered
her into the back. Then he reached under his console and
pulled out a SIG Sauer and laid it in his lap.

He debated only a moment. He shouldn't be driving. He
had planned to spend the night in the parking lot. But he
knew it would be too much provocation if the bikers found
him still here when they came out. He'd move a few miles
down the road, cautiously and opposite from the way they'd
come, and find a safe place to sleep off his now dead but
legally still active buzz.

He put his cruiser in gear and roared out of the parking lot. If they were going to come after him, he'd be ready.

"You plan on being shit for company all night?"

X didn't reply to his companion. He hated conversation. Right now, he needed to think, hard.

Rhino was the guy's biker name. Hollywood action-hero made-up shit. But weren't all their names? Now he knew Rhino was a cop. Probably a narc.

Undercover narc.

He hadn't spent the previous five years of his life eating shit and living like a coyote to lose it all to a city kitty rookie with a hard-on for his first bust. He owed that prick.

X stared half interestedly at the young woman over by the bar in a cowboy hat, as a plan formed. "I got the license plate. All I need is an address, and a little time."

His partner shifted uncomfortably. "We're seeing our way into some real cash for a change. Don't need no cop-killer bounty on our heads."

"I don't plan on killing him."

"What then?"

X smiled and it was like watching a corpse come to life.

CHAPTER ONE

"Here you go. One good bite deserves another."

K-9 Officer Nicole "Cole" Jamieson placed the doggy bowl on her kitchen floor.

Her partner, Hugo, greedily gulped down the first of his two daily meals then checked her out with a hopeful stare from soulful black eyes.

Cole shook her head. "No more for now."

Hugo's ears drooped as he came forward and nudged his big heavy head under her hand.

Cole squatted down and scratched under his chin and then behind his ears. "Okay. You've earned it. But only one." She stood and reached for the jar of dog treats she kept handy for special occasions.

Hugo scarfed down the treat without even bothering to chew then jumped up against her, huge paws resting above her waist, to deliver a lick of thanks before turning toward the spacious dog kennel in Cole's kitchen. Before he went in he looked back at her. She waited. Bouviers liked to think about things before they acted. When satisfied by whatever his doggy instincts were telling him, Hugo barked gruffly once and entered his crate.

The Montgomery County Police Department wasn't initially impressed by her choice of a Bouvier des Flandres over the more popular law enforcement canine choices such as Belgian Malinois or German shepherd. But research backed her up when she had gone on the hunt for a self-motivated, hard-driving, even-tempered pup. When she'd found the six-month-old black brindled Bouvier with uncut ears but docked tail, he'd looked like a fuzzy puppy-faced teddy bear. But as he grew, he morphed into a powerfully built canine with an intimidating bark and a menacing set of teeth. Topping out at ninety-five pounds, Hugo was now a force to be reckoned with.

Cole yawned and reached into the fridge for a sports beverage and drank from the bottle. Usually she went straight to bed after a night shift. Today, she didn't even have time to take a nap.

She glanced at the clock. Seven A.M. She had a job interview in Baltimore at ten A.M.

"Damn! I'm going to be late!"

She hurried toward the shower.

This is big. That's the only hint her K-9 sergeant had given her when he told her about the interview. When the Drug Enforcement Administration approached local law enforcement agencies for manpower, it usually involved mounting a task force.

Visions of covert operations, undercover, and SWAT team takedowns danced through Cole's thoughts, none of which calmed her nerves.

Forty-five minutes later, she came tearing back through the kitchen in full dress uniform. Her blue shirt and trousers had been professionally pressed, all starchy crispness and sharp pleats. Her boots reflected back the ceiling lights as stars. But her expression was anything but self-possessed professional as she lifted one end of a sofa cushion and then another. She was fretting over the possibility of being late.

"I just had them. I know—" She stopped talking to herself and turned back toward the kitchen, propping a fist on each hip. "Hugo. Come here."

Moments later a big black shaggy head with a pink tongue appeared in the doorway.

"Where are my keys? Bring me my keys. Now."

The big head disappeared. Twenty seconds later all of Hugo reappeared with keys hanging from his mouth.

Cole shook her head even as she made a come-here motion with her hand. "Hand them over."

Hugo trotted over and put them in the palm of her hand, black eyes shining with pride. He sat and barked, ready to be praised.

The only thing wrong with this picture of doggy obedience was that Hugo had hidden them in the first place. The game he'd made up himself usually amused her. Not today. That's because she knew that he knew she was about to leave him alone for hours, and he didn't like to be left. She couldn't account for his sixth sense about such things. He was scary smart at reading people, especially his handler.

She shook her head. "Maybe you should be going to this interview instead of me."

Cole sat stiffly on one of several chairs placed at intervals along the hallway of the Baltimore office of the Drug Enforcement Administration, waiting for her name to be called.

All of her tactical gear had been left behind at security, making her feel unusually light. She looked cool and professional, but she didn't feel that way. Her tie felt as if it was a hangman's noose. Her starched collar rubbed the back of her neck. And, where her hat sat on her brow, a thin sheen of sweat had begun to form. Normally she didn't wear much makeup. But today, she had applied a heavy-duty concealer to try to hide the worst of the black eye she had gotten while subduing a suspect a week ago.

"Officer Jamieson?"

Cole jumped to her feet at the sound of her name. She hadn't even noticed the door opening on her right.

A youngish man in a tie and rolled shirtsleeves gave her a brief impersonal smile. "Follow me please, ma'am."

He moved down past half a dozen closed doors until he arrived at the last one on the right. He knocked then opened the door. "Agent Lattimore will see you now."

Cole stepped into the room to be met by a tall, middle-aged, balding man in a nondescript off-the-rack suit. He had Fed written all over him.

He came forward and extended his hand. "Officer Jamieson. I'm Agent John Lattimore. It's a pleasure to meet you."

"The same, sir." Cole shook his hand firmly.

"Have a seat. And please make yourself comfortable. We aren't being formal today. I understand you go by the name Cole. May I call you that?"

"Yes, sir." She felt his gaze, though seemingly casual, following her every move as she sat and removed her hat, balancing it on her knee.

He sauntered back behind his desk, his gaze never leaving her. "I'm sure you're wondering why you're here."

"Yes, sir." Cole made herself relax back into her chair. "I expect you're looking for local personnel for some sort of team." He nodded. "Would you like me to tell you a little bit about myself?"

"Not necessary. I know everything I need to know."

Cole saw him glance at the open folder on his desk. "You're a first-year K-9 officer with the Montgomery County, Maryland, Police Department. You grew up around dogs. Your first canines were a yellow Lab named Homer and a Bluetick Coonhound by the name of Marge. You were athletic in high school. Played soccer, correct? You also participated in dog sports competitions. Your college transcript is well above average and yet, after you were waitlisted for law school, you joined law enforcement. Your background in Agility training and AKC rallies made you a natural fit for the K-9 law enforcement program. You have one sibling, a sister named Rebecca, who's a veterinarian. From time to time you still serve as an instructor for her obedience classes."

"Wow, sir, that is a thorough investigation." Someone had done his homework on her. Which meant DEA had been thinking about her longer than a few days.

Cole wondered fleetingly what else was in that report. Did they know she needed to do laundry and sometimes failed to remember to put out her trash cans in time for the weekly pickup? Did they know about more private things, like her marriage to undercover Agent Scott Lucca, and what a disaster that had been? Of course they would.

That's when reality hit her. This wasn't just an interview. It was more like a security clearance check.

Her pulse ticked up with equal amounts of excitement and anxiety. Was she being considered for some kind of task force? Or was Scott in trouble again? Were they looking to her for information about him? Had the two-year-old case made its way to court, after all?

Her heart began to pump in heavy thuds. She wasn't going to defend him but she couldn't imagine testifying in any way against Scott, even if he was her ex.

At that moment the door opened and the young man in rolled shirtsleeves appeared. "Your next appointment has arrived, sir."

"Good." Lattimore smiled at Cole. "I'd like you to meet the team leader and your potential partner in our task force operation."

"Great." *Task force operation.* Not about Scott. This was about her, after all.

Cole stood up, preparing a smile of welcome for whomever stood on the other side of the door. Perhaps she was doing better in the interview than she thought, if Lattimore was prepared to introduce her to the team leader.

"Show him in, Pierce."

One second, Cole was rising with a polite smile of welcome on her face. The very next, she was trying to control her breathing.

"Hello, Nikki."

She knew that voice. That face. And those damned seductive dimples.

It wasn't supposed to happen like this.

For two years, she had engineered things so that she would never again have to be in the same room with Scott Lucca. That plan had been working just fine, right up to a second ago.

CHAPTER TWO

"Come in, Agent Lucca."

While Lattimore shook Scott's hand, Cole gave in to the dozen conflicting emotions surging past her defenses. She was a police officer. She knew how to take care of herself in tense and dangerous situations. Yet, she had no idea of how to handle her reaction to this man.

He seemed taller. Or maybe it was his hair. He was no longer a skinhead, only one of the things she had hated about his undercover persona. His dark hair grew thick and tousled, as if he'd been riding his Harley without a helmet. God, how that habit had worried her. And he'd lost that prison-time, balloon-muscle physique he had deliberately cultivated their last few months together. The body beneath his dress shirt and trousers was leaner, more sinewy. Like his face.

Something inside Cole twisted with painful longing. He looked as dangerous and wild as the night they'd met.

The last time she saw him—two years, three weeks, and one huge heartache ago—he was being detained for public lewdness and suspected drug possession, and she was one of the arresting officers. Now she was being confronted with—

Task force leader?

"I don't suppose introductions are necessary, in this instance."

"No, sir." Cole turned back to Lattimore while her mind and body continued to react to her ex's surprise appearance in so many ways she couldn't keep up. Even worse, some of the sensations were more pleasurable than they had any right to be. That was a very bad sign.

She felt Scott move to stand behind her. "Officer Jamieson and I go way back. At least there won't be any awkward getting-to-know-you period for us."

Cole shifted uneasily as Scott spoke. He gave off the kind of sexual energy women craved and other men envied. She felt it now, a vibe she knew too well. It said, *Pay attention, danger here.*

Cole focused her attention on Lattimore though she could feel Scott's gaze on her back like radiant heat from a fire. "Sir, Agent Lucca and I are—were—we're divorced."

"So I've been informed." Lattimore's knowing gaze moved back and forth between them. "That's not a problem, is it?"

"That depends." Cole felt the embers of anger stir within her as she turned fully to confront her ex. "Why is he here?"

"We're going to be working together." Scott hadn't moved and he didn't smile. Yet, for a moment, it seemed as if his aloof tough-guy expression shifted as he stared at her.

Once she thought she'd seen the full measure of her worth in his sea-green gaze. That's why it hurt so much when she realized her mistake.

He had let me go.

Cole did an about-face and smacked right into the back of the chair she had been sitting in. Ignoring the sharp pain shooting through her kneecap, she looked at her interviewer.

"Sorry, sir. I—ah, thank you for the opportunity but I'm not the best choice for whatever position I have been interviewing for."

Lattimore held her in a stare just short of a disapproving glare. "I understood you had a cordial relationship."

"I believe I said professional."

Cole turned at the sound of Scott's voice. He offered her a sketch of a smile. "We have a professional, cordial relationship. Right, Officer Jamieson?"

Cole ignored his attempt to get her to join in his little joke, praying that no signs of her volatile emotions were on display. She would be a professional, if it killed her. "I haven't seen you in two years. If that's your definition of cordial, then we are cordial."

She shifted her attention back to Lattimore. "If I am being interviewed for a position that would require me to interact with Agent Lucca, then I must respectfully decline."

Lattimore frowned. "You're saying you won't consider an offer because Officer Lucca is part of it?"

"I'm saying Officer Lucca can—" Cole swallowed hard, appalled that she had allowed emotion to leak into her voice.

She squared her shoulders, resisting the urge to simply walk out. "There is a history between Agent Lucca and myself that did not end well. Future association would not improve that history. But thank you all the same."

Lattimore rose from his seat with a sour expression. "Then we're done. Thank you for your time, Officer Jamieson."

Cole shook the hand he offered, more eager than her interviewer to have the meeting over with. "Sorry to have wasted your time, Mr. Lattimore."

Scott hadn't moved from his position. He waited, arms loosely folded, until she was close before he spoke. "Don't you even want to hear why you were chosen to be part of this task force?"

"She works on paper." Lattimore turned a world-weary gaze on Scott and shook his head. "But I doubt, in any case, that she would have been able to get close to our target."

Scott, who managed to lounge on the hard unforgiving chair his ex had abandoned, frowned. Two minutes before, she had stormed out past him without a reply. "Why? Who's the target?"

His superior toyed with the pencil on his desk. Scott knew it wasn't nervousness powering Lattimore's fingers. It was a diversion while he calculated how much to reveal. That bland expression on his everyman's face hid a sharp and perceptive mind. He was an old hand in the bureau, and tough as nails. "Let's just say our prime target is a young, wealthy, and hip female."

"How hip?"

"Hip-hop hip."

Scott got a mental picture of Beyoncé, followed by one of Nikki in her unisex police officer's uniform. Okay. Big gap. But he knew something practically no one else knew about her. "What if I can bring her up to speed?"

Lattimore's eyebrows climbed to skeptical heights. "Officer Jamieson said no in terms that left no gaps between the *n* and the *o*."

"True. But I know her. She'll want this. Give me a few days."

Lattimore seemed to consider it, for three seconds, before shaking his head. "We don't have much time. The series of canine competitions we hope to insert our undercover operation into begins in just three weeks. We can't train a green agent to play against type, bring her up to speed on the technical aspects of the competitions, and set up sufficient covert surveillance in that space of time."

"She won't be surveillance. That's my job. You need a female agent who can believably compete on the dog competition circuit. As you know from the department research, there aren't half a dozen females in law enforcement East Coast division who've had experience. Nikki has. She's here. She's ready. As for her appearance? She's a woman. Change her clothing and hair, you change her attitude."

Lattimore's lids lowered. "You'd trust her with your life?"

"Yes." Scott didn't allow himself to think before he spoke. He knew the truth would come out. "She's what you need. Let me prove it."

Lattimore laughed, as if astonished he was going to give in. "She hates your guts."

"I noticed." Scott shrugged. "So when she pulls off what I'm thinking of, it will be proof she's got the acting skills as well as the canine skills to go undercover."

Lattimore's gray eyes turned into ice chips. "How badly did you hurt her?"

"It wasn't like that." Scott knew Lattimore was thinking of the awful record of law enforcement personnel whose marriages blew apart because of issues stemming from physical abuse. "Our marriage was collateral damage from my time undercover."

Lattimore turned and stared out his window so long Scott began to think he was dismissed. When he turned back, his face was grim.

"Don't lie to her about the risk. Or the likelihood of failure."

"No, sir."

"And don't think I won't change you out for another team leader if that's the only way to get her agreement. You are right in that her skill set is the priority. DEA has other K-9 drug teams."

"Yes, sir."

Scott was on the other side of the door before allowing himself to consider how he thought he might convince Nikki to let him near her, let alone close enough to make other people believe they were a couple who shared the love of competition in the canine arena.

CHAPTER THREE

"How did you get my address?"

"You forgot this yesterday." Scott held up the deputy's hat she'd left behind in Baltimore.

Cole stared at him through the storm door of her home that separated them. "Leave it by the door."

Instead, he twirled it around his finger.

Cole folded her arms, unimpressed by the smile beneath his reflective shades. He had caught her just as she returned from night patrol or she wouldn't have bothered to open the door.

Scott whipped off his shades and pocketed them, then reached for the door handle. "I've come to tell you about our task force."

Cole didn't move to open the door. There was something very intimidating about looking her ex in the eye, even with a locked door between them. Force of personality. Scott had it in spades.

"Why don't you just tell me from there?"

He slid a finger along the length of the door handle. "If

you're nervous about being alone with me I can wait while you call a fellow officer for backup."

"That won't be necessary. Hugo. *Hier!*"

From deep within the house Scott heard guttural growls followed by deep otherworldly barking that would not have been out of place in a horror movie. Two seconds later, a huge shaggy black canine appeared and struck fist-size paws on the glass of the storm door at chest level. Scott stepped back instinctively, despite the barrier between them. Crap. Nikki's K-9 partner looked like Batman in a black bear suit.

"Hugo. *Platz.*" Cole used German, the official language for canine instruction for most police K-9 teams nationwide. That way Hugo would know he was on the job.

Hugo immediately dropped prone at her feet but his ears remained pricked forward, his doggy body trembling at full alert for her next command.

Cole smirked as she looked up at Scott. "You still think talking is a good idea?"

He met her hostile gaze through the now smudged glass. "Is that an invitation to enter?"

She watched him for maybe four seconds longer. "Stay there." She turned away from the door, taking the fuzzy Dark Knight with her.

She was gone a while. Two years ago he would have been banging on the door in irritation after thirty seconds. He'd learned a few things since then. To distract himself, Scott pulled out his cell phone and checked his mail.

She seemed surprised to find him still waiting when she returned but she didn't say a thing. She simply unlatched the door before swiftly stepping back.

Scott remained in the foyer as he gave her living area a thorough perusal. No dog. Then he saw the gate across the kitchen entry at the far side of the room. Hugo must be behind those bars. Big-ticket item on his list of possible concerns accounted for.

The living area was small. Neat. He didn't recognize a single stick of furniture or see any other evidence of their married life. Nothing to remind her that she had once been part of an "us." That realization stung as his gaze came to rest on her. Had she really left *them* behind, or was she still running from memory, just as he had done?

Nikki had put enough distance between them so that she could maneuver, if necessary. She had also stripped off her windbreaker but she had not removed her weapons belt.

A frown tugged his brow as Scott dropped her hat into a nearby chair. Did she really think he presented a danger to her in any way?

He watched her check him out, as if he were a suspect. He was wearing his favorite pair of jeans, so faded and worn and frayed at the cuffs they looked like he lived in them, which he pretty much did off duty. His faded Redskins T-shirt hugged his torso, making it difficult but not impossible to conceal his badge and gun. As he watched, her gaze paused fractionally to check for telltale bulges of weapons in all the usual concealment places.

Fine. If that's the way she wanted to go. He assumed an at-ease posture and returned the inspection.

She wore a fitted dark blue T-shirt with her police department insignia. The dark cargo pants tucked into her tactical boots emphasized both her narrow waist and female hips. Her sun-streaked light brown hair was pinned up in a messy ponytail that left loose strands to frame her face.

At first glance, a man might not think of her as a babe. Oh, pleasant enough, with those big hazel eyes and so full lips, but vulnerable, not at all law-enforcement material. He knew from intimate experience that there was another

woman just under the calm exterior Officer Nicole Jamieson showed the world. That woman could kiss like it was
the last kiss at the end of the world and make a man okay
with that, because she was there with him.

Yet when she looked directly at him, as now, that level
law enforcement gaze from beneath her brows came across
as forceful and defiant, yet compellingly female in a way
that still got under his guard and messed with his mind
without permission.

His brother Gabe called it her Kate Winslet look. Nikki
had gone all girly blushes at the comparison to the actress.
He, Scott, had noticed the resemblance first. His fault that
he'd not told her first. Gabe had always come out the win-
ner with women.

Shit. Not now. A muscle tic appeared in Scott's jaw as
he pushed the thought of his older brother aside.

"Seen enough?" Her voice was cold and clipped.

Not hardly. But he wasn't about to start out that way.
He stepped away from the door. "How'd you get the black
eye?"

"The normal way. Connected with something harder.
Your arm?"

He glanced down at the bandage covering the stitches
in his right arm from wrist to elbow. He'd forgotten about
it. "Dark alley. Concertina wire."

She winced and he was embarrassed by how grateful
her simple sign of empathy made him feel. He wanted very
badly to make her feel something, anything for him. Then
he'd have some emotional connection to work with. So far,
all she was giving him was attitude.

He moved toward the center of the room as he slipped
free the manila envelope he had tucked into the back of
his jeans. "Here. Lattimore sent these for you to look at.
He doesn't like being turned down before he's made his
case."

"Put it on the table." She pointed to her dining area table.

Scott checked the impulse to respond as he would have when challenged by anyone else. He was lucky to be in the same room with her. "Have it your way."

He dumped the folder on the table and took a few steps back. "If you can say no to this task force after you've viewed what's inside, I'll leave."

She hesitated only a moment before moving toward the table. She rounded the far end, putting its width between then. Even then, she kept her gaze on him as she pulled the folder toward her. He didn't blame her for her caution. Police officers worked in close quarters with felons on a daily basis. One wrong move could put her on the defensive with some very unsavory characters. Maintaining control was about narrowing the options for your suspect while keeping your own options open.

She slowly opened the folder, gaze flicking back and forth between it and him. He saw the exact moment the contents registered with her. Her face went slack and then she flipped the folder closed.

The look she leveled at him said that she held him personally responsible for the contents. "That's disgusting."

"Damn straight." He grabbed the folder and shook out the contents, then spread out between them a series of eight-by-ten color glossies. "Take a good look, Officer Jamieson."

She took an involuntary step back. "I've seen enough."

He rounded the table and pulled out the chair nearest her. "Sit down."

She stiffened but moved the few steps it took to reach the chair. He immediately retreated to the other side of the table, offering a little respect for her pride.

Scott saw her gaze move toward the pictures then dance away, so he shoved them closer to her. "What? You can't handle a little blood and gore?"

He was being a manipulative bastard but he also knew that what he had placed before her was real hard evidence of a crime. He needed her help to find and arrest the perpetrators.

He stabbed a particularly gory shot with his forefinger. "This is what these scumbags are doing to move their product."

Cole gave him a long hostile glare and then lowered her gaze very reluctantly until she was staring at the series of pictures of dead puppies in a Dumpster. It looked like a slaughterhouse. Their once sleek fat bellies had been slit open and disemboweled.

She swallowed carefully. She had seen bodies of people who had died violently, had even attended an autopsy once. No way was she going to show vulnerability over dead puppies to the one man in the world she once thought she could always count on, but no longer trusted with her emotions. Was. Not. Going. To. Happen.

Scott was suddenly there beside her, a hand on her shoulder meant to steady her in her chair.

Cole squeezed her eyes shut, willing tears not to fall. "I'm okay." Her voice sounded strong in her own ears but when she tried to stand she realized she had no strength to accomplish the task.

He knelt down next to her as his other hand settled heavily on her opposite shoulder. "Deep breath." His voice hadn't risen above a whisper but it made her suck in a long ribbon of air.

The growl from the kitchen doorway surprised both of them. Hugo stood with paws on top of the gate. That's when Scott realized that the gate was a polite fiction. It was a barrier as long as the big guy played nice. If he changed his mind?

Hugo cleared the gate seemingly without effort and came forward, rear end wagging. A suspect might be deceived by that shaggy-dog tail wag but Cole knew it meant Hugo was ready for action.

She straightened immediately. "Hugo. *Platz! Blieb!*"

Hugo plopped his body on the tile floor but his gaze remained on the stranger as he wriggled and whined in place. He barked twice, the sounds guttural and loud.

Cole looked up at Scott. "Take your hands off me. Slowly."

He did just as she asked and then sat back on his heels to put space between them.

She rose and, without even a backward look, headed for the kitchen. As she passed Hugo she said, *"Hier."* He turned instantly and fell into step beside her.

Once in the kitchen Cole paused. Hugo stood gazing up at her, ready for any directive. *"Lass es."*

Hugo turned his big head back toward the dining room and growled deep in his throat, a sound that left no doubt about his opinion of her guest.

Cole couldn't help but smile. "Yes. He's a pain in the ass. But we don't attack DEA officers." She reached for a treat. "Here you go. *Gute Hund.*"

Hugo swallowed then looked back toward the dining room a second time. She knew how things must seem to him. Trained to protect, Hugo wanted nothing so much as to get rid of the stranger who had put his hands on his partner while she was spilling pheromones of anxiety. But he couldn't be permitted to fixate on Scott.

"Lass das sein."

His handler's command tone snapped Hugo out of whatever doggy thought process he was having. He turned with surprising agility and trotted over to scoot headfirst into his kennel.

Cole shut the gate behind him and went to the sink to splash water on her face, hoping to gain a moment to compose herself before she dealt with Scott again.

She was gone so long, Scott decided to check on her. He found her leaning over the kitchen sink.

A slow warmth spread through him at the sight of her bending over the sink in a way that pushed her hips back in his direction. One of the first things he'd learned about her was that she liked to wear very feminine panties under her uniform. Lacy near-nothings. She said she did it to remind herself that she was, at the end of the day, a woman. Once upon a time, he had enjoyed the privilege of peeling off her uniform and showing her just how very happy all parts of him were that she was female.

His body responded instantly to thoughts he probably shouldn't be having. Confirmation of that thought came as he clocked the exact moment she became aware of him. She spun around and stood upright, eyes wide with wariness.

Maybe she had a right to be nervous. He was now swinging serious pipe.

Hoping to distract her from that realization, he gestured back toward the other room. "Look, about before."

"I'm good." She lifted her hand and pushed it palm flat into the air between them, as if it was a solid thing against which she could pit her will. Officer Jamieson was back on duty.

Scott nodded. He had seen her in action at the scene of more than one murder when she was D.C. police. But this was different. Nikki had a soft spot for innocent creatures, especially dogs, and he had deliberately played into that. Looking back into her hard eyes and too pale lips, he felt like a bully. He knew how to intimidate and how to apply pressure. But maybe he'd gone too far. Nikki wasn't a suspect. He needed to give her back her pride. But he knew enough about her not to come at it directly.

He slanted a look at her kenneled partner. "Enjoy your patrol last night, rattling doorknobs and checking locks?"

"We do more than that." A flash of temper. Temper was good.

"Yeah. Saw a recent background photo of you on guard duty at an event where Miss Maryland put in an appearance. Tough job. Must have required all your skills."

Definitely the Kate Winslet stare. "A week ago we were called in to track and arrest an abusive husband after he got away from the responding officer."

"Fun, huh?" He smiled and nodded. "A chance to really show what you could do?"

He watched her gaze go inward as she reached up and touched her wounded eye. Then a tiny smile tugged her mouth.

He leaned back against the wall and crossed his legs at the ankles. He saw her gaze slip for an instant and realized his action had practically served up his hard-on for her inspection. She didn't seem impressed or intimidated. Either she didn't care, or she'd mastered nonresponsive behavior to provocative situations. For pride's sake he chose possibility number two.

"You and Hugo are wasted as glorified security guards. You can do more."

Instead of answering, Cole reached to unbuckle her rig. The fact that she sometimes thought that herself didn't make it any easier to accept coming from him. She wasn't going to share her new hopes and dreams with the man who'd once wrecked her life. But he had roused her curiosity about the DEA project.

"How long has that been going on?"

Scott glanced back in the direction of her nod. She was thinking about the photos. Good.

"Using dogs as drug mules? There've been reports since the nineties in Belgium, the Netherlands, even France and Italy. Most of those dogs were imports from Mexico and South America. It's tougher to import dogs into the U.S.

but we've caught a few cases in the last decade. Even cattle moved up from Mexico have been found to be stuffed with drugs after gelding. However, the pictures I showed you are an entirely different matter. These dogs weren't imported. They were used to move product around the U.S."

"Why would anyone go to all that trouble? The surgery required to implant the drugs would seem to make the practice problematic."

Scott waited to see where her thought process would take her. Besides, she had drawn her weapon and was in the middle of unloading it. No need to distract her.

When she finished, she leaned her hips back against the sink and crossed her legs at the ankles in imitation of his pose. "Must be cocaine. Nothing else on the street is worth the effort."

Scott smiled and straightened away from the wall. "Forensics found traces of cocaine in the incision sites. The stuff was very pure. The potency alone should leave a near permanent trail, if you know where to look. We didn't, until this happened."

Her frown deepened into two exclamation points between her brows. He longed to smooth them away with his thumb. Wanted, really, any excuse to touch her again.

Cole stared off into the distance. "Who goes to all that trouble and then leaves a slaughter as evidence?"

"Could be a case of careless traffickers." He moved a little closer to her, in spite of good sense telling him to keep his distance. "Maybe whoever they sold them to didn't care that they left behind evidence. Either way, it was a break for us. Now you know what we're up against."

Her gaze shifted back to him. "We? There's no *we*."

Hugo's crate creaked as he stood up. A rumble like distant thunder issued from within as he pushed his big black nose against the bars.

Scott saw her gaze shift sideways toward her partner,

an action that irritated him. She was trying to block him out.

He moved deliberately into her line of sight, forcing her to refocus on him. "You're going to turn down the DEA? Why, Nikki? Because you're afraid you can't handle yourself in the field with me?"

Those hazel eyes widened. "This isn't about you and me."

"Damn straight. It's about the scumbags who use animals to transport drugs. And who will continue to do it until someone puts a stop to it."

He reached past her and braced a hand on the counter, angling his body toward hers. He knew he was amping up the provocation. But if he didn't break through soon, she'd put him out. "Tell me you don't want to be part of the task force that takes these bastards down, Nikki."

Cole placed a hand flat on his chest to halt his encroachment. The contact alarmed her more than it should have. Maybe because she knew what lay behind his shirt. Once she had claimed all that hard muscle and warm skin as hers. Now here he was, two years too late, and the solid reality of him was still doing things to her heart rate. This was not fair. She did want the assignment. But at what cost?

She lifted her head to search his sea-glass gaze between a tangle of thick black lashes. He was so close she could see the faint throb of his pulse under his jaw stubble. The heat of his body had seeped through his shirt to warm her palm. The register of the slight uptick of his heartbeat under her little finger meant that he wasn't as detached as he seemed. His impact on her was still visceral, physically and mentally, overwhelming in minutes two solid years of careful repair of her emotions.

She closed her eyes briefly. That was long enough for memories she had had on lockdown for two years to stage a jail break.

Legs tangled in sweaty bedsheets. Warm wet licks in all the right places. Harsh breaths punctuating the action of pumping bodies. Laughter. Always laughter at the back end of bliss. And then a refreshing shower that more often than not ended in another round.

Cole opened her eyes. Those extracted memories made her body flush with desire and intimidated her more than a little. They felt real and fresh, like a morning rerun of a previous night's sexual highlights. And her ex, standing right here before her, was at the center of every delicious aching moment of recall.

She saw reflected in his expanding pupils the exact moment he realized the effect his nearness was having on her.

Suddenly it wasn't two years later but the day before ever after. Oh shit. She was still mad-bad attracted to the man whose pulse raced under her fingertips.

Her hand clenched on his shirtfront and she lifted her face, lips parting in an invitation her brain hadn't given her body permission to make.

"Nikki?" He sounded as surprised as she felt.

Hugo's vocal vibrations, so low they could barely be heard, were warning her of the danger of this close encounter with a man too potent for his own good.

Cole lowered her lashes, trying to handle the yin-yang tug-of-war going on between her reason and her feelings. Yes, he was still as dangerous as ever. However, those enticing lips hovering just an inch above hers had also spoken the words that broke her heart. It was too good to be true to think they could just pick up—

Wait! Something didn't add up here.

She stiff-armed his shoulder and with a flex of her hips launched herself away from the sink, and past him to safety.

She didn't go far before turning back. "Why me? Why

did Agent Lattimore choose me?" Her voice sounded winded as she refused to look directly at him.

Scott jutted a hip against the counter and folded his arms, ignoring the fact that—*Shit*. She'd nearly kissed him. He dragged in a breath instead of giving in to the urge to drag her back in against him and finish what she'd started. "You're experienced with dog competitions."

"That was a long time ago. Who recommended me to him?"

"I did." He could see the idea didn't please her, though it didn't show anywhere except in the tiny jiggle of her left foot.

"Why me?"

He knew what she meant. She wanted to know why he wanted to work with her. He wanted *any* reason to be near her again. That truth would blow this operation all to hell. He opted for a lesser truth. "Let's just say this operation is more important than the odds against us being a success-ful U/C team."

"What, exactly, do they want us to do?"

"Follow a lead the DEA has developed that points to the dog-competition circuit as a major means of drug smug-gling. We're to get in close and gather more evidence."

She looked over at Hugo, who stood alert to every word they spoke. "We don't have time to qualify for any kind of serious competition. That would take months."

"DEA will see to it that you have the credentials you need to make the cut."

"Why not just hang out at the shows or use drug dogs to search behind the scenes until you turn up something?"

"We have a suspect and don't want to spook her."

"Her?" She looked at him, finally. "Working the female-suspect angle is more in your line of undercover work, isn't it?"

Scott ignored the barb. "This is how it will go down. We pose as a couple. You'll compete. That'll give me cover to nose around with my K-9 partner without suspicion."

"You work K-9 drug detail for DEA?" The surprise in her voice said it all. "Since when?"

"A year. Her name's Izzy. A chocolate Lab." He smiled. "You'll like her, Nikki."

"Stop calling me that. Everyone calls me Cole."

He couldn't stop himself. "Your husband called you Nikki."

"License revoked. And don't change the subject." She launched herself toward him. "What about your SWAT and undercover work? The boys' club where females are good only for recreation? You lived for it. Traded us for it."

Her sudden blast of anger caught him off guard. "That's not what I wanted."

She stopped right before him. "Oh right. Then why are you on record in our divorce proceeding? I quote, 'Marriage? Screw that. There're too many women to fuck and there's only one lifetime.' "

His eyes flashed anger for the first time. "That was taken down by the duty officer the night I was arrested. I was drunk as a skunk, and I'd been working undercover in a biker bar. I was still in character."

"I know what you were doing. I was there. Remember?"

Guilt knifed through Scott's gut. He remembered. Would never forget it.

"You weren't supposed to . . ." He groped for a better beginning. He wanted to explain how jacked-up miserable he had been juggling two lives and knowing he was losing on both ends. He wanted her to know that after she left him he'd staggered under so much regret he could barely function. So many things to say, to admit, to account for.

He heaved his shoulders. "Things change. If you'd let me explain—"

"Don't even go there." Her eyes, only two feet from his, were throwing off sparks that should have burned him to the ground. "Bastard. Rat *bastard*. For you to come here, after all this time and—and—"

The catch in her throat so appalled her that Cole did an about-face. "Get out."

"Right."

Cole waited until she heard the front door close. Then she released Hugo, who bolted past her.

She followed and watched as her partner sniffed every spot where Scott had stood or touched. He was memorizing the scent of the man who had upset her. Too bad she couldn't explain to her partner all the complex reasons why. Especially, the long-absent feelings of familiarity coursing through her the entire time Scott had been here.

When Hugo was done, he came back to her and leaped up to place his front paws square in her chest. She wasn't a small person but Hugo didn't have any trouble planting a big slurpy kiss on her face. His way of saying, *I got your back*.

"I love you, too." She leaned her head against his and hugged him tight.

Working nights was not something her body had ever completely adjusted to. When Cole woke up late in the afternoon, her head felt stuffed with cotton balls and her head throbbed. And then she remembered. She'd fallen asleep with tears staining her face.

She was still angry. The emotion beat faintly behind her gritty eyes. But on another level, she felt calm. The confrontation she had longed for and dreaded for two years was behind her. There was just one teeny-weeny little problem left.

She should just admit the hard pathetic truth.

I still have feelings for Scott.

She also hated Scott's guts. And after what he'd done, hate still topped love.

Cole let out a breath she hadn't even realized she was holding, and scooted off her bed.

She made coffee and toast then brought the items to her dining room table where she sat and looked as objectively as possible at the pictures Lattimore had sent her.

Someone needed to catch the assholes who had done this. She'd been asked to be part of that. But what about Scott? How much was seeing him again going to cost her?

She opened her computer and ran him through the law-enforcement background-check system via her police department. He hadn't remarried. Lived in an apartment in a less than desirable part of D.C. After nearly a yearlong gap in his work record he was now listed as a DEA agent, SWAT K-9 division. No Facebook, Twitter, Tumblr, or other social network accounts under his name. No record of that missed year, either.

To learn more personal details, for instance if he had a girlfriend, she would have to reach out to her personal connections. However, law enforcement became an unbelievably small, gossipy world when an officer went snooping about a colleague. She couldn't go further without the risk that Scott would learn about it. Not knowing was better than him discovering she was checking on him.

Instead, she called Agent Lattimore, just to confirm that she was still eligible to be considered for the task force job. That would be a yes, he told her.

Cole sat and nibbled her thumbnail.

Did she dare grab this opportunity the DEA was offering to prove herself? Even if it meant agreeing to spend a few weeks in close quarters with the one man she didn't know how to handle, didn't trust, and was pretty sure she still hated?

Tall order, in the name of the law.

CHAPTER FOUR

"You said no, right? Right?"

Cole shrugged off her sister Becca's question. "It's an opportunity not many local law enforcement officers get."

"It's an opportunity to find yourself in more danger than necessary." Becca sat back as their waitress set grilled chicken salads down before them.

Cole noticed the waitress eyeing her nervously as she put her plate down. Some civilians welcomed a police presence while for others the mere presence of a uniform and all that went with it was seen as some sort of hostile provocation.

Cole smiled at her. "Thank you."

"Sure." The waitress's gaze skittered away. Maybe she'd been on the wrong end of an encounter with law enforcement recently.

Cole gave up and picked up her fork. It was her lunch hour. She had exactly fifty minutes left to explain to her sister the big decision she was about to make.

"So here's the thing. If I did accept the task force position, the assignment may take me out of town from time to time."

Becca gasped. "You're going undercover!"

"Loud, maybe?"

"Right." Becca's voice dropped to a whisper as she glanced around the busy restaurant. "Are you going undercover?"

"I can't give you details. Just don't say anything to Mom and Dad until it's a done deal, okay? Then I'll tell them."

Becca dipped a forkful of salad into the side dish of dressing. "Why do you need to do this? You're doing great with the county police department. You made the K-9 in record time. You don't need to do anything else. You're set."

Cole leaned forward. "That's just it. I want to do something more, Becca. Something important and exciting. Use my skill set where it's most needed. You've got a husband and a career. You're set."

Becca grinned. "And we're expanding the franchise."

"The vet's office— Oh!" Cole's expression widened into a gape as Becca patted her tummy. "You're pregnant? I'm going to be an aunt!"

The two sisters jumped up and hugged each other, all girly squeals of joy.

"You're the first to know." Becca's smile couldn't stretch any wider. "I had to check on the results of some extra tests this morning before I told the folks."

Cole's smile dissolved as she sat back down. "Why extra tests?"

Becca made a sad face. "I'm thirty. It's a bit late for a first pregnancy, since we've been trying for three years. But everything's fine."

Cole searched her sister's face. "You would tell me?"

Becca nodded. "You first. Just like always."

Cole felt the tightness in her chest ebb as they tucked into their salads. Though three and a half years apart in age, they were closer than most sisters. Really, BFFs. Their attitudes and tastes were so similar that, more often than not, they could finish each other's sentences and predict what the other would order for a meal. And, they always told each other everything—no matter how personal—eventually.

Cole ducked her head on that final thought. She had decided to wait until the end of their meal to bring up the matter of Scott Lucca.

Meanwhile, there were dozens of other catch-up topics to discuss since their last sisters' lunch four weeks ago. For instance, the new assistant in Becca's office whom she had to fire because she kept "borrowing" boarded pets.

"The first weekend she took a cockatiel because, she said, birds need more attention than dogs. I told her never to do that again. But the following weekend she takes home a pet ferret, and loses it. I mean, really? So there I am, on my hands and knees in her apartment, searching. Turned out the little guy had climbed in under her dishwasher. Probably to get away from her. I finally lured him out with a thawed mouse. I was so done with her."

Cole laughed. "The gla-*mouse*-rous life of a vet."

"Speaking of gla-*amorous* lives, tell me you're finally seeing someone. Anyone?"

Cole met her sister's mischievous expression with a sour one.

"Harper knows this guy. Don't make that face. He's new in the area, a podiatrist in Harper's clinic. A real looker."

"I don't need a man to make my life complete, Becca. I'm not you."

"Ouch, and unnecessary."

"Sorry, I didn't mean it like that."

"It's been two years, Cole. When do you move on? If you need a challenge, go back to school. With your five years of law enforcement experience, you could get into law school like that." A snap of her fingers accompanied the thought.

"I doubt it. There's the little thing called the LCAT."

"Which you passed once."

"It's been years since I cracked a textbook."

"Okay, not so easy—but once you graduated, you could do something important. Instead of chasing the bad guys, you could make certain they went to prison. That's where your talents are needed, where you can make the biggest impact. D.A. Jameson. Sounds good, doesn't it? Any Tom, Dick, or Jane with a badge and a gun can arrest perps."

"Suspects. We call them suspects. You watch too much TV."

"You know what I mean. You told Mom and Dad you didn't intend to stay in law enforcement, you just needed a breather after college."

Cole sighed. She had told them what they could handle at the time. "After I'd worked summers for the sheriff's department between college semesters they should have guessed I was interested in law enforcement."

"They hoped you'd be interested in law without the en-*force*ment part." Becca pointed the tines of her fork in the general direction of her sister's weapon.

Cole rolled her eyes. "This is one point that we won't agree on, *okay*? I love being a cop. Hugo and I do important work every day. We help people and protect people. Sure, we chase the occasional bad guy. But a month ago, we helped locate an Alzheimer's patient who'd gotten away from her caregiver. We make a difference. Now we're being asked to step up to something even more important."

"Tell me more about it. Maybe you can make me believe it's a good idea."

Actually, what she was about to say was guaranteed to do the opposite. Time to confess. "Scott called me."

Becca's final forkful of salad paused halfway to her mouth. "What? When?"

"Three weeks ago."

"Three weeks . . ." Becca stared at her so long Cole began to feel a blush creep up her neck. "Your anniversary. That's the day he called?" Becca dropped her fork back into her plate. "What did he say?"

"He said wrong number and hung up."

"The bastard!" Becca's usually mellow voice lost all tone. "I can't believe even he has the nerve . . ."

"Isn't it my place to be the one upset?"

On a roll, Becca didn't pause. ". . . after all you tried to do for him, defended him against the family, and his family, and everything. For him to betray . . ."

Her sister sputtered to a stop as Cole's gaze narrowed. "Right. We can't talk here." Becca glanced around to signal for the check.

A few minutes later, they were walking toward the park where Becca had scheduled a mid-afternoon dog obedience class.

"So what, exactly, is going on? Why did you wait to tell me about Scott's call?" Becca's head turned back toward Cole. "DEA task force. Hah! There's more to it than you're telling me."

No moss growing on her sister. "When I went in for the initial interview Scott showed up. He's part of the team."

"He's what?" Becca paused momentarily on the sidewalk, uncaring that they upset the park traffic of strollers, runners, and lunch-hour walkers. "Scott calls you out of the blue and then just happens to be part of this DEA business? That's just a little too convenient. He's up to something. This is a trick."

They were so in tune it was scary.

"It's what I thought at first. But my sergeant got a visit

this morning from a DEA representative. It's been cleared through my department for me to go. I have this lunch hour to think it over and say yes or no."

"Say no."

"As my big sister, you're supposed to tell me that I shouldn't let a great job opportunity slip through my fingers just because there's a bump in the road."

"Bump? Scott Lucca is an axle-busting deal breaker. The last time you saw him, he was screwing another woman."

Cole winced.

"Okay. You're right. I'm sorry. Picking a scab." Becca embraced her sister's waist and leaned her head against Cole's as they continued walking. "I saw what Scott did to you. You fell so hard, when you landed there were scarcely enough pieces left to collect to put you back together. I'll never forgive him for that."

"It wasn't all Scott's fault."

"No. You should have known better than to get involved. He had bad-to-the-bone written all over him."

"Then why did you point him out that night?"

"Come on, Cole. It was a game. Find a hot guy. Turn him on. Then turn him loose. You were supposed to know better than to take it seriously."

Cole looked out across the park. Is that what she had done? Taken the game with a sexy stranger too seriously?

Truth or Dare on a girls' weekend. After dinner they decided to move out of their comfort zones and find a bar that didn't cater to middle-class twenty-somethings. They found one on the outskirts of D.C. Another round of drinks, and the game was on.

"Him." Her sister and three girlfriends had pushed her out of the booth. "We dare you to kiss that guy."

Cole had noticed him even before her sister pointed him

out. He was hard to miss, even in a room full of men. Even from the back. He wore a leather jacket with a lot of miles on it and jeans that hugged his hips and thighs like they were happy just to be along for the ride. And then he turned around.

He was gorgeous; hard-eyed, hard-bodied, and so laid back it seemed as if he didn't care if the world kept on spinning or not. Thick black hair with a tendency to wave, light eyes. He didn't show any emotion, just went very still as their gazes met.

Maybe it was the adrenaline rush of the dare. Maybe it was what she'd been drinking. Or maybe it was just lust. She wanted him with an awful urgency that felt truer than any sexual craving she'd ever had before. Like steel to a magnet, the force of attraction was undeniable.

It was as if she'd been waiting all her life for this moment, even if it was a total lie and he probably was everything he seemed, bad-news-dangerous, and then some. But she was just drunk enough to want to find out. She had reached up on tiptoe and kissed him.

A few more kisses and a couple of slow turns on the tiny space that served as a makeshift dance floor, and she'd left with him. She never looked back.

"Earth to Cole."

Cole glanced up.

"Where did you go?" Becca had her serious face on. "And why are you blushing? "Oh. My. God. You still have a thing for the bastard. You're thinking that if you spent time together you might patch things up? You're an idiot!"

Several nearby park visitors glanced their way.

"Uniform, Becca." Cole said the words quietly.

Becca's turn to blush. "I'm sorry. I forgot. Respect for the badge."

She turned to the people looking their way. "She's my sister. We fight. Get over it." She looked back at Cole. "Better?"

Cole pulled her sister to a nearby bench and made her sit. "I know this won't make any sense to you but I need something from Scott. Maybe just to hear his side of the story of what went wrong."

"How can there be another side to what you saw with your own two eyes?"

"I don't know." Cole closed her eyes for a moment. "But I never heard what he had to say. I ran away."

Becca stared at her for a long time then nodded slowly. "You need closure."

"I hate that expression. But, yeah, I guess that's what it is." Cole took a deep breath. "It's been two years. I have to do something. You, more than anyone, know I haven't been able to move on."

Becca brushed a stray hair from her sister's cheek. "Promise me you won't let him hurt you again."

"I'm armed, Becca." She grinned as her sister eyed with alarm the pistol she wore. "That's not what I meant. I have Hugo."

Becca smiled. "How is that bruiser of yours?"

"At home alone, probably ready to chew my upholstery. He hates days when I'm called in for desk duty."

They rose and hugged. "You be careful. And tell your ex if he so much as makes you tear up, he'll have to deal with your newly edgy hormonal big sister."

Cole laughed and hugged her sister. "Love you, too."

As she walked back to her cruiser, Cole realized the decision was made. She was going to do this.

She had made only one other rash decision in her life, and it had cost her, emotionally, everything she had. At least this time, she knew what to expect.

Trouble.

As she slid behind the wheel her cell phone beeped with a text.

Fool me once, shame on you.
Fool me twice, shame on me.

Cole laughed. Becca could so read her mind.

CHAPTER FIVE

Scott pulled into the driveway of a modest-sized two-story Colonial house on Eastern Avenue in New Brunswick, New Jersey. There were no other cars parked there yet. He was early. That didn't help his state of mind. Going home was like taking a dive headfirst into murky waters with unknown hazards. Showing up early only meant he'd have more time to think about that dive.

When fellow D.C. law enforcement officers found out he was originally from New Jersey they teased him about being "connected" à la *The Sopranos*. That, or that his life growing up must have been a version of *Jersey Shore*. Neither could be further from the truth. His parents were scholarly professionals. His dad was a professor of political science at Rutgers University. His mother was a judge in family court. Today, his father's sixtieth birthday, marked the first time he'd been home in more than a year.

Izzy, who had been a silent passenger all the way up, poked her big snout through the doggy door of her back-seat kennel and rested her chin on Scott's right shoulder. He reached up absently to scratch her head. That was all the invitation she needed. She was through the opening and onto the front seat in a long chocolate-fur movement.

Unlike most times, the sight of his partner didn't improve Scott's mood. "Down, girl." He gently stiff-armed her head aside. His mother would notice if he came in smelling of dog.

Undeterred, Izzy made a few turns then stretched out to fill the bench seat and rested her large head on his thigh. A thin thread of doggy drool traced across his chinos as she bounced her chin in a comforting motion. So much for spotless.

In no hurry to get out of his truck, Scott pulled Izzy in close to his body and studied the house he had been reared in, as if the outside would give him clues to the mood inside.

The house could stand a coat of paint. His father would be certain to point that out to him, as if he should have thought of it beforehand and brought along cans of paint, brushes, scrapers, and a ladder in order to get started. His father never thought anything Scott did do was as important as what was not being done. Only Gabe had ever gotten a pass. Nearly three years after his older brother's death, the pain still felt raw for the entire family.

Gabe was the stuff of legend. His father never spoke about his eldest son without a catch in his throat. Gabe had graduated from a military academy while Scott was still trying to make his way through public junior high school. Gabe went to college and then into the Marines. In no time he was Special Ops. By the time of his death, he'd made SEAL Team Six.

"Stay, Izzy. I'll be back for you later." No point in bringing her in until he decided if he was staying long, and/or if the number of people his mother promised were coming would be too much for Izzy to deal with on an informal basis.

Scott wiped a hand across his mouth as he headed toward the back door, nervous in the way chasing an armed suspect down a dark alley made him edgy. Gabe had been his lodestar for as long as he could remember. He used his older brother as the measure of how he was doing in the world. Success was according to how close he could come to Gabe's scores on everything: college grades, physical endurance, drinking, even women. He'd always come up short. Except with Nikki—Cole. "Shit." She would always be Nikki to him.

When he'd asked her opinion of his brother, after the one and only time they met, Nikki had said Gabe had obviously inherited the Lucca charm and good looks, but he wasn't her type.

Her response had made Scott want to take out a full-page ad. Always before, when Gabe was around, Scott was an also-ran for women's attention.

And then three years ago, six months into Scott's marriage to Nikki, Gabe was gone. Killed in action in a covert operation somewhere in the Hindu Kush mountains of the Kunar province. The military returned a small locker with his personal effects. They said Gabe's body wasn't recoverable.

Scott sucked in a long breath as he reached for the back-door knob. His compass and direction, his benchmark, his nemesis, and his much loved brother, all of it was gone. He knew to whom his father had looked to fill those shoes, and how miserably he had failed, and was still failing.

"Scott!" His mother greeted him with a big hug as soon as he entered. "I thought I heard your truck."

She held on to him for so long Scott began to color with embarrassment. Message clear; he'd visited so rarely these last two years, she couldn't control her joy at actually laying her hands on her only surviving child.

Even when she released his body she held on to him at

the elbows, smiling despite wet eyes. "You look good, Scott. Your hair's longer. And you're tan." Her gaze fell to his arm. "But what's this?"

"Zigged when I should have zagged. It's nothing, Mom."

She touched the bandage very gently, biting back the urge, he knew, to warn him to be careful. "As long as you're okay."

He grinned and leaned down to plant a kiss on her cheek. "You're looking good. You stepping out on the old man?"

"Smart mouth."

Scott looked up past his mother's shoulder. "Happy birthday, Dad."

John Lucca stood a few feet away. He looked much younger than the sixty years they were gathering to celebrate. Tall and still lean from a regimen of handball and swimming, he had a full head of gray hair that suited his professorial status. According to his mother's e-mails, his father's students still adored him, though four decades now separated him from most of them.

When his mother released Scott, his father came forward and held out his hand. "You're almost late."

Scott shook it. "A worse offense than actually being late, right, Dad?"

His father immediately frowned, making Scott wish he hadn't been so fast with the comeback. But, damn, his father always had something negative to say about whatever he was doing or not doing. No way to win.

"Now, John, don't tease Scott."

"I wasn't—"

"He wasn't—"

Father and son exchanged uneasy glances before looking away.

"Please come in and relax. We're waiting for your father's sisters, and cousins Edward and Sharon. And, of course, Ashley and Teddy's brood before we get started."

His mother waved a hand toward the kitchen table that all but groaned under the weight of dishes waiting to be served. She was prepared to serve an army. "Would you like a beer?"

"Maybe later."

"Come through." His father turned and headed toward the living room. Scott joined him.

His mother followed. "What do you hear from Nicole?"

His father rolled his eyes. "Now why would he hear from her, Cathy?"

"You never know." His mother smiled at him. "I did so hope you two might, well, talk things out after a while."

"If he hasn't heard from her by now it's because she has nothing more to say to him. He screwed up and made certain of that."

"Thanks for the benefit of the doubt, Dad." Scott held back the sharper words that came to mind. His father didn't even know exactly what had happened between them, yet he'd come to the conclusion that it was Scott's fault, and it was unforgivable.

"John, that's not fair. When two people love each other the way they do . . . did . . ." She glanced at Scott for help.

Scott retreated to the safety of professional detachment. "Leave it, Mom. Please."

He sat on the family room sofa opposite his father's well-worn leather recliner. He looked around, hoping desperately for some topic of interest to appear. Not sports. His father was a Giants and Yankees fan while he had long ago moved to the Redskins and Orioles camp.

"Just to spite the old man," Gabe had once declared in front of them. Not true, but Scott saved his breath. Gabe had said it, it was now fact.

"So, sixty years." Scott nodded slowly. "That's some achievement, Dad. Anything left on your bucket list?"

"I thought I'd be a grandfather by now." John's voice rose

in challenge. "You were supposed to make me a grandfather."

The jab hurt. It was supposed to. Scott, even knowing better, shot back. "What made you think that was going to happen?"

"Nicole promised us."

"John!" His mother looked thoroughly put out by her husband's disclosure.

Scott felt his stomach drop into his shoes. "When did Nikki say that?"

His father merely hunched a shoulder and looked away.

His mother frowned, biting her lip. "The last time we were all together for Thanksgiving. At your little apartment in D.C. At first we thought Nicole was teasing us. But she looked so pleased with herself. So then, well, we decided you two were waiting to make the big announcement official when you came up here at Christmas. But then, things didn't . . . work out."

Scott was still waiting to reach bottom as his thoughts were in freefall. "There was no baby. You misunderstood."

"Wishful thinking, I guess."

His mother glanced at her husband, and Scott caught the disappointment in her eyes. They had hoped to be grandparents and once again he had let them down. The cold queasy feeling of failure slithered through him.

He quashed it, replacing that emotion with annoyance with Cole for leading them on. He raked a hand through his hair. "I don't understand why she would make that promise, even in jest."

His mother's face filled with sympathy. "Maybe, Scott, because she wanted it to become the truth. She was ready to start thinking about a family."

"Maybe she would have told you what she was thinking if you'd been around long enough to listen." His father looked on with a fault-finding gaze. "Nothing was more important than what you wanted. You didn't even make it through carving the Christmas turkey. One text and you're out the door, leaving your wife to serve the meal by herself. Typical of you in those days. So self-absorbed you couldn't see past your nose."

"I was working twenty-four-seven. Nikki understood that."

"So you say."

"John, please." Cathy laid a hand on her husband's thigh.

"Fine. But the truth is you left that girl on her own too damned much while you rode around on that damned bike, pretending to be, what? What was it that was so damned important?"

"I was SWAT, Dad. I had people whose lives depended upon me showing up, ready, at a moment's notice."

"That's right. Your father just means that we loved Nicole. She was just naturally part of the family from the beginning."

"Best thing that ever happened to you was her. You should have held on to her."

"I know, Dad. You've said so before. I got the message. You would rather have divorced me and kept her."

His father started. "That's not what I said."

Scott didn't bother to respond. Sometimes what wasn't said was a helluva lot clearer than what was. He'd ruined his life, Nikki's life, and now he knew he'd ruined his parents' hopes for the future, too, by losing her. Fine. Fucking great!

Scott got up and headed for the kitchen. "Need some water. I'll be back." He tossed words over his shoulder so his mother wouldn't come after him.

But once in the kitchen he just stared at the refrigerator without opening it. There was a small color photo attached at eye level by one of those magnetic frames a little smaller than a Post-it note. It was of Gabe in full battle gear with a thousand-watt chick-magnet smile that outshone the reflective surface of his silvered sunshades. Gabe could live off the land with only a knife and two days of water in a two-week wilderness training. Gabe could do anything, and everything.

"Except come home safe, you bastard!"

Scott snatched the picture off the silver face of the refrigerator and looked around for somewhere to toss it. Instead, his fist closed around the frame and he squeezed until the metal rim digging into his palm and fingers threatened to draw blood. He missed his brother so damned much. He could really use some advice.

After a few moments, he carefully replaced the photo, adjusting it to his mother's eye level. Gabe wasn't here. The world inside his own head was all he had left. Piss poor as that might be.

He braced an arm on the fridge and lowered his head against it as he tried to think his way logically through the revelations of the last few minutes.

Nikki had thrown their history and his failings in his face when he went to see her the other day. He didn't think she'd held anything back. If she had been pregnant, she would have told him then. She was too honest to do otherwise.

She hadn't mentioned wanting to start a family, not in any concrete way, the last few months of their marriage, either. Of course, even before the wedding, they'd agreed that one day, in the future, they wanted children. Later. After things settled. When they were financially stable and their careers established.

Yet some long-neglected memory was wriggling its way to the surface of his thoughts. Their last Christmas Eve, she'd placed something on the tree. What was it? Something about Christmas wishes. A tiny red stocking with a white fur trim. She'd said . . .

Scott sighed and shook his head. He couldn't remember. After he left that Christmas afternoon, he'd been gone for three straight days. She wasn't talking to him by the time he returned. And not much after that. By spring it was over.

Emotion welled up inside him, a longing for so many things he was afraid he might never have and knew he didn't deserve. What was a man supposed to do with this huge wad of longing? He'd chased down armed felons, run with one percenters, even squared off with hopped-up addicts who didn't know they'd been shot. But the emotions coursing through him now scared him more than anything ever in his life. It felt as if the only answer was that deep abyss he'd crawled out of just last year. He could feel it, just beyond the edge of his consciousness. Waiting, in case he got tired.

Get in touch again with who you really are. Department counselor's advice. Great advice. If he'd had any idea who he was in the first place.

He reached into his pocket and pulled out his cell phone. The background photo was blurry because Cole almost caught him taking it in her kitchen. But the sight of Nicole's face gave him a jolt of life. He knew he could go on living without her. He'd done that. But the sight of her, after all this time, made him want to find out if there was a way back to having her in his life again.

His involuntary smile at that thought surprised him almost as much as the relief that coursed through him with that decision. He was about to make an all-out assault on Nicole Jamieson's heart. And this time, nothing was going to screw it up.

The doorbell rang as he came back into the living room.

His mother sprang up. "Right on time. Thank goodness. I was getting worried about all that food getting cold or overcooked."

As she moved to open the door to their guests the scream of a motorcycle engine disrupted the quiet.

Scott looked up, every nerve alert. "What the fu—heck is that?"

"New neighbors." His mother pressed her lips together in disapproval. "The son comes and goes at all hours. The neighborhood association has filed a noise complaint with the city. But what are you going to do? He says it's his only mode of transportation to and from work."

"He can buy a muffler, for starters."

"I'm sure he'll do something after the next town hall meeting. Your father's on the agenda to speak on the subject."

Scott was only half listening. That motorcycle didn't belong to a kid, not unless he'd joined a biker gang. This was a serious machine. "I'll be right back. Left Izzy in the truck."

He was through the back door and across the neighbors' backyard in seconds. He only caught sight of the back end of the rider and bike. It was enough. Denim-clad sleeveless jacket and a patch he knew so well he didn't need to be close enough to read. Pagans.

Every hair on his arms lifted. His parents had some disturbing new neighbors, or the rider was not passing by by accident.

He stood several minutes listening as the noise from the bike faded like a fire engine's siren once it's passed by. He noticed the rider didn't stop in the neighborhood.

He supposed he needed to think about why this was the second time in a month he'd seen a Pagan biker. First outside his apartment in D.C. and now outside his parents' home. Was it coincidence, or something more?

"Scott?" His mother had poked her head out of the back door. "We're waiting for you."

Scott held his breath. Nothing stirred in the air. He went

deeper, sensing through whatever extra survival instincts being undercover had honed in him to the point that sometimes that edgy energy kept him awake for twenty-hour hours at a time. He felt . . . nothing.

And yet, he didn't buy it. Something had just occurred. Instinct told him that was no random biker passing. And yet he had not a single shred of proof to the contrary. Maybe being at home was messing with his head.

"Scott?"

"Yes, Mom. Coming."

He wrenched up the driver's side door and let Izzy out. He'd be happier knowing she was safe inside.

CHAPTER SIX

"Our target is Shajuanna Collier, the wife of the D.C.-based hip-hop mogul Eye-C."

"Didn't he do time for racketeering in connection with illegal dogfights?"

"That's the one."

"Jeez. What's with these guys? Getting sent up for running illegal gambling isn't enough. Now he wants to breed these killers."

"Dogs aren't killers by nature." Cole sat up straighter as the room of task force people glanced her way for the first time during the morning overview. "Even volatile breeds are often subjected to mistreatment, like starvation and abuse, in order to make them vicious killers, sir."

Lattimore, standing before his PowerPoint presentation, nodded vaguely in her general direction. "Officer Jamieson has a valid point. Her expertise in the matter of canine behavior should be useful in the field."

"I'm no expert." Cole's voice was lower this time.

"All the same, every person here has a part to play."

Cole didn't doubt that hers was a small part. This

was the first meeting of the task force team. It consisted of a joint investigation by the Drug Enforcement Administration—Baltimore District Office, DEA's Wilmington, Delaware, Resident Office, the District of Columbia Division, the Philadelphia Field Division, an FBI advisor, and a Montgomery County, Maryland, police K-9 officer. The men gathered in the room knew more than she ever would about drug trafficking and interdiction. The fact that they were all male and shared previous experience with the DEA didn't improve her standing.

As Lattimore continued his overview, Cole reminded herself of the chain of command. As the newest, least experienced member of the team she was supposed to keep her head down, mouth shut, and learn.

She bent her head to study the proposal that had been handed out to the team, and to give herself a moment to think. Despite programs like Dropbox, shared files, and so on, they were using good old-fashioned paper documents as reference materials.

Cole followed her notes as Lattimore recited them. "Our prime target is Shajuanna Collier, wife of hip-hop artist Eye-C, real name Isaac Collier. Three years ago Collier was arrested for gambling on illegal dogfights and sentenced to prison for two years. While he served twelve months of that sentence, his wife Shajuanna began breeding dogs, specifically the Argentine mastiff and the Japanese Tosa. These expensive and rare imported breeds are banned in many European countries because they were most often brought in for illegal fights.

"Shortly after Eye-C was released on probation, Shajuanna announced that she intended to redeem these 'precious loving animals' from their undeserved reputations as vicious brutes by showing them off at companion dog sports competitions sanctioned by the AKC. She has stated repeatedly since that by doing so, she would prove to the public that her husband has learned his lesson and become a passionate advocate for these maligned dogs."

The FBI and DEA agents around the table snorted their opinion of Shajuanna's motives.

"Those carved-up pups were all Argentinean mastiffs." The speaker, an FBI agent named Hadley who had headed up the FBI portion of a successful multistate dogfighting ring a year before, reared back in his chair. "If they are so damned valuable then why are they used to smuggle cocaine? I don't buy a word coming out of her mouth. This is a front. Pure and simple."

Cole absorbed without comment the pointed look the FBI advisor sent her way. There was no point in challenging him. Everyone at the table was convinced that Shajuanna and Eye-C were using these sports dog activities as a cover for everything from illegal gambling to drug trafficking. They had, as Lattimore now reiterated, the means and opportunity. As for motive? Money.

Lattimore clicked to bring up a chart that represented Eye-C's revenue flow for the past six years. "As you can see, despite the street creed of a rap sheet, Eye-C's rap career hasn't recovered from his forced absence from the charts."

"Money's a bitch." Cole didn't lift her gaze quick enough to identify the speaker.

"Even money says Shajuanna's going to file for divorce if he can't keep her upgraded," the FBI agent, Hadley, offered in response.

Ignoring the general laughter, Cole scrolled through the pictures she had been given to download on her computer tablet. The photos of Shajuanna were of a tall and beautiful woman dressed in that expensive-to-know pampered way of all celebrities. Okay, so yeah, she looked like a gold digger. That was the life. It didn't mean she was a gold digger. But what was she?

Every shot of Shajuanna included one or more of the dogs in question. Some were on a leash. In a few she was in the ring, coaching one of her dogs in mid-performance. Finally, there was a close-up of her hugging an Argentine mastiff. The dog was big and muscular and pure white, with small pink-rimmed eyes.

Cole winced at the severely docked ears. And there was Shajuanna, squatting down beside the animal in six-inch platform heels and a very expensive fur and diamonds, planting a big kiss on the dog's face. She wasn't just posing. She clearly had affection for her pet. And the dog—Cesar the notation said—seemed as close to smiling as was possible for a dog with a big pink lolling tongue. Happy dog. Not a tortured killer.

Something didn't add up.

She rechecked the notes she had typed into her notebook so far. Comments by Eye-C about how his wife had made him think differently about dogs. Shajuanna's statements about her intentions to rehabilitate the public perception of these dogs. She'd even hired a celebrity image consultant who had gotten one of her pets placement in a national commercial. Why would they draw so much public attention if they were doing something illegal?

"Too easy."

She did not realize she had spoken aloud until silence in the room made her lift her head. Ten pairs of male eyes were staring at her.

Lattimore spoke. "Do you have something else you'd like to contribute, Officer Jamieson?"

Scott, who sat across from her, gave Cole a slight shake of his head in warning. That only spurred her to speak up.

"Why would Eye-C be so obvious? He's got to know law enforcement's going to be looking at him for the slightest indication he's slipped back into something illegal. Why draw attention to himself by breeding dogs known for their popularity in dogfighting if he intended to use them to smuggle drugs? Not smart."

"Smart?" Hadley's bark of laughter sounded as rude as it was meant to be. "Smart's not a category I'd put Collier in. He needs money. His music's gone bust so he falls back into old habits. Pre-music enterprise, he dealt drugs. Once a slinger always a slinger."

"But—"

"When you hear hoofbeats, think horses, not zebras, Officer Jamieson." Lattimore gave her a sharp glance to see if she understood his meaning. *Don't look for unlikely possibilities when the probable answer is the obvious one.* "Collier's our prime suspect. His wife is our conduit to him."

"Yes, sir."

Cole ignored the smirks exchanged around the table though her face stung. It wasn't embarrassment, it was anger. They might know what they were doing as far as drugs and task force business went. But she knew dogs and their handlers. On Shajuanna's side, at least, there was a genuine interest in and affection for her dogs.

"We need eyes and ears on the ground at dog competitions where the wife shows her dogs, something that will give up probable cause to go after them in a more aggressive way. Actually finding puppy drug mules at an event might be too much to hope for. But if any of the animals carried drugs at one time, or was kenneled with those who did, traces of cocaine should remain with them. The vet told us the packets aren't always leakproof. The potency should leave a permanent trail."

"That's where our dogs come in." Scott flashed a reassuring glance at Cole.

"Exactly. Officer Jamieson's Bouvier des Flandres is one of the breeds registered to compete in dog sports. We'll be using them to infiltrate the dog competitions. With her training experience they should pass inspection as competitorworthy. Meanwhile Agent Lucca's K-9 will work drug detection backstage at the shows."

Refusing to make eye contact with Scott, Cole angled her chair toward the front of the room. "Why not go in separately, sir? There's no need to pose as a couple."

"Actually, there is. Being a couple keeps you and your partner from looking suspicious. You will be expected to have dogs with you wherever you go. The fact that Scott's canine doesn't compete won't look suspicious if he's paired with you. I'm told Shajuanna Collier's a very outgoing young woman. Likes to chat with other dog handlers when on the road. The dog competition circuit is very clubby. You'll be status seekers, new to the game, looking to learn the ropes. We need you to buddy up to Shajuanna. Get in. See what you can stir up."

Cole nodded. "How long do you expect this is going to take?"

"The faster you do your job the quicker it's over. Two, three weekends of shows should be enough to tell us if this operation can yield anything of value."

Cole smiled. "So I'm home during the week? I can work my patrols?"

"No. You have to have a home base in case Shajuanna decides to befriend you." Lattimore clicked through a few slides. "Lucky break for us, Shajuanna owns a home in Potomac, just off River Road, where she breeds her dogs."

"That's Montgomery County. My patrol area."

"But you won't be patrolling. Weekdays the two of you are to cozy up at home and work the dogs for the next show."

"Great."

"Shit."

Cole and Scott eyed one another, not sure who had said what. But, clearly, neither was happy about the proposed arrangements.

"I'd prefer not to use Officer Jamieson's home." Scott didn't glance at Cole. "It's risky. What if something went wrong? She'd have to move."

"It does seem invasive, sir." One of the Baltimore reps spoke up. "If anything goes wrong, they'll know where to find Officer Jamieson. Even if she moved, with a bit of snooping they'd have her name, her badge number, everything."

Lattimore's mouth lifted in one corner. "That's why we're looking for suitable housing. First order of duty is to get our K-9 teams in sync. To get you up to speed ASAP, I've made arrangements for you both to spend a few days at Harmonie Kennels to refresh your skills. So when you go home pack a bag. The training begins in the morning. Ms. Summers has agreed to supervise your training herself."

Cole was impressed. Yardley Summers, owner and operator of Harmonie Kennels, was nearly a legend. Everyone in the K-9 law enforcement world knew of her. Her kennel was one of the top training facilities for K-9 services in the United States. They trained canines for law enforcement, local, state, and national, as well as for military and Special Forces use. And Lattimore had arranged for Cole to train under her. Cole was impressed all over again.

When the meeting broke for the day, the FBI agent slapped Scott on the back. "Sweet deal you got going there, Lucca. All the perks of a live-in girlfriend without the baggage. Tough break, you're the bracelet on this one."

Over Scott's shoulder Agent Hadley snagged Cole's eye and winked.

Cole winked back, pleased when surprise was reflected in his expression. Good. She would rather have given him the finger. But that, she suspected, was what he'd wanted, as proof that his needling had gotten to her.

Beyond exhausted after spending hours in a boardroom when she would rather have been doing, well, anything else, Cole stifled a yawn as she gathered her things and headed out the door, not making eye contact with anyone else.

"Hey. Officer Jamieson."

Halfway down the hall, Cole turned back at the sound of Scott's voice. She'd almost made it out without having to deal with him face-to-face.

He waited until he caught up with her before he spoke. "Lattimore wants to talk to you."

Cole went still. "What about?"

"My guess? He wants to know what you saw in those photos."

"How could he know I saw something of interest in the photos?"

"Same way I did. By watching you. I saw your face as you went through those pictures of Shajuanna. You saw something the rest of us missed."

"Maybe." Cole found she was having a hard time looking at him. The last time they'd been this close she'd thrown him out. *Because I wanted to kiss him.*

If he had guessed her thoughts Scott didn't give any indication. "Don't underestimate Lattimore. He's got as many eyes as a spider. But before you go in there you need to tell me exactly what you're going to tell him."

Cole shrugged. "It was Shajuanna and the dogs. She's not pretending to like dogs. There's real affection there."

Scott was nodding when she finished telling him her impressions. "I saw it, too."

"Then why didn't you say something? Back me up?"

He tried to take her elbow but she lifted her arm out of his palm. Undeterred, he angled his body so that his shoulder touched the wall, forming a shield between them and the rest of the hallway. He lowered his voice, as if they were sharing a personal private moment, but his expression was dead serious.

"I know you're angry as hell at me. But we've agreed to give this a go. That means we have to trust each other to have the other one's back on the job. I'm trying to do that, if you'll let me."

"You didn't back me just now."

"That's right. You have to be seen as holding your own weight and taking the heat when it comes, too. This is the big leagues. You can't be viewed as needing a protector or you lose your credibility."

"Okay. I see that." Cole held his gaze. "Does everyone on the task force know our history?"

"Hell no." Scott's eyes narrowed. "Only Lattimore. And it will stay that way."

Relief tumbled through her. "I wondered, the way that FBI guy Hadley is acting."

"Hadley's a douche. Smart, good at his job, but a douche."

"What did he mean about you being the 'bracelet'?"

To her amazement, Scott's face reddened. "It's a term for the undercover agent who is acting strictly as cover for the main undercover operator. Like a girlfriend."

Obviously, not a term of respect. "So in this operation you're my stud muffin arm candy?"

Scott scowled.

Suddenly, Cole felt better than she had all day. "Better go see the boss."

Scott leaned in closer, making her aware of his superior height. "Here's the thing. Lattimore's position requires that he do some political grandstanding. Task forces are funded by public money. There's never enough of that to go around. So, there's no room for any weakness in our plan. If you convince him we have the wrong target, he'll pull this operation."

"You're telling me to lie."

"I'm telling you to ask yourself if you're a hundred percent certain you're right. Or if you'd like a chance to test your theory against the weight of developing evidence."

Cole nodded. "That's smart. Someone's using puppies to move drugs. One way or the other, this is our best lead. At best, we get the right people. At worst, we could develop other leads while discounting our hypothesis."

Scott's mouth twitched. "I wouldn't use the word 'hypothesis' with Lattimore. He's not always dealing with heavy artillery when it comes to seeking congressional allocations of money. He needs small-word explanations to pass on."

"There is something else." Cole flipped open her tablet and pointed to the graph she punched up on her screen. "Eye-C's lost money on his recordings, but I did a little surfing at lunchtime. He's making good money on residuals and his protégée, PaTreeZ. She's gone platinum this week. He may be a criminal but he knows how to make money without dealing."

Scott grinned at her. "You may make detective one day. But don't lay all your cards on the table, not even with Lattimore. Hunches are just that until you have hard evidence. Now go get 'em."

He turned and walked away.

Cole had to stop herself from calling him back. To say thank you. To express gratitude to the man who still made her body hum just by entering a room.

She shook her head. She had some serious mental issues she needed to deal with. Serious. Because she was grateful for his little pep talk. And she was excited about the next few weeks.

She squared her shoulders and went to find Lattimore.

* * *

"The Pagans made you?" Dave Wilson stared at Scott across the tiny table space in a D.C. corner deli/grocer. "You didn't think that was something you should have reported before now?"

Scott shrugged. "A cop gets made on the street on any given day. No big deal."

His former undercover handler shook his head. "An ex-undercover agent gets made two years after a nasty bust, that's news. You got a name?"

"Calls himself Dos Equis. X for short. We rode together for several months."

Dave made a note in his cell phone. "I remember him. Biker from out West. Always thought it suspect he should choose Pagan affiliation. Anything else?"

"Nothing I can't manage, now I know to keep an eye open."

Scott had planned to keep to himself the incident that occurred on the road a month ago. He could handle himself. But the drive-by of his parents' home in New Jersey over the weekend hinted at something altogether different. If some sick bastard was scoping out his family, he needed backup. So he had decided to reach out.

Undercover operatives were assigned a handler while undercover. Dave Wilson had been Scott's only point of contact while he was on the job. Dave had monitored him, provided instructions, and assistance. When it all went sideways, Dave had been there with the manufactured backstory that extracted him before he was exposed.

Usually the handlers had some form of cover themselves, creating a convenient excuse for why the agent would be in contact with them. Dave had been Scott's uptight coke-head brother-in-law whom he sold to from time to time.

"You sure you've told me everything? Is there anyone else we need to include in the scope? A regular girlfriend?"

"Don't have one." Scott's expression didn't alter but his handler changed the subject. Dave knew more than anyone how messed up Scott had become after his divorce.

"It's just as well this new task force assignment is taking you off the street for a while. If there's a real threat, the Pagans will either give up when they can't find you, or intensify their efforts to pick up your trail. If they choose door number two that will make it easier for us to track them, and protect you. Meanwhile, I'll check with ATF and see if they've picked up any talk of a bounty on a narc's head. When are you leaving?"

"Tomorrow. DEA is anxious for us to get under way."

"Where will you be?"

Scott shrugged. "How about I call you?"

The former handler looked over his notes. "For the record, can you think of anyone else who might want you dead?"

Scott smiled. "A name or two comes to mind."

"Want to share?"

"Maybe I'm wrong." His smile widened as he recalled how close Nikki had come to kissing him that day in her place. He'd been able to remember little else when not on the job. She was still attracted to him. Even if she did hate his guts.

"You're wasting my time."

"Yeah. Sorry."

Long pause. "If I get anything you'll hear from me. Meanwhile don't get yourself fucking dead playing the hero." This was Dave's standard parting line.

"Yes, sir. I won't be leaving myself open to approach again."

CHAPTER SEVEN

"What the hell?" Yardley Summers crossed the parking lot of Harmonie Kennels to greet her latest students, her expression reflecting her thinking. None of it was good.

Officer Nicole Jamieson grasped the leash tightly as her K-9 Hugo went airborne at the end of it. His repeated jumps were impressive, all four feet off the ground as ninety-five pounds of black Bouvier cleared more than two feet of air with each leap.

Six feet away, straining at the end of her own leash, Agent Scott Lucca's chocolate Lab, Izzy, stood at full alert, growling at Hugo's antics.

The mixed doggy messages were clear: Hugo was gonzo happy to meet Izzy while Izzy thought Hugo was a bad idea in every possible way.

Yardley already knew the reason why, though Agent Lattimore had neglected to mention it. It's why she always did her own background checks even if she'd been sent the official files. Trust but verify. This tiny oversight was a time bomb. Agent Scott and Officer Jamieson were once married.

She could tell them she knew, but she wanted to hear it from the pair themselves. Their explanations would reveal a lot and tell her if, and possibly how, to proceed.

She reached Cole first. "Control that gorgeous beast, Officer Jamieson."

"Yes, ma'am." Totally embarrassed, Cole barked orders to her canine partner. "Hugo. *Nein. Fuss.*"

Hugo stopped jumping and trotted back to heel at Cole's left side. But his happy-to-see-you-let's-play attitude had him squirming. *"Sitz."* He sat but his butt continued to do a happy dance.

Yardley moved in close then waited until Cole gave Hugo the go-ahead to greet their instructor. "Hello, you handsome devil." She bent down and Hugo moved to let her pet him. "How fine and strong you are, Hugo. What a sweetheart."

Yardley stood and turned to Scott.

Scott curbed his dog before she could speak. "Izzy. *Fuss. Blieb.*"

When Izzy had moved back next to her handler, Scott let out her leash and took a couple of steps forward himself, leaving her behind to offer a smile and his hand to Yardley. "Morning, ma'am. This is my fault."

Yardley ignored his offer of a handshake. "Don't fall on your sword just yet, Agent Lucca. This unacceptable behavior is on both of you."

Once again, she moved into range, of Izzy this time. Izzy, whom she'd helped train, immediately came up to lean against her leg to be petted. "Pretty girl. How sleek you are. Like an otter." She bent lower. "Yes, you are a beauty, my girl." Izzy licked her trainer's face.

Yardley treated her dogs like small children, unashamedly doting on them in a singsongy voice of affection. It was humans she seldom gave a second chance.

She stood again, allowing her gaze to move between the human pair. "What exactly is the issue here?"

"It's my fault, ma'am." Cole ignored Scott's look of surprise. "A misunderstanding occurred between Agent Lucca and myself when he was introduced to Hugo last week. Hugo misread my reactions."

"I doubt that. Hugo is so tuned into you that if you sneeze he licks his nose." Yardley folded her arms and jutted out a hip. "Want to try again?"

"Officer Jamieson and I were once married, Ms. Summers." Scott noted Cole's glare but continued. "As you might imagine, we have a few unresolved issues."

Something between a grunt and laughter erupted from Yardley. "DEA must be really desperate to even consider putting exes together undercover. The probability of disaster is astronomical, and John knows it."

Cole and Scott exchanged glances at Yardley's use of Agent Lattimore's first name.

"What the hell. I can't make things worse than they are. Let's move out." Yardley pointed in the direction of the practice field. "Officer Jamieson, lead the way."

"Yes, ma'am. And you can call me Cole, ma'am. Hugo. *Hier.*" Hugo moved instantly with her as Cole turned to walk away.

Cole's hands were shaking as she held Hugo's lead. She had met the K-9 legend once before but she was more intimidated today than the first time. Yardley was her idol. Cole cringed. After the way Hugo behaved, her idol must think that she couldn't control her emotions any better than her K-9. And why did Scott tell her they were acrimonious exes?

In the male-dominated field of K-9 law enforcement, Yardley Summers was both an enigma and a rock star. Rumor tagged her as everything from a retired Special Ops to a sometimes still-operative spook. What she did have was access to the highest echelons of both political and military arenas.

Cole hadn't missed the look of admiration on Scott's face when Yardley appeared. Okay, she couldn't blame him. The entire male population probably responded like that when Yardley appeared.

At five feet nine inches tall with long dark red mahogany tresses and coal-black eyes, Yardley was what Cole's grandmother would call a striking woman. Yet she most often hid her long-legged Victoria's Secret curviness beneath military fatigues and windbreakers. Today, as usual, her hair was stuffed up under a fatigue cap.

Some said there was a man out there who had her complete and utter loyalty. No one seemed to know who he was or what he did. Yet, almost every man who passed through here envied him. A few learned, to their regret, that she wasn't interested in second-best.

Above all, she radiated a no-nonsense intensity and competence that made even SWAT teams and military Special Ops call her ma'am with absolute respect.

Cole led the way past a sprawling facility that housed classrooms, a dining hall, a series of canine training suites, and farther on, barracks for handlers. Next they passed the temperature-controlled low-roofed barn that served as the kennel for the animals Harmonie Kennels bought and/or trained for law enforcement and the military. At any given time the kennels might be simultaneously hosting law-enforcement K-9 handler classes on the local, state, and national levels. Only military classes and drills were held in seclusion.

As she followed them, Yardley reviewed what she knew of the pair she'd promised to whip into shape. She knew them both, though Scott Lucca much better than Nicole Jamieson.

Officer Jamieson had come to her attention six months

ago as part of Montgomery Police K-9's annual training week at Harmonie Kennels. Most law-enforcement K-9 departments made certain their officers got professional refresher training at least one week a year. Though a rookie, Officer Jamieson had a gift for working with dogs. And she was eager to prove herself, pushing Hugo and herself every day. At the time Yardley had wondered why. Now watching Agent Jamieson's posture as she gazed at her ex, Yardley suddenly understood a lot more. Something to tuck away for use later.

Scott, on the other hand, was one of her salvage projects. Undercover operatives often had a miserably difficult time trying to fit back into even normal law-enforcement routines. Scott had suffered the double whammy of an extraction from a tough undercover situation just after the breakup of his marriage. Surly and feeling sorry for himself, he'd had almost gotten himself kicked out of K-9 training the second day.

Yardley smiled to herself. Handsome and used to getting his way through charm or intimidation, Scott would not allow anyone in close enough to help. Yardley understood about wounded warriors. What he needed was an intimate relationship, though not the sexual kind. He was the kind of man for whom sex was as easy as entering a room. Part psychologist and part dog whisperer, Yardley personally paired her dogs and handlers and so chose Izzy for Scott. Izzy, calm, sure of herself, and yet absolutely attuned to the world around her, was Scott's perfect K-9 partner. The fact that they worked bomb squad duty allowed Scott to stay part of SWAT, work dangerous situations, and still bond with a partner who doted on his every action. Of course, Yardley doubted Scott realized that pairing them was her idea, not his. The reports she was getting back on them reinforced the appropriateness of her choice.

Now she was saddled with partnering a team of four,

who at the moment weren't making eye contact. She did like a challenge, though.

The slight smile on her face betrayed her decision. "I'm told this undercover pairing requires you to pose as a married couple?"

"Significant others." Cole rushed to supply the answer. "I—we thought it might be more believable if we're just a couple. In case it's obvious to others that we won't, you know, work out." Oh, God. She sounded like a teenager.

Yardley folded her arms. "From where I'm standing, this mission is already flirting with failure."

"We just need a little adjustment time." Cole reached down to pat Hugo and remind herself she was a police officer who had chased down badass criminals. "Hugo's really good at warming up to people." She glanced at Izzy, avoiding Scott's eye. "I'm sure Izzy will do the same. With time."

"Right. Hugo and Izzy are the problem." Yardley pushed her hat back on her head. "So here's what's going to happen. First we're going see what Hugo can do on an Agility course, or this mission is a nonstarter. Cole, take him out behind the kennel barn. We've set up a course for you to use. Warm him up for me."

"Yes, ma'am." Cole hesitated. "Alone?"

"Do you need help working your dog?"

"No, ma'am."

"Dismissed."

Cole didn't look at Scott as she moved away. She knew her face must be hot to the touch. She'd been sent to detention.

She couldn't believe that she'd allowed Hugo to get so out of control in front of the one person who could send her back to the Montgomery County Police Department with a black mark against her K-9 skills. But then, she'd never seen any dog excite Hugo the way Izzy had. Other dogs seldom caught his interest, unless his alpha position was being challenged. Besides, Izzy was female. *Female*.

She glanced sharply down at her partner. "Don't tell me you fell for that chocolate-brown hussy?"

Hugo looked up at her, his jaws slack in a pink-tongued Bouvier smile.

"You dog!" She chuckled. "She is cute. But I've got news. She's fixed. So it would be an exercise in futility. Let's go exercise off some of that excessive energy."

Cole took a deep breath as she surveyed the Agility course that had been set up on the other side of the kennel. It had been more than ten years since she'd been in the ring with a dog. But something about the familiarity of the course kicked up her heartbeat with pleasure.

Dog Agility was one of several dog sport competitions. In Agility, the handler directed his or her dog through a complicated obstacle course. The judges gave points for both time and accuracy. Winners were determined by the dog that made the most accurate and rapid path around the numbered obstacles. The dogs were always off leash and handlers could use only voice cues and hand signals to direct them, no toys or food or other incentives. It was a team effort, which was what she loved best about it. The dog ran the course while depending on his human partner to point out which obstacle was next and the quickest path to it. No two courses were ever the same.

Cole let out a slow breath as she mentally ran this course. The jumps of various kinds would be no problem. She and Hugo often practiced jumps and Hugo liked to show off by leaping higher than necessary. The A-frame and Dog Walk were about negotiating ramps. No problem there, either. K-9s were trained to go into buildings with stairs and, more rarely, climb over barriers between a suspect and itself. It was the officer's responsibility to judge if there was probable danger on the other side. One of Cole's favorite trainers liked to say, "If I can't see what's on the other side, I ain't sending my dog over that wall."

The Tube Tunnel and Collapsed Tunnel obstacles were about maneuvering through tight and dark spaces. Dogs instinctively don't like tight spaces but K-9s were trained to navigate them because suspects often chose dark, restrictive spaces like closets, under stairs, or even a drainpipe to hide in.

Cole stopped short as she spied one obstacle they had never done: the Weave. The Weave was like a slalom for dogs, requiring a series of in-and-out motions between upright poles placed close together. This was not something a K-9 team trained for. It was also, unfortunately, the most difficult obstacle to master.

Cole looked quickly away. She didn't want Hugo to get wind of her nervousness about the Weave before he'd even tried it. Maybe she'd wait until tomorrow to introduce it.

Cole glanced back over her shoulder, expecting to see Yardley rounding the corner of the building at any second. She would be expecting perfection. So far, no one was watching them.

She bent down and unclipped Hugo's leash. "I know you don't understand most of what I'm going to tell you but this is important. We have work to do. Important work." She pulled a ball with a jingle bell inside, his favorite toy, from her pocket. "You get this if you try very hard."

Hugo sat up and barked. He sounded ferocious but she recognized that this was his happy bark. She gave him a pat. "*Gute Hund.* Come on, let's see what you've got."

Hugo bounded a few steps away from her and barked happily.

Cole was sweating by the time she and Hugo had cleared the A-frame, the Ring Jump, and the Pause Table, and not from exertion. She kept expecting Yardley and/or Scott to pop up. Where could they be and what were they doing?

Yardley and Scott had been watching Cole and Hugo from a viewing space inside the kennel barn. Yardley didn't want to spook Cole but she needed to access the younger woman's ability to handle her K-9 in the ring.

To her credit, Cole was working Hugo through the course with the skill of someone who was familiar with ring work. Hugo, in turn, seemed to be delighted by the challenge. Though it was obvious he wasn't familiar with every obstacle, he seemed game to try. With concerted effort, they just might pull off their end.

So now, to kick-start the other half of the team.

She turned on Scott suddenly. "What the hell were you thinking? Agreeing to work with your ex? How many kinds of stupid are you?"

That backed him up, as it was meant to. He had been staring out the window at Cole with every thought in his head reflected in his expression.

But he switched effortlessly to good cop mode, and smiled. "Officer Jamieson and I are professionals. It's about the needs of the task force. Nikki's very talented. I'd not seen her work Hugo in the field but I can tell—"

Yardley held up a hand. "You can't tell me about what you don't know, Agent. As for the rest, you need to shut it down. Or have you already told her?"

Scott's charming smile faded. "Told her what, ma'am?"

"The reason for that dopey look on your face every time you gaze at Officer Jamieson?"

His eyes narrowed. "Nikki's not in the mood to listen to me at the moment."

"Cole's a good K-9 officer. In a few years she'll be great. You undermine her confidence in herself. You're the reason she's not at her best today."

Scott looked like she'd thrown a bucket of ice water over his head. But, again, he recovered quickly. "Okay. Maybe we've still got unresolved issues."

"That maybe and a dollar won't even buy you a cup of coffee these days. You hurt her once. You're capable of doing that again. That's why she's put you behind her."

Scott looked away, genuine anger tightening his jaw this time. "Right."

Yardley was silent for a moment. If she didn't set this up properly, she'd destroy any chance of them pulling off their assignment. "The first relationship was on your terms. Don't bother to deny that. You know how that turned out. What would be different this time?"

Scott sent Yardley a glance that had nothing to do with attraction. It was a "get the fuck out of my face" reaction. But he didn't act on it. "I've changed."

Well, damn and good for him. But she couldn't let him off the hook on one step forward.

"Take a second and feel nice about yourself, Agent. And then realize everybody changes. Before you make another mistake, be certain you like the woman Officer Jamieson has become—not the person you think you remember."

Scott's jaw worked for a moment. She decided not to give him the chance to ruin his admirable self-control. "I don't like being in the middle of anyone's personal business. But you brought this hot mess to me. So suck it up and tell me. Can you two work this out in a week?"

His anger suddenly dried up, reshaping into concern that softened his expression. "Whatever happens, Nikki's not to blame. I pushed for this. I'll take the weight for making it work."

"Don't waste your breath on me. Go get shit done. For starters, that woman out there you knew as Nikki?" She hooked a thumb toward the window. "She calls herself Cole."

Yardley turned and quickly walked away. She'd probably given him too much to think about too soon, but she didn't have time for subtlety.

God, she hoped he was as much of a quick study on relationships as he was on anger management. But when a man's heart was in a struggle with his pride?

"Damn you, John Lattimore. I will get even with you for this one."

CHAPTER EIGHT

Cole entered the women's barracks at Harmonie Kennels to hear Hugo growling low in his throat. Her gaze went instantly to the shadowy figure sitting at the table at the far end of the common room. Her free hand moved to her waist until she remembered she wasn't wearing her weapon.

"Where the hell have you been?" The cranky male voice was familiar.

"Scott?" She reached for the nearest light switch.

Scott occupied a chair on the far side of a small table while Hugo stood guard on the opposite side, tracking him with the single-mindedness he reserved for cornered suspects.

Cole's lips twitched. "Hugo, what's that you've cornered? A *schmutzige Ratte*?" She glanced at Scott. "That's German for 'dirty rat.'"

Hugo came to his feet, barking his agreement.

Scott stood up. "Very funny. Now call him off."

"Hugo. *Lass es.*"

Hugo looked disappointed at the command to leave the

intruder alone. He turned and came readily toward her, but looked back several times at his would-be prey.

Amused, Cole deposited her bag of groceries on the counter then retrieved a ball from her pocket, bouncing it toward Hugo. "*Gute Hund. So ist brav.*"

When Hugo had caught and bounded away to play with his reward, she turned to Scott. "What are you doing here?"

"I came to see you." He rolled his shoulders. "While I waited I thought you might have something to munch on. I had just found your chips when Batman there took exception to my presence. Don't you ever keep his kennel door shut?"

"That would defeat the purpose of having a guard dog. Still, you seem to be in one piece." She looked him up and down, ignoring the wave of super self-awareness that seemed to be part of her every encounter with him. "I'd say you got off lucky."

Scott glanced at Hugo, who was chomping so hard on his toy the jingle bell inside tinkled constantly. "We were actually negotiating pretty well until I ran out of chips."

"That's when he cornered you?" Cole bit her lip.

"What's so funny? He could have taken a chunk out of me at any second."

"I'm not laughing." But Cole had to press a hand to her lips to keep back the chuckles bubbling up inside her.

"You're enjoying this." He scowled at her, a decidedly sexy scowl that she remembered all too well.

She nodded, trying to hold in a breath that escaped in soft puffs of humor.

"It's not funny. Well, maybe it is a little." He cracked a smile. "Don't tell Yardley about this."

"What? That I found you hiding behind the kitchen table like a little girl afraid of a mouse?"

"You're enjoying this entirely too much." He tried to maintain a scowl but her laugher was infectious. Before long his dimples popped into view. "I had almost forgotten your laugh. Your whole face lights up."

Cole sent him a sidelong glance. "Don't make too much of it."

"Why?"

"Because, just don't."

Their gazes met, hers turned a deeper blue than usual, as if something had disturbed those depths and brought up shadows of things past. Maybe she was remembering how much they once laughed together, often in bed. In bed, nothing mattered but them. In bed they were perfect.

One glorious second his dick sprang to life along with the sudden urge to capture her laughter in his mouth. He longed to scoop her up, slam and lock the door, and carry her to the nearest horizontal surface where he could screw his wife until they were both too exhausted to move.

My ex-wife. And I can't touch her. Can't do any of the sexy nasty things streaming though my mind.

A man who lived his professional life observing and making split-second judgments about the emotional status of others, Scott clocked the exact moment she began to read his thoughts. Her eyes widened and her lips parted in a soft expression of alarm mingled with resistance.

He looked away first, not because she intimidated him. The exact opposite. If she saw more deeply into the dark dangerous desires swirling through him, she would refuse to continue to work with him. And who could blame her?

So, he slammed the door on his libido and put his emotions on lockdown before he put his hands on her.

All he had left was a jittery anxiety he channeled into the most useful emotion he could find. Anger.

"This is not a game." He gestured toward Hugo. "How the hell do you expect Hugo to accept me when hostility rolls off you as regularly as waves on the shore?" Lust to anger in less than three seconds. A new record for him.

She didn't back down. She crossed her arms. "I'm not hostile."

He took a few steps toward her. "You hate my guts. Admit it. Stands to reason Hugo isn't going to cuddle up to me."

Cole bit the inside of her lip. He was pushing harder than the moment seemed to call for. "Are you finished?"

"I haven't begun."

"Then this isn't going to work."

"Oh, it will work." He paused before her, reaching out to tug the end of the ponytail slung forward over her shoulder. "But you're going to have to warm up to me. For the sake of the operation."

Cole jerked her gaze away. Warm up? She was much too hot already with him just standing so close.

The deep dark secret that had kept her awake for hours each night since Scott had reentered her life was that the connection between them hadn't eroded during the past two years. She might resent him, blame him for ruining everything, have every sane reason to distrust him. Yet their bodies still knew each other. The attraction held. Easy for him to make light of it. Impossible for her.

When she looked up again he had moved away from her. Was, in fact, peering into the grocery bag she'd brought in. "You can stay for dinner."

He looked up with the delight of Christmas morning. "Great. What are we having?"

She unhooked Hugo's leash from around her waist. "Whatever you make. There's an hour of daylight left and I need to give Hugo all the time I can fit in on that Agility course." She was out the door before he could reply.

Scott unstrapped his watch and washed his hands before unbagging the groceries. There was a whole raw chicken. Sweet potatoes. Kale. "Beets? Seriously?"

He held up the plastic bag to inspect them. Damn. Some of them were orange. He was all for healthy eating. But beets? He set them aside. Nikki never cooked beets when they were together.

Scott turned and glanced at the door Nikki—Cole, the door that Cole had left through. Yardley's comment about how Cole had changed skimmed his thoughts. Maybe Cole liked beets. So just maybe there was a way to do something with them even he would eat. Laptop in his cruiser. Recipes at his fingertips.

He finished unpacking bread, milk, and coffee. Onions. BBQ sauce. "Okay, now we're talking."

"We need a cover story."

They were sitting on the steps of Cole's barracks watching twilight slide into night in the sky overhead. Hugo lay stretched out beside her while Izzy had deigned to join them, but only at the far opposite end of the porch. At least no one was barking or growling, not even she and Scott.

Cole stretched out her legs, letting her boots make gullies in the gravel walkway. She was full of barbecued chicken, mashed sweet potatoes, and, surprisingly, roasted beets. "How elaborate will it have to be?"

"The best lies are those that stay close to the truth."

Scott pulled free another beer bottle from the six-pack he had fetched from the barracks he shared with five other male handlers and offered it to Cole.

She shook her head. One was enough. "Could we be brother and sister?"

Scott choked on his beer. "The way I look at you could get me arrested for incest in twenty-five states."

He said it lightly but Cole found it hard to smile.

"How about this? We're exes who recently got back together after you blew us up by screwing around. I'm giving you another chance but I'm not betting on this being a permanent arrangement because I don't trust you."

Scott took a long pull on his beer. "Is that what you think? That I'm just doing this because I don't like being the bad guy?"

Cole gazed at him for several seconds. "I think you don't know what you want. I don't think you ever have." She waved a hand around. "If this task force assignment is your way of trying to make something up to me then know that it doesn't make up for a thing."

He reached out and touched his little finger to hers. "What do you want?"

Cole looked down at their touching fingers, wondering how such a tiny thing could set off such huge seismic quakes in her middle. She shifted her finger away.

"I want to do something important. I want to prove I didn't make a mistake in choosing a career in law enforcement." She lifted her gaze to the night sky. "I want to prove I'm good enough."

Scott heard an echo of her words in his chest. To do something important. To prove he was good enough. That had been the be-all, end-all of his entire life. And still he'd managed to screw up everything that mattered.

Cole shook her head at some internal thought. "I wasn't the perfect daughter with As because I wanted to be. I just knew it would have killed my parents if I'd become a rebel after they divorced. Becca and I had to show them we were okay, that they didn't ruin us."

Scott pulled up a knee and rested his elbow on it, letting the beer bottle dangle from the hook of two fingers. Unlike his own, he'd always thought she had the perfect childhood. After all, even though they were divorced, her parents had presented a united front to him. They didn't like him.

"You never told me how the divorce affected you before."

She glanced at him, for once without her guard up. "We didn't do much real talking the years we were together."

He couldn't argue with that. Too hot to cool down. Plus, to allow her to open up would have meant she would have expected the same from him. He hadn't wanted her to see him as he really was, not when she gazed at him like he was Superman, the Socrates of law enforcement, and the Sexiest Man Alive all rolled into one. How could he have been so blind?

"So circumstances prevented you from being . . . ?"

She smiled. "Who knows? Goth, maybe, or I might have gotten a nose ring and tattoos—"

"Tattoos? You hate tattoos."

"Not hate. I just didn't want you to ruin a great body with one of those ugly biker tats you kept threatening to get. And I certainly didn't want some biker-gang scum with an ink gun anywhere near you. Hepatitis? HIV?"

Scott let her explanation sink in. He didn't recall any of their fights on the subject including such a reasonable argument. Or, maybe he had just stopped listening before she could make it.

"Of course, I'm not inflexible." The corner of her mouth lifted though she didn't glance at him. "I found a licensed artist who is working to pay her way to become a nurse practitioner."

He sat forward suddenly. "You've got a tattoo?"

She nodded. "Not that it's any of your business."

Scott's gaze swept over her. She'd showered and changed before they ate. Her hair was swept up in a ponytail he longed to tug at. No designs on her slender neck.

The sleeveless vee-neck tee and shorts she wore couldn't be hiding a tattoo on her arms or her legs, which meant no thigh or chest tattoos. It had to be in a secret place. A variety of possibilities invaded his thoughts, each one more intimate than the last. He felt himself begin to sweat. "Can I see it?"

To his astonishment, she gave him a secret naughty-girl smile. "In your dreams, Agent Lucca. In your dreams."

Well hell. Now he was going to have to see it. Somehow.

Cole reached for the beer she had earlier refused. "We need to get back to business."

She did, maybe. He wanted to continue to think about her hidden tattoo. He stretched, deliberately allowing his legs to spread until one of his denim-clad thighs leaned against her bare one. When she didn't immediately shift away, he smiled. Now they could talk business.

"Lattimore called this afternoon. He's sending out people in the morning to evaluate our progress. We need to get our story straight and prove to them that we can do this before we take it on the road."

"How do we do that?"

"Glad you asked." He clinked his bottle to hers. "We need to move in together."

Cole bit back her initial reaction. Of course, they had to move in together. They were going to pretend to be a couple. A real couple.

"Is that a problem?" Scott leaned toward her. "You got a boyfriend somewhere who won't like it?"

Cole had been expecting he would ask, sooner or later, if there was a man in her life. She even had a story ready. "He understands."

"Does he?" The question came out of Scott in a huff of surprise.

Shit. That wasn't the answer he'd wanted to hear. But he tried to play it off casually.

"I most definitely wouldn't understand a woman I cared about moving in with another guy, even if it was strictly for the job. I'd be a wild man."

"Yes. You would." Kate Winslow was in the house. "That's why he's nothing like you."

Scott reared back, bracing his elbows on the porch. Cole tried not to notice how his sprawl showed off his long lean body to good effect. "So, what's he like?"

"He's a podiatrist." She saw his jaw drop a little before a smirk punched dimples into his cheeks. "I know. Feet. That's what everyone thinks. But he's a surgeon. Sports medicine. Specializing in injuries to the foot, ankle, and lower leg."

"Sounds like a busy guy."

"He is. Sports medicine is very lucrative."

He gazed at her between narrowed lids. "Interesting."

"What?"

"You haven't mentioned his name."

"Robert Dawson. Dr. Robert Dawson. Becca introduced us." She had looked up the name of the doctor her sister had been trying to set her up with, in case Scott decided to check. She just hoped the guy would never know how she was lying about him.

"Doc Rob? Cute." Scott rocked back into a seated position. "You've known him long?"

Cole crossed her toes inside her boots. "Nearly a year."

"Sounds serious." He picked up her left hand and turned it palm down. "But I don't see an engagement ring. I thought you'd be remarried by now."

"No. You cured me of the habit. You?"

He merely shook his head, sucker punched by her candor. He'd cured her . . . of what? Wanting to be married?

She'd loved being married, said so practically every day they were together. She talked about a house and kids . . . kids.

He glanced at her sharply. He didn't know how to start that conversation.

"What about you, Scott? Got a girlfriend?"

"I was seeing someone. Sort of." No point in telling her there hadn't been anyone special in his life since she walked out of it. He had gone back to strictly one-night stands. Even so, it had been months since he'd been with a woman. Next to Doc Rob, it would make him sound like a loser. "Nothing serious."

"I seem to remember you prefer your women raw and raunchy, like that skank who gave you a blow job in public."

Shit. Back to the heart of their split. "It was a biker initiation."

"Oh, and that was supposed to explain everything?"

"I'm not making excuses. I screwed up. Got in a situation where I couldn't back out without causing suspicion. Who the hell knew the bar owner would call the police?"

Cole leaned in, her shadowed expression going from serious to pissed off.

"You were in my precinct, Scott. Even if I hadn't been one of the officers who answered the call, those who did would have seen you and talked. By the time the night was over, everyone we worked with would have known it anyway. This way, at least, I got to walk out first."

Scott's expression went dark with anger. "You should have waited to talk with me. You owed me that."

"Did I? If I had waited for you, what would you have said?"

"Shit. I don't know. Something." Anything to make her stay.

He stood up suddenly and heaved his beer bottle across

the yard so that it smashed against the telephone pole a healthy distance away.

After a moment she spoke, her voice quiet. "You had enough of tiptoeing down memory lane?"

He sucked in a breath, trying to regain control of his temper. "Yeah."

He offered her a third beer.

She shook her head. "I'm in rehab. Have been for a while."

"Rehab?" His gut tightened. "For what?"

"Stupid heart syndrome." She rose. "I'm going to bed. You can, whatever."

She reached the door before she looked back at him. "Just so you know. I forgive you. I just don't want to go back. Hugo. Come on, boy."

Scott sat in the silent darkness and finished a third and then the fourth beer.

He felt bruised deep down in the most tender parts of himself. And he knew he didn't hurt as much as she had. He wanted her back but he needed to face facts. She didn't love him. She was over him. And he couldn't promise her, even if she'd listen, that he wouldn't make any more mistakes with her.

But the need inside him didn't diminish with these thoughts. That deep-rooted need for her wasn't rational or to be reasoned with. That need made him wonder how much longer he could go on without showing her in a very real and physical way just exactly how he still felt about her.

Whoever said love conquers all didn't know shit.

Cole lay awake wondering why she hadn't just kept her mouth shut and drunk another beer. She had behaved like a bitch. And she really didn't mean any of it. Not anymore. They had hurt one another, badly. She understood that now.

She wanted only to comfort him, and herself, and she didn't know how.

She was afraid. It was dangerous, what she was thinking. Dangerous to her pride, and her sanity. She wasn't like some of her friends who could just contact an old boyfriend for a quick booty call. If she got in Scott's pants, she was going to want to stay there, and then return on a regular basis. And if he didn't want that, too, she'd die inside.

She knew what it was like to be made love to by him. Her body was aching even now with the need to be touched by him. And there he was, just on the other side of the door, closer than he'd been since she left him or ever would be again. All she had to do was open that door. He wouldn't make her beg. She'd seen the need in his face. He would welcome her. It was real. He felt it, too.

Ego be damned! She needed him, needed him deep inside her, moving with that body-slamming rhythmic push-pull so uniquely his own that made her cry out in ecstasy.

She sat up and tossed off the sheet.

Once upon a time she knew just what to do to bring him to the brink, so close that he would beg for it in his deep voice made ragged by lust. It had been so long. Too long.

She opened her door.

The sounds of deep sleep rumbled through the dark. She moved to the front screen door and looked out.

He was still stretched out on the porch where she'd left him. He'd removed his shirt and bundled it under his dark head to make a pillow. His lean muscular torso gleamed in the moonlight. He could have been a toppled Greek statue, if statues wore jeans. Those jeans gaped at his waist, leaving enough space between them and his bare skin for a hand to slide in. She knew that because she'd done it often enough in the past.

Cole sucked in a careful breath and wrapped her arms about her middle as goose bumps pebbled her arms. She wasn't cold. She felt her hunger for him rising. This time she let herself feel it and many other things for a change.

His face was turned away so that moonlight played along the lobe of his ear and the slope of his cheek, and brought into relief the corded muscles of his neck. With his hair ruffled and eyes closed she could almost see the little boy he had once been.

She'd been a little shocked the first time she had watched him sleeping. They had been together for weeks but it was their first time to spend the entire night together. It stunned her to realize how innocent and vulnerable he seemed with his eyes closed. The man so vividly alive no person passed him without feeling it had let down his guard with her. He was the protector, a criminal's worst nightmare, the first and last defense. But not then, and not now.

She pushed open the screen and came forward on bare feet to squat down beside him. She wanted to touch him but didn't dare. Fascinated by every breath that caused his chest to rise and fall, she fell in love all over again with every separate bit of him, the hard places and the softer smooth ones. They had been playing games for days. Finally, he was real and mortal to her again. This was the man she once loved.

She also saw the shadow of sadness in the furrow of his brow. He never talked about that. Things she could only guess at, yet had once tried to protect him from.

A pang of regret shot through her. She had failed him. And now it was too late.

Cole returned to her room but didn't go back to bed. The restlessness that had driven her to the brink of temptation could not be put back in the box so easily.

She moved to the window of her room, propped an arm on the jamb, and rested her head against it. She must be nuts. Nothing had changed since Scott came back into her life. Nothing had been said to change one unalterable fact.

Cole lifted her head to stare out across the field to where night escaped into the impregnable black of the forest. He had simply let her go.

Most divorces were messy. She'd seen it up close when her parents uncoupled when she was ten. There were fights and accusations, digressions, petty ugliness, strategies large and small. All done to wound the partner in the break. At the time, she had thought the fighting and screaming and ugliness was the absolute worst way for a marriage to end. Now she knew otherwise. Silence was worse.

Scott hadn't bothered to fight with, or *for* her.

That's what hurt the most, what she hadn't thought she could forgive. She might have been the one who walked out, but he'd let her go. Because it was what he'd wanted.

The reason for walking out had dimmed after two years. But the knowledge that he wanted out had not.

That's why she hadn't tried to go back, couldn't offer a reconciliation. After everything else, she couldn't bear to hear him tell her face-to-face why and when their marriage had disintegrated to the point he no longer wanted her.

That's what made the desire tugging at her now so hard to deal with. They might want each other again, for now, but there would come an after. And if she gave in to the reckless raw need raging through her and then he walked away? It might just stop her heart.

Cole wiped a tear from her chin, surprised to find it there. She wasn't a crier. She never cried. So whatever was leaking out of her didn't have her permission. And neither was she a quitter. She'd chosen to do this. She was just going to have to find a way. But how?

She thought about the weeks ahead, being forced to be constantly in Scott's company. *Look but don't touch* was already stretching her nerves to the limit. Even her anger was taking more and more effort to keep up.

She was tired of fighting. Tired of being on guard. This

wasn't going to work if she didn't figure out a way to get past this constant aching need for him.

Hugo nudged his big head under her hand. She turned toward him. Blacker than the darkness, only his eyes gave away his presence.

"Love you, too." But sometimes, like tonight, it wasn't enough.

CHAPTER NINE

"That's it. This is impossible. I can't do this anymore."

Cole wheeled away from the table of people who had been coaching Scott and her on their new undercover roles for the past three days.

Scott reached out and grabbed her wrist as she passed his chair. "Wait up, Nikki."

Cole swung around on him. "My name's Noel. Remember? Noel Jenkins. God! Even you. Total fail." She jerked her arm free and stalked away.

Her head ached and her chest felt too tight. If she didn't get away from Scott and the two DEA agents who had been sent from Texas to prep them for going undercover she would explode from shame and anger.

Head down, she hurled herself forward out the doors of the Harmonie Kennel classroom complex and into the late afternoon where the sky was turning golden along the rim of the Shenandoah Mountains to the west.

Three days. Three days of prep and she couldn't even remember her own alias: *Noel Jenkins*.

They had said choose something close to her real name because it would be easier to remember.

They said think of herself as being in a play. Real time, live, but not only on a stage.

They said be spontaneous, the character was hers to create. Elementary school children playacted every day. It came naturally to most people. Not to her.

"Unnatural acts. That's what they should call this mission."

Cole wiped the sweat trickling down her forehead with the heel of her hand. It wasn't as if she wasn't giving it everything. It was all she thought about when she wasn't in the ring working Hugo. But this was like trying to learn Greek from a Dutchman.

She was too self-conscious to let go and "inhabit the role" as her high school drama teacher would have said. Maybe if she'd been dealing with total strangers she could have pulled it off. But she was also dealing with Scott.

Sam Lott not Scott Lucca. *Noel Jenkins* not Nicole Jamieson. Not hard to remember. Except that keeping her volatile feelings under wraps around Scott was keeping her from being able to pretend anything else when he was being Sam.

If one more person said, "Loosen up and show us how Noel feels about Sam," she was going to lose it. No, make that, had lost it. Unprofessional or not, she was done.

As if that wasn't bad enough, there was a worse disaster looking to spoil their plans. Hugo had decided to balk at the Weave Poles obstacle.

The ability to weave in and out of a set of poles spaced fourteen inches apart usually took a dog weeks to learn. Like a skier learning the zigzag of a slalom race, speed and close maneuvering were the key. But Hugo didn't like the idea of moving back and forth. After three weaves, he was done. Trouble was, there were always ten to twelve poles in the competition. And so that was that. Deal off.

She could not do this. Absolutely could not. That's what she was going to tell them. But first she needed to get away from here to cool off.

Cole glanced around, surprised to find herself in the parking lot near the truck she had been loaned by the DEA. First law of undercover, separate yourself from your personal life. She reached for her keys but they weren't in her pocket.

"Damn!" She kicked the front tire with her boot.

"That's a lot of temper."

Cole looked up, prepared to do battle with Scott.

"Don't snarl at me, little lady. I'm just the messenger." It was DEA agent Jeff Richards, one of their pair of tutors. He must have followed her.

She bit back the angry words that had rushed to the tip of her tongue. She'd made enough of a fool of herself. She stiffened into a professional pose. "Sorry, sir."

"No need to be professional out here. I don't see any cops, do you?"

Cole wilted. Right. She was supposed to be playing at *not* being a cop. Epic fail.

Richards leaned against the front fender of her truck and pulled out a cigar. "I'm not supposed to have this. My wife thinks I'm into vaping these days. But once in a while, when I'm away from home, I cheat. It's okay because she knows I do it, but we pretend she doesn't so I can have my guilty pleasure."

He stacked one heavy scarred cowboy boot over the other as he reached for a lighter. He was tall and broad. With his shirtsleeves pushed up to reveal burly forearms bristling with the same red-gold hair that sprouted in a buzz cut from his scalp, he looked more like a day laborer than a government agent. That didn't explain why he was out here.

Cole bit the inside of her lip to control her emotions as she waited for him to finish lighting his cigar. She expected him to lay into her about her performance. She had it coming. He might even be about to fire her. Not that she'd give him the chance. She was going to quit.

He exhaled a perfect doughnut ring of smoke before he spoke. "You know what your problem is?"

"I have a problem? How about that. I had no idea." Okay, she couldn't control the snark.

He chuckled. "I'm going to tell you, anyway. The trouble is you see Scott when you're supposed to be dealing with Sam."

Cole opened her mouth to shut him down but his words echoed in her head. *You're supposed to be dealing with Sam.*

"You got to buy into the story about Noel and Sam. They're in love. Hot sweaty heat for each other. Can't keep their hands off each other. That's why he's following her around like a puppy on a leash. The man's got it bad. You're in charge, pretty lady. So cowgirl up."

She stared at him, a dozen thoughts whipping through her mind. But in the end, there was only one. "I don't know how."

"That's because you've been trying to reason your way to Noel. A good cover is all about feeling. That means knowing deep inside you that Noel's actually a part of you."

Cole looked down and to the right as something flickered to life in the back of her mind. Part of me. That was the trouble. Nothing felt like part of her anymore, except the ache of being in the same room as Scott and doing nothing about it.

Richards blew out another ring and watched it float away. "You've just graduated vet school and are waiting to see if you passed your exams so you can get a license to practice. Meanwhile you've decided to try your hand in ring competition."

She nodded. "That's my cover story."

"Doesn't that strike you as atypical behavior? Here you are an animal doc, spent all those years on schooling, but suddenly you're just kicking back and doing nothing. Why would you do that?"

"Because she's—I'm dog tired of school. I've sacrificed everything for so long, worked so hard. I just want to have a little fun."

He nodded. "Makes sense. I suspect there's a whole other personality inside Noel Jenkins that hasn't been let loose in a while. Probably even a wild streak. Otherwise, how could you explain Sam's interest?"

Cole blushed as he winked at her.

"He's a hellion, that Sam. Yet, he's sniffing at your heels. You got something that man wants bad, sweetheart. Figure out what it is, and you'll do just fine."

He pushed off her vehicle and bent to carefully break off the ash of his cigar against the road gravel. When he was satisfied the tobacco was out, he stuck the remainder of the cigar in his pocket. "I don't have to smoke it all to enjoy the experience. This way, I save a bit of fun for later."

He reached into his pants pocket and pulled out several keys. When he had unhooked one, he looked her up and down, from her tee to her jeans to her patrol boots. "You got a license to ride?"

Cole gazed in amazement at the motorcycle key he held out to her. "If I say I know how to ride?"

He grinned. "Close enough." But as she reached for the key he snatched it back. "Only one rule. Don't scuff the chrome." He pointed out his motorcycle before handing her the key. "Helmet's hanging on the back and there's a jacket in the saddlebag. Be back before dark."

He didn't even look back once to see what she was going to do.

Cole laughed when she had swung a leg over Agent Richards's bike. It was big, a little bigger than anything she had driven before. It had been years since she even straddled a motorcycle. When they were married, Scott seldom let her drive his bike. Most often she was the unhappy and totally intimidated chick on the back.

"But not Noel," she whispered under her breath. And her boyfriend Sam would be cool with her borrowing his bike.

She tightened the strap of her helmet and zipped up the too-large leather jacket she'd pulled from the saddle back. Finally, she turned the key in the ignition. The engine thrummed to life between her legs. Yes! Suddenly, she felt the possibility of having fun. The worries and concerns of Nicole Jamieson might even take a backseat for a while. She was Noel Jenkins, and Noel was a bit of a badass.

Harmonie Kennels was located in the hills of Shenandoah National Park. Traffic was sparse on the back roads that led in and out of the compound. Even so, concentration was in order. Once out on the empty two-lane blacktop, Noel let out the throttle a little more.

Riding a bike was about confidence. Noel had confidence for days. Noel rode with Sam regularly. They loved the open road and being together.

Sam was ex-military and now manager of a motorcycle shop in New Jersey. They'd met six months ago at a mutual friend's wedding in Baltimore. She had learned to ride to be with him. In turn, he was supporting her desire to compete in Agility competitions. They share a love of dogs, and the wicked urge to keep their freedom. Oh, and a wild desire for one another that ran so hot that people sometimes felt closed out in their company.

Cole's body quivered under the vibrations of the engine

locked between her thighs. Yes, Sam would be hot and heavy and thumping just like this. When she got home to him.

A small smile began.

After that, Noel stopped thinking and just concentrated on the ride as the gorgeous scenery of Virginia flew past her in a hundred shades of forest green and late-afternoon blue-gold sky.

Scott began to worry when Cole didn't show up for dinner. No one seemed to know where she was. No one but he seemed particularly worried. She'd been very angry when she ran out on the meeting. He checked his watch. No, his empty wrist. He hadn't been able to find his watch this morning. He pulled out his cell phone to get the time.

Cole had been gone four hours. She hadn't taken Hugo or her cruiser. How far could she have gone on foot?

For the fourth time in an hour he stepped out onto the porch of the bunkhouse that he and Cole now shared. It was almost dark , the sky streaked by deep purple fingers that seemed to point to where stars twinkled into view. That air was still and warm. Mosquito weather.

Hugo padded out onto the porch beside him and stared off into the distance.

Scott looked down. At least they had come to some sort of truce in the past couple of days. "Where the hell is your owner?"

He was answered by a brusque bark that sounded remarkably like a doggy imitation of his own gruff tone.

Izzy lifted her head from her sprawl on the porch. The trio had formed an uneasy truce when Cole hadn't returned in time to feed Hugo.

Irritation whipped through Scott. If this was her way of forcing him to deal with her K-9 at least she could have warned him.

He glanced at his wrist. "Where the hell is my watch?"

Hugo looked up at Scott then turned and went inside. Great. Even Cole's dog was giving him the cold shoulder.

Scott rubbed his brow. It wasn't like Cole to be irresponsible. It wasn't like her to disappear. It wasn't like— Oh, hell.

Yardley was right. He didn't know what Cole was like two years down the road. She must have changed. Everyone changed. She was a seasoned law officer. Still, he didn't like to think of her wandering around in the dark. She could have gotten turned around, lost. Or, she could be sitting in a roadside café somewhere sulking.

That thought soured his bad mood even more. If she was waiting for him to turn himself inside out and go chasing after her, she would be waiting until hell froze over.

Scott turned back toward the door as the distant rumble of a motorcycle reverberated through the hills. For a moment every muscle in his body tensed as he listened intently. This wasn't a Harley. It was the rumbling purr of a well-muffled engine. Sighing, he opened the door. "Izzy. *Geh rein.*"

Izzy climbed to her feet and shuffled through the door.

When the Lab was inside, Hugo emerged at a trot. "*Nein,* Hugo. *Geh rein.*"

Ignoring him, Hugo stood on the porch a moment longer listening, Scott supposed, to the motorcycle. Irritated, he repeated his command more sharply. "Hugo. *Geh rein.*"

Hugo turned his big head in Scott's direction. That's when Scott noticed he held something in his mouth. "My watch."

Hugo put it down. Then with a huff that sounded all too human, the Bouvier went back indoors.

Great. Everyone was giving him attitude tonight.

He picked up his watch and then rubbed the back of his neck. It felt gritty. He needed a shower. If Cole wasn't back

by the time he got out, he supposed he'd have to go looking for her.

The sound of the shower curtain being pulled back was his
first clue that he was no longer alone.

"What the fuck?" Scott scowled as he turned to face his
intruder.

Cole stood there staring, taking in every wet inch of him.

She looked wild. No longer long and straight, her hair
was chopped off above her collarbone, the ends wild and
uneven, and whipped in all directions. Her cheeks were
bright red and in her eyes was a frank "do me" invitation.

The impact of her wide-open gaze connected him instantly to every primitive impluse in him. Nothing rational
about the sudden desire to take, conquer, seduce, and
possess the woman before him.

Mercifully, just enough of his self-command remained
to take control of his mouth.

"Cole?" His control didn't have much breath to operate
with.

She cocked her head to one side, eyes sliding down from
his face, past his soapy chest and navel to where rivulets
of water snaked into dangerous territory. "Who's Cole?"

She sounded annoyed, yet there was also mischief and
definitely heat in her expression. His dick understood that
before his brain did, rising proudly to the occasion he wasn't
yet certain he was being invited to.

Smiling, he braced a hand flat against the tile beside the
shower head and propped the other in a fist on his hip.

"Shut up."

He hadn't said anything.

She undressed quickly. First one boot and then the other
kicked off in opposite directions. Then she was unsnap-
ping her jeans. He watched her hand slide her zipper down
as if she were reenacting his favorite wet dream. The glide

of denim over her hips had him drawing in breath through his open mouth. He must be dreaming. It couldn't be happening this fast, this easy. Her jeans slipped down legs that were slim and smooth yet well muscled enough to pass the physical endurance required in the police academy. She stepped out, kicked them aside, and reached for the hem of her tee.

Scott licked his lips. Breathing no longer seemed to be a necessity.

Then she stood in only her bra and panties. He smiled. He'd been right. She still wore lacy little nothings. Pale blue scraps that hugged all his favorite parts of her.

She came forward slowly, a seductive invitation in her eyes. The heat was all his. He half expected steam to rise from his skin where the shower rained on him.

She ran a finger down his chest, streaming with water. "Like what you see, Sam?"

Sam? Who the hell— Oh yeah.

"I like."

"It could get better."

The hand he'd braced on the tile wall clenched as Scott struggled for air. *Don't touch.* The two words were scrolling across his mind's eye like a news alert. Somehow he knew if he touched her too soon he'd break the spell. But oh how he wanted to touch and hold and squeeze and stroke until he made her purr.

She stepped one foot over the rim into the shower. He moved back to give her space. Water splashed across her shoulders, soaking her hair and lacy bra as she joined him and closed the curtain behind her.

They were just inches apart. He could feel the heat rising off her skin while his own seemed to sizzle under the assault of the water's warm cascade.

He glanced down. The telltale dark buds of her nipples had appeared and pushed against the damp lace of her bra.

Definitely, a world-class dream. Only much, *much* better. She was here.

She lifted a hand and pressed it palm flat against the middle of his chest. "Did you miss me, Sam?"

"Uh-huh." *Geesh*. Where was his brain? Oh yeah.

"It's been a while." She added her other hand to the first, brushing her palms in outward circles over his dark flat nipples.

He sucked in a breath as the flesh-on-flesh contact sent whatever remained of the blood flowing through his brain surging south to his groin. This was her game, for now. He was letting her take the lead but, damn, his balls felt about to burst and he hadn't even touched her.

"You look good. No more Hulk." She ran a finger around one of his nipples and smiled as it beaded up. "All this lean smooth muscle is very tempting. But you know that, don't you?"

"Whatever you say, Noel." He let out his breath when she smiled. He'd guessed right. She was trying to find a way into her alter ego. He liked this way just fine.

She moved in on him until they touched from chest to knee. She pressed a knee hard between his, wiggling it until he widened his stance. Her thigh slipped between his, nudging them farther apart until her hip pressed against his erection. Then she did a little hip wiggle that wrung an involuntary sound of lust out of him.

"Now that I've got your attention, I need to know that I can trust you, Sam." She reached up and traced her finger across his damp lips. "Can I trust you?"

"With your life."

She looked up into his face, her gaze narrowing as she assessed the truth of his reply.

He gazed back steadily at her, letting her in a little more than he was comfortable with doing. He owed her that. But only that. He still loved her but he had begun to realize he no longer had the right to burden her with it.

After a moment she tossed her head and smiled to herself, as if she had captured some secret he didn't know he had given up.

She eased up off him and raked a hand down his chest. She took her time, letting her nails graze the shallow ridges of his ribs, tickle his belly, and finally lower until her fingers touched his cock.

"You like me to touch you?"

"I do." Scott felt his blood scorching though his body. But this could be a really bad idea.

"Really bad." Her whispered reply came as a shock. Had he spoken?

"Shut up, Sam." She squeezed his erection, pumping it a little with her hand.

His laugh came out a bit strangled. "Question is, can I trust you?"

"I suppose we'll find out. If you want to."

"Hell yes." He leaned forward and kissed her, his tongue slipping through to entangle with hers.

She grabbed his neck to hold his mouth to hers as she began a sinuous caress of his tongue with her own. Not content with that, she drew his tongue into her mouth and tugged, imitating the motions of sex until she heard him moan.

He moved quickly, backing her against one wall of the shower. Leaning his weight on her, he fit his body to hers in every possible way from shoulder to knee. Without breaking the kiss, he urgently pumped his body on hers until she turned her head away.

"Hey. No fair." She grabbed his biceps and pushed.

Scott lifted his head. "What's wrong?"

She placed both hands in the middle of his chest and pushed harder. "Get off."

Surprise raced through him but he moved back from her. Breathing hoarsely he mentally stomped on his disappointment. He hadn't expected any of this but—damn.

He spread his arms wide. "Look, I don't know what you—"

She moved quickly to press a finger to his lips. "My way. Okay?"

A slow smile of understanding spread across his face, stretching his lips taut beneath her finger. "Lady's choice."

She pushed him until his back was against the wall. "When I was in the eighth grade my friend Evy told me that sucking dick was technically not having sex. I always thought she was a liar."

Scott watched her through half-lidded eyes. "And now?"

"I'll let you know."

Once more she reached for him, sliding her hand up to where she could thread her fingers into the rough silky hair at the base of his cock. Leaning up on tiptoe, she put her lips against his ear. "I love these curls, Sam. Will you give me one to carry in my wallet?"

"You can have the whole damn bush."

She turned her head and he felt her smile stretch against the damp skin of his neck. "I think it's time you kissed me again, don't you?"

Her mouth was wet, and hot, and delicious. He'd forgotten how good it was to kiss her. He cupped her head with one hand and reached to turn off the shower with the other.

"No. Leave it." She whispered the words against his mouth. "I like you slippery and wet."

His whole body jerked at her words. His wife had always been a bit reluctant to talk dirty to him. Always a bit shy, Cole had seemed like a wallflower to his friends, who teased him about being the hellion who married a nun. That wasn't the case tonight.

Cole's low suggestive laugh tugged directly on his dick. She was hugely enjoying the role of aggressor.

In amazement, he watched her lower herself to her knees on the tile. Lust roared in the same direction, stretching him to his fullest until his dick throbbed with each heartbeat.

She grasped his cock with one hand, the pulsing heat of it rigid proof of his virility, and cupped his balls, full and weighty, in her other hand. "You're a lot of man, Sam."

"I'm all yours." He pumped his hips against her hand.

"In a hurry?"

"What do you think?"

He was breathing harder now and, despite the cooling water jetting from the nozzle, beginning to sweat. He wasn't touching her but he knew she was as excited as he was. He could see it in the wicked gleam of her gaze between her water-spiked lashes. There was still a connection between them. It was sexier than ever.

She ran her thumb over the smooth dome that topped his shaft, catching a pearl of liquid on her nail tip. He jumped in her hand, his breath sucked in sharply as she squeezed the tip.

"What do you want, Sam?" Her voice was so low he wasn't certain he heard her.

His answer was no more than a gust of desire. "I want you to suck me."

"How?"

"Hard."

"How long?"

"Till I cum."

"Cum where?"

"Shit." He flung back his head, gave a heaving breath, struggling to control himself. "In your sweet mouth, Noel Jenkins."

She braced herself by gripping his bare hip with a hand,

and then leaned forward, stretched her mouth wide, and extended her tongue to taste the drop of moisture from his cock.

She licked him a second time and his cock jumped from her hand. Smiling, she gripped him more firmly, opened wider and took as much of him as she could into her mouth.

Scott squeezed his eyes shut and moaned low in his throat. He also braced his legs wider apart to give her better access.

Using her hand, she worked the full length of his cock, sliding the skin back and forth, lips crimped to hold him tight. In and out, pumping hard and harder, she used her tongue to increase his sensation, licking the bottom of his shaft, tonguing the eye of it, and then swirling it around the length of his cock.

Unable to help himself, he began moving his hips in time to her rhythm, the thrusts growing strong and harder, his harsh breathing the only sound in his ears.

Finally he leaned forward, bracing himself with a hand on her shoulder while the other cradled her head. "Yes, yes, take it all." He was whispering very low but his voice seemed loud in his own ears. "That's it, Nikki. Yeah!"

He came in jetting streams that flooded her mouth and throat, all but choking her. But she hung on until his hips stopped pumping and his cock stopped jumping and wilted a little on her tongue.

He felt her swallow several times, trying to hold on as tears flooded her cheeks.

After a few seconds, Cole opened her mouth a little reluctantly, sorry to break the contact. She felt overwhelmed by the emotion of his climax, and her own. That had never happened before. Without touching her, his responses had roused her to reach in simple reaction to his own fulfillment.

Did this happen to other women? Or was she romanticizing something that people took for granted every day? What would he say if she asked him? Would his answer hurt her feelings?

He reached down for her, lifting her to her feet before he pulled her close and wrapped his arms about her. "Damn, Cole—Noel."

Cole stiffened, her face pressed to his chest. "Was it good?"

"Hell yeah." He kissed the top of her head and then he lifted her chin and kissed her full on her cum-drenched mouth. He'd never done that before.

He kissed her a long time, touching her and caressing her until she knew what he intended and reached out to stop his hands. "I'm okay."

"But you didn't come."

She pushed against his chest and said softly, "Yes, I did."

He snagged her arm as she tried to turn away and pulled her back.

"Not so fast."

CHAPTER TEN

"Turnabout is fair play."

Scott had pulled her in against his chest, hugging her to him so hard she couldn't catch her breath. When he turned her around, his kiss this time wasn't slow and seductive. It was a Red Bull jolt that electrified all her senses.

The blood began to pound in her temples, her stomach, and her womb. Her nipples budded, eager for his hands. He hadn't touched them yet tonight. She arched her back in invitation and whispered against his lips. "What do you want, Sam?"

His voice above her head in the dark sounded almost strangled by his full arousal. "Everything you got."

His hands found and unhooked her bra and then moved lower to shove down her panties.

Freed from the barrier of her clothing, her body became his playground. He found and teased her breasts with his fingers while his tongue explored her mouth. And then he bent his head and sucked a nipple into his mouth.

Cole caught her breath as he tugged and tongued it to full peak. It felt as if her nipple was attached directly to her sex, each tug sending a tiny electrical shock wave to her womb. As long as she had been in control she'd felt safe, even from her feelings about him. But now he was overwhelming her power and the feeling was both exhilarating and terrifying. But he didn't need to know either of those things.

She grabbed his shoulders to try to control her body's response.

Scott took her by the wrists and placed her arms down at her sides. "My turn." Leaning in, he kissed her quickly and then backed her up to the end of the shower stall where the spray ran fully over.

"This is for you." Bracing a hand on the wall above her head, he pressed his body firmly against hers for a moment, as if he were absorbing her through his own skin.

His chin rested in her hair. "I like your hair, all wild and messy." He slipped a hand behind her head and slowly massaged her neck. "Just relax. Close your eyes and enjoy the water sluicing over your skin. Think of this as your personal Sam Spa."

Cole did as he suggested though she would rather have watched him. Curiosity made her open an eye when he lifted himself off her.

He placed a hand over her eyes. "Close. Just feel."

He dragged a soapy cloth over her face then trailed it slowly down her body, fingers spread wide so that his thumb and pinkie brushed her nipples as the cloth moved down between her breasts. When he reached her navel his forefinger began a slow circling as the cloth trailed over her belly. It was such a simple touch but the heat pooling in her belly began to chase the movement of his fingers until she was trembling. At last the tip of one finger dipped into her navel. Her vagina tightened as if he had pushed in a finger there instead. It didn't linger. The drag of his fingers and the cloth moved lower, causing a fluttering in her lower belly.

He combed fingers through her mons. "I'm glad you don't go Brazilian." He nudged her with his hand. "I like how your curls tangle around my fingers, welcoming me to this place. Are you happy to have me here?"

"Yes." Her voice sounded far away.

The cloth abandoned, his fingers slipped lower, parting her curls. The lips of her sex parted for his fingers but he was careful not to touch her clit. He chuckled as his fingers slipped into the slick wetness. "Oh yes. You feel very happy to have me here."

He just rubbed his finger back and forth along the edges until she began to wiggle. "I like it that you're wet for me here, Noel. I want to kiss you here. May I kiss you?"

"Oh yes." Cole felt as if she was floating, like she would simply skim away if not for the anchor of his hands. No one else had ever handled her this way, made her feel as if her body was something special and precious and appreciated.

He knelt before her and lifted one of her legs over his shoulder and behind his back so that she had to balance on one foot. He nuzzled her mound. "You smell like sex, Noel. Like a woman. And it makes me hard as a rock."

His mouth on her sex felt as warm it had on her mouth. His kisses were soft and delicate. And then he was sucking each petal into his mouth, tugging and then blowing his breath upon the tender wetness. Then his hot tongue slid forward and into her.

Cole rocked her head back and forth on the wall. She was weeping for him, desire flowing from her, and he lapped it up with greedy flicks of his tongue.

She came suddenly and hard. He held her in place with firm hands on her hips while he gently nibbled her clit until she stopped erupting in little rhythmic cries of pleasure. Even as she tried to come down, the flicks of his tongue were urging her toward another peak that rose steeply in tension that bordered on pain

"Too much." She sagged against him, bracing her hands on his wet shoulders. "Oh, what are you doing to me?"

"Easy, sweetheart." He rose and pressed her body to his so that she understood how ready he was once more. He leaned in, putting his wickedly talented lips against her ear. His voice was dark and rough with sexual energy. "We got all night."

Cole hid her face in his armpit. "I don't think I can stand all night."

His laughter rocked her whole body. "In that case, I need to take a little for myself right now."

"Oh yes, please."

"You're sure?" He pulled back so he could look into her flushed face.

Cole grabbed him by both ears. "I want you to fuck me right now. Hard."

She saw his micro expression of surprise at her words. But then he was grinning again, so deep his dimples had dimples. "That's my girl."

He pulled back the shower curtain and scooped up his jeans from the floor. Out of the pocket came a packet. A man of economical actions, he donned the condom so quickly she decided it would be hypocritical to wonder why he was prepared when she was so glad he was.

Ready for action, he hitched up her leg and pressed his cock to her opening. One hand came under her butt as he hoisted her up against him. Then he turned so that he was the one leaning against the wall of the shower.

"Come on up and ride me." The hand under her naked butt again urged her upward.

Cole wound her arms behind his neck and wrapped her legs about his waist as he hoisted her up. In that position the head of his cock was angled so perfectly that when he flexed his butt muscles and thrust forward, he slid into her easily. A series of little inarticulate cries erupted from her as he slid home.

"Ah, that's good, baby. Now hold on tight." Back braced on the wall, his hands tightly clamped under her butt, he began to move her body in a slow circular in-and-out grind, his whole body flexing when he ended each circle with a deep thrust into her.

Cole couldn't catch her breath. Each one came out as a little hitch ending on a pant of desire. She came again but he didn't alter his rhythm. He just kept up that slow mesmerizing grind. Sweat glistened on his forehead. His face was tight with concentration. Finally she felt it, the sudden tension in his shoulders and back and the swelling of his cock inside her.

He came in long hard thrusts that made him gasp with each. He clutched her tighter, whispering a word that astonished her. "Home."

CHAPTER ELEVEN

No one mentioned Cole's new haircut as she walked into the classroom. She had a to-go cup of steaming coffee in one hand and a bagel in the other. She'd been up since dawn, working with Hugo.

"You're looking happy this morning." Richards grinned at her. "You get something out of your system?"

Cole offered him a cryptic smile. "Yes. Thanks for the loan."

"What loan?" Scott was the last to arrive. He was rumpled and unshaved and looked much too grumpy for a man who'd had fantastic sex the night before. In fact, he looked like a man who'd been rode hard and put away wet, which is exactly what had happened. He'd actually slept alone. Cole/Noel left him toweling off and locked her door.

"Hey, babe." Cole walked over and placed a kiss on Scott's lips but moved back before he could touch her.

From the corner of her eye she caught the puzzled look he sent her. Tough. She was going to play this her way. "You need a cup of coffee, Sam?"

"Sure." He sounded uneasy but that was his problem.

He moved closer to Richards. "What's this about a loan? Is Officer Jamieson running short of funds?"

"Naw. I sent her on a mission yesterday to find Noel. Looks like she's done a good job." Richards grinned. "Should have known that sometimes change for a woman is as easy as a new hairstyle. Gives her whole new personality."

Cole set a cup of black coffee before Scott then casually braced her arm on his shoulder. "Sam likes it, don't you?"

Scott looked up at her, cop face in place. "Sure. It's okay." He did not sound like he meant it but Cole ignored that.

"See that. Practically a new girlfriend without the pain of a breakup." She dropped a kiss on the top of his head, as if he was a six-year-old, and then moved away to take her usual seat on the other side of the table. "What are we doing today, gentlemen?"

Smiling, Richards exchanged glances with his partner, who nodded. "Looks like we can move on today to surveillance techniques."

At the end of the morning session, Cole swung by Richards's chair. "The ride yesterday helped. Mind it I take your bike again this afternoon?"

That caught Scott's attention. "What bike?" He stared at Richards. "I didn't take you for a fan of ten-speeds."

"*Shee*-it, son. We're talking serious wheels. I ride a hog. Noel, here, took it for a spin yesterday."

Scott looked at Cole. "You hate bikes."

Cole rolled her eyes. "Men. The fact you manage a motorcycle dealership is what first attracted me to you. You know I like bad boys." She slapped him on the butt.

The astonished look on his face was priceless.

"Got to put Hugo through his paces again. Be back after lunch."

Scott came after her, catching up quickly with his longer stride. "We need to talk."

As they stepped outside, out of view of their trainers, Cole turned and offered him a cool gaze. "Let me make this simple for you. Last night was about Noel and Sam. They are in love. They are hot together. Cole and Scott have issues but they don't matter a damn at the moment. I needed to know that I could separate that. Now I do."

She veered away quickly before Scott could use his cop instinct to read more into her expression than she could afford to divulge. He was good at that, when he bothered to pay attention.

That's why she'd left him standing in the shower, grabbed a towel, and locked her bedroom door. As if sex with her ex wasn't crazy enough, he had scared her at the end, scared her in a way she didn't know was still possible.

Home.

That's what he'd murmured as he slid into her body the night before. She wasn't at all certain he knew he'd said it. She definitely hadn't wanted to hear it.

Home is where the heart is. Home is wherever you are. Home is where, when you go there, they have to take you in.

Cole shook her head as those clichés swam through her mind and sped up her step. Let Scott think she was running away from him. It was better than him seeing an echo of his sentiment in her eyes.

As she crossed the yard toward the kennel, Cole fluffed her new haircut with both hands, making it look even choppier and wilder.

"Nice." She looked around to see a soldier in desert fatigues wink at her as he passed.

She grinned back. It was a badass hairstyle with lots of angles and pieces, both long and short, the front raking across her forehead on a slant. She'd even put on eyeliner and doubled her mascara, something she never did for work. The haircut could handle it. She might even add highlights, when she got home.

Home.

Scott—dammit—Sam was messing with her mind.

It meant nothing. Men said all kinds of crazy things in the heat of the moment. And last night had been scorching hot.

Cole ignored the twinge of soreness between her legs as she walked on. She couldn't afford to be mad or hurt over it. She most certainly couldn't afford to be "home" for either Scott or Sam right now.

Cole watched Hugo weave his way around five poles before pausing to see if he'd done enough.

"*Geh voraus.* Go ahead." Cole motioned to him with a hand.

Hugo, ears flattened and head low, moved in and out of another pair of poles then looked back again.

"That's one unhappy dog."

Cole spun around. She hadn't heard Yardley approaching.

Cole smoothed her sweaty slant of bangs off her brow with her forearm. "We've got an issue, ma'am. Hugo hates the Weave. Even if that weren't true, it takes weeks, sometimes months, to learn this obstacle."

"That's usually true, with an average dog. Hugo's not average. And, he's been trained to the peak of his ability. He's just not concentrating. That makes me wonder who is really afraid of the Weave."

Yardley knelt down to call the big black dog. "Here, boy."

He came running over to her. "Who's a good boy? Who's

so handsome? Who's going to learn this trick for his handler? You are. Yes, you. You, handsome boy."

Yardley's voice, often pitched at drill-sergeant level, became soft and high and girlish when she interacted with her dogs. She rubbed him and chucked him under the chin until he just fell apart, lying down and rolling over on his back like a puppy.

Yardley looked up at Cole, a grin in her face. "Why are you training him in German for Agility?"

"He knows I mean business when I give commands in German. That improves his concentration."

"Smart. But now you need to up the ante." Yardley reached into a pocket of her windbreaker and tossed Cole a hard rubber object that looked a lot like a bright orange snowman.

"It smells like peanut butter."

"That's because I put peanut butter in it."

Cole smiled. "Hugo's a peanut butter maniac."

As if to prove it, Hugo rolled to his feet and leaped straight up in the air and barked.

"Continue using other rewards for other obstacles. This reward is only for the Weave. Once that's mastered, he should only get it after a successful completion of the entire Agility circuit."

Cole eyed Hugo closely as she wagged the new toy before him. "How much do you want it?"

Hugo's little stump of a tail worked back and forth while his breath accelerated as he sniffed the object. He began salivating and repeatedly licking his chops with his pink flag of a tongue. Finally, he barked.

"Well, big boy, you're going to have to earn this puppy."

Cole moved back toward the Weave poles, wagging the toy behind her. Hugo bounded after her. "Come on. Come on. Show me what you've learned."

She made the motion with her hand for him to go in between the first poles. He darted between them, rounded the second and swept through the opening of the third then back through the fourth. And paused.

Cole shook her head and made the hand motion for him to continue.

Hugo huffed but launched his big body between poles four and five, hesitating only a second before entering the slot between five and six. He paused longer but did not look at Cole for encouragement before angling back between six and seven then weaving right back between seven and eight. After that, he stopped, sneezed twice, and craned his head back toward his handler.

Cole waited several seconds while her canine partner gazed at her in stubborn resistance. And then she moved ahead of him, calling out, *"Hier, Hugo!"* Running, she wove her way through the remaining poles with Hugo in close pursuit.

When they had completed the obstacle together, he barked loudly and triumphantly.

Cole paused and ordered him down. *"Platz."*

He had dropped to the prone position at her feet.

"Blieb." After giving the command to stay, she moved a few feet away and put the orange snowman on the ground at the end of the Weave obstacle. She pointed. *"Lass es."*

Leaving it alone was the last thing Hugo wanted. He stretched up his front paws and groaned in frustration but remained prone.

Cole began walking back to the beginning of the obstacle. *"Hier."* Hugo fell quickly into step behind her. Only then did she glance over at Yardley, who had been watching them near the first pole with a fist propped on each hip.

Yardley waited until Cole reached her. "Teamwork between the dog and handler is the main objective of canine competition. Hugo adores you. Will do anything for you. Make him earn your approval." She cocked her head to one side. "While you're at it, take a second and feel nice about yourself. You're doing better than you think. Then get the hell back to work."

Cole watched Yardley walk away. "She likes me. She really likes me."

She looked down, expecting Hugo to be staring at her in all his doggy admiration. Instead, he was intently staring down the poles at the orange Pillsbury Doughboy. So much for handler adoration.

Right. Back to work.

Cole ate dinner alone. She had carried her plate back from the general mess hall to the bunkhouse she shared with Scott, though he wasn't here. He was working late with the Harmonie Kennels drug detection team to bring Izzy up to speed on the latest detection-avoidance techniques and how to get around them.

Hugo was so tired from their own efforts of the afternoon that he lay sprawled on his back at her feet snoring like it was 2 A.M. He hadn't won the orange beehive—she really did need to settle on a name for his new toy—but he certainly knew now what the goal was, and the prize that lay at the end of it.

She reached for her iced tea and walked out to the porch to watch as the last of the gold of the setting sun slipped down behind the western hills. For the moment, she didn't think about anything. She couldn't afford to think about what the night would bring. Couldn't afford to recall the night before or anything related to the past.

This was the first peaceful evening she'd had since she arrived. It felt, in a way, as if she'd dropped off the face of the earth as she knew it. That's what happened when routine was scrambled all to hell.

She sat on the top step and pulled out her phone to make a call. "Hey, sis. How are you?"

"I'm fine. But I haven't heard from you all week." Becca sounded peeved. "Where are you?"

"In Virginia."

"You left the state without even telling me?"

"Aren't you supposed to be psychic about things like where I am?"

"It would be a whole lot simpler if you just told me. Are you, you know, doing that thing we talked about?"

"I don't think anyone's tapped my cell, if that's what's bothering you. It's not that kind of operation. And, yes, and no to your question. I'm here for training."

"What kind of training? Are they teaching you how to raid crack houses?" Her sister's voice dropped to a whisper. "Defuse bombs?"

"My partner's a dog, remember? We don't do SWAT. We do search, apprehension, and rescue." Cole heard an engine in the distance. "So tell me, how's it feel being pregnant?"

"Like I'm on a rowboat in the middle of a hurricane. Any and everything makes me want to hurl. I can't believe I once liked bacon or tuna fish. Do you know how nasty over-easy eggs are? It's scrambled or nothing from now on."

"Yep, sounds like you're preggers." Headlights of a truck swung onto the gravel lane that led to the barracks. It was moving fast, when it braked suddenly and gravel went flying. The door opened and Scott leaped out with Izzy at his heels. He stopped short when he noticed Cole.

"Oh. Sorry. I got to pack."

Cole stood up. "Why? What's wrong?"

Scott kept walking past her into the barracks.

"Who is that?" Becca's voice could be heard clearly though Cole had lowered the phone from her ear. "Is that Scott? That sounds like Scott."

"Sorry, Becca, I have to go." She pressed the end button and went after him.

She paused at the threshold of his room. He was cursing and tossing things into a backpack. "Scott, what's going on? You can tell me. Maybe I can help."

He wasn't listening. "Have you seen my shield? I took it off my wallet. Fuck. It should be here." He grabbed up his pack and headed straight for the door.

Only she was blocking it. She braced herself for impact.

He didn't touch her but his snort of hot breath in her face would have been enough to back off a smart mortal. Cole set her jaw and glanced up into his face.

He was looking beyond her with a fierce don't-fuck-with-me expression. But she wasn't about to back down.

She gripped his biceps, digging her thumbs into the muscles until she knew she must be hurting him but he didn't even blink. "Scott?"

It took him a full three seconds more to focus. When he was looking down at her panic grabbed her by the throat. The truth was there in his eyes. Something awful had happened.

She'd seen that look on his face only once before, after the phone call telling him Gabe was dead. "Scott?"

"My mom called. There was a break-in at home. Dad's in the hospital. They say he had a heart attack."

Hearing the anguish in his voice, Cole felt as if her own heart had been stepped on. But she shoved those feelings aside in favor of the law-enforcement training that kept her on track in crisis. "Okay. You're ready. I'm coming with you."

He shook his head. "Don't have time." He shook off her touch and tried to push past her.

She stepped in front of him and grabbed his chin in her hand to jerk his face back to hers. "I'm coming. Don't give me any bullshit."

He didn't glance at her again but after a second he nodded once.

When she ran to get her purse, Hugo appeared. He moved in close to Scott and butted his shaggy head under Scott's dangling hand.

Scott reached down to absently pat Hugo and felt metal press into his palm. Hugo had Scott's DEA badge in his mouth.

CHAPTER TWELVE

They rode to New Jersey in silence. Izzy was in back, in her crate, while Hugo rode up front, wedged between them. Not ideal, but neither of them wanted to have to stop and break up a dogfight if their partners decided they didn't want to share a crate.

For once, Hugo ignored Scott. In sleep, he even stretched out and leaned his big head against Scott's thigh. Cole noticed that, when Scott thought she was sleeping, he reached out under the cover of darkness and stroked Hugo a couple of times.

They made the two-hundred-plus-mile drive in under three hours. Scott had always had a heavy foot. This time it was concrete. Yet she knew he was in complete control, all emotions shut down to get the job at hand done.

When he stopped for gas, Cole had offered to call his mother and check on his dad. The look Scott sent her way made her back off. She suspected what he was afraid to say aloud. He didn't want to know if he would get there too late.

Having grown up in New Brunswick, he knew the way

to the hospital. The fact that he parked his car in the emergency lane was the only betrayal of his state of mind.

She trailed behind him through the emergency door, figuring that no one was going to tow a truck with two dogs wearing collars emblazoned with the word POLICE.

Scott flashed his badge at the desk. "John Lucca. Heart attack."

The receptionist nodded. "Let me check."

Scott watched her make a call with laser-focused attention, while Cole scanned the waiting room. She didn't see his mother there. Enough time had passed since her call that perhaps Scott's father had been admitted. Best-case scenario.

"He's still in Emergency Intensive Care. If you'd like to wait over there." She pointed to an area filled with families and friends, and those patients not lucky enough to yet be seen.

"What I want is to see my father. Now." Scott's voice hadn't risen but the menace in it sent the tension in the emergency room skyrocketing. Even the hospital guard's head twitched in their direction.

Cole didn't touch him but she slid in beside Scott and addressed the receptionist. "Can you locate Mrs. Lucca for us? We're worried about his mom, too."

"Sure." The receptionist didn't glance at Scott again. This time she got a more positive response. "She'll be right out. You can wait—"

Scott wasn't in the mood to be told what he could do. He walked over to the doors that opened to the emergency room ward and stood there, his stance braced for anything.

Cole hung back, not certain now that she was here what if any part she had to play. She just couldn't allow him to drive for hours back, alone, especially if the news wasn't going to be good.

The doors opened with a whoosh. Cathy Lucca was already in motion. She looked much as Cole remembered her, dark hair cut into a sophisticated bob and well dressed for the evening out she'd shared with her husband earlier.

"Scott, you're here. Thank God." She plowed into her son at full force, wrapping her arms about him and hugging him tight.

Cole saw the spasm of anguish on Scott's face as he briefly shut his eyes and hugged his mom back. He was a head taller than she was, making her seem almost frail by comparison.

Finally his mother released him to reach up to touch her son's face. "Your father will be so glad to know you're here."

"He's alive?" The wonder in Scott's voice surprised Cole.

"Yes, he's awake and complaining." Cathy smiled and patted her son's cheek. "You're exactly alike, you know."

Scott shrugged. "So, he's going to be okay?"

A cloud appeared in Cathy's attractive face. "We're waiting for tests. They said something about—Nicole?" She had turned to lead Scott away from the doorway when she noticed Cole. "Oh, my goodness. That *is* you."

Cathy left Scott's side to rush over to hug her. The hug was so huge and long Cole reeled a bit. "Whatever are you doing here?"

The question might have been directed at Cole but Scott's mother turned almost immediately to him. "I'm so glad you brought her with you." She smiled at Cole. "We can talk later. Come with me."

They followed Mrs. Lucca back through the emergency room doors to a private waiting room just inside. "I'm expecting the doctor any minute. They had to do some tests and said someone would be in shortly to talk with me about what comes next."

"So, Dad's going to be okay?" Scott asked in doubt.

"Oh, Scott, I hope so. He was fine earlier. No hint of a problem. We had gone out to dinner. I had a coupon for two-for-one pricing if we ordered before six. So then we decided to take in a movie. We went to see that—"

"Mom." Scott raked a hand through his hair in irritation.

Cole saw his mother's face crumple and didn't know who she felt sorrier for, her or his son. Cathy's lip began to quiver. "I'm so sorry, Scott. I don't know why I'm rambling on about a stupid movie. It was just so awful. So awful. We walked in and . . . and . . ."

"Mom, Mom, it's okay." Scott reached for her and again she collapsed against him. This time he directed her to a chair and made her sit as his hands continued to support her.

"I'm so sorry. I didn't know what to do. We walked into the—the destruction of everything. Your father's face turned this awful shade and then his legs buckled. I called 911 and told them to send the police, the ambulance, everyone."

"You did exactly right." Cole located a box of tissues and plucked one for her. "Your fast thinking is the reason John's getting the attention he needs right now."

Scott made eye contact with her over his mother's bowed head. There was a hollowness there she had seen only once before. She reached out and laid her hand over one of his cradling his mother's and squeezed briefly.

"How about I find us all some coffee and maybe a few of those bad-for-you items in the vending machines? This could take a while."

Cole rose quickly to her feet. She wasn't the least bit hungry but she knew they needed a few minutes alone. This wasn't her family anymore.

"Come back."

Cole looked over her shoulder. It was Scott who had spoken. She smiled. "Absolutely."

* * *

"Angioplasty and a possibility of stents." Scott had pulled Cole out into the hallway when she returned with coffee. His mother was keeping his dad company while they waited. "They are just waiting for a room."

"That's good news, isn't it?"

Scott nodded but yet his eyes were hollow and the stubble shadowing his lower jaw seemed to weigh down his face.

"Something else is wrong, isn't it?"

He didn't answer directly. "I need to go and secure my parents' house. Can you stay here and wait with my mother?"

"Of course. If you think she'd like that."

A ghost of a smile flickered in his expression. "I think she might be happier to see you than me. I'm certain my father will be."

"Don't." Cole moved in close to him. When he didn't respond, she leaned her head against his chest. After a moment, his arms came up around her, tightening until she was having trouble breathing but she didn't complain. His crushing embrace told her all he could not say.

He released her quickly and headed for the door. He had climbed into his truck before she remembered Hugo was still in the front seat. She ran out after him but he had pulled away.

She debated calling him but decided he must think he knew what he was doing. After all, she couldn't bring a dog into the emergency room. If she hadn't been so worried about Scott and his dad, she might have been amused by the thought of Hugo and Izzy and Scott together.

CHAPTER THIRTEEN

"Looks worse than it is. Strictly amateur hour."

The New Brunswick patrol officer who had accompanied Scott to his parents' home turned the key to let Scott in past the police tape.

On alert, Scott gazed around the living room of his parents' home, looking for a clue. Pictures and mirrors had been smashed. Lamps, the flat-screen TV, and small tables knocked over.

Scott shut his eyes briefly, imagining his parents' horror when they walked in on the destruction of their home. *My fault*.

"You getting a picture?"

His expression void of emotion, Scott turned to the officer who had followed him in. "Yeah. The scumbags didn't miss a trick."

"Yep. Real bad boys. They shit and pissed on things upstairs. Cleaned out the medicine cabinet and all the liquor. Your dad's a professor, right? We're thinking maybe he gave some frat boy a grade he didn't like. Got his friends in here to toss it."

"My mother's a family court judge."

"For real? Then it could be some juvie miscreant sending a message he didn't like her decision. No real harm, but ugly."

Scott got the message. The local police weren't all that concerned about vandalism. Any excuse to write it up and file this case away would work. He knew the drill. It might have looked bad to the owners. So horrifying, his dad had had a coronary event. But to the hardened gaze of law enforcement, this was a minor incident.

They didn't know what he suspected and he couldn't tell them without jeopardizing both present and former undercover work. Besides, he had no proof.

He looked around for some clue to the identity of the intruders. Even his parents' CDs had been dumped from their chest in one corner and stomped on. The intruders didn't steal. Just set out to do maximum damage. This was intimidation masquerading as rage.

"Can you get DNA from the piss and shit?"

The officer shrugged. "Took samples. But I doubt it's going to be a high priority with the lab. We've had a stabbing plus a rape case just this week. Could be months before results, even if we make an arrest. No one was injured. No weapons displayed. Say, did your parents have guns in the house?"

Scott shook his head. His mother didn't even like him to bring his weapon into her home, though she'd never said so. So many silent displays of disapproval of his life choices. And now this. His father would never forgive this, if Scott was the cause.

Scott treaded cautiously around the main room. "You did collect other evidence?"

"Some. Without suspects, fingerprints are next to useless with this kind of thing. We don't have much to go on. No neighbor heard or saw a thing. That's about all we can do. Vandalism is not that big of a crime, on the scale. Know what I mean?"

"You go tell that to my mother."

The cop shook his head. "I don't envy what they're dealing with. But tell them to look on the bright side. No personal harm was done. These are just things. They can replace them."

Scott didn't reply. He'd been the responding officer on many break-ins during his early years on patrol. He had always thought people made way too much of things being lost, stolen, or broken. They were, after all, just things. But looking at the accumulated contents of his parents' lives broken into so much landfill turned his stomach, and set rage burning in his belly.

"What about the fact this incident put my dad in the hospital?"

The patrol officer gave him a palms-up shrug. "He had a heart attack when he came home and saw the damage. That's not a direct connection. The D.A. won't want the bother, unless we catch the perpetrators. Or do you know something we don't?"

"Just a hunch." Scott did a systematic search of the room, eyes doing a thorough sweep, looking for the clue that must be here somewhere.

He moved quickly through to his father's study. File drawers had been pulled open and the contents tossed. Books had been dumped from their shelves. His father's computer had been dropped and either smashed with something heavy or repeatedly stomped on.

He turned into the dining room with a heavy heart. The intention had been to inflict pain. They had succeeded. His mother's good china lay in shards all over the floor. His grandmother's crystal had been smashed on the shelves of the china cabinet, gleaming wetly like icicles in the light.

Even the chandelier had been struck repeatedly. The floor sparkled where bits of broken crystal had fallen.

He doubted this was random, though it had been planned carefully to look that way. Until he had evidence that said otherwise, no one else would believe it. He wouldn't either, if he didn't have this big fucking hunch sitting on his shoulder.

It was a little past noon when Scott left the hospital a second time. He'd slept, sort of, in the waiting room, giving his mother the recliner in his dad's room. She wouldn't leave and he couldn't encourage her to go home. Fuck it all! He didn't want either of them to come home to the wreckage he'd left behind last night. That's why he was stopping at the house, instead of going to the motel where he'd sent Cole after his father's surgery was over. At least someone was getting some rest.

His eyes felt as if he'd rubbed sand in them. His back had a hitch in it, and his breath must be as rancid as his attitude. Still, he had work to do.

The sight of his mother's car parked out front, instead of the garage where she kept it, set Scott's heart into action mode as he pulled up in the driveway. The front door was open. The police tape gone. He reached for his gun, which he'd kept in the glove compartment while he was at the hospital.

Even before he reached the front door he heard music, up-tempo and heavy on the beat. Hip-hop. And a woman's voice, singing regrettably off-key. He was pretty sure he recognized who was singing.

Suddenly he felt a little foolish and tucked his weapon in his jeans.

He didn't knock, just walked in. Amazingly a bit of the clutter had been removed from the living room. But the music was coming from the dining room. He walked quickly in that direction.

Cole had laid towels over the surface of the dining room table, which now held pieces of crystal and china that had escaped damage, and some that looked like they could be repaired. She was doing salvage.

She still wore her clothes from the day before, just as he did. The music coming from her cell phone speaker was loud and rude, and slightly familiar. But it was like a desecration in his parents' home.

"What the hell do you think you're doing?"

Cole straightened up from where she'd been sweeping glass into a dustpan. She smiled when she saw him. "Hi, Scott. How's your dad?"

He nodded, feeling too raw to talk about it. Still, he had to say something to her. "What are you doing here? I thought you'd taken a hotel room."

"Couldn't sleep." Cole yawned. "The keys you gave me last night to your mother's car also included the house key, so I decided to come over and make myself useful."

"Could you turn that off?" He pointed to the music source.

The resulting silence seemed to vibrate with relief.

"You left Izzy and Hugo in a motel room?"

Cole looked at him as if he'd pulled a rabbit out of his ear. "I put the dogs out back in your parents' dog run. Your mom told me Kato died last year, which I was so sorry to hear. She was a good dog. They should replace her for safety's sake. Still, it was nice to have a place for our pair. They were tired of being caged up. I figured they'd probably get along just so they wouldn't be put back in your truck."

"Okay. But you don't need to do"—he waved his hand around—"this."

She frowned. "You don't want your parents to come home to it. They've suffered enough."

He tucked in his chin. "I planned to take care of it."

"You have two people depending on you already. Let me at least clean."

He looked around. Cole saw a twinge of pain in his face each time his eyes alit on something broken or damaged. He was looking at them through his parents' eyes and feeling their pain. All the more reason why she, one step removed, should be doing the heavy lifting in this situation.

"I have a little coffee left." She pointed to a cup. He didn't have to be invited twice.

"You shouldn't have touched anything." He frowned hard, scratching at the day-old growth on one cheek. "Now I don't have an inventory."

"I took pictures of everything." She held up her camera. "Better than that, I called your parents' insurance company this morning, like your mom asked me to. They sent an agent over an hour ago. The claim's already being filed. So we've got permission to straighten up."

He just stared at her. Okay, maybe he was all out of thank-yous at the moment.

Cole held up a clipboard. "I'm making a list of everything I recognize. Once we know exactly what's salvageable it might help your parents to make a list of what was destroyed or missing." She glanced at the pile of glass and porcelain she had swept into one corner to make a walkway. "It's kinda impossible for me to tell the remains of a champagne flute from a crystal candy dish."

He continued to stare at her until discomfort made her continue talking.

"I put some of the pictures and mirrors in the car. Thought I'd take them over to a glass shop and see if I can get them redone before they return home."

"Did you clean up the shit upstairs, too?"

She flinched at the ugliness in his voice even while she reminded herself that he was hurting and worried, too. But she wasn't going to be provoked into being his punching bag so he'd have a release.

"Why don't you start in your father's office? I couldn't begin to sort his files. Maybe you'll have better luck."

"Is that the washer and dryer running?"

"I'm washing some of your mother's things. She'll need a bag to stay at a hotel for a while. Then I'll tackle your dad's. Piss washes out."

His mouth tightened. "The fucking bastards."

From the corner of his eye, Scott saw her reach for her phone. "What in the hell were you playing?"

"Eye-C's latest album. Thought I should familiarize myself with it. In case I have an opportunity to pal around with Shajuanna." She rolled her eyes. "It's just what you'd expect; misogynistic, homophobic, and crude. Never say I don't like culture."

Her little joke fell flat. Scott's expression didn't alter a muscle. He just turned away.

Ten minutes later, he was on his knees sorting the paper chase that had once been his father's files when he heard her call.

"Scott?"

His gut turned watery at the odd note in her voice. He didn't even consciously move from his father's office. He was simply there in the kitchen.

She was standing with the refrigerator door open. She pushed it wider when she saw him.

A bloody hog's head sat on the middle shelf with an *X* carved into its forehead.

He moved forward and stared at it.

This was the clue he had been looking for. The break-in wasn't random. It wasn't amateur. This was a warning, to him, made at his parents' expense. How was he supposed to explain that to them, and then make it up to them?

He didn't even look at Cole as he walked away.

* * *

"A hog's head?" Dave Wilson, Scott's former undercover handler, whistled over the phone line.

"Yeah, the kind you can find in the frozen food section at Walmart."

"You figure all this was just a way to deliver a message to you?"

"Pig. Police. The *X*. Doesn't take Einstein to connect the dots."

"What's local law enforcement saying?"

"What you'd expect. Despite the implied threat, it's not the kind of case they can classify as potentially lethal without further evidence. But you called me. Talk."

Dave snorted on the other end of the line. "For starters, someone out of criminal investigations up in Philly requested your file a month back. It wouldn't have come up on my radar if you hadn't alerted me to look into things. The officer claims he pulled it by mistake."

"Uh-huh. What did he get?"

"The standard stuff. Age, rank, general background. Nothing about U/C or SWAT. That's classified."

But enough to cause trouble. Anyone who was interested would have enough to take even basic information and find out where he went to school. From there it wouldn't be at all difficult to locate his parents because they had lived in the same house for more than thirty years.

"Second. You were right. There's money on the street in D.C. for information about a former undercover narc. No name attached. Info says it's not gang-related but the Pagans know about it."

Scott nodded. "So there's a bounty on me?"

"More like reward for information. Maybe you. Okay, after your parents' vandalism, probably you. So far, we got shit on this Dos Exquis scumbag. But his paperwork looks suspect so I'm digging. He's been out of prison for six months. Visits his parole officer like clockwork."

"He got a job?" *Somewhere I can find him,* Scott thought.

"You hear about the economy? Jobs are scarce even for the good guys. I'll ask you again, can you think of anyone else who might want to get at you?"

"I'm pretty sure X is the guy trying to punch my ticket."

"What did you say your girlfriend's name is?"

"I didn't say I had one."

"Don't get cute, Lucca. I know you. There's a woman somewhere."

"Is this really necessary?"

"If she's a regular booty call, it's necessary. They found your parents."

Scott glanced toward the kitchen where Cole was still cleaning. "It's delicate."

"Surgery is delicate. Murder is messy."

"It's personal."

"It can't be personal. You said this is related to your former U/C assignment. That makes it my business, too."

"She's on the job and owed some consideration."

"Police? Then at least give her a heads-up." Dave waited three heartbeats before he changed the subject. "I'll check with ATF. See if they've picked up any additional info about a bounty on a narc's head. When are you leaving for your new assignment?"

"Tomorrow. DEA is anxious for us to get under way."

"Where will you be?"

"How about I call you?"

Longer pause. "If I get anything else you'll hear from me. Meanwhile, don't get yourself fucking dead playing the hero."

"Yes, sir."

CHAPTER FOURTEEN

"So I explained that it was just a business-related coincidence that we were together when I got the phone call. Because you remember them fondly, you offered to come along." Scott looked out across his parents' backyard to where their pool lay smooth as a mirror reflecting back the sky and trees in the late-summer evening light. "They needed to know that you coming with me didn't mean anything was going on between us."

Cole nodded. "Okay."

This was the first real conversation they had had since they had left Harmonie Kennels late the night before. They had done a lot of cleanup in one day. But the house needed more, and then he needed to get professionals in to handle the stains and furniture repair. She and Scott had both showered at the hotel, separately, after she'd bought a pair of capris and a tee and a few other necessities. She was going to catch the late bus back to Virginia shortly. She'd already obtained tickets and a pass that allowed a police K-9 to travel with her. In less than thirty-six hours round-trip she would be back at Harmonie Kennels.

She glanced sideways at him. His hair, still damp in the warm summer air, lay in little C-hooks along his brow and collar. Her heart swelled—stupid heart—at the sight. She longed to run her finger along the column of his neck. Or maybe pull him close into her arms to offer the comfort of her body touching his. But she didn't dare. Every tense line of his body told her to Keep Out.

Just as well she was going back because she didn't know what to do with any of the feelings running through her. It wasn't just lust this time. This was something much more risky. Something neither of them could afford to acknowledge right now.

Scott was staying on two days longer to shore things up for his parents. His dad would be released from the hospital in the morning. Other than out of necessity, Scott had scarcely spoken to her all day. She had gotten the message. She had barged in without thinking and without welcome. By doing so, she'd made things awkward with his parents. Scott was trying to be civil but it was hard.

Cole licked her lips, her throat suddenly dry. "I hope my appearance didn't upset your parents."

Scott looked pained. "The exact opposite. Dad's still in a hospital bed and they were already making plans for us to come visit when the house is redone. Insurance is going to pay for a lot."

"I see."

Cole picked up and tossed a ball to Hugo, who went hustling after it. Izzy was asleep on top of Scott's feet. "I'm sorry if my presence is an embarrassment for you."

"You aren't an embarrassment." He sure seemed interested in something going on in the yard behind the fence. Or, he really didn't want to look at her.

"I just wanted to help." To cover her acute discomfort she launched herself out of the patio chair as Hugo came hurrying back. He spit out the ball at her feet in the hopes of another toss.

She didn't look around when Scott stood up beside her. She just gave Hugo's ball a mighty toss. The ball took a bad bounce and landed right in the middle of the pool.

"Crap." She started to go after it but Scott wrapped a hand around her upper arm, halting her. When she turned to him his expression was still closed off, all but the beat of pain in his eyes.

"You did more than help. Your being there." She could see him struggling with the words. She let him. Finally he lifted a hand to her cheek, cupping it so gently she felt the sudden foolish push of tears in her eyes. "Your being here was a good thing for them. Thank you."

He dropped his hand and turned away. Izzy, feeling bereft, pulled herself to her feet and stared after him.

Cole watched him walk back into the house that had once been his home, thinking that she was watching the loneliest man she'd ever known. Yet that didn't make sense.

His dad was going to be fine. His mother was already talking about new drapes and paint chips this afternoon, mostly to have something positive to hold on to, Cole figured, when she dropped by the hospital to say farewell. His parents would be staying at a long-term residency inn while their home's interior was redone. Scott had already found a place for them, close enough to the hospital so that if his dad should need care they could get there quickly.

Something else was wrong. He just wasn't going to tell her.

The huge splash had her shaking her head before she even turned around. Hugo, all ninety-five pounds of him, was paddling for dear life to retrieve his ball from the pool.

Izzy did a head kick, cocking her head to one side, and woofed her opinion of his action.

Cole glanced down at the chocolate-brown Lab and smiled. "I know. Males. Right? At least you don't have to share a bus seat with him tonight. Don't suppose you know where a hair dryer is?"

Hugo scooped up the orange prize and pranced around the Harmonie Kennel course as if he was taking a victory lap after winning a race.

"Show-off." Cole smiled and clapped for him.

For the first time, Hugo had completed the Weave obstacle without stopping or faulting. A week's effort. It was tenuous at best. Yardley was loaning her the poles so that they could practice every day, wherever they went. They would need all the practice they could squeeze in. Hugo was still tentative in the beginning and slower than she wanted because he was still thinking his way through it.

She allowed him to chew on his prize for a few minutes to extract some of the peanut butter before asking for it back. Hugo reluctantly brought it to her and put it down. She picked it up and tucked it under her arm. "So now you know the joy of winning. Show me what else you've got."

She ran back into the ring and put him through his paces, all the jumps and tunnels, the teeter-totter, and even the A-frame, before bringing him back to the Weave poles.

Hugo slid through the first four zigzags like butter. But he overshot coming out and went in between six and seven, skipping five-six.

"Nein." She waved him back to the beginning.

Hugo gamely tried again, this time going more slowly, as if he was thinking his way through it again. He paused briefly twice but actually made it through. She didn't hand him the prize this time but called him back to the beginning. *"Hier.* Again."

The third time through he made it without mishap.

Cole tossed him the orange peanut-butter-flavored prize. "Good boy! *Zei brav!*"

Exhausted, she made her way back to the bunkhouse. Scott was expected back tonight, or so she'd heard from Richards. He hadn't called or even texted her. Something wasn't right. She couldn't put her finger on it but the more she thought about it, his actions didn't seem to be related only to the bad scare of almost losing his father. The hog's head, which seemed just an ugly prank at the time, had begun to creep into her dreams. Who brought a hog's head to an act of vandalism, unless it had a purpose? What purpose? A message. But for who?

"Always a cop, Jamieson," she murmured to herself.

She'd become accustomed to putting the worst interpretation on every suspicious event. Perhaps the hog's head had already been there in the Luccas' freezer. Although she really couldn't imagine Judge Lucca making roasted hog's head in her immaculate kitchen.

Or possibly the only thing wrong with Scott was that he'd had sex with his ex.

Cole briefly covered her face with her hands. "Stupid move, Jamieson."

While it had seemed a good idea at the time, during, and right afterward, Scott could be having second thoughts. Being a fuck buddy was one thing. The thought of having your ex back in your bed and under the same roof twenty-four/seven until the task force operation was over might be more than enough reason for him to back off and cool down. Maybe he thought she would start wanting more.

Home. Yeah. That unintentional slip had probably meant no more than the baseball scoring system junior high-schoolers still used to determine their sexual progress with a girl. Scott had made it to first, second, third, as well as accumulating a few more advanced scoring stats, before he slid into home.

Yep. That should be enough to send her running for the hills, too.

"Hey, Noel!"

Cole automatically smiled as she looked up. She was becoming accustomed to her new name.

Richards had pulled up in a truck beside her with what looked like a motorcycle under a tarp in the back.

She leaned in the window. "New wheels?"

"That's right. Come and tell me what you think."

While he climbed out, she moved to lean over the side of the truck bed on the opposite side. He pulled loose a couple of knots holding the tarp then whipped it off.

"It's green." Grasshopper green. Cole laughed. "I can't imagine you on anything green."

"You'd be right." He grinned at her. "Like it?"

"What's not to like? What is it?"

"A Kawasaki Ninja 250R. Great little sports bike for a female, I'm told. Not too much power but a sweet goer. Wouldn't get on the interstate with her. She's more a weekend-out-in-the-country bike, or for a city gal."

He loosened the grips on the wheels, dropped the tailgate, and, using a built-in ramp, rolled her down. He patted the seat. "Try her out."

Cole could feel her excitement building but resisted. "I'm sweaty from working Hugo. I wouldn't want to get something so pretty dirty."

"Up to you. You can try her now or later, but let me show you a few things before you take her for a spin." He shut the tailgate and began folding the tarp.

"You're leaving it for me to try out?"

"I'm leaving it for you, period."

Cole was touched, and a little embarrassed. Just because they'd been flirting the past couple of days, innocently on her part, she hoped Richards hadn't gotten the wrong idea about her interest in him. "That's so nice of you but I can't accept a gift this expensive."

He grinned at her in a way that let her know he'd read her thoughts. "You're cute but I'm taken." He held up his left hand and tapped his ring finger.

Cole felt herself blush, hard. "Oh, I wasn't thinking . . ."

"I'm still flattered. But put your mind at ease. I requisitioned this for the task force. I purely did like what a ride on a bike did for your confidence. Probably saved this operation. So, this is undercover operational equipment." He patted the seat. "For the duration, this little honey belongs to Noel Jenkins."

"Seriously?" Cole ran her hand over its sleek and sexy surface. It looked very modern and fun, like something from a movie. "I'd be afraid I might damage it."

"Hell. Don't worry about that. Worry about you. I can't requisition another dog whisperer."

"Dog whisperer?"

"That's what the boys are calling you. Ms. Yardley says you're remarkably good with Hugo. She didn't expect you to progress so quickly. Says you have a gift for training K-9s."

Delight sped through Cole. Yardley certainly had kept her praise a secret this week. In fact, every time she noticed the kennel owner watching her put Hugo through his paces, her heart rate had doubled in apprehension. Yardley seldom said a word, just watched her and Hugo's every movement with eagle-eyed intensity.

"You take care now, you hear?" Richards opened the driver's side door. "Wait up. I forgot something." He pulled a big shopping bag out of the cab and came around to hand it to her. "I figured you wouldn't have a helmet or jacket. Hope they fit. I had to guess your size."

Cole pulled the items out. The jacket, thankfully, was black. The helmet a bright green to match the bike, as was the trim on the motorcycle gloves. "Wow. Let me pay you for these."

"Not a penny. My pleasure."

She waited until Richards drove away to throw a leg over the bike. It felt lighter and easier to manage than the bigger, heavier one he rode. Yes, Noel just might be taking up a new hobby.

She looked down at Hugo, who was sniffing the bike suspiciously. "Too bad you can't hang on or you could ride bitch."

Hugo barked twice, sniffed the bike a little more, and then backed up and barked a few more times. Clearly he recognized competition when he saw it.

Cole leaned down and scratched the top of his head. "I will always love you best." But, obviously, a test ride was in order.

One shower and a change of boots, jeans, jacket, and helmet later, Cole was cruising down a back road dappled with sunshine and leaf shadows.

The Kawasaki was a sweet ride. The engine buzzed like a motorboat, the sounds revving into a higher range, and she shifted gears.

Noel was riding, confident, sure of her skills but no squid, a rider overconfident of her abilities. She hadn't seen Richards's note tucked into the helmet until she went to put it on. "Better wary than roadkill." That, of course, put things in perspective.

She was thirty minutes from Harmonie Kennels when she heard the sound of another bike, big and powerful, screaming up fast behind her. Cole glanced in her rearview mirror, thinking it might be Richards. It wasn't. The guy didn't wear a helmet. And he was straddling a vintage Harley.

She automatically glanced ahead. No oncoming traffic. She checked her speed and moved closer to the shoulder, expecting him to roar past her in a cloud of exhaust and earsplitting engine noise.

Instead, she heard him shifting down, coming up behind her until he was so close she could no longer see all of him in the mirror.

She waved him around her. Nothing.

Looking steadily ahead, she decided to ignore him. From what little she'd glimpsed of him, black shades, bearded, with a bandana holding back long greasy hair, he wasn't anyone she wanted to deal with.

Suddenly he came around her, engine roaring, until he had pulled up alongside.

Cole glanced at him. He wore jeans and a dirty white T-shirt, revealing arms lean and sinewy and so browned by the sun and wind they looked like tree roots. As he moved a little ahead of her she spied his denim vest and the insignia on the back. The name PAGAN was emblazoned on a patch between his shoulders. Below it a separate patch depicted the god Surti, the Norse god, sitting on the sun and wielding a sword.

Her stomach did a flip as her hands flexed tight on the handlebars. As a law-enforcement officer she was familiar with gang symbols. After all, Maryland was the reputed home of the outlaw motorcycle gang. But meeting one on this lonely stretch of the road was not a good feeling. Not good at all.

He grinned and motioned for her to pull over.

Cole shook her head and motioned him to go ahead then looked away, hoping he would get the message.

Instead he swung his bike inward toward hers and, reaching out, grabbed her butt.

Shocked by the intimate gesture, Cole swerved sharply away from him, almost onto the shoulder. She caught herself before she could spin out. The bike wobbled as she corrected the drift but she didn't go down.

She looked around as he roared away, just past a bend in the road. She had lost speed and rolled to a stop, hoping he'd just go on now, content he'd frightened her.

Woman on a bike. Har har. Go away.

Sweat had popped out on her face and neck, and began to trickle down her chest as she debated what to do. She turned and squinted, trying to see if there was on-coming traffic, but the ribbon of road behind her was empty. If she went on, he might be lying in wait for her.

No reason to go ahead. She was just testing out her new toy.

Returning was not retreat, she reasoned calmly. It was, in this instance, a calculated maneuver to defuse the situation.

She was barely a mile back down the empty road when a rising whine, keener than a chain saw, signaled that he had turned around and was coming back, fast.

"Shit. Where the hell is a traffic jam when you need it?"

She forced herself not to speed up. It was clear that his hog could overtake hers and she didn't want to get caught in a confrontation at high speeds with an unfamiliar bike.

This time, he screamed past her, leaving her choking on dust.

He began braking almost immediately and turned quickly, kicking up dust and leaving, she knew from the smoke rising under his rear wheel, rubber on the road.

Her heart began to pound in earnest. He wasn't done with her. And that wasn't good. She blinked the sweat out of her eyes, afraid to take a hand off the handles.

He had rolled to a stop 50 yards in front of her, teeth gleaming through the tangle of his beard. As she neared him he signaled for her to pull over.

Cole's gaze shifted left and right, calculating if she could get around him by using the other lane. Maybe. Or he might kick her bike as she passed, sending her spinning off into the trees. Then what?

Control the situation. Survive. Police Academy 101.

It took her a few seconds to remember she wore a weapon in a pancake holster at the small of her back. She had gotten out of the habit of being armed at all times while on Harmonie Kennel property. But leaving the property had prompted the habit to return. She owed another thank-you to the police academy for that.

She stopped ten yards away and cut the engine. Not pausing to use the kickstand, she let the bike drop as she dismounted, jerked off her gloves, and reached with both hands for her gun. Though her hands were sweaty, the weight of the Keltec PT3A pistol felt reassuringly good as her fingers closed over the butt.

She took a wide-legged stance as she brought her weapon forward and braced it with both hands. "Police officer. Dismount, slowly, and get down on your knees."

She was happy to hear the strength of command in her voice.

He didn't move to dismount but he did raise his hands.

She pitched her voice louder. "Police officer! Dismount!"

He dismounted.

With the light at her back, she could see him better now. With eyes sunk deep in his head and razor-sharp bones beneath sunken cheeks, his face had an almost grinning-skull quality to it.

He started walking slowly toward her, moving on the balls of his feet, arms held away from his sides. She calculated the odds of hitting a target at this distance. Keltec PT3A was a close-in weapon best used at a distance of less than seven yards. He was closing in rapidly.

"Halt! On your knees!"

He was grinning, seemingly unimpressed by her gun. "You wouldn't shoot an unarmed man."

"Try me." She slipped free the safety. "Halt. Now."

He grinned. "You're afraid of me. Yeah. I smell pussy fear."

"Move a foot closer and you'll smell blood as a bullet tears through you." She moved her aim a little bit lower, smack at the center of him.

He paused. "Just fucking with you, bitch. You can't take a joke?"

Cole was done talking. Her full concentration was on when and if she'd pull the trigger.

He seemed to sense she was serious. "Pussy cops. Fuck you!"

He began backing up but he didn't turn his back.

She watched him, keeping him centered in her sight as he retreated. No way would she release her stance until he was out of sight and hearing.

She heard road noise before she saw the car in the distance coming up behind him. He heard it, too. He slung a leg over his hog and started it. He revved the engine until the air seemed to bleed and then he came straight at her.

Cole held her breath and pretended she was doing firearms training simulation. He was just a target she had hit many times before.

At the last second, he veered away from her, catching her in the heat of his exhaust as he passed.

Cole swung around, coughing fumes, gun still on target. She didn't move until he was a blur and the car at her back began laying on the horn.

She sheathed her weapon as she turned toward the approaching car and waved at the driver to stop. She didn't know what he'd seen, so she reached for her wallet to show her ID.

The driver, a kid of about eighteen, and his friend hopped out of opposite side doors. "You spin out?" Apparently they hadn't seen anything, or been paying attention until now.

Cole nodded and pocketed her wallet, still straining for the sounds of the retreating Pagan biker.

"You need help?" asked the companion.

"No. I got this. Thanks."

She moved to her bike and put the kickstand down. Then she came around and squatted down, put her butt against the seat, grabbed a handlebar in one hand and the back of the bike with the other, and pushed with her feet and legs until it was upright.

The two teens clapped in approval. "That's a pretty nifty maneuver."

She smiled. Nothing like what they would have witnessed had they come along a few minutes earlier. She could take care of herself.

Even so. The acceleration of her heart was giving her a head rush and she had begun to tremble.

"Here you go." One of the teens scooped up and handed her her gloves. "That's a beauty of a bike."

She nodded, then sucked up a breath and pushed pride out of the way. Ninety-five percent of police officers went their entire career without ever using their service weapon in the line of duty. She'd almost switched sides to the other five percent this afternoon. She owed herself a little protection while she decompressed.

"Would you guys mind following me back to Harmonie Kennels? It's just a few miles. If my bike has suffered more damage than it appears, I might need a lift."

"Sure thing."

She slung a leg over and started the engine. If Hugo had been with her, she wouldn't have needed to rely only on her weapon.

Bikes were fun but she'd had enough fun for a while.

X waited until the sound of the bitch's bike had faded before he stopped on the side of the road to take a leak and grab a smoke. When those two urgent needs were handled, he pulled out a bottle of Southern Comfort from his saddlebag and took a deep swallow.

He was pretty pleased with his plan so far.

After that night in Georgia a month ago, he'd had no trouble tracking a DEA K-9 unit's license plates to D.C. Then it had become a matter of spreading a little cash around for eyes to watch the office building until Rhino was spotted and followed home.

Rhino was a narc, all right. A narc named Scott Lucca.

X spit a stream of liquor between his teeth just to watch the golden stream arc through the afternoon air like piss.

He could have killed the bastard a dozen times that first week. But that would have been too easy. Over too quickly. He didn't want him dead so much as fucked up.

So he'd waited.

The wait gave him a chance to spread a little more money on the street and weave together a web of informants who watched Rhino when he wasn't watching. He'd hoped to find a wife and kiddies, someone he could easily terrorize. But Rhino was being a monk. And then came a break: an informant spotted him headed up Interstate 95 in his private vehicle.

It always took luck. Anyone who lived on the edge knew that luck counted as much as preparation and heart when it came to survival, and the hunt.

Rhino had gone north to visit his parents. Weakness number one.

The sighting of Rhino with a woman by a pansy-ass wannabe biker out of Baltimore had been the next piece of luck.

She, too, was a cop. Weakness number two.

X poured a bit of whiskey on the ground then ground it into the dust with his heel, homage to a pagan god all his own. Then he twisted the cap back on his bottle and re-mounted.

He now had all he needed to take the son of a bitch down. He was just going to do it bit by bit. Like checking out the reason Rhino was in Virginia had given him a chance to follow his woman's movements.

So, that was Rhino's bitch. She didn't look like much of a good time. But maybe after he'd had Rhino's piece of ass, he'd toss her to the informant as payment. If there was anything much left of her.

Patience was a virtue. Payback was a bitch.

Scott didn't return until after she was in bed for the night. She lay listening to him move about, speaking occasionally to Izzy. He came near her closed door once and stood there so long she almost called out just to end the suspense. Finally, he moved away without even tapping to see if she was awake.

Was he avoiding her?

Or, was she avoiding him?

She sat up, disturbing Hugo, who was curled in a pile of fur at her feet. She reached out and stroked him until he resettled.

Hugo seldom slept with her but tonight she needed comfort. She had wanted it to come from Scott. The longing surprised her in its intensity. Yet she was afraid he would misinterpret her need as sexual. She couldn't handle that option tonight.

She certainly wasn't going to go whining to him about the incident with the Pagan biker this afternoon.

A shiver rocked her hard. She sat up

She had yet to tell anyone, even Richards. The fact she'd been harassed by a douche bag on a motorcycle would only reinforce to the men on the task force team her vulnerability as a woman. She'd fought too long and hard to gain respect as a female police officer to go running to the DEA, or even Yardley, with a Big Bad Wolf story. Red Riding Hood had saved herself. That shit was standard operating procedure these days.

The ease with which she'd not only changed her mind about Scott, but felt this sudden intense urge to rely on his big solid strength for emotional support was dangerous, and foolish.

She squirmed around on the bed until she could lay her head against Hugo's bulky back, and pushed her hand into his fur for reassurance.

As she drifted off to sleep, she pretended it was Scott's warmth surrounding her.

CHAPTER FIFTEEN

Scott woke up at Harmonie Kennels to find Cole gone. He hadn't wanted to awaken her when he came in after midnight. But he had expected—correct that—hoped they could talk this morning in private. Hugo wasn't here, either. They must be training already.

Scott let his anticipation of seeing her ebb into disappointment as he crossed to her room. He'd been a jerk to her from the get-go on their trip to New Jersey, and all she'd wanted to do was help. He wanted to apologize and explain. If he could find the words for the guilt, sense of helplessness and fear that had been motivating him.

He paused in her open doorway, taking in the twisted sheets on her bed and the shed of telltale dark dog hair at the foot. On a nearby chair lay a biker helmet and gloves and a jacket.

What the hell?

Newly awakened, Izzy padded in behind him and went to sniff the bed and then the biker gear before circling back to be petted.

Scott bent and stroked her. "Looks like we've missed a few things." She licked his face in response.

It had taken him longer than he expected to get his parents settled at the residence inn. His father demanded to see the house but his doctors recommended he wait at least a week before he subjected himself to anything that might upset him. So Scott had stayed on two extra days to make certain the details of insurance and police reports were taken care of. That required an inventory that, much as he would have liked to, he couldn't compile alone. He hadn't lived at home since he went to college. Things could be missing or broken that he would never remember or know were part of the household.

He had taken his mother to the house yesterday morning, after hiring a nurse to sit with his father. He had tried to prepare her, even made her promise to not tell his father the worst of it, no matter how distressed the experience made her. Teary-eyed, she'd promised. Then she had shocked him with her reaction to the cleanup.

"Who did this?" she kept asking as she wandered from room to room, astonished by the progress she had not expected. While not anywhere near restored, the house was no longer a homeowner's worst nightmare.

He told her who was responsible.

"Nicole did this for us? Why?" That question had been on Scott's mind since the moment Cole piled into his truck for the drive to New Jersey.

After she had finished making her preliminary list, his mother had come into the kitchen where he was sitting. "Tell Nicole thank you from the bottom of our hearts." Her eyes had softened and she'd put a hand on his shoulder and added very quietly, "She still loves you, son."

That couldn't be right. Little more than two weeks ago, Cole hated his guts. She had ripped him a new one and then kicked him out of her home. His ulterior motives shot to hell, he had given up on her when she suddenly changed her mind and decided to join the task force, despite his participation. She ran hot and cold with no stops in between. Even the sex, he suspected, was a game designed to keep him off balance and at a distance. "Noel" had had sex with "Sam."

She'd certainly worked to keep him at arm's length at every opportunity. Until his mother's call.

Cole had waded into his family's disaster as if it was her own, helping out without asking. Even when he'd behaved like a douche toward her, she'd kept her temper. Through it all she'd had his back.

He felt a lump of an unwanted gratefulness forming in his throat. He wasn't accustomed to anyone having his back. He worked best alone or with Izzy. He might not have Gabe's finesse for making chicken salad out of chicken shit. But he knew how to survive. Until Cole.

Scott swore under his breath, reluctant to acknowledge the damn ache in his chest every time he thought about her. And he thought about her almost constantly these days.

He moved across the room to pick up one of her socks and toss it into an open drawer. Instead, he found himself gazing at a drawer of pretty but impractical underthings.

He felt like a perv but he couldn't stop himself from snagging a pair of purple lace panties and holding them up for a better look. It didn't take much imagination to picture what she'd look like in them or, better yet, out of them. After the other night, he'd been hard-pressed to think of anything else in the solitude of his bed. He was pretty sure he'd dreamed about her each night. This scrap of purple satin and lace was the last thing anyone would expect the sensible, logical Officer Jamieson to wear.

Yet he knew that she was wholly, sensually female.

A rush of lust pushed hard down through him. He would

remember that night in the shower with her for the rest of his life. And always want more.

Scott rubbed an eye, fighting the urge to return to bed. But that wasn't going to stop thoughts of Cole from running through his head. Was he misjudging her? In dealing with everyone else he could think of, Cole was warm and generous, if intense. Even when called on the carpet with Lattimore, she'd rallied and defended her point of view. Only around him was she defensive and hostile.

Maybe that was because she didn't know where she stood with him. How could she? For fear of running her off before he had a chance to get close to her, he hadn't given her anything but attitude. But she scared him this time in a way she hadn't the first time around. She was no longer an impressionable young woman who thought he made the sun rise and rest. She'd seen and known the worst about him, and held it against him. And yet, when he needed her, she'd been there, no, insisted on being there to help take care of the two other most important people in his life. The emotions he'd felt behind that nearly undid him. And so he'd doubled down on locking out his emotions out of fear that, if she saw how really badly he wanted her back in every way, she'd run. No wonder she kept her own emotions on high alert.

And yet, she had blown his mind a few nights ago by simply walking into the shower with him. She had been all satin skin and smooth places and sweet curves and warm, wet dark places he could not get enough of. She'd been that brave. And he'd said nothing. He'd been a goddamn coward, pretending that because they called one another Noel and Sam, he couldn't confess then and there that he wanted her back.

Even as he shifted through these thoughts, Scott knew they were correct. In so many ways, large and small, he hadn't been giving her a chance to want him back. Nor had he been trying to learn the new woman she had become. He'd been so busy trying to go slow and be cool, he hadn't even dared ask for her cell phone number. Something he didn't realize until she was headed back to Harmonie Kennels and he needed to talk with her. In trying not to crowd her, he was pushing her away.

So, again, he was the problem.

The sting of that accusation felt familiar. His father had been his usual self just before Scott had left this morning. Why couldn't Scott take time off to look after his mother until his father was on his feet again? Why wouldn't he simply demand the time off? Didn't he want to help out? And why had Nicole left so quickly? Couldn't his son keep up his end of a relationship long enough to get his wife back for more than a day?

All that disapproval, and his parents had no clue that the trashing of their home was more than likely his fault, too.

Scott dropped the panties back in the drawer and turned toward the door.

He would bet money that X, with or without the Pagans' direct involvement, had frightened his parents to send him a message. The hog's head couldn't be coincidence. X had figured out who he was, knew he'd been an undercover narc, and was going to make life hell for people he cared about until he provoked a confrontation.

The New Brunswick police had promised to keep an eye on his parents, after he explained the "pig" reference. But they didn't have an official obligation to do so. This was simply a courtesy extended to a fellow law enforcement officer. He couldn't tell them more without jeopardizing both his new and old U/C operations.

Scott ran a hand down his face. Even after a few hours' sleep he was still exhausted and hungry, and tired of thinking about things that tied him up in razor wire. He knew—gut level—that everything that was wrong in his life was his own damn fault.

His responsibility. His mess to clean up. He was going to have to do something about X. He just didn't know what yet.

As for Cole, he guessed it was time he fessed up about how he felt about her, and took the consequences. However painful that might be.

"Come, Izzy." He grabbed a bag of dog food and headed out for Harmonie's cafeteria where there'd be coffee and sweet rolls and, with luck, Cole.

"Handlers are permitted to talk, praise, encourage, clap, pat their legs, and use verbal means of encouragement. Multiple commands and/or hand and arm signals are allowed. Handlers must not touch the dog or make any other physical corrections. If during the performance, loud or harsh commands or intimidating signals are used, the handler will be penalized."

Cole listened to the rules being read by the judge, along with the dozens of other handlers competing in Agility at the open-air competition. At nine A.M. the sun was making itself felt through the canopy of park trees. She'd been given all her team's paperwork and a sheet of the course. Hugo was listed as Open Standard, an intermediate class designation that meant that Hugo had already earned the Novice Agility title, thanks to Lattimore's machinations. At the moment, she was more worried about showing the judges that she and Hugo belonged in competition.

When the announcements were finished, Cole looked around for Yardley. This was her doing, a surprise announcement at six A.M. that Yardley had entered them in an Open Agility competition in a suburb of Richmond, Virginia. Cole hadn't had time to do more than gulp her coffee, prepare a show bag containing treats, toys, leads, water bowls, water, and pooper scooper, and set off.

She had thought two seconds about waking Scott, but he was stretched on his bed in only a snug pair of knit shorts, dead to the world.

The fact that he looked amazingly vulnerable and cuddly in that prone position did nothing to encourage her to wake him. She was mad at him. Well, hurt was a better word. And annoyed. But she also had world-class reserves of self-preservation stored up. Going anywhere near him was just asking for the kind of trouble she could not afford now that he had redrawn the personal space lines.

Cole adjusted her sunglasses and refocused. Scott was a problem that wasn't going anywhere anytime soon. At the moment, she had bigger issues. This was her first official dog competition in a decade. She was as nervous as the first time, a fourteen-year-old with sweaty palms and a pulse in overdrive.

There was no mention of Shajuanna Collier on the list of competitors, and no reason to think she would be here. Shajuanna lived in Maryland, just outside Baltimore. Yet there were enough things going on to keep Cole off balance. For instance, she was listed on Hugo's paperwork as Noel Jenkins. So, not only was she road-testing her Agility course skills for the first time in years, she was also undercover.

She wished—No, she was glad Scott—no, Sam—wasn't here. His dual-personality presence would have been one thing too many to keep track of today.

When the smaller dog classes ended, Cole rechecked the course map. Because each course was different at every event, handlers were allowed a short walk-through of it before the competition started.

This one seemed much more difficult than the ones she'd been using with Hugo. Her worse nightmare was that she would get lost on the course and Hugo would make mistakes because of her.

"This is just a test run." The sound of her own voice was small comfort. If they didn't do well, what did it matter? Not a disaster if Hugo popped out of the poles on the Weave obstacle. Except that all the other competitors would wonder how they had achieved Advance status with a team who didn't seem to know the basics.

She smoothed the exhibitor's entry labels stuck on her T-shirt after making certain it matched Hugo's paperwork. Despite the heat of the summer day she felt clammy.

You backed down a Pagan yesterday, Noel Jenkins. Put your big girl panties on and get out there!

"Hi, Noel."

Cole started at the sound of Scott's voice at her back. Before she could turn around a hand slid around her waist from behind and pulled her up against him as he dropped a kiss on her neck just behind her right ear. Pleasant sensation zinged through her as his warm breath fanned over her skin. So did confusion. Oh, right, they were Noel and Sam in public from now on.

She turned within his one-armed embrace. "What are you doing here? Sam?"

He nodded, offering her a very wide grin beneath the shades that shielded his eyes. "Sorry to be late, babe." He dropped another kiss, this time on her lips, before he released her waist. "Got held up in traffic. Isn't that right, Izzy?"

Cole looked down at Izzy, who was on the leash, and bent to pet her. "Hi, Izzy."

Scott pushed back his sunglasses and looked around. "Where's the dog of the hour?"

"This way." She pointed to the cordoned-off area where participants had set up crates and stations for their dogs.

As they fell into step, he swung an arm behind her and anchored his hand on her opposite shoulder.

Cole looked up to find him smiling at her, a grin that managed to be easy and intimate and slightly intimidating all at once. She smiled back and received a shoulder squeeze. Oh, he was good at this. He was at ease. If she didn't know better she would believe his possessive lustful gaze was genuine. It seemed so natural. It was, for Noel and Sam, she reminded herself. Simple and easy because they were totally into one another and everything between them was new and fresh. No baggage.

No baggage.

She repeated that line in her thoughts as she reached up and hooked her thumb in the back of his jeans. She was only momentarily disconcerted to feel the impression of a pancake holster against her knuckle. He wore his weapon under his shirt in the small of his back. It was a reminder that this wasn't a free and easy day. They were on the job. She had two huge tasks ahead of her. Complete the Agility circuit competently. And make every observer believe she was infatuated with Sam.

"Hey." Scott paused. When she did, too, he steered her around to face him and tilted her chin up with his curved forefinger. "I missed not waking up to you this morning. Just so you know." He kissed her again, this time taking time to really leave an impression.

When he lifted his head she stared into green eyes edgy with emotion she didn't dare ponder. Yep, he was good. And that scared her because all she wanted to do now was kiss him again, and go on kissing him until the rest of the world . . . oh, she was in trouble. She gave him a distracted smile and moved on.

Accustomed to patrolling in crowds, Hugo was standing alert in his crate when they approached, watching his surroundings but not anxious about them.

Cole let him out and snapped on a leash. He walked straight over to Scott.

"Hey there, Hugo. How's it going, big fella?" Scott tapped his hand against his jeans leg. Hugo came over and allowed himself to be petted.

"Advance Agility for Large Dogs is open for walk-through."

The loudspeaker's announcement startled Cole. Her pulse began to pound. She wasn't ready. She knew it and so, in short order, would everyone watching the competition.

Astonished at her own reaction but unable to control it, Cole took a step backward, bumping into Scott. This was going to be a first-class disaster, in front of Yardley, Scott, and the Agility world. She looked up at Scott. "I can't do this."

Scott ignored the panic in her tone, though it amazed him. "No, you can't. The Agility course is for dogs." He pulled the course map from her hands "Hell. If he could read, Hugo wouldn't need you at all."

Kate Winslet peeped out of her gaze. "Give the map back."

"I don't think so. You're a natural-born competitor. You and Hugo are a team. You read each other like you've got a psychic connection. He trusts you. You trust him. You got this."

Cole could hear his words but they weren't getting through to her mind. She reached for the map. "I need that back."

He backed away from her, holding it higher than she could reach. "Tell you what. I'll walk the course with you and you can explain it to me."

Cole nodded, mostly because she didn't want to get into a physical struggle with him she knew she couldn't win.

They walked the course with the other handlers for fifteen minutes. By the time they exited, Cole was silent but feeling a bit more calm.

They went back to get Hugo.

Once on the leash, Hugo remained aloof from the other dogs, some barking and yipping with excitement, too certain of his alpha status to get caught up in the noise of those intimidated by strangers and unfamiliar animals.

Scott leaned against the crate and watched Cole continue to study the map as if it contained the answer to some cosmic mystery. He'd seen SWAT team members get over-focused just before a bust. It never went well. He needed to get her mind off the map for a second or she'd blow this.

"I was a jerk to you in New Jersey."

She looked up, gaze scattered. "Yes, you were."

"I'm trying to apologize."

She nodded and lowered the map. "I'm trying to hear it."

"Your being there meant everything to my parents."

"Your mother already sent me an e-card saying thank you."

"How did she know how to find you?"

Cole cocked her head to one side. "We exchanged e-mails and phone numbers."

He murmured, "I don't have that information."

"Wonder why?"

He scowled. "Geez. You're tough."

"Just say the words."

"Give me—" Scott stopped himself as she raised an eyebrow. "May I please have your contact info?"

"Oh, you smooth talker, you." She smiled before whipping out her phone so they could exchange information.

"So, that's settled." Scott reached back to tuck his phone into his pocket. He missed and it fell onto the top of the crate but he didn't notice.

Cole was about to point out his mistake when Hugo

came up. She smiled at Scott but watched as Hugo picked up the cell in his mouth. Holding it delicately he immediately made a dive for his crate. "You were apologizing for being an arrogant ass."

Scott looked away from her but his cheek in profile popped a dimple. "I'm glad you came with me. I needed you in ways I hadn't known I would."

"You're welcome."

He slipped off his shades and turned back to her. For a moment his expression softened into a smile that tugged her heart. "Thank you."

She nodded and stood up.

"Hugo is up!" The gatekeeper's cry didn't startle her this time.

Adrenaline kicked up her heart rate in anticipation of the challenge ahead. But this time it felt on-the-job familiar, not out of control. Hugo, alert to Cole's change in energy, barked twice and leaped into the air. He was ready to go.

Scott caught her hand and squeezed it. "Ready?"

Cole smiled at him. "Absolutely."

He leaned in and kissed her again, lingering long enough this time to signal an intimacy she didn't expect. Oh, right. For the benefit of the crowd. "I trust you to do this. Go kick some doggy ass."

Scott found a place to watch in the shade by the portable picket fencing used to cordon off the one-hundred-by-one-hundred-foot space.

"Down in front, good-looking!"

Scott glanced back over his shoulder. Two older women in sunshades and floral-print tops and white capris sat beneath portable umbrella chairs, each with a can in hand.

The redhead waved. "Nice butt, but I can't see around it. Want to back it up over here?"

Tucking in his smile, Scott and Izzy moved back from the fence toward the women.

The redhead lifted her shades. "I don't know you. You're new. Who are you?"

"Name's Sam, ma'am."

"My name's Jennifer. This is Lorene. Want a beer?" She pointed to the cooler at their feet.

"No. Thanks all the same. You got a dog in the ring?"

"My daughter's got a boxer named Tobey. Lorene and I used to compete but these days my legs won't move as fast as they need to. Lorene's got the damned MS. So we just come for the joy of watching." She pointed back in the direction of the parking lot. "We recently got a 2008 Winnebago Sightseer 35J. Hardly ever miss a show on the Atlantic Coast, Maine to Florida. Who are you here for?"

Scott pointed out Cole and Hugo, who were entering the ring.

"Nice dog. Cute girl. They belong to you?"

In my dreams. But he was Sam today. "Yes, ma'am. My lady friend."

Jennifer looked at Lorene. "He means they're sleeping together."

She looked back at Sam. "Looks like a nice girl. So, here's a tip. If you don't treat her right you better be packed and out of town before that beast of hers knows about it. I had a friend with a daughter one time, owned one of them Bouvier dogs. She brought home a guy who didn't know how to behave. Next thing he knows her pet's got his total attention. Crotch bit, right through his ding-a-ling."

Laughter burst from Scott before he could control it. "I'll keep that in mind."

As they watched, Hugo flew over the first three jumps and then headed for the first tunnel. Out the other side, Hugo followed Cole's signals

"That's a lovely soft turn at that jump," Jennifer commented.

After Hugo cleared a few more obstacles, Jennifer leaned toward Scott again. "See the way she counterrotated back toward her dog on the approach? That was a very nice backy-uppy."

Scott held his breath as Hugo made the final turn into the jumps. When he had cleared them he came bounding back to leap into Cole's arms. Amazingly, she caught him, though she staggered around for a few seconds before releasing him.

Jennifer tugged his pants leg. "He wasn't the fastest time but he won't be at the back, either. Your lady friend's got talent. I can tell she's new at this but she'll learn."

"Thanks for the lesson. I've got to go congratulate Noel."

Scott tugged on Izzy's leash to urge her off but she resisted. It took him only a second to realize she was *signing,* sitting at attention as she stared intently at Lorene, who was using an electronic cigarette.

He gave a subtle hand signal for Izzy to back off. He couldn't afford to blow his cover before they'd even begun. She did but looked questioningly at him.

Too bad Izzy couldn't tell him exactly why she was signing. The older woman could be carrying any of several legally prescribed medications like oxycodone or medical-grade opiates that would be on Izzy's inventory of drugs to "sign" on when detected in a raid. Besides, Izzy wasn't one hundred percent correct every time. A record of ten percent false positives in the field was considered an excellent rating for a K-9 drug dog. They should probably just walk away. Or maybe he should confirm his suspicion.

Scott casually took up the slack in Izzy's leash as he eyed the woman. "What flavor are you smoking, Lorene?"

Lorene's eyes widened guiltily before she glanced uncertainly at her friend.

"You into vaping?" Jennifer asked quickly.

Scott shook his head. "But Lorene sure looks like she's enjoying herself."

Jennifer tried to wiggle up out of her slinglike chair then gave up and waved Scott over to her. When he was close enough she pulled him down by the arm so she could whisper. "Lorene uses THC vapor to help control her spasms from MS. They've been giving her fits this morning. It's legal where she bought it but not everywhere so don't give us away, okay?"

Scott held up his hands. "None of my business."

Jennifer grinned and turned to Lorene. "I told you he's a good guy. I can always spot 'em."

At that moment, there was a rustle of interest at the opposite side of the ring by the parking lot. The deep bombastic beat of 808 basses shattered the day as the hip-hop sounds of Eye-C blared from some unseen place.

A few seconds later, the music died and Scott watched the crowd part for a woman in a radically cropped tee and batik-printed drawstring harem pants hanging off spectacular hips and showing lots of toned caramel skin stretched over smooth abs. Shajuanna Collier was in the house.

CHAPTER SIXTEEN

"What do you mean I can't participate?"

Cole, who was signing off as having completed the ring course, looked up in amazement. Shajuanna Collier, the person she was tasked with befriending, was standing next to her.

Shajuanna pointed at the registrar inside the booth and then pointed that same sequin-studded fingernail at the paperwork in her hand. "Shujaa is listed to compete in the Excellent A Agility level." She pointed to the dog at heel on her leash. "Shujaa is here. I am here. We are ready."

Cole glanced past the striking woman to the Argentine mastiff named Shujaa. People found Hugo intimidating, with cause. But this was a different kind of brute. A hundred pounds of muscle budged beneath its short pure-white coat, leaving no doubt the jaws in his massive head could easily snap the bones of the toy poodle being hurried past in its owner's protective embrace.

However, Cole noted, Shujaa seemed at ease. That could be because he and his owner were accompanied by a seven-foot-tall wall of muscle in a suit.

Cole flicked her gaze back to the registrar, who responded. "The rules state that the team handler must come in person to pick up his or her registration so that the judges can review the dog for eligibility." She was eyeing Shujaa with some trepidation.

Again, Shajuanna tapped her papers. "Show me where that is written."

Another woman behind the counter with a cap of gray curls pulled at the registrar's elbow. "Excuse me." Moving a little away, they whispered together.

Cole caught only a few words. "Vicious animal" and "criminal" among them. Curious about the outcome, and hoping it might provide the opportunity she needed to meet Shajuanna, she didn't move away from the booth.

When the registrar returned, her expression was stiff. "It's more a policy. An unwritten policy. Which we abide by. I'm sorry."

"Not as sorry as Bravo is going to be." Shajuanna flung a handful of shiny straight black hair back over her shoulder as she glanced toward the parking lot. "See that? We brought a full camera crew and a producer to do a piece for my reality show, *Shajuanna's Swag-Grr.* We're on cable so I know you've heard of it."

The women followed her gaze to where a crew of ten were streaming into the park carrying an array of bulky black cases as well as chairs and a folded-up tent.

Shajuanna looked back at the registrar. "This is a fundraising event, isn't it?"

The registrar blinked behind her glasses. "Yes, for our local county animal rescue shelters."

"I'm all about animal shelters and rescue. My sweet baby Shujaa was a rescue." She bent over to pat her pet on the head, snaring the eyes of men standing nearby who noticed how her top gaped away from her chest.

When she stood up again she turned away from the

booth to address the curiosity seekers who had started to gather. "I'm a passionate advocate for animals other people would kick to the curb. So are my girls."

She signaled to her bodyguard and he produced from behind him two young girls. One wore tiger-striped leggings and a chiffon top, the other was in jeans with a sleeveless white military vest. They both wore identical worshipful expressions as they gazed at their mother.

Shajuanna shifted them in front of her. "Leila and Miya are the ones who told me about your event and encouraged me to participate in order to provide you with PR. I'm supposed to be on a flight to L.A. But here I am, trying to help out your event for a good cause." She looked back over her elegant shoulder at the registrar. "But if you don't want your event to be on TV or the teams competing here today interviewed so that lots more people know about the good work you do . . . oh well."

Shajuanna gathered up Shujaa's leash. "Come on, baby. We'll have to find an arena where shelter dogs are really welcome."

"Wait a minute." The registrar looked back in surprise at her adviser, who had spoken up.

The older woman stepped forward, her face bright pink beneath her gray curls. "Since you're here to help promote our good cause, we should be able to see our way past this hiccup. We could list you as a celebrity guest. That way, you can do your show and our policy remains in place."

"Just a minute." Cole, who had been shamelessly eavesdropping, moved in closer. "Are you saying that her team's score won't count?"

The registrar eyed Cole with a cool glance. "Under these circumstances, no."

Cole felt her temper building at the woman's superior tone. "I don't know squat about your polices but I do know that this person paid the entry fee and so her scores should count."

"I'm sorry you feel that way, miss. But no."

"Then expect a complaint to be filed with the Agility association." Cole let her voice rise so that passersby could hear her. "Everyone knows Ms. Collier is a nationally ranked Agility handler. You accepted her qualifications. If you can make her scores ineligible based on some arbitrary rule that isn't even written down, how do we entrants know you won't do something unethical with our scores?"

The registrar pinned Cole with a hostile look as several of the other participants paused to listen in.

"Very well. Since Ms. Collier is a ranked handler, her scores will count. If she wants them to."

"That's what I thought." Shajuanna looked over at her daughters with a triumphant smile. "What do I always say, girls?"

"No is just the opening of a ne-*go*-tiation," they chorused together.

A cameraman, who had been crouching unseen with his lens aimed at the registration booth, stood up saying, "Got it, Shajuanna."

Horrified by the realization that she had been caught on camera, Cole turned and hurried away. *Dumb. Dumb.* Her big mouth might just have blown her cover.

"Hey!"

Cole swung around.

Shajuanna had followed her, leaving girls and dog in the Wall's care. "Why'd you do that? Get all up in the judge's face about my participation?"

"I don't like people who switch the rules to suit their needs—or biases. I'm sorry if I butted in."

"No. You were just what the scene needed. Disgruntled outsider saves the day. Up till then it was strictly amateur hour. I knew their policy. Still, I was worried I wouldn't be able to generate enough heat to provoke a 'moment' for the camera."

Cole's face fell. "You wanted an argument?"

Shajuanna laughed. "I was doing this for my girls. They haven't had much to do on our reality TV show the past few weeks and they really love shelter animals, so I wanted to make certain they would both get screen time. That's why I created the drama. Reality TV is about drama, even if you have to provoke it."

"I guess I messed up your drama."

"No, girl. You did good. I always reward good. In fact, if you'll sign a release, you can be on TV, too."

Cole swallowed. *TV?* That's the very last place she wanted to be seen while she was undercover. "No, thanks. I don't feel comfortable with the idea of being on TV."

Shajuanna subjected her to a shrewd look. "You don't want to be seen on my show?"

Cole shook her head. "It's not about your show. It's just that, well, I like my privacy. I'm sorry if I messed things up for you."

"You didn't. My producer can do some clever editing and fuzz your features where she can't."

"Thanks." Cole's look of relief was genuine. "I only got involved because I don't like it when people start making up rules to suit their own purposes."

"You're sweet. Naïve as hell but sweet. What's your name?"

Cole took a breath to recall the correct answer. "Noel."

"Hi, *ahh* Noel." Shajuanna mimicked Cole's breathless reply then held out her hand. "I'm Shajuanna Collier. So what do you do when you're not rescuing people from themselves, Noel?"

Cole chuckled. "Do I seem like a do-gooder? I'm a vet."

"For real?"

"Once I've passed my licensing exam. I'm waiting for

the results in October." This rehearsed biography came more naturally. "Meanwhile, I'm hanging out, teaching a few dog obedience classes. I'm so tired of school, and not ready to work quite yet."

"I hear that. After law school— Whoa, I saw your expression. You think a lawyer wouldn't marry a hip-hop artist? You should know, Eye-C went to Howard University, just like P. Diddy and Chris Rock. Anyway, I passed the bar but then married Eye-C so I haven't practiced in a formal way. However, I creep all over every legal document before he signs. See you later."

Cole watched her walk away, hips moving to some inner rhythm possessed only by women supremely confident of their desirability. Cole consoled herself with the knowledge that now that they had met, she had an "in" with Shajuanna the next time they were at a competition. When she checked in with Lattimore to tell him about her luck today, she would ask him to check when her next competition was scheduled. Yardley's spur of the moment notice today had rattled her. Speaking of which, here came Yardley and Scott.

"Nice work with your objective, Noel." Yardley patted Cole's shoulder. "I need to get back to work. You're riding back with Sam."

Cole stared after her teacher. Yardley couldn't have known about what Shajuanna said was a last-minute decision to participate. Could she?

"Shit! I think I lost my phone." Cole looked back to see Scott patting down his pockets.

She grinned. "Ask Hugo about it."

An hour later, Cole and Hugo watched Shajuanna's team breeze through their Excellence A course. The woman had exchanged her teetering heeled sandals for sports shoes. Every eye in the park was on the curvy Amazon as she led her dog through a much more complex course than the one Cole and Hugo had run.

A little cheer went up from Shajuanna's daughters as Shujaa finished the course in record time.

Cole added her own applause. Shajuanna was the real thing, a skilled handler who loved her dog and whose dog adored her in return. That, of course, didn't prove that she wasn't a drug smuggler.

"You could beat her, with some practice."

"I don't know about that." Cole looked over at Scott, who had walked up with Izzy on a leash. "How was your visit with the other competitors?"

"We met some characters. Sniffed some butts. Izzy signed on medical marijuana. Nothing serious."

Cole nodded. The chances of them stumbling across criminal acts at a competition were slim. The competition setting was Cole's chance to make personal contact with their target.

Cole gave herself points for having made a bit of progress with that. Shajuanna Collier now knew her name.

Scott bumped her shoulder with his. "By the way, you owe me an apology. Your dog's a klepto. He had my cell phone in his crate."

"Consider yourself complimented. He only steals from those he likes. If he didn't like you, he'd have chewed it up and buried it."

"Seriously?"

"It's a game he plays when he's bored. He takes something. You ask him to find it. He retrieves it. You give him a treat."

Scott looked down at Hugo. "That's called extortion."

Hugo woofed.

Cole laughed. "You hungry?"

"Starved. Let's get out of here."

As she neared the exit with the last of Hugo's competition gear in her arms, Cole heard the name Noel being called. She turned back.

Shajuanna was walking toward her with her girls in tow. Even after running a very taxing course, she looked as fresh as she had when she arrived. Of course, her crew included a stylist.

"We need to talk." Shajuanna glanced up as Scott approached, her gaze narrowing in appraisal.

Cole made the introductions. "Sam, this is Shajuanna Collier. Shajuanna, this is Sam."

Shajuanna smiled at Sam like he was on the menu as the featured dish, but spoke to Cole. "My daughter Leila wants to become a junior showman competitor." She waved the daughter in tiger-striped leggings over. "I don't have time to teach her but you do training, right? You want the job?"

"But you don't know me."

"Oh, I'm going to have people check you out. Count on it. But you've got passion. You stand up for what you believe in. And you can't be bought. That's three giant steps forward over most people I know. You say you're free to do what you want until October. By then, Leila will be back in school. So, you game?"

"I don't know."

Cole glanced at Sam, who shrugged. "Your time, babe."

Play it cool, Cole told herself. "I don't know where you live. It might not be practical."

Shajuanna nodded. "True enough. I live in the greater Baltimore area."

Cole smiled, eyes going wide in fake surprise. "So do I."

Cole turned to Leila. "My name's Noel. Would you like to have me show you some beginner techniques for the ring?"

Leila looked up at her mother. "Would that get me more airtime?"

"No."

Both mother and daughter turned their heads to stare at Cole, who had spoken.

Cole kept her focus on Leila. "Learning to be a handler is first about your love of dogs and a commitment to learning how to teach your dog how to compete. If it's just for the camera I won't teach you."

Shajuanna tapped her daughter on the shoulder. "Looks like you found someone as demanding as me."

Leila shrugged, her gorgeous brown eyes throwing sparks. "I guess, in the beginning, it would be okay. But when I compete, I want it on TV."

"You get that good and we'll see." Shajuanna offered Cole her hand. "Deal?"

Cole took it. "How about a trial period? Two weeks. Let's see if Leila and I hit it off."

Shajuanna nodded. "She'll need five lessons a week. Three hours a day. Will a thousand a week cover it?"

"Whoa. Daily training is good but three hours a day is too much for a beginner."

Shajuanna gave her a shrewd look. "I'm covering your travel time to and from your home, plus an hour lesson. You need to start thinking like a business person. For instance, you should have asked extra for travel. Or asked me to put you up somewhere for the five days a week I'm hiring you for so you don't have to travel. We can renegotiate after the two weeks." She whipped a card out of her bag. "Monday, say eight A.M.?" Both Leila and Cole protested. "Fine. Ten A.M. What's your cell?"

Cole waited until mother and daughter were out of earshot before she spoke. "This is all happening way too fast."

Scott grinned at her. "Sometimes it happens like that. Be grateful. It will get hard."

Cole stared at Shajuanna's card. "She said she's going to check me out."

"That's what a backstory is for. Lattimore's ready."

They finished stowing Hugo's items and made certain Hugo was settled in beside Izzy then climbed in for the drive back.

Cole reached for her seat belt. "I like her."

"That's a rookie mistake."

Scott didn't continue until he had exited the parking lot. "This isn't real life. You're playing a role. Your job is to get close to people, maybe bad people. You get to know them. You may begin to understand how they view things. It starts to make a certain kind of sense, even if they're criminals with blood on their hands."

He glanced at her, his expression serious. "But at the end of the day, if the people you've come to know and even like are dirty, your job requires that you betray the trust they've put in you. You need to be ready for that."

Cole was silent.

Scott pulled off the road when he spied a burger place and drove through the takeout lane.

Cole didn't realize how hungry she was until she had finished her burger and was working on a mouthful of fries. "So what now?"

Scott didn't look at her. "Lattimore called this morning. Our new residence is ready. Looks like we start playing house tomorrow."

Cole looked away. Oh yeah. That.

CHAPTER SEVENTEEN

"You got a license for that?"

Cole spun around to face the bathroom door. She hadn't heard a sound. Nor had Hugo reacted to the presence of someone in the apartment. "Oh, I didn't know you were back."

Scott stood in the doorway dressed in a dark T-shirt and low-slung jeans. He didn't say anything else but there was a dark, intense look on his face. After a few seconds more, he crossed his arms and leaned a shoulder against the door-jamb, and waited. Finally, she realized why.

She stood there wearing next to nothing. A see-through lacy red bra and matching hip-hugging panties that left the lower curves of her butt exposed didn't quite count as clothing. Perhaps he thought she was about to offer him an invitation to remove those next-to-nothings. If so, he was out of luck.

"If you need to use the facilities I'll be done in a second."

She turned away from him but the four-by-four-foot vanity mirror gave her a crystal-clear image of the very sexy, if seriously unhappy man standing behind her. His stance was deceptively relaxed. In contrast, his mouth had formed a hard line. His gaze narrowed as it tracked down her body with a single-mindedness that sent a zing of longing through her.

"You've got a wedgie."

She reached back automatically before she could stop herself. But she let her hand slide away without adjustment. If he was trying to throw her off balance he needn't have bothered. He'd done that just by appearing.

Scott had also discovered the location of her tattoo. Below the small of her back a little red heart with delicate curlicues on either side sat just above the lacy red edge of her low-rise panties.

She picked up her brush. "Please close the door on your way out."

"I don't think so."

He leaned away from the jamb, moving with a deliberate slowness toward her. She knew he was trying to ratchet up her awareness factor of her half-dressed state. A rush of warmth moved up and down her torso as he came within two feet of her. It was as if the heat of their last encounter in a bathroom had followed them to the condo. Did tummies blush? She didn't dare release her gaze holding his to find out.

She put the brush down, handle rattling slightly, but she didn't turn toward him.

"How are your parents?"

"Good."

He had taken off before dawn to drive up and check on his parents. That's what made her decide to treat herself to a grooming day—the kind of self-pampering that she couldn't do with a man around twenty-four/seven. It included deep conditioning her hair, a facial, and complete body buffing. She'd even splurged and paid to get her brows waxed, and her nails and toes done. The new undies were her little gift to self.

Now he was back.

The strain of being in close proximity without really connecting was wearing on both of them. They were police, accustomed to donning armor both real and mental to step out into the world each day not knowing what to expect. That was the job. Most days it was boring as hell. But the possibility, that's what kept the blood pumping and the adrenaline flowing, and the mind focused and set.

Two weeks of enforced idleness had tightened their frustration to the buzzing level of a high-tension voltage wire. It was a wonder the lights in a room didn't spontaneously light up when they entered. They could no longer speak to each other without the words being barbed, pointed, aggravating. Nothing to grind the irritation of inactivity against but each other's nerves.

It was a stalemate she didn't know how to end.

She'd thrown herself at him that night in the shower. And he'd been more than happy to oblige. Correct that. Blown her mind and satisfied her body in ways she had begun to think her memories of him had exaggerated. Yet, he hadn't made a move on her since. Why?

Each day that that question went unanswered made it more difficult for her to approach him. She'd offered—okay, Noel had offered Sam everything. Conclusion, Sam was not that into her. So, she'd withdrawn the offer. And, damn him, he hadn't even complained.

Cole watched him wander around the small space, picking up first her hair dryer and placing it in the linen cabinet, then hanging up her towel. Each task brought him closer to her. He was scowling, as if he didn't want to be here, but neither could he back away. Wary, alert, they watched each other like adversaries looking for a weakness they could exploit.

If something didn't happen soon, she was going to walk away from the mission. Her first instinct was right. This wasn't working. Correction. They weren't working.

For nearly a week they had shared a two-bedroom Baltimore suburb condo with a fenced-in area for their dogs. Other than the three hours each day she spent commuting to teach Shajuanna's eldest daughter the basics of Agility, there was precious little for her to do.

Lattimore was happy she'd made a connection so quickly but she was limited, so far, to one hour of training in a ring set up in a side yard of the Collier estate. Shajuanna wasn't even there, having flown out to L.A. for business, Leila said. No chance for her to better infiltrate the Collier inner circle. In fact, she hadn't actually seen inside the kennel where the Collier dogs lived and bred. They wouldn't get to start using a dog until Leila had mastered the basics, so she wouldn't confuse her pet when she began training it.

Meanwhile, she and Scott had tried to find reasons to stay busy and excuses to avoid one another. But doing nothing was tearing at both their tempers.

For instance, right this minute she was about two seconds from hurling her brush at Scott's head and ordering him out of the bathroom he did not have the decency to vacate.

Cole picked up her brush again, her gaze never straying from his reflection in the mirror. He looked pissed off. She was, too. Playing house! Whose dumb idea was that? Why didn't Sam and Noel have jobs? They needed reasons not to be constantly together. Only idiots wouldn't have known the sexual tension couldn't be infinitely denied. Something in this arrangement needed to change.

"Lattimore called. There's an Agility meet in Baltimore on Saturday."

He had come up behind her, so close she could feel the

heat from his body on her bare skin. But he didn't touch her.

"Why didn't he call me?" Cole frowned at him in the mirror. "The competition ring is my assignment. I should be the one he calls about that."

Scott met her glare in the glass. "He called me because I'm the task force leader."

"Oh, sir. Sorry, sir." She gave him a little mocking salute.

Scott's gut tightened as he absorbed her disrespectful gesture. He'd forced men twice her size by sheer determination and force of personality to respect his authority. But, hell. This wasn't about control or authority, or respect for the badge. This was about the woman inside the too brief red lace undies.

During the past six days, he'd burned through his lifetime supply of honorable intentions.

He had tried to stay the hell away from her. But that wasn't working. He was in a foul mood all the time, and it got worse every time she walked into the room. Because. Because.

He wasn't that good. He wasn't that honorable. What he was was in heat for her. Constantly.

Maybe that wasn't entirely her fault. He wasn't gelded by guilt. She might as well learn that he had limits and she, just by being Cole, had pushed him way past them for the last time.

She was daring him to touch. He could see it in the steadiness of her gaze and the slight uptilt of her chin when he moved in behind her. Didn't she already know how dangerous an idea it was to wave a red flag—particularly a red-lace-panties flag—under his nose? Maybe she needed a reminder.

He leaned in, angling his head so that his lips came within a fraction of an inch of the tender place where her neck curved into the beginning of her shoulder. "You smell good."

He saw her lids flutter before she released the brush and braced herself with both hands on the countertop. Was she expecting the touch of his hot mouth on her? It didn't happen that way. It was going to happen his way.

Their gazes met in the mirror. "You look even better."

He reached around and touched her, his forefinger sinking into the shallow well of her belly button before he rimmed it.

Cole's belly quivered, as did all parts farther down.

"Was all this primping for me? I promise to be very, *very* appreciative."

His voice was pitched so low it was little more than a deep breath of rough air across her shoulder. And then the impression of his lips was on her right shoulder blade. He had a hard-on so impressive she had to feel it pressing against the back of her lacy panties, in search of its target.

The shocking heat of arousal sped through Cole, lighting up every pulse point in her body before rolling down to lodge deep between her thighs.

He glanced up at the mirror, daring her to look away. "Last time we did things Noel's way. This time it's Sam's turn."

She didn't answer. She didn't have to. He had slipped a hand down the front of her panties. She closed her eyes and stopped thinking as his hand sank into the warmth behind the lace.

He pumped his hips against her a little. She bucked forward, and his fingers slid home. He watched in the mirror as her mouth opened in an O of desire then her lids fluttered against her flushed cheeks.

He closed in tighter behind her, using his fingers when he really wanted to press into her with the best he had to offer. He wasn't being cocky—ah, what a great word. He *was* cocky. He was packed to the balls with lust for his ex-wife.

The problem was, he decided on the drive back from New Jersey, she had started thinking after that night in the shower. When Cole started thinking, she usually erred on the side of caution. That wasn't working for either of them. He was taking charge.

She couldn't make up her mind? He had just made it up for her.

Step one. But no more quickie bathroom trysts. They were going to have a normal couples' evening if it ruptured him. And when they slid between the sheets in his room it would be because neither of them wanted anything else.

He slid his hand very slowly and reluctantly out of the front of her panties. "Let's get out of here."

Her eyes flew open and their gazes met, hot reflections of what had just occurred.

"What? Where are we going?"

He backed up a step. "Out."

She hesitated. Maybe because he sounded like he had a stranglehold on his own throat. She, in contrast, looked dazed and bereft, and hungry. Just what he wanted.

"You've got two options. Okay or no."

She nodded once. "Okay."

"Okay. You've got five minutes to get dressed, or you don't get to make any more choices at all."

Promises. Promises. He was pretty sure she didn't say that out loud but his eyes caught fire just the same.

Good as her word, Cole was at the front door in four minutes. She had her cop face on, revealing nothing. That was okay. Her outfit revealed enough, for now.

Scott did a quick inventory of her scoop-neck slouchy long-sleeve top and short flowy skirt as he held the door for her. With her new, messy, shorter hair she looked younger, more carefree. He liked it. He even liked her strappy sandals that revealed shell-pink toes. Most of all, he liked the fragrance rising from her skin as she brushed past him. She smelled of flowers warmed by sunshine. In this case, the heat of her own body. Oh yeah. He was going to enjoy every last minute of this night.

"Where did that come from?"

"I manage a dealership, remember?"

Cole stared at the motorcycle. It was big. A cruiser. She thought about the Kawasaki Richards had loaned her. This must be from the same source. "I'm not dressed for riding on that."

He tipped his head to the side and smiled at the sight of her strong smooth legs revealed by her short skirt. "Looks like you'll have to sit sidesaddle." He produced from behind his back the green helmet that matched her bike. Her suspicion was confirmed.

She watched him strap on his helmet and throw a leg over the bike, much newer and nicer than the one he'd ridden while undercover. She'd only seen that bike once and its faintly menacing silhouette reminded her of the biker who had accosted her on the road.

Cole pushed the thought away. One bad memory not worth the effort to recall.

He started the motor and reached out a hand to her.

She strapped on her helmet and hopped up behind him, straddling the seat. Her skirt was worryingly short once she sat, and the breeze caused by a moving bike hadn't even begun to inch it up her thighs. She tucked the back edge under her butt and the front down between them.

Scott looked back over his shoulder with a smirk. "Nice view from here."

She was more worried about the view for passersby. "Maybe I should change."

"Screw that! Hold on tight."

She grabbed him about the middle, fitting her chest to

his back as she laced her fingers together across his abs. They were warm and solid beneath his shirt. "What are we doing?"

"You and I are taking Noel and Sam out for a hot night on the town." He revved the engine and took off.

Cole released her fingers and grabbed his shirt in both fists, hugging him closer. It felt so good. He felt so good, that she stopped worrying about her skirt hem.

CHAPTER EIGHTEEN

"You really were hungry." Scott lifted a hand to wipe a smudge of pizza sauce from her chin. "I never knew playing air hockey could rouse such an appetite in you."

"You mean winning at air hockey." Cole grinned at him. They had gone into town and found a video arcade that included table games like foosball and air hockey. Right next door was a pizzeria and bar. "It is just me or is this the best pizza ever?"

"Best pizza ever," he agreed. "And you didn't win. I threw that last game, just to see you smile."

"You are such a liar." She was laughing and trying to scoop stringy cheese into her mouth. "I totally beat you. Just like the first time we played."

"I lost that night, too. So I could get lucky."

"Liar!"

"Did I get lucky?"

She paused to chew but her eyes were shimmering with challenge. "So, we'll have to have a rematch. And, you'll see. I'll win."

He bobbed his head. "And I'll get lucky, just like that first time."

"In your dreams."

Cole gazed at Scott with shining eyes. It swelled his heart. He had forgotten so many little things about her, like how she put her hand up before her mouth when big laughter erupted from her. Or, that she was as fierce a competitor as he was when it came to games. Or how her happiness made his own.

Regret prodded him. How could he have been so stupid as to risk missing out on her smile?

During their short marriage there'd been little time to reminisce about their courtship. If sex before they knew each other's last names could be called the beginning of a courtship. But it wasn't a hookup. They both knew that before the sun came up. Something profound had occurred and they never looked back. Still, there had been little getting-to-know-you time before they wed.

She must have seen the many thoughts cascading through his expression because she sobered. "What are you thinking?"

"I'm remembering your parents looking at me like I had erupted from the earth fully grown when you introduced me. They must have been shocked to learn I had parents who both had advanced degrees."

"That's not true. My parents really like you, and your parents."

"I'm sure they wanted to ask how they'd happened to rear a son like me. A bad-boy biker cop. Soon to be skinhead son-in-law. What did your sister call me? Nine miles of bad road?"

Cole dipped her head to hide her smile. Becca's precise words had been, "My God! What's gotten into you, besides nine inches of bad trouble?" The estimate was generous but not the effect. Becca, she just knew, had never experienced the body-quaking sex she had with Scott. But it wasn't enough to sustain the reality of marriage.

"Don't be like that. My parents knew I loved you and they love me so—"

"So they tolerated me."

"They were prepared to love you."

"Until I screwed up. They must have told you they expected something like that would happen when you left me. That I couldn't be trusted."

Cole wagged her head. "They never said anything like that."

"You expect me to believe that?" Scott picked up his beer and took a long swallow. "What about after what you saw? A public orgy with their son-in-law front and center?"

Cole glanced down, the final piece of pizza on her plate untouched. "I told Becca. But never my parents. I just told them we weren't getting along. We had discovered we wanted different things. I knew I wasn't right to try to tie you down. But I thought I could make it work. When I realized I couldn't make you want what I wanted, I left."

He set his beer down carefully. "What did you want, Cole?"

"To be a family."

"With children." Her gaze jerked up to meet his. "My parents told me. You wanted children."

Annoyance and embarrassment made quick impressions on her face. "I wish they hadn't. I told them you and I hadn't had that conversation yet. It was our last Thanksgiving. While we were waiting for you"—she ducked her head—"they started talking about grandchildren. They were teasing me, saying you and I were their only hope for grandchildren. One thing sort of led to another."

Scott watched her with such intensity she felt like she should hatch. Finally, he said, "Were you pregnant?"

"No. No." Cole shook her head back and forth several times. "Don't you think I would have told you?"

He slid a hand through his hair. "It's old news, I guess. My parents didn't even mention it until a few weeks ago. Just before Dad's heart attack." He cursed under his breath and sat back in the booth. "They thought you were pregnant. So sure, they expected us to announce it at Christmas."

"So you think I was pregnant when I left you, and didn't tell you?" It sounded so awful even in her own ears that her throat closed over the final words.

He shrugged, sorry he'd stepped into this tonight. "Look. I was fucked up in so many ways in those days I wouldn't blame you if you didn't want me to be any part of our child's life."

"Stop." She reached out and grabbed his wrist and squeezed hard. "Look at me."

She waited until he lifted his eyes, dark with the expectation of rejection, to meet hers. "I've never been pregnant. Ever. If I had been carrying your child I would have told you."

She released his arm as if touching him had become painful. "And I sure as hell would have fought harder for us."

They sat in silence, the music of the restaurant filling that lull with a silly tune about foxes.

Finally, Scott shrugged. "I didn't mean to upset you. Or bring up bad memories. We were having a good time."

Cole moved a hand toward him. "I would never try to hurt you, Scott. I love you."

The present tense of that sentence didn't escape either one of them. It just hung there in the air between them because Cole realized that it was true. Love had never been the problem. Priorities and trust, those were the issues.

Scott just stared at her, afraid to probe in any way those

three words. If she took them back, it would kill him. If she didn't, it would change . . . what?

"You hear from Doc Rob lately?"

It took Cole three seconds to remember who he was talking about. Oh yeah. Him. She shrugged. "I might have exaggerated our relationship a bit."

"How much?"

Good question. Was she ready to say she had lied just so she wouldn't sound like a loser in love, or let him think she was still pining for him? They had barely reconnected when she told that story about the podiatrist. Now, after all that had happened in the past two weeks, that reasoning seemed meaningless.

"Let's just say we haven't been in touch in a while. A good while."

Scott tried not to feel too happy about her news. But it had him grinning from ear to ear inside. "So, we're free to exercise our options."

Cole ducked his suggestion. "You sure you don't have any issues I should know about?"

Just like that, all the issues Scott had pushed aside when he walked in on her in the bathroom came roaring back. Hell yes. He had issues.

He had an ex-con on his tail. Had he forgotten? His parents were in a shaky situation, living in a motel until their home was redone. His father's health was compromised and he didn't yet know what the full ramifications of that would be. He was a task force leader with a mission barely under way. He had no damn business trading confessions with her while these things hung over his head.

Panic stabbed his gut. He wasn't ready.

"Let's get the fuck outta here."

His good mood gone to shit, Scott strode out of the restaurant, pushing past customers mobbing the bar while waiting for a table.

Cole followed closely behind him, confused by his sudden mood swing and getting more than a little annoyed herself. Noel and Sam were on the town. She should never have dredged up the problems of Scott and Cole. Except that he had been the one to bring them up.

Near the front door she stepped on someone's foot and tripped. She would have fallen if she hadn't been caught by strong hands grabbing her by the arms. She looked up into the face of a smiling man. "You okay?"

"Yeah. Fine. Thanks." Cole straightened up only to realize her purse had slipped from her shoulder and fallen onto the floor. She looked around. "My purse! Someone must have kicked it."

"Let me help you look." Her savior craned his head to look around the crowded space. "What are we looking for?"

"It's brown leather with— Oh, there it is." She reached between the legs of a customer and snatched it up.

Her savior smiled as he helped her hoist the strap back onto her shoulder. "Can I buy you a beer to say sorry?"

"Get your hands off my wife."

Cole looked up into Scott's very angry face. He grabbed her arm. "Come on."

They were out on the sidewalk of the nearly empty street before he released her.

As he expected, Cole swung around on him, spitting mad. "What the hell was that?"

"That guy was hitting on you."

Her eyes narrowed at his words. "So what?" She flung her hair back from her face with a hand, fury glinting in her eyes.

"Come on. You don't need that kind of cheap thrill."

Cole marched up to him and poked him in the chest to punctuate her words. "You have no idea what I want, Lucca."

"Oh, I know. I know exactly what you want." He grabbed her by the arms and hauled her to him until she was plastered to his body from shoulder to knee.

There was no question in Cole's mind that he was aroused. She braced a hand on his chest and pushed hard. "Let me go."

Scott's usually mellow baritone was reduced to a dark hiss. "You came with me. You leave with me."

Cole looked into his angry face, her feelings too complex to pull apart. She lifted a hand to touch his hot cheek, genuine puzzlement in her voice. "Why? What is it you really want from me, Scott?"

A few latecomers rushed into the alley, their laughter bouncing eerily off the brick walls of the narrow lane before they disappeared into the pizzeria.

Cole didn't hear them. She was locked in Scott's arms and his mouth was on hers, lips and tongue explaining in explicit detail just exactly what he wanted.

Scott's promise to himself that he wouldn't touch her until she asked him to was shot to hell. Now, he'd probably made her so angry hell would freeze over twice before she forgave him.

His closed his eyes, dragging his mouth away from hers. But his hands didn't loosen their hold of her waist. "Bad idea."

"Really bad." Cole's whispered reply was almost lost in the folds of his shirt where she clutched it with both hands. But she had been miserable for so long, been lonely without him so long, that getting hurt again might feel better than feeling nothing at all.

At the moment, nothing hurt. Kissing Scott felt like the most right thing she'd ever done. She wanted nothing more than to kiss him and go on kissing him until she was saturated with his taste and smell and touch.

She lifted her head and curled a hand behind the nape of his neck.

"Cole—" He sounded as desperate as she felt.

"Shut up, Scott."

She lifted her face and brought his head down for another kiss.

He moved a hand from her waist down over the fabric that covered her hips where he flexed it under her butt and pressed her sex hard against his throbbing groin.

Yet the hunger building between them was more urgent. It blocked out light and sound as they concentrated on the warm sinuous play between them of lips and tongues. Kissing had never felt better, sexier, hotter.

For two years Cole had been replaying over and over in her head the reasons she had fallen for him. And wondered, had her imagination played her false? First love was like that, swamping good sense with the ecstasy of the moment. He couldn't have been as good as she remembered. They hadn't been as happy as memory said. She just needed to be clear about what she had walked away from, to erase memory with reality. That's all she wanted, a little hard evidence to counteract too many lonely, sweaty nights alone in her bed.

She felt sorry for women who claimed no man had ever kissed them in a way that made them want to strip and get busy right then and there. She'd said as much once, and gotten a tableful of ugly female glares.

All evening long she had been hypersensitive to Scott's every move. He had sat so still as he drove, as if only a certain set of muscles were required while the rest of him remained at ease. As they had walked in silence to the pizzeria, his posture was militarily erect. It was as if he'd only trusted himself on a very short leash.

She'd thought that his attitude was her fault; that he didn't want to be here with her. But now his restraint was broken. Desire, liquid and molten, was surging between them, connected by soft damp lips and warm tongues. He wanted her. He was all but screwing her through their clothing.

Suddenly she had a much bigger problem. She wanted to feel it all again. Everything she'd felt that night in the shower. Only she didn't want this time to be a game between Noel and Sam. This was her very real life. She needed it to be about Scott and Cole.

She breathed in a long shaky breath and tried to think. But his mouth was so warm and inviting, and the hands on her back were cupped and holding her body so perfectly against his that she couldn't catch her breath. And she needed, badly, to do that.

She pressed against him, trying to gain a little space between them, until finally he lifted his lips from hers.

"Right." He shook his head, as if to dispel a dream. She could feel the tension in him where his hands still held her. The breath he inhaled shuddered through his chest. He wanted her. But he was backing away from her. His fingers were flexing away from her body, one by one.

In the space it took him to unhand her, she clocked about eight good reasons why this was insane before her mind sputtered to a stop.

She reached out to—something, shove him farther away, out of her way, some decisive move that would end the madness. Instead, the moment her fingers touched his shirt-front they curled and grabbed, jerking him closer to kiss him again.

Scott resisted her kiss, not quite trusting her lust. Yet there were no words for what he was feeling. A kernel of desperation struggled to life within him. At any second she could decide that this—that *he*—was not really what she wanted.

He muttered something urgent against her lips but her overstimulated senses couldn't work out the words.

She did register the instant he tried to move away from her. Pride tossed aside, she grabbed on to him. "No. Don't—"

He looked down into Cole's face, which expressed the sexual invitation he so badly wanted to see there.

He smiled at her in perfect understanding. "I'm not going anywhere. We just need to get off the street, okay? Come on."

He scooped her about the shoulders and urged her across the street into an alley opposite the pizzeria. A few yards in from the street he guided her into the shallow dark alcove of a bricked-up warehouse entrance. He backed her up against the wall, his body blocking out all other impressions of the night. Bracing himself with a palm flat against the wall above her head he leaned into her until they touched everywhere from thigh to shoulder.

His free hand moved from her waist to lift her chin as he dipped his head, blotting out even the distant light.

She murmured something she thought would be a protest but in reality was relief as his lips settled over hers in slow but complete possession.

Her mouth opened under his as he began a slow grind, his engorged cock rubbing insistently against her lower belly through the barrier of their clothing.

She could not catch her breath but this time it didn't matter. She didn't need to breathe. She only needed to feel Scott inside her, as quickly as possible.

"Please," she whispered raggedly as she clutched the powerful muscles of his upper arms.

Scott was exerting too much control on his body to answer. If he didn't get inside her sweet body and soon, he would explode in his jeans.

He shucked her short skirt up to her waist. Using both hands, he ripped off her lacy panties and tossed them away. He slipped up between her soft thighs and her moan made him growl in response. She was moist and warm. As he parted the wet silk of her lower lips with a finger she whimpered in response.

Cole did a little dance on the tips of his fingers, grinding her sex against his hand, frantic for release and afraid it would once again be snatched away. In spite of where they were, in an alley in sight of anyone who might come their way, she could only urge him on.

This was wild. This was madness. Someone might see them. She didn't care.

She lifted her leg and hooked her heel behind his thigh.

Scott used the advantage of her parted thighs to slide two fingers deep into her sex. Sighing, she pressed her lower body into the push-pull of his fingers. But that was not how he wanted to be inside her. He wanted to cram the full length of his rigid cock into her.

He unhooked his belt buckle and reached for his zipper as the sounds of music and laughter burst from the opening door of the arcade opposite them on the street.

Scott stilled and swung his head in that direction, ever alert to danger.

Cole grabbed his neck. "Please don't stop."

"The hell I will." A fire hose couldn't get him off her now. But he watched, his pulse pounding in his cock, until the gamers moved on down the street.

He had her pinned to the wall so tightly the bricks dug into her back. There'd be scrapes and bruises in the morning but she didn't care. She was about to screw Scott Lucca, right here, right now.

She pulled his shirt from his waistband and ran her hands up under it, exulting in the heat of his skin and the solid ripple of muscles on his back. He grabbed one of her hands and pushed it down to his zipper. She didn't need any more encouragement.

She jerked it down and then her hands were inside his waistband pushing jeans and shorts down over the rock-hard contours of his butt.

He grabbed her by the waist and hoisted her up off the ground. His lips directed his quiet words right into her left ear. "Hold on tight, Cole. I'm going to give you all of me. As much as you can stand."

She kicked off her sandals and wrapped her legs around his waist, locking her hands behind his neck.

He reached between them to direct his shaft at the right angle, felt the slick heat of the outer folds of her sex part against its head, and shoved toward the goal.

A faint cry escaped her as the fat head of his cock entered her. At this angle, he felt even bigger than she had expected.

"*Shhh*. Take it slow." His whisper was thick with a sex-drugged urgency.

"Slow?" she responded, sounding offended at the idea. "I need fast."

Gritting his teeth he took her firmly by the waist, and drove her hips down on his swollen shaft with an upward thrust. A series of little inarticulate cries began erupting from Cole as he slid home.

The sounds exploded in wonder by Scott's ear as the ripples of her climax massaged the length of his cock.

Damn. She was so responsive he almost lost control and he hadn't even begun to move. She might need only one thrust, his body demanded many more. Now. While her body was sucking him in.

He bucked under her, pounding into her hot wet darkness like a jackhammer. The old Scott Lucca finesse deserted him. He was running hot and wide open. She was so wet, and felt so right. This was how it had been with them from the first. It shouldn't feel like the first time after all this time. But even the miracle of it was losing fascination to the seeping urgency of sensation that locked their bodies together.

He felt her climax rising again and she was calling his name in little breathless whispers that feathered his ear. A second later she gripped him hard, her fingers digging into his shoulders as he continued to pump her. Afraid she would cry out loudly, he reached up and stuck his thumb in her mouth to distract her. Her lips clamped down on his thumb as she began sucking it like it was a lollipop.

Her second climax went on much longer than the first. The clutch and caress of her sex echoed by her firm sucking of his thumb finally wrung from him a helpless "Holy shit." She really was going to be the death of him.

Then he lost control.

He buried his head deep in her neck to keep from shouting in relief as he flooded her with his climax.

For a moment the world stopped. When it came back it was distant, shadowy, muffled, a dim shadow beyond the vivid touch and scent of their coupled bodies.

Scott threw back his head and sucked in a breath. He felt as if he'd run a marathon—no, a hundred-meter sprint—and won the race.

Finally he looked down at her, still wrapped tightly around him by her arms and legs. Her forehead had fallen forward against his chest. Her shoulders were quivering and he thought he heard little sobs. He lifted her face up to his. Her cheeks gleamed with tears.

"No, now. Tears? Did I hurt you?"

"No." She looked up into his shadowed face, a smile quivering on her kiss-swollen lips. "You're just so . . . intense."

He grinned. "You're the one. Damn, Cole." With his

thumbs he swiped the tears from her cheeks. "You're sure you're okay?"

"I—" She shook her head. Even now, trembling from the backwash of desire, she hesitated to admit her weakness for him. "I'm okay."

He took her by the waist as she slid off his body and then held her against him a moment, as if to absorb the last of her ecstasy.

Finally he leaned a little away from her, but not enough so that she felt in any way abandoned.

She saw him check the street again, ever the police officer, as he hoisted his jeans back up over his hips and quickly fastened them. He didn't bother to button his shirt. He helped her pull her top down from where it had rolled up her torso as they coupled and smoothed her skirt back over her hips.

Cole let him do most of the work. She was too spent to do more than sag against the wall.

The sudden roar of motorcycles into the alley from the opposite side they had entered sounded like a helicopter landing overhead.

Two riders rolled to a stop just yards away from them, their headlights throwing a glare that blinded them.

Fear, bright and icy cold, splashed through Cole. It was as if her skin had suddenly been ripped off.

"Oh God, oh God, oh God."

Even as Scott moved in against her to shield her, she was already backing into the wall, flattening herself as if she might be able to slide between the bricks. The police officer in her had fled, leaving behind a trembling and vulnerable woman.

CHAPTER NINETEEN

"Don't move."

Scott's whisper wasn't necessary. Cole was too frightened to do more than shake. She heard the motors die and then sounds of jackboots scrape the pavement.

"What have we here?"

"Pussy on the half shell. Served up and waiting." The second man dismounted.

Scott made a move with his hand, an action that was hidden by his body. "Don't move, I've got this."

"Come on, bitch, let's see what you're giving out in the alley."

Cole felt him work to free his weapon but the holster tucked into the small of his back had been dislodged by their lovemaking. She heard him swear softly as the men neared them, two chilling silhouettes backlit by their headlights.

"Cole." His breath feathered across her face as his hand slid up and gripped her shoulder hard. "When I turn around, get my weapon free."

Before she could answer he turned toward the men and

208   D.D. AYRES

took a step, completely blocking her from view, and raised his hands. "We don't want any trouble."

"Shit. He thinks we want trouble."

The second man chuckled, spacing himself in case they needed to tackle Scott. "Don't try to be a hero, friend. It's just a bitch. Back off and it'll be like you were never here."

"You don't need a knife. And I'm telling you, you don't want to start anything." Scott's voice was calm, his words a signal to her that this wasn't going to go well unless she did something. Fast.

Heart pounding so hard she could scarcely breathe, Cole slid a hand under the tail of Scott's shirt and slowly moved it up until her fingers closed over the butt of his gun. The holster had gotten twisted. She needed both hands to free his weapon, and she was going to get only one opportunity.

"Let's see her, junior. We want to play, too."

"Sure." Scott took a step forward as she jerked hard. His gun came free.

"Hey. What's going on?"

The sound of more male voices was the last thing Cole thought she wanted until she heard them say, "Stop. Police."

"Fuck that." The bikers moved back to their bikes, gunned their motors, then burned rubber as they swung their motorcycles around and roared out of the alley in the opposite direction.

Scott turned his head toward Cole, a ghost of a smile on his features. "Reholster my weapon, and then don't move or speak."

He turned, arms raised, toward the police officers coming their way with drawn guns and flashlights. He remained so that his body almost completely shielded her.

"Step away, slowly, sir."

"I'd rather not." He turned his hand slowly to show he held his badge in his right hand. "DEA law enforcement."

One of the officers shone his light on the badge.

"Who do you have with you, sir?"

"My wife."

"Ma'am, are you okay?"

"I'm fine." Cole stuck her left hand out from under Scott's right sleeve and offered them a little wave. At the same time she reached up under his shirttail with her right and tucked his gun into his waistband.

"She's shy." Scott smiled at the two officers. He saw them exchange glances. "I know. We were breaking a few rules. We were just warming up for the ride home. No fault no foul."

One of the officers snickered. "Take it home. It's not safe out here."

"So I noticed. Thanks."

When the police had turned away Scott pivoted toward her. She plowed into him and gripped him as tight as she possibly could.

"You're shivering." Scott took her by the shoulders and tried to push her away so he could see her face. "Cole?" But she clung to him like he was a life raft.

He closed his arms and held her. "It's okay. We were never in serious trouble. I would have announced I was in law enforcement next. I just didn't want—" He felt her body heave and shudder inside his embrace. It felt suspiciously like a sob.

He couldn't quite believe it. Nothing made her cry but slaughtered puppies and—him.

"Shit. I'm sorry, baby. I know I shouldn't have brought you out here like this. I didn't think . . ." He closed his mouth. That was the problem. He'd been too horny to think—about her, about the possible dangers, about her reputation, and worse.

Bikers. Coincidence, or something more? He needed to get her off the street to find out.

After a few more seconds he bent and kissed the top of her head. "I'm sorry but we need to get off the street. Now."

She dropped her arms and stepped back. In the dim light he could see tear tracks on her face. He scrubbed one away with a thumb. "You poor kid."

Cole pushed his hand away. "I'm sorry. I freaked. That was unprofessional."

Scott didn't reply to that. It was one thing to be a police officer in full gear facing down the bad guys you knew were out there. It was another thing altogether to be caught butt naked in a public alley. "Don't worry about it. It's over."

For a few seconds Cole didn't move, locked in the creepy-crawly sensation of nightmare memories hatched by the last few minutes.

The outlaw biker grabbing her butt on the empty stretch of highway.

His leer as he moved in close to let her know he had rape, and probably worse, on his mind.

If she hadn't had her gun . . .

If Scott hadn't been carrying tonight. . . .

"Cole?"

Cole jerked as if slapped. Scott was standing in front her with her shoes in his hand. Slowly the chill of the alley asphalt under her bare feet began to penetrate her senses. She took them. "My panties?"

Grim-faced, he moved a little away and scooped up a rag of red lace from a darkness her eyes could not penetrate. "There you go."

She waved them away. The action helped move her back to the edge of rational thought. The way she had behaved required an explanation. She put on her shoes saying, "I need to explain."

"Later."

He glanced back up the alley, still as Hugo on alert. She

could feel the air around him vibrate with watchfulness and something she couldn't guess at.

He turned and grabbed her hand. "Let's move."

As he moved toward the street, he pulled her in under the protection of his arm until he could get them off the street.

Instead of returning to the pizzeria, he hurried her into a coffee shop and ordered two double espressos. His expression was harsh as he waited for her to take a sip. "Tell me what happened out there."

"I had a flashback, sort of." Cole felt her cheeks catch fire with embarrassment. "There was an incident near Harmonie Kennels last week. With a guy on a motorcycle."

Scott went still as stone. "What guy?"

"I didn't know him. But he wore a Pagan jacket."

"Start at the beginning. I want to know everything." The passionate lover in the alley had been replaced by the law-enforcement officer interrogating a witness.

She told him the story as matter-of-factly as she could.

Scott tried to hear what she was telling him about how she'd pulled her weapon on her assailant and held him off. But the primitive protect-my-woman rage building in him was quickly blocking reason and logic, or even his relief that she was a trained and prepared law-enforcement officer who knew how to protect herself.

"Why didn't you tell me about this at the time?"

Cole met his hard stare. In the bright lights of the shop she felt that she had overreacted. Scott's pissed-off expression seemed to confirm that.

"You were with your family. But that's not the only reason. I didn't tell anyone."

Scott's gaze sharpened. "What about Richards? He loaned you the bike."

"No. I didn't want to come off as a victim." She paused. She'd probably blown whatever credibility she had on that score in the alley just now. Even so, it helped her ego to say the words out loud. "I'm a cop. I was armed. I can take care of myself. I did that."

When she was done Scott's expression was so hard and cold his face might as well have been made from local Cockeysville granite. His eyes were scary. His once kiss-able mouth was pinched to a white line.

After a second he scraped back in an almost violent action and left the table.

Worry curled through Cole's middle as she watched him stiff-arm his way through the front doors of the coffee shop. But she had seen the look on his face. It said *Follow at your own risk.*

He needed space. She would respect that. For five min-utes. And then she was pretty sure she'd be in need of some-thing to smash, too.

Scott paced back and forth in front of the shop, trying to marshal his emotions. Three years earlier he wouldn't have stopped on the sidewalk. He would have thrown a leg over his motorcycle and roared off into the night in search of X. He would have searched until he found him or, if not him, some Pagan with whom he could start a fight so he could pound on him until he felt better. The outlaw way. He'd absorbed that part of his undercover persona a little too well. He'd been a Ranger, and SWAT. He knew how to inflict pain. But his temper was what had washed him out of the most elite Special Ops.

"You think with your heart, dickwad" was Gabe's affec-tionate explanation after Scott had been told he was out. "You can't do what we do and think with heart or dick or any part of you that is attached to emotion. You're a good man. Lots of good men aren't cut out for this. That's not a bad thing. Hell, it might be a good thing. Learning to live without essential parts of yourself comes at a great cost.

The folks got one idiot for a son. You be the upstanding citizen."

Except his parents were minus one son. And "the upstanding citizen" was not how he was viewed by at least one of them. Not that that mattered a flying fuck at the moment.

Scott wiped his mouth with a hand. Even in the so-called real world emotions could fuck a guy up. Rage roiled within him, making the coffee in his belly feel like lit jet fuel.

A year of anger management teetered on being blown to hell because something had finally gotten under that bunker of control he'd built between "then" and "now" with real blood, sweat, and unshed tears. That something was Cole's safety.

The thought of anyone hurting Cole made him want to tear up shit.

Instead, he gulped back the hot tangle of rage and anxiety choking him, and continued pacing until the action began to slow the hammering of his heart.

Cole had had to face X without any idea of who he was or why he had accosted her. If she'd been any less prepared, or unarmed, that meeting might have had a far different conclusion. And that would have been on his head. He hadn't warned her.

Scott's sudden burst of profanity, while spoken low, startled a couple coming toward him. They hesitated on the sidewalk then gave him a wide berth as they hurried past into the coffee shop.

He gave himself points for continuing to pace but the need to punch something took a while to control.

When the blinding haze of anger lifted he noticed Cole standing a few feet away, arms and legs crossed as she leaned against a lamppost.

When he stopped before her, she tilted her head to look up at him. "You done?"

His face was still hard with anger. "You should have told me."

Worn out and battered by ecstasy run over by terror, Cole could no longer be calm or accommodating.

She launched herself away from the pole, getting up in his face as righteous anger powered her words. "I'm not your damn girlfriend."

She lowered her voice but not its intensity. "I'm your partner. So you're going to tell me what it is that I don't know. Now."

Scott found he still had the capacity to smile. "You want to take this somewhere private?"

"What part of 'don't get yourself dead' did you not get?" Dave Wilson rubbed his forehead, an action Scott could perceive through his cell phone, because they were doing FaceTime.

"The essential part." Scott shifted on the park bench where he sat. "You know as well as I do, he's calling me out. First my parents, now my task force partner. X will continue to escalate. I need to stop him before people instead of things get hurt. At least this way I can control when and where."

"I can't get you backup on this, you know that."

"Right. No probable cause." By the time he got hard evidence people might have been injured, or worse.

"What about the woman? If she pressed charges that would change the game."

"She can't do that without blowing her cover." At least X didn't know about their undercover operation. They weren't undercover when he'd accosted Cole. Since then they'd been living under aliases. Still, X had been savvy enough to put them together, and have them terrorized in an alley. Which meant X or the people he was paying were watching Scott's every move.

That sent Scott's temper flaring a few degrees. It was like he was a damn lab rat, watched for his reactions to stimuli X applied.

"What about the task force?" Dave's pale face seemed to float forward, free of his body. "You could put that in jeopardy if you go after X. You can bet your ass Lattimore will have something to say about it."

"I'm not telling him anything, unless I have to." Scott shoved a hand through his hair. "I'm the expendable part of this operation. I can be replaced. But that doesn't mean X will back off from my partner."

"What's your number one priority here?" That had been Dave's favorite phrase three years ago when he thought Scott was about to screw up because he'd become too passionate about an idea or a cause.

"The job." Scott's tone gave nothing away. Protecting Cole was actually his number one priority. But that wasn't something Dave needed to hear.

"Then act like it. Let me handle X. You complete your mission and then we'll talk to the right people about this."

Scott nodded but they both knew it was only to move the conversation along. "I need you to dig deeper into X's background. There's something we're missing. Not even the Pagans would dare go publicly after a cop. He's after me. Yet I haven't been knifed in the dark. I need to know why."

"Maybe he's just a sick twisted sumbitch. He doesn't need a reason for what he does."

"Screw that. Even crazy has motivation. I need to know what kind his crazy is."

"Meanwhile?"

"I'm going to have a little talk with the ass wipe. What's his parole officer's number?"

Dave shook his head like a disappointed parent. "Let me know what you're going to do before you do it, just so I can keep the paperwork current."

Scott punched to end the call and stared out at nothing while his thoughts rearranged themselves.

Eventually the park and Cole came into focus. She was on the far side of the green lawn park where they'd come so she could exercise Hugo in an Agility-ring-sized environment for the competition tomorrow in Baltimore.

She wore shorts and a tee that read *AGILITY: BE THE DOG*. As she ran, taking Hugo over the three jumps she set up, he could hear her voice offering her partner encouragement. Hugo's happy barks carried back to him more clearly than her words but he understood them both. They were in sync. The running and sudden swerves and double backs were a game. The flash of tan legs caught his attention for a while. Then he let her laughter echo in his ears like some sort of goddamn sultry siren wind chimes.

He had thought what might bring them back together would be the sex. Damn. It was better than before, if that was possible. Cole had become a woman very sure of herself and her needs, and of how to get what she wanted.

He'd learned something else last night, after every lustful feeling had been satisfied. Standing in that alley in that awful moment when he realized his actions had put her in jeopardy, he'd understood what he had only given lip service to before. She was a good police officer. Afraid, sure, but she still unconditionally had his back.

And he knew now he would willingly protect her life with his.

Not just because it was his sworn duty to protect and serve. Not because it was the right thing to do. Not even because he was responsible for their trouble.

I love her. That simple. No greater reason.

He'd known it all along but buried it so deep he thought he could live with it thumping underground like an undead thing. Yet the moment he heard her voice on the phone a month or so ago, those feelings shot from the earth like a phoenix from the ashes of their marriage. And now he knew something more.

He wasn't going to make it without her in his life.

Even her blistering anger was a hundred times better than the bitter lonely regrets that had gnawed at him these past two years. The first time she set eyes on him in Lattimore's office, it had been like she'd set fire to him. He felt fully alive for the first time since she walked out. This feeling wasn't something he would willingly give up again.

What they had was still searing hot. But this humming feeling inside him, even when she wasn't looking at him, was what she did for him. He was one mangy lovesick sorry-ass bastard not to own it all along. She made him feel worthy.

No one before Nicole Jamieson had ever made him feel *worthy*. Not his parents. Certainly not his untouchable older brother, Gabe. Only Cole did that for him. And he was grateful enough to learn that lesson a second time. He would never, no matter what happened now, squander it with less than his best.

X was after Cole, had been stalking her while Scott hadn't even considered that possibility after his parents' home was wrecked. Once again he'd allowed passion to overrule methodical good sense. Gabe would be laughing his ass off at the mistake.

Scott swallowed hard, forcing down personal emotions as he tried to think objectively. X had not succeeded. Cole was not helpless. Twice she'd made the correct judgments. He could trust her professionalism and instincts to keep her safe now that she was aware of the danger X presented.

They had talked after they got home last night. He'd told her about X, and his suspicions about the reason his parents' home was wrecked. She was surprised but not frightened. Law-enforcement professionals, particularly local police officers, knew it was just a matter of time before they were confronted by a felon they had had a part in putting away. Occasionally one of them came looking for vengeance. Most of them could be faced down by simply calling them out on the spot. Big talk was cheap. Even felons knew that taking on one police officer meant taking on the entire force. The Blue took care of their own.

So now Cole was warned.

But that didn't exactly solve the problem.

Dave was right. He should tell Lattimore about X. But if he did so, Lattimore might pull him, probably would pull him, off the task force. The Pagans ran drugs, among other things, for a living. If X continued to track him he could learn enough to jeopardize the task force operation. However, if he, Scott, bowed out there was no guarantee that X would follow him and leave Cole and the operation alone.

Scott rubbed his jaw, trying to think dispassionately like the DEA agent he was. He'd never before let personal feelings get between him and cold hard reality.

But Cole had never been up against anyone like X.

And that made it personal.

He was probably breaking protocol, maybe even DEA rules, but he needed to stay very close to Cole until he had neutralized X. He wasn't going to give Lattimore an excuse to pull him. He'd deal with the consequences if and when he needed to. Until then, Cole's welfare was his main objective.

His past couldn't be allowed to further jeopardize his family or Cole. He'd have to find a way to take X out before the prick had a chance to make his next move.

X wanted his attention? He had it. One hundred and fifty percent. He just hoped the bastard made it easy for him to take him down the hard way.

Cole came running up with Hugo bouncing along beside her as if he not yet had a workout. Cole was another story. Sweat plastered her slant of bangs to her forehead and made her face gleam. But it was her smile that pushed the air from his lungs.

"Help me gather the Weave poles?"

Scott spread his legs and pulled her in between them. "What do I get for helping?"

Laughing, she pushed against his chest. "You're awfully sure of yourself today."

"Believe it." He was in deep trouble, and about to go deeper. All to protect the woman in the circle of his arms.

"You've been idle too long. Want to let me beat you at a game of racquetball later on?"

"Maybe another time. Tonight I've got to see a man about a dog."

Cole's smile disappeared. "If this is about X—"

He put a finger to her lips. "You need to trust me."

She frowned. "I do. But—"

He cut off her protest with a kiss so long and deep a couple of teenagers on skateboards passing by started making kissy sounds of derision.

CHAPTER TWENTY

"Hey there. Your girlfriend's up next, gorgeous."

Jennifer and Lorene waved at Scott as he cut across the grass toward the Agility ring. The two women were again decked out in sunshades, matching floral this time, bright solid tops and khaki capris. As he recalled, Jennifer was the talky one. Great. She'd want to chat.

He tossed a wave in their general direction. In no mood to be social, he increased his pace.

He'd just come from a task force meeting and the news wasn't good. One further lead had developed in their puppy mule case. One dog had turned up alive. It belonged to a family in New Hampshire who had gotten the puppy from a friend of a friend of a guy who ran into a guy on the street in Nashua selling a box of puppies he wheeled around in a Red Flyer wagon. He was "just one of those anonymous people" who turn up periodically in neighborhoods selling flowers in June, corn and watermelons in July, and extra cheap Christmas lights in October. Lucky break, the puppy had developed an infection at the site of his neutering. The family took him to a vet who discovered a heroin packet had been left inside him.

DEA had got to the vet who reported it and buttoned up the discovery before it became front-page news.

Good result: The smugglers didn't know they were under surveillance and so could be caught in the act.

Bad result: Puppy mules contaminated with heroin were showing up in homes of unsuspecting families with children who might get exposed to other packets.

Dilemma: Put out a bulletin warning people off buying puppies from unknown dealers, or not? If news of the drug find leaked out, the smugglers would simply quit using that method.

Compromise: Send out a public health bulletin warning people that buying puppies from unknown dealers might expose the buyer to diseases like roundworm, hookworm, and rabies, and hope that people would be more careful.

Meanwhile, Scott and Cole were still point persons in the operation to find and shut down the smugglers. The meeting took two hours. They could have just sent Scott an e-mail. He hated committees.

"Hey. Sweet cheeks."

Annoyed, Scott refused to look back as he reached the edge of the ring. No way was he going to answer to that name.

The major irritation in his life was X. According to his parole officer, X's address was a flophouse for street people. Scott checked. The reality was X flopped wherever and whenever the mood struck him. Never the same place twice in a row. And usually during the day. Nights, X was on the prowl.

His parole officer was unimpressed by this minor parole violation. "I should be so lucky all my parolees are like X.

He follows the rules. He's clean. I don't give a flying fuck where he sleeps. You got no legal authority to know about my meetings with him. You follow me, I'll have you arrested for interfering with an officer of the court."

"Hey there." Jennifer had sidled up beside Scott in hot-pink jelly sandals that matched her top. "Didn't expect to see you in Baltimore, hot buns. Thought you lived down near Richmond."

Scott smiled tightly. No way to ignore her now. "It's Jennifer, isn't it? Actually, my lady friend lives here in the Baltimore area."

Jennifer tilted her head back until she stared fully into his face. The gaze in her cherublike face was speculative. "Where do you come from?"

"Philly."

"That's where we're going next. Then back to Maryland for the CPE because my daughter's competing there. Guess we'll be seeing a lot of each other."

"Maybe." Wanting to change the subject, Scott looked back over his shoulder to where Lorene, silent as ever, sat and waved. "I see you have your umbrella chairs and ice chest set up."

"Oh, we're always here early to pick our spots. The Winnebago gives us the edge. We park the night before and sleep in the parking lot, if they allow it. We've got the next three months charted out. Started out in Florida. We're working our way up the coast to Maine, more or less, depending on the competitions we choose to attend. Won't be home until fall."

That surprised Scott. "Where do you call home?"

Jennifer lifted her shoulders. "These days, our motor home is home. We're retired, you see, me and Lorene, and on a fixed income, which isn't much considering—"

So sorry he'd asked. To cut that off he interjected another question. "Is your daughter competing today?"

"Not this time." As she shook her head, rows of perfectly formed cylinder-shaped orange-red curls bobbled. "We got Lorene's granddaughter with us on this leg of the trip."

She pointed to a little girl who appeared to be about six years old. She was squatting in the grass in denim shorts and a floral top pulling at weed flowers.

"That's Mimi. We call her Boo Bear. Her mother works most days and weekends and has to pay a sitter in the summer when school's out. So we just brought Boo Bear with us. Want a beer?" She pointed to the cooler at Lorene's feet.

"Maybe later." It was only eleven A.M. These women started early.

"You know where to find us. Oh, here comes your lady friend."

Scott turned to watch Cole and Hugo approach the entry to the ring, which was on the opposite side. He waved but didn't call her name. He knew she was concentrating on the course and didn't want to break her focus.

"There's a lot of nervous energy in the contestants today. Bunch of beginners in the first round. Just pitiful, some of them handlers. Several dogs did flyoffs."

"What's that?"

"When a dog leaps off an obstacle too soon it's called a flyoff. Most often it happens on the teeter-totter. What you Yankees call a seesaw?"

Scott shrugged. Chatty people wore out their welcome with him pretty fast.

She pointed to the obstacle on the side of the ring. "Once that high end drops to the ground some of these excitable rookie dogs figure they've done their part. But they need to come down the other side and touch that yellow area near the end. If they jump off before they touch yellow they get a penalty."

"Interesting."

"Not only that. There've been two backweavers this

morning. That comes from sloppy teaching technique. You never correct a dog in mid-weave. You let him finish and then take him back to the beginning. If he misses a pole and you stop him and make him go back and catch it while he's in the Weaves, he'll do it in the competition if he misses a pole. Backweaving reflects on both the handler and dog. Big fault."

Scott felt his stomach tighten with something more than a lack of breakfast as he surveyed the ring. He supposed Cole knew about such things as flyoffs and backweaves. He had admired her and Hugo for what they had accomplished so quickly but he was beginning to think he didn't fully appreciate all that went into it.

"Where's your dog?"

Scott tried not to let his irritation show but decided he'd answered enough questions for one day. "I'll bring her by the next time I see you. Bye." He turned and walked away.

Undeterred, she called after him. "You do that. We make all the big tournaments and lots of the smaller ones."

"Next up, Hugo." The announcer's voice rang out over the sunny day as Scott approached the entry gate of the ring.

He was late because he had had to check in with Lattimore, privately, after the task force meeting. Lattimore was pleased with Cole's ability to form a relationship with their target so quickly but Scott was less enthusiastic. He was beginning to share Cole's hunch about Shajuanna.

He just wasn't getting a vibe that said she might be involved with puppy mules. That didn't let her off the hook for drug use or dealing. But this particular method required a calculated indifference toward animals that he didn't see in Shajuanna. Whatever else might be going on at chez Collier, Shajuanna was taking good care of her children and her dogs.

Scott leaned his folded arms against the uprights that

held up the ring fence. Of course, if criminals all looked and acted like criminals he wouldn't have a job. The local police could just go out and round up the suspicious on a daily basis.

Hugo was fast off the start, flying over jumps. Scott watched with new interest as Cole ran with him and then ahead, sometimes stopping short as she used both vocal and hand commands to direct her partner through the course. Hugo barked a couple of times in exhilaration, for instance, after he made it through the Weave poles. She had slowed him down and that cost them both points, but he completed it without mishap.

It wasn't until Hugo shot through the tire jump at the end that Scott realized he had been holding his breath. A little shot of pride sped through him as they completed the course with no major fouls.

This time at the end, Cole turned away as Hugo came racing toward her. When he jumped up on her back, she caught him behind his rear legs. With his front legs clamped over her shoulders, she carried him out of the ring, piggyback style. That earned them extra applause.

Happy to have an excuse to act on his genuine feelings, "Sam" embraced "Noel," Hugo and all, as they exited the ring. "Great run. You've got a real talent."

Grinning, Cole released Hugo from her back and ran a forearm over her sweaty brow. "You really think so?"

"Absolutely. You and Hugo could become champions." Scott snatched up the towel sticking out of her backpack and handed it to her.

She shrugged as she toweled off her face and arms. "It's too much for him to do both, patr—I mean, compete often." He saw the pain of her almost-gaffe cloud her gaze but she continued. "Because he's so big, Hugo's tendons and joints get a lot of pounding in the ring."

"But you could be champions. Believe it." He slung an

arm around her neck. "You'll have to show me the different moves next time you practice so I can learn this stuff."

Cole frowned but didn't remove his arm. "You don't need to do all that."

"You know men and sports. We need to know all the terms and nuances so we can talk the talk with the boys."

"Don't you mean the girls? I saw you talking to those women. Weren't they at the last meet?"

"Yeah. I guess they are like Agility groupies. One even has her granddaughter with her.

"Ah, and here's your favorite person."

Scott pointed out Shajuanna and her entourage turning into the parking lot.

What they actually saw was a big motor coach emblazoned on the sides with the *Swag-Grr* TV show logo in purple and gold and diamonds.

Scott shook his head. "Does she ever go incognito?"

"Don't hate the playa, hate the game."

Shajuanna arrived sans cameras this time, Cole noted. Even her glam factor was muted as well, sort of. Shajuanna stepped out wearing sequined basketball shorts and a navy racer-back tank and high-tops that cost, if Cole remembered the ad correctly, half her apartment's rent. Her cap matched her shorts and her sunglasses covered half her face. She waved high and dramatically when she noticed Cole.

"Looks like you're on." Scott slipped his arm from Cole's shoulders and took Hugo's leash from her hand. "See you later."

"But you just got . . . here." Cole let her protest trail off. Scott was moving away at an easy lope but she knew he was getting out of her way.

"What's up with your boyfriend?" This was Shajuanna's greeting.

Cole smiled. "He's taking Hugo for a cooldown and a drink. We just left the ring."

"How'd you do?"

Cole glanced up as her numbers were posted and felt the warmth of satisfaction. They had improved slightly from the week before. "Not bad."

"You want to come help me decide who I should bring into the ring today?"

Cole fell into step with her as they headed toward the back of her vehicle. "Not Shujaa?"

"Oh, I've got a kennel full of dogs. All with the potential to become champions. Today I brought Akita and Mmumba."

"How was L.A.?"

Shajuanna adjusted her sunglasses. "Sample sale. Snatched from Rihanna's shopper. You ever been there? No? Then whatever you heard about the place is true. I keep my bags packed from the time I land until I'm home. It's a drive-thru type place. I make my order, fly through to get what I need, and I come home. But enough of that. Tell me about Leila's lessons. She talks about nothing but you."

"Really?" Cole didn't want to contradict Shajuanna but Leila had been pretty much a handful during the week of lessons. When they weren't testing each other, Leila was sandbagging. It's too hard. That's dumb. I'm tired.

"She showed me three things she learned this week. She knows I'm going to test. Miya said she spent an hour every day after you left practicing what you'd taught her that day. You're a good teacher."

"She's a good student." More likely she was afraid to disappoint her mother. Whatever worked.

Shajuanna decided to compete with the Argentine mastiff named Mmumba. Without the docked tail or ears, the pure white dog looked almost cuddly, more like a Lab on steroids.

"Mmumba reminds me of my little brother as a teen. Loved him but couldn't stand to be in the same room with him half the time. Which was bad luck for me since we were so poor we had to share a bedroom." She stroked her pet. "Male and cocky. Always showing off, trying to have his way. Thinks he knows more than me. Mmumba is a trip!"

Half an hour later, none of that conflict showed as Shajuanna and Mmumba breezed through the course, until the final jump. Mmumba first balked and then walked around it.

Shajuanna was so pissed she didn't even say good-bye, just climbed in her motor coach and left.

Cole looked at Scott as she pulled out of the parking lot. "I'm ready to head out."

The child's cry of alarm didn't penetrate the noise of the crowd at first. It was the second shriek of terror that dampened the noise.

Scott and Cole reacted as one, turning and running in the direction of the cry.

They found a few people gathering where the competitors set up for the day. A pen of chicken wire had been set up next to a camper to make a dog run. Inside the enclosure a black-and-white border collie had a little girl backed up against the camper wall. The collie was making high yips of excitement. Head held low, ears up, legs braced and teeth bared, the dog made a lunging movement forward every time the little girl tried to move.

"For pity's sake! Someone get me a stick. I gotta git my Boo Bear outta there!" Lorene stood by the pen, her eyes wide with fright. "That dog's got my little Boo Bear cornered. Where's the dog's handler? Somebody find the handler before my grandbaby gets bit!"

Scott stepped up to the woman, who had never before spoken directly to him, and took her by the shoulders. "I will get her out, Lorene, but you need to get calm. You're scaring your granddaughter."

The little girl was crying and dancing in place. "Me maw! Me maw!"

Scott turned Lorene to face her granddaughter. "Tell her in a calm voice that everything's going to be okay. She's going to be okay."

"Hey there, Boo Bear. It's okay. Everything's going to be okay. This nice man here," Lorene patted Scott's arm, "this nice man's going to get you out of there."

"What's going on here?"

A woman had come running from the direction of the refreshment stands. She had an ice-cream cone in one hand and a leash in the other. When she saw what was going on, she dropped both. "Oh my God! Bebe. No! Bad girl! Bad Bebe!"

Scott looked at Cole. "Let's lock this circus down. You get Hugo to distract the dog and I'll grab the kid."

Cole nodded. She reached out and unclipped Hugo's leash but held on to his collar.

"Everyone, back up five feet. Now." Scott's tone demanded and got obedience. The crowd shuffled backward though those in front did not want to relinquish their positions.

Cole motioned to the owner. "Ma'am, I need you to back out slowly. I'm about to release my dog."

When the owner was once again outside the fence, Cole opened the gate and let go of Hugo's collar. "Hugo, *wache! Wache!*"

Hugo nimbly jumped inside and shot straight toward the dog and child.

The little girl screamed to see another, bigger dog racing toward her. But Hugo wasn't targeting her.

He slowed at the last minute, ears forward, his stance strained as he targeted the border collie.

The collie had been intent upon the child and he didn't notice Hugo until the bigger dog was right up on him. Startled, he backed up.

All bulky black coiled muscles and piercing gaze, Hugo moved into the space between the collie and child and swung around, putting his body between them. His head was low and his stance unequivocal. It said: *Back off before I bite your ass.*

The border collie seemed confused by the sudden change in dynamic. Uncertain if he wanted this particular fight, the dog backed up a few more steps but his ears stayed flat and his eyes remained round with excitement.

"Hugo. *Pass auf.*" Satisfied that Hugo would only guard and not attack, Cole motioned to Scott to go ahead.

Scott swung a leg over the fencing nearest the camper. The child looked toward him and he motioned to her with a hand. "Hi, there, Boo Bear. My name's Sam."

The child looked at him and then at the dogs, her eyes so round with fright it seemed she would never blink again.

Scott edged closer, not wanting to draw the attention of either dog. In a situation this tense, even a handler could get bit by his partner if he or she made a mistake.

Scott held out his hand and said softly, "Come to me, sweetheart. Slowly, like you're sneaking away. That's a girl. Come on."

She moved one foot and then the other in great exaggeration of each step. When she got close, Scott grabbed a handful of her shirt and hauled her up into his arms and put her down on the other side of the fence before climbing back over.

Lorene was there to scoop her up. "Oh, Boo Bear, are you all right?"

Her lower lip trembled as she shook her head. "I wet my pants."

"That's okay, sweetheart. Pants can be washed." Scott ruffled her hair and turned to watch Cole handle Hugo.

Cole waited for Scott to nod and then opened the gate. "Hugo. *Hier!*"

Hugo didn't hesitate. He shot past the border collie like a black comet, out of the gate before the other dog had a chance to do more than yelp his surprise.

"Gute Hugo*! Gute Hund. So est brav."* Cole tossed him a bell ball, which he happily chased after.

The crowd, having witnessed his furiousness, applauded but backed out of his path.

"I never saw anyone handle a dog like that." The owner was staring at Cole in wonder. "I don't know what happened with Bebe. He loves children."

"You just better thank your lucky stars he didn't bite my granddaughter." Lorene held the child protectively. "Keep your damn animals away from the public until you learn to control them. My little granddaughter could have been mauled."

"Oh no. But he would never, ever harm . . ." The woman's voice trailed off as two friends or relatives herded her away. "I just can't believe it. How could he have behaved that way?"

Lorene snorted her opinion. "They should never let novices attend these big events. Too many people and too much noise. Dogs get all nervous. If the handler does, too, it torques up the animals even more. That gal doesn't know the first thing about how to train a dog. But you sure do." Lorene smiled at Cole.

Cole smiled back. "Thank you."

Lorene looked up at Scott. "Treat her right. She's a keeper."

Scott looked at Cole. "I already knew that."

Cole looked up to see Leila come running up to them.

"Well, hi, Leila. Where did you come from?"

"Mama sent me back with our bodyguard." Cole looked up to see the Mountain standing a few feet away. "Mama said to ask you if you like jazz."

"Yes, I guess. Some of it."

"Not that esoteric sh—stuff. Mama likes smooth jazz, rhythm and blues, that kind of thing. She said if you do, there's a birthday party for Shujaa at our house tonight. So, tenish. Bring Hugo." Leila's gaze shifted to Scott. "She says you can bring him, too."

With that she turned and hurried away in the direction she'd come, the Mountain following.

CHAPTER TWENTY-ONE

"Wuss up?" Eye-C studied Cole and Scott out of distrustful deep green eyes tucked under a heavy brow framed by long thick dreads. Everything about him was broad. His face, his nose, his shoulders, even his waistline. It was a linebacker's physique except for his height. Shajuanna towered over him in six-inch platform sandals.

She folded her arms and leaned them on his shoulder, hip cocked, as she greeted them. "You're late."

Cole glanced at her watch. "Leila said tenish."

"I'm teasing. You're way too serious. Collier, this is Noel, Leila's Agility teacher, and her friend Sam. And this." She kissed his dreads. "This is my husband, also known as Eye-C. He's just home from a tour."

"What's up?" Scott, expression cool, put out his fist.

After a second's hesitation, Eye-C gave him a fist bump. "It's cool." He looked at his wife. "I'm home. Need to lay it down. Now."

Shajuanna gave her husband a look that didn't need interpretation. "You hit the shower then I'll hit the sheets."

He gave her a look that took advantage of the fact that

her towering height put her bosom nearly at his eye level then reached out and snagged open her neckline and leaned to look in.

Shajuanna smiled. "You good to go?"

"There's no question." He released her top and walked away.

Chuckling to herself, Shajuanna hugged Cole. Next she bent down to greet Hugo. "And this ebony sugarplum I know is Hugo." She waited until the Bouvier nudged her hand before she petted him.

After a moment she looked at the chocolate Lab. "Now who's this?"

"Izzy." Scott gave Izzy permission to approach Shajuanna.

Shajuanna smiled and patted her. "Just what I need under my roof, another beautiful bitch." Her laughter carried through the entry.

"Come here, boyfriend." She gave Scott a full-bodied hug that Cole noticed included a pat on his butt. She winked at Cole. "See you guys later. My man's waiting. Grab a drink and then tell Isaac I said show you the kennels."

It turned out Isaac was the man-mountain of a body-guard. He was still dressed in a suit, as if it were armor. He led them into the main part of the house, a large family room, casually but expensively decorated with leather furnishings and granite flooring. Shajuanna had come a long way from sharing a bedroom with her brother.

"Get your drinks and something to eat first." For a man so large his voice was curiously soft. "No food or drinks allowed in the kennel. I'll be back in fifteen."

Scott and Cole looked around, clocking the people, the mood, and the numbers.

The party was much more low-key than either of them had expected. The music was jazzy, Brazilian in tone. Less than thirty people were in attendance. However, every other person had a dog on a leash, everything from toys held protectively under the arm to a Neapolitan mastiff spread out like a hundred-and-fifty-pound throw in the far corner.

Scott leaned in toward Cole. "Let's hope he had a good meal recently."

Cole nodded and patted Hugo, who had just discovered the worthy rival for his position as alpha male in the room. "Hugo. *Pfui.*"

Hugo glanced up at her for confirmation. *"Lass da sein."* In other words, forget about it.

He woofed under his breath and sat down, deliberately glancing away.

"Why do you talk to Hugo in German?" Leila had appeared before them, dressed in curly poodle ears on a bandeau. She had two more in her hands and offered them.

Cole took a pair.

Scott looked at them as if they might bite. "No."

"I speak to Hugo in German because it's the international language for dog training." A white lie but not totally untrue. It was the dominant language for *law-enforcement* dog training.

Leila looked very serious, as usual. "Can you teach it to me?"

"When you've learned all the commands for Agility in English we'll see." Uncomfortable with a promise she knew she'd never be around to keep, she changed the subject. "Where's the birthday boy?"

"He's with Mama. It's a surprise party. He's got a cake and everything." Leila pointed to a table in the breakfast area. "Want to see?"

Scott gazed longingly at the food spread out nearby. "You girls go see. Izzy and I are thirsty. You want a drink?"

Cole nodded. "Something light."

"Your ears?" Leila pointed.

Cole slipped on her polka dot Dalmatian doggy ears. "How do I look?"

"Bitchy." Leila's giggle made her sound like the nine-year-old she was.

After a turn about the Puppy Table, Leila went to look for her mother. Cole came back to show Scott her plate. "Look what I found."

"Sweet." Scott grabbed the biggest of the two cupcakes from her plate.

"No, no!" Cole grabbed his wrist. "That's for Izzy. It's a Pupcake."

Scott stared suspiciously at the confection in his hand then sniffed it. "It smells like peanut butter and cinnamon."

"With real cream cheese frosting. I took that off. But Hugo loved the cake part. You should see what they have for the dogs. Sweet potato pretzels. Dog bone cookies. Puppy Chow mix. There's even a three-tier cake. It's a doggy's wet dream."

To confirm that, Hugo barked. Unfortunately his deep woof rattled the composure of every lapdog within hearing and drew the frowns of the other guests.

"Oops. I suppose we should head outside. I heard there's pit beef barbecue on the patio. For us humans."

"That sounds more like it." Scott grinned and lowered his Pupcake for Izzy to nibble on.

After consuming a plate of melt-in-your-mouth BBQ, they followed Isaac to the kennel. It was designed with a façade that matched the house. Inside the temperature-controlled space, large open crates provided individual space for a dozen Argentinean mastiffs.

The presence of Hugo and Izzy on their home turf set off a barking and growling contest. That didn't prevent Scott from walking Izzy down the line of crates.

Isaac's eyes narrowed. "Why's she sniffing like that?"

"Oh, Izzy has this thing about new scents. Until she's sorted out which scent belongs to which dog she won't be happy." Cole hoped that explanation put Isaac off the fact that Izzy was meticulously sniffing for contraband.

At the end of the kennel, Izzy turned and came back, walking quickly with nose to the ground but never pausing long.

Scott nodded when they were done. "Nice accommodations. What's in that area?" He nodded toward a short unlit hallway.

"The infirmary, for when the vet comes."

"Can I see?"

Isaac shrugged.

Scott came back quickly, his expression neutral. "Impressive."

Cole smiled. Nothing here to implicate the Colliers in puppy drug smuggling.

As they walked back toward the house, Scott's cell phone vibrated in his pocket. He looked at the text and paused, his mouth tightening.

Cole, alert to his every shade of mood, looked back. "What?"

Scott looked up. "I got to take this. Can you get home if I'm not back in an hour?"

Cole met his gaze but he'd locked her out. "Okay." She laid a hand on his arm, and squeezed. "I need to hear from you in an hour, either way."

He nodded and left, taking Izzy with him.

Shajuanna and Eye-C reappeared five minutes later, with the birthday boy in tow. Shujaa wore Snoop Dogg fake braids and sunglasses. After the birthday song, the Birthday Dog was allowed to take a huge bite out of his specially prepared cake.

Afterward, Eye-C sat down at the piano in the living room and began playing.

Cole smiled as Shajuanna came over to stand by her. "He's good."

"Of course he's good. He minored in music but jazz won't pay the bills, not like hip-hop. You learn to play what the audience is buying. Who does his style remind you of?"

Cole thought about it. "Maxwell, and some D'Angelo, definitely. And Marvin Gaye."

Shajuanna leaned back with an arch expression. "Listen to you, sounding all hip and shit." She glanced around. "What happened to Boyfriend?"

"He remembered he had to be somewhere."

Shajuanna swung a sharp glance her way. "He left you?"

"He said he'd be back in an hour."

"Uh-huh."

Cole turned away from her hostess's long appraising look. "It was a much cozier party than I expected."

"Eye-C and I agreed that once the girls became aware of things, he couldn't bring Eye-C's gangsta attitude under this roof. He leaves it at the door. I don't question what happens when he's not here. It's about respect."

Cole nodded, biting into the last of the barbecue on her plate. "The food is outrageous."

Shajuanna stole a sliver off Cole's plate and popped it in her mouth. "Growing up in Baltimore, I always wanted to own a restaurant. That way I thought I could be certain everyone in the neighborhood had enough to eat. Those that could would pay. Those that couldn't would get a voucher for one free meal a day. My brother told me it was a crazy idea. He was going to be a professional baller and move us out of poverty." She smiled. "This is his barbecue."

"Really? I'm impressed."

Shajuanna grinned. "Funny story. He took home economics in high school just to be in a classroom full of girls. Turns out, he was better at making yeast rolls than baskets. He went on to culinary school and now owns the restaurant I always wanted."

"Did he follow up with your ideas?"

"He did better. Opened a soup kitchen near a shelter last year where all the meals are free, one per day. He asks for donations from the restaurant's patrons to keep it going."

"Your family sounds like self-starters."

"We had to be." Shajuanna paused as if deciding how much of herself she wanted to share. "Mom died when we were little and Dad worked two jobs to keep us in school. I was lucky enough to get an academic scholarship to college. I like nice things." She spread her arm to include her room. "But I earn them. So does Eye-C."

When Eye-C finished his set to lots of appreciative applause, Shajuanna nudged Cole. "You got a minute?"

Shajuanna led her away from the party into a media room and closed the doors. "Have a seat."

Cole sat on the edge of a plush leather media chair and put Hugo in the down position. Shajuanna had been eyeing her speculatively while Eye-C performed but now Cole was getting a distinctly uncomfortable feeling there was more to this one-to-one than girl talk.

Shajuanna sat next to her, dark eyes shining. "How long have you and Sam been together?"

"A couple of months."

"You know him before that?"

Get Noel's story straight, Cole reminded herself. "No. We met at my cousin's wedding in Baltimore back in the spring. Why?"

"I can read people. I know, you probably don't believe in that kind of thing. But for me, people have auras."

Feeling uneasy, Cole nodded. "That must be fun."

"Not really. Auras can tell you more than you want to know. Ever since I was a little girl I've never known if or how much to tell people. Most of the time, I keep it to myself." She paused to gaze steadily at Cole. "You've got this really intense thing going on with Sam. And you're really jacked up about it. It's all through your aura. So I thought you should know."

"Know what?"

"Sam's not who he seems. His aura tells me Boyfriend's a cop."

Cole couldn't quite master her surprise, so she went with it. "Wow. I don't know what to say."

"It's no secret Collier was recently released from prison so he's still paranoid as hell about every new person he meets. I'm not paranoid. But I'm definitely catching a vibe about your Sam."

Cole tried to look casual as she reached for her soda. "He told me he manages a motorcycle shop in New Jersey."

"You seen it?"

Cole shook her head. Stick to the truth as much as possible. "He was in the military before that. He doesn't talk about it."

"That could be why he's got that watchful-eye thing going on. He's hard in a way that says street experience, deep and long."

She pulled a card out of her pocket and handed it to Cole. "You need to do a background check on your man." She tapped the card. "Kelli will get all deep in anybody's shit. Maybe he's PoPo. Maybe something else. Shajuanna's never wrong about a man who's packing."

Cole let her surprise show again. "You know Sam carries a gun?"

"You see me hug him when he came in? I do that to all the new men crossing my threshold. Yardmen and plumbers think I'm fresh. What I am is thorough. Every ass I pat is about the patdown. I guard my home. You hear me?"

Cole was a little surprised. "Don't you trust your security?"

"Security gets lazy. That's why I'm always changing it up for them. They work for me but they don't know when or how long, or even which days I'm doing what. If I'm constantly changing it up, they have to stay on their toes. And they can't tell anyone ahead of time when or where I'll be. I know I sound hard but I have to be, for the sake of my girls."

"Why? Has someone tried to abduct them?"

"Tried and succeeded, once. Collier's been married before. Crazy woman. So crazy Eye-C got custody of Leila. Five years ago, I left Leila with an au pair to take Miya in for a well-baby check. Ex-wife snatched Leila in the park, thinking she could up her alimony with extortion. Got her skinny butt put in jail, instead. Thank you, Jesus." Shajuanna raised a hand palm flat to the sky. "Everybody wants a piece of our world."

"I see." Cole did some quick calculation about her options. "If you don't want me and Sam around—"

"I didn't say that. I like you. Sam makes you happy." She smiled and patted Cole's cheek. "As long as you're happy, I'm happy. Trust, but verify, Noel. Anything changes, it all changes."

"Thanks for the heads-up."

Shajuanna stood up. "I need a drink. You like blood orange margaritas?"

"I'm game to find out."

As she followed her hostess back into the party, Cole felt as if the world had shifted under her feet.

Scott had been identified but it didn't seem like a major problem. Had she been believed? Or was Shajuanna suspicious? Either way, that couldn't be good. She needed to reach Scott before he turned up here again.

She reached for her phone but decided against sending him a message. It might be the wrong time. She'd just have to make certain she caught him at the door.

CHAPTER TWENTY-TWO

The sign over the door read B'MORE BILLIARDS & ARCADE. ADULTS ONLY.

This was the address Dave had texted him without any assurance that X would be here.

When Scott called Dave for more intel, Dave said X's parole officer had voluntarily called him with the address. "He said X had been in touch to ask him to meet him there tonight. Something about a birthday celebration but he said he doesn't party with his parolees."

Scott grunted. "Birthday? I thought X crawled out of the gutter fully formed."

"That's all I got."

Cole might have done him a favor by not telling him about her attack immediately after the fact, Scott thought grimly. Twice X's attacks had gone unanswered. Perhaps he was getting cocky, or careless. Both attitudes would work in Scott's favor.

Still not satisfied about what he'd be walking into, Scott called one of the task force guys who lived in Baltimore to ask about the place.

"It's a recreational bar. Caters to youngish commuters who like to think they're still the shit, and college students with IDs that say they're twenty-one. Then you got your hard-core video gamers and assorted sports fans. The drinks are cheap and the food's a step up from movie-theater popcorn fare. Got enough of an edge that it some-times lures the fringe element looking for a weekend experience."

When he pulled into the parking lot, Scott noticed the patrol car parked at a discreet distance. Message: As long as everyone played nice, the doors would remain open.

At least it wouldn't take long for law enforcement to re-spond if things went sideways.

Even so, he walked Izzy around the lot. He counted sev-eral motorcycles. Two sported Pagan insignia. Izzy didn't sign on anything except a couple of joint roaches on the pavement. Satisfied that he had been as thorough as he could without backup, he tucked Izzy back into his truck and headed for the door.

Scott paused just inside the huge open space, cop senses on full alert as his eyes adjusted to the gloom.

The atmosphere was downscale Vegas. Despite air-conditioning, the sultry heat of the August night penetrated as far as the entrance. The place smelled faintly of beer and bodies. Strategic lighting that pierced the darkness was all aimed downward, offering the illusion of intimacy for the hundred-plus customers playing pool, paddle boards, darts, shuffleboard, or arcade games.

The bar area itself was dark—dark walls, black tables and chairs. On the far wall above the bar a bank of big-screen plasma TVs offered a variety of sports broadcasts. Here and there signs spelled out popular beer brands in electric neon lettering.

Closer in, a stage whose spotlighting barely penetrated

beyond its immediate arc was occupied by a local band running through a cover of "Home" by Phillip Phillips.

To one side a line had formed under a sign that read KARAOKE COMPETITION for patrons to sign up for when the band took a break.

Scott took it all in quickly. It was a good place for a confrontation. Plenty of witnesses. Yet the half walls that separated the different gaming areas gave a sense of privacy that would make it easier to deliver the warning he'd come to give—if X was here.

A watchful suspicion tightened in his gut as he moved forward. Something else stirred as well, tied to that darker side of him. The lust for life on the edge. The rush of knowing that you were the biggest, baddest SOB screaming down the road. He would never be quite free of it.

Scott swallowed, as if the old life had a flavor he could taste.

But the image didn't hold. The reality was that he was a cop, first and last. The sheepdog guarding the flock from the real wolves. He had come here to corner a vicious wolf who called himself X.

It turned out not to be a problem to locate him. Three Pagans and their girlfriends lounged in and around the seating along the far back corner where two pool tables formed a ninety-degree angle. They were watching two men play pool. One of those men was X.

The smile that stretched Scott's features would have sent a civilian ducking for cover. The thrill of the chase lit his eyes. It was on.

He came up behind X and grabbed the back of his pool cue just as he was about to sink the final shot and jerked it out of his hands. X's body motion carried him forward in an action that nearly had him sprawled on the table before he caught himself.

"Fucking shit!" He spun around, one hand going to his

waist where Scott knew he kept his Ka-Bar in a hidden sheath.

Scott brought the pool cue up in a defensive position.

"Hello, birthday boy. I hear you've been looking for me."

The biker's lean leathery face looked ghoulish in the stark overhead lighting. There were so many seams and ridges that shaving must be a bitch. His gaze narrowed down to slits. "Who the fuck are you?"

"I'm the guy you'd been throwing spitballs at from the back of class. If you wanted me to ask you out all you had to do was say so."

A smile jittered at the corners of X's mouth. "I don't know what the hell you're talking about. Fuck off. I don't know you." He turned his back and reached for another pool cue.

As he did so, Scott stepped up and sank the shot X had been about to make. Scott grinned at X's astonished expression as X looked around. "Can't say I didn't give you a present. Now I'm going to give you a little advice. Stay outta my shit."

Snickering from his friends arrayed in the booth jerked X's head around. "Shut the fuck up."

X turned slowly back to Scott, fingers of his right hand running lightly up and down his new cue. "Like I said, who the fuck are you?"

Scott met the man's glare. X was a little or maybe a lot drunk, or high, or both. "You wanted to dance. Here I am. Two years ago you would have stepped up like a man. You should have stayed like that. Wrecking houses is junior high crap."

All the crags in X's face shifted under the seismic pressure of his temper. "Fuck that. Fuck you."

"Take him, X. Don't let no asshole talk to you like that."

"Yeah, X. Let's dance." Scott made a move with his cue as if he was going to stick X in the ribs.

X's eyes flew wide. "Motherfucker!"

His tone had the heads of nearby customers swiveling his way.

Scott's voice never rose but the edge to it sharpened. "You might want to watch your language. Contrary to the sign over the door I'm sure there are minors present." Scott took the cue and laid it gently on the table. "You should get a hobby. Yard work, maybe."

X's face cratered into a smile. "I prefer knife work. It's so much more personal, don't you think?

Scott held that empty-eyed gaze for a beat. And though it was like looking into his own grave, he did not even blink. "Let's do this. Outside. Now."

"I ain't stupid. There's a cop outside."

"So that's a no?"

The air vibrated with tension, drawing the eyes of the curious but also backing up those nearest them. The tables on either side of them had been vacated. Scott knew the exact moment a bouncer headed their way. X's gaze shot past his shoulder and then his stance relaxed a fraction as he mumbled something more obscene than usual.

"We got a problem here?"

Scott glanced toward the tall man with sloped shoulders but forearms like hams. "I just came to extend my felicitations to the birthday boy." He saw X's squint deepen at the use of the word "boy." "I'm all done." He handed his cue to the bouncer.

X took a step toward him. Scott would swear he could heard X's teeth grinding. "I will break you."

"You had your chance. Don't waste my time."

"How's your daddy? Hear he's all laid up. Your mama's gonna be looking for company."

Scott smiled. Checkmate. X had just admitted that he knew about his parents, and made a new threat. But he wanted X for more than that. He wanted to take him in carrying the kind of weight that would put him behind bars for a long time.

Scott didn't turn his back as he moved out of range. In fact, he made it to the front door with the bouncer following without losing his line of sight to X.

He had pushed as hard and fast as was possible, considering their surroundings. He might have just increased the bounty on his head. But he was also pretty sure the next move X made would be aimed at him, and not those he cared about.

Scott was back in the truck with the doors locked before he took a deep breath. He really didn't want to get dead. In fact, he wanted to live so much the ebb of adrenaline was making it hard to put his key in the ignition.

But those were the parameters of the job, protect and serve. Forget that. He'd do just about anything for those he loved. Even if he couldn't be sure she loved him back.

His cell chimed. It was Cole.

He smiled as he answered, not waiting for her voice.

"On my way, babe. See you in thirty."

CHAPTER TWENTY-THREE

"There are two of them." Becca's voice was hushed with fear on the telephone.

"Two what?" Cole rubbed her forehead where a tiny Spanish dancer in heels and castanets was pounding out a rhythm in her head.

"Two babies!"

"What?" Cole sat up and immediately regretted that decision as her stomach rolled over and dived steeply.

"You're moaning. What's wrong?"

"Something I ate—" A big gassy burp erupted from her, carrying bitter reminders of the nachos and enchiladas she should never have eaten the night before.

Cole sagged back against her pillow. She was not going to be sick again. No. No. No.

"Did you hear what I said?" Becca sounded insulted.

"Two babies?" The room was spinning slowly on an axis attached to the ceiling.

"I'm carrying twins. The doctor said she missed it the first time because they were stacked, one in front of the other. But, Cole, I saw them. Just now on the sonogram. Two tiny people. What am I going to do?"

"Enjoy the bonus?" Cole took a deep slow breath.

"I can't do it. I can't handle two babies at the same time."

Despite her misery, Cole smiled to herself, thinking of her sister with a cherubic angel in each arm. "You were born to be a mother. You're a vet. You birth babies all the time."

"I watch. And assist. Animals. Animals have all the instincts humans have lost to civilization and baby experts. Have you read a book on child care recently? So much can go wrong. Oh my God!" The sentence ended on a sob.

Cole tried to rally, to focus her eyes.

"You have to come home. Now. I need you. I can't handle this alone."

"You're not alone. You have Harper."

"Harper knows nothing about babies. He's never even held a newborn before. He's an orthodontist. You should have seen his face when the doctor pointed out baby two on the screen. He went green. Wobbled around like a Weeble. How can he help? He can't help. He's useless." Becca's voice edged toward panic. "You need to come here now."

"Hold on." Cole gazed up at the ceiling, which was going in and out of focus. She must have a fever. Not a good idea to visit a pregnant lady when she had a fever.

"You're abandoning me!"

"No. No. It's just that I'm an hour or maybe two hours away and—"

"And you've got a hangover." Becca's voice was full of accusation. "Do you know how much I could use a margarita right now? Icy cold, lots of lime and salt. But, *nooo*. I'm pregnant. And there's two of them!"

Her sister's wail actually shocked Cole. Baby hormones. Wow.

"Becca, what do I do for nausea?"

"Acupuncture." Cole turned her head at the sound of Scott's voice to find him in the doorway of her bedroom.

He came in and reached for her wrist.

"That was Scott's voice, wasn't it?" Becca's tone sharpened. "You're in bed with your ex while your sister is in crisis and you won't even come and help. I'll never forgive you for this. Never!"

Cole flinched even though there was no sound as Becca disconnected.

"What was that about?" Scott had taken a seat on the bed and was pressing his thumb into a point on her wrist directly below her middle and forefinger.

Cole breathed in through her mouth. "Becca's having twins."

"Whoa. That's good news, right?"

Cole would have shook her head but she was certain her stomach was about to catapult itself out of her body. "She thinks I'm sleeping with you and won't come to her aid."

"That could be arranged—again." Scott slanted a glance down at her that singed her eyelashes.

Cole knew she must be pretty sick because, in spite of how her body reacted to that smolder of an invitation, she wasn't interested at all, at the moment. "Maybe later."

"I heard you up during the night. But I didn't know you were sick. You look pretty rough."

"Just what a girl wants to hear." She looked down as he released her wrist. "What did you just do?"

"Pressure point therapy. Thirty seconds of pressure. Feel better?"

"Maybe. I can't tell."

He rose off the bed and went into her bathroom. He came right back carrying a wet washcloth and a bottle of mouthwash.

"You're cute, even when you're sick. But you're rank,

babe." He wiped her face before folding the cloth and applying it to her forehead. "I'll just get a pot in case you need to throw up."

Cole's phone chimed. It was Becca.

"Oh, sis, I'm so sorry. I didn't mean it. I love you."

"Becca, don't cry. Please. I know you're upset and I don't blame you. I will come. I just need to stop hurling first. Okay?"

"You're really sick? Of course you are. You need to lie still. Get that bad boy to open a window." Cole punched speaker as Scott returned. ". . . fresh air. And ice chips with just a sprinkle of salt, to get fluids back in you. No sports drinks. Crackers. If they stay down then a banana or applesauce—"

Scott snatched the phone from Cole. "Hi, Becca. Scott here. I got it under control. And by the way, congratulations on being preggers."

"You hurt my sister in any way and I'm coming after you with a dull scalpel."

"Geez, Becca. You're about to be a mother. You shouldn't be thinking ugly thoughts like that. Could upset the baby."

"Oh. Do you think so?" Becca sounded very concerned.

"I'll take care of your sister. You take care of your growing family. The rest of it is none of your business. How about that? Cole will call you back when she can think. Bye." He disconnected.

Scott handed Cole her phone. "You don't need that kind of upset, whatever that was about."

"Thing One and Thing Two."

He nodded. "That explains it then. Twins. Double the hormones. I don't envy Harper."

Cole tried to think through what Scott might mean by that statement but the flamenco dancer in her head had gotten a second wind and moved into overdrive. "Ice chips?"

Scott nodded. "Coming up." He looked down at her a

moment longer. "When you're feeling better we need to talk."

She waited until he left the room and then sprang from the bed and ran into the bathroom and slammed the door.

"So that's where we stand." Scott watched her sip ginger tea he had gone out and gotten, along with a few other items like crackers, bouillon, and bananas. "X makes the next move or it's over for now."

Cole leaned back against a pile of pillows. He had added his bed pillows to her stack. He watched her with troubled eyes. She was too pale but she'd stopped hurling and wouldn't even entertain the idea of a trip to a doc-in-a-box. "I don't think it's over with X, do you, Scott?"

"No. That's why I've been doing some reconnaissance the last few nights."

"Is that militaryspeak for staking out our apartment from your truck all night?"

He looked grim. "I do what's necessary."

"Then you might have warned me away from El Ptomaine."

"I never ate there before, either."

"And you didn't get sick. I hate you."

Scott smiled at her. It wasn't an important conversation. It was an ordinary conversation, the kind millions of couples had every day. Hope clutched his heart.

He moved a swath of hair back from her brow. "Next time, I'll be sick. Okay?"

Cole tossed back the sheet. "I have to walk Hugo. And he hasn't practiced the Weave today."

"He's been walked and fed. Guess it's my turn to try the Weave."

Cole opened her mouth and then shut it. Hugo and Scott practicing the Weave. This could be fun.

When she had instructed him on how to set the poles

up Scott nodded. "I'm leaving Izzy here with you. She's not Hugo but she's trained to protect and track, as well as do drug detection. Where's your weapon?"

When she pointed to the bedside-table drawer, he pulled it out, checked to see if it was loaded. He put it down without comment. "So, you're good for now?"

She nodded. "I'm good. We've sort of worked this out, haven't we? I mean with the dogs."

"Yeah. With the dogs."

He had a hard-on that made it tough to walk when she was around but he wasn't a complete asshole. She was ill. He wouldn't take advantage of her weakened state to wring a concession out of her.

"Thanks for nothing," he muttered to his conscience.

A minute later Cole heard Scott's command voice. "Hugo! Where's my shoe? And while you're at it, find my keys. Keys. *Such!*"

Cole snuggled down in the pillows with a big fat grin. Yes, her boys were learning to play nice.

An hour later Cole saw the look on Scott's face as he came in with Hugo. "What's wrong?"

"Lattimore called. He read our report. He wants to see us in the morning."

"Oh." Cole knew what that meant. Their undercover work could be over.

CHAPTER TWENTY-FOUR

"I'm not convinced." Lattimore tapped the report displayed on his computer screen. "Just because you haven't turned up any evidence at the Collier home doesn't mean their smuggling business isn't taking place somewhere else. As you pointed out, Officer Jamieson, Mrs. Collier is very protective of her children. She may not want them exposed."

"Yes, sir." Cole sat on her urge to defend Shajuanna. That wasn't her job.

"So I'm continuing your undercover assignment. Are there any questions? Issues?"

"Sir, Hugo needs a rest. I'm concerned about him training to compete constantly." Cole didn't glance at Scott because she hadn't mentioned this to him.

"Is he injured?"

"No, sir. But he wouldn't let that stop him if I put him in the ring. That's why I'd rather not push him this weekend."

Lattimore studied the computer screen before him. "That might be helpful. If you're not competing, you can concentrate on making friends, getting to know more about the persons traveling for Agility competitions on a regular basis. Our smugglers aren't operating in a vacuum. They have contacts, messengers."

He fell silent, letting his fingers play over the keyboard as he seemed to be debating something. He was a man who adhered to the on-a-need-to-know protocol. "We're doing DNA on the puppy found in New Hampshire. The AKC has begun collecting voluntary DNA profiling for their registered animals. We might get lucky and find its lineage in their records."

"Have we tried DNA matching with the slaughtered animals, sir?"

"No, Agent Lucca. We didn't know about the profiling service until the vet in New Hampshire mentioned it. We are, of course, doing so now. But there's every chance, since it's a voluntary system, that the smugglers aren't among those to register their dams and sires. In any case, you will continue undercover while we track backward from the New Hampshire incident."

"Yes, sir." Cole and Scott spoke together, more than ready to be out of there.

It had been a very quiet drive into Baltimore, each lost in their own thoughts about what it would mean if the undercover assignment was suddenly scrapped.

Cole slanted a glance at Scott. He wore a button-down shirt, very rare for him, with his best jeans and boots. His jaw was close-shaven today, the sight of that smooth hard angle making her want to touch him. But she didn't touch and hadn't touched him since the night in the alley. And he hadn't touched, either, though she'd seen the dark look of desire on his face several times in the last days.

Something had come between them. That something, she suspected, was X. Scott was being noble. Worried about her, he was spending his nights in his truck with his gun

on the seat so that no one could creep up on them unex-
pectedly.

Was he that worried?

Or, was he just loving the idea of playing gotcha with
one very scary scumbag?

Cole waited until they were on the highway before she
brought up the subject that had been simmering between
them silently for several days.

"About our living arrangements."

Scott glanced over at her sharply, his expression unreadable. "You're not thinking anything I haven't already
thought of."

"Oh." Because she hadn't been thinking anything in particular and it sounded as if he had, she decided to let him
take the lead in the conversation. Except that he didn't say
another word.

He drove on for another few miles and then took a sudden turn off the highway.

She didn't ask where they were going or why. But grad-
ually the city gave way to the suburbs and miles later turned
into countryside. After a few more turns he had left state
roads to drive a two-lane blacktop ribboning out before
them in the afternoon sun.

It was apparent that Scott had something else on his mind
before they went back to their apartment. If he wasn't going
to say more, she would have to force the issue another way.

Cole lowered her window and let the cooler country air
stream her hair back from her face. After a few minutes
she kicked off her heels. She'd dressed professionally for
her visit to their boss, even wearing a suit. But the heat of
summer had her sizzling in her clothes. She began struggling out of her jacket.

Scott noticed how her actions put a strain on the buttons
of her blouse so that they gaped a bit, giving him a glimpse

of baby-blue satin. That gave him a rush. He was so very glad she was a girl. Even if she was off-limits for the moment.

Once the jacket was tossed in back, she began to unbutton her blouse.

Scott swerved suddenly.

Cole grabbed the dashboard to steady herself. "What was that?"

"Squirrel." Scott supposed he should keep his eyes on the road. But if she wanted safe driving she needed to stop the striptease. No, what was he thinking? The squirrels would have to take their chances.

She pulled her arms out of her white blouse, revealing a baby-blue cami. The blouse followed the jacket into the backseat, and then she pulled the hem of her cami out of her skirt, letting the scalloped edge float free. As she did so, one tiny strap slipped down her arm.

Scott skimmed it back up onto her shoulder with an index finger. The feel of her warm soft skin riding under his rough finger struck a match to his libido. Didn't she know what she was doing to him?

"I'm glad you're feeling a lot better than yesterday."

Cole screwed up her face. "Almost any feeling would be better than what I was feeling yesterday. I was ready to dig a hole and crawl in."

Only if he could crawl in after her, and then into her. Yep, he was an asshole. He had wanted her even when she was sick. Now he just wanted her. With that wanting came the need to be territorial.

Scott kept his eyes on the road as a question he wanted an answer to came to mind. "You planning to tell Doc Rob about Noel's relationship with Sam?"

Propping an elbow on the window frame, Cole looked straight ahead. "I told you I embellished that relationship a bit."

Scott's head snapped toward her. "Which part?"

Cole slanted a coy glance at him. He looked mad. Was he jealous? Could that be it?

Her pulse did a happy dance. Men could be so dumb even when the proof of the opposite was right in front of them. Jealous! That had possibilities.

"All of it."

He did a ninety-degree double take. "You lied. A total lie? Why?"

She shrugged. "Why does anyone lie? Self-protection."

He couldn't argue with that.

She played with her hair, wrapping a few strands about her finger. "I may still have feelings for you, Scott. But I have more to lose than you do."

His expression stiffened. "Oh, I see." He said each word distinctly, as if each were a whole thought by itself. "For instance?"

She forced herself not to jump to defense mode. She had some things to tell him and he needed to hear them. "For instance, I could very easily fall for you all over again."

She saw his eyes widen in response and went on before he could speak. "But I'm not going to let that happen." She touched his arm lightly. "I don't need a man who's afraid to be a friend as well as a lover."

He glanced away from her to check on the dog crossing the road ahead. When their gazes met again it ignited in him a smile so slow and tender it lit up his eyes long before his mouth began to cooperate with the feeling. He reached out and snagged the strap of her cami and slipped it back down her arm. "You don't think I'm your friend?"

Every nerve ending in her body urged Cole to agree with him. But this was about making him come her way, at least a few steps. She leaned toward him, as far as the seat belt would allow. "Are you my friend, Scott?"

When he reached out an arm to pull her closer she put

up a hand to halt him. "Because right now you're acting like a jerk."

She pushed away from him and moved back to her side of the seat. "I'm talking friendship and you're trying to use seduction to avoid the discussion."

Scott felt something like a wasp sting begin at the back of his neck and rise into his cheeks. *Well shit!* She'd made him blush. And she was right.

He pulled the truck off the road under a canopy of trees that shaded this section of road, killed the engine, and turned to her. "Okay, let's talk."

She shrugged, arms crossed.

Unhooking his seat belt he turned to her, stretching a long arm on the back of the seat until his fingers could tangle in her hair. "You want honesty? I'm glad there's no Doc Rob. Because I'd have to call him out or something. This time I will fight for you. I'm not sure what we've got but it's good, Cole. It's so damn good."

She couldn't call him a liar. But . . . "Damn good is not a relationship. It's a feeling. We ran out of good feelings the first time." She stole a look at his expression. He seemed to be listening very hard. "I need more. I need to share lives. Some things you want and some I want, and lots and lots of things we both want. That's what I mean about friendship. When we're not in bed, what do we have?"

He reached out and cupped her cheek in his broad hand. "For the moment, we've still got a job to do. The fact that we were both thinking about lying to Lattimore in order to keep being together a little longer shows you just how far this situation has taken us."

"How did you know what I was thinking?"

Two fat dimples popped into his cheeks. "I didn't *know* know but I was hoping like hell that it was true."

She shook her head. "You're talking work. This task

force won't last long. And then there will be no reason for us to ever see each other again."

"So then we need to do something about that."

He ran his thumb over her lower lip. The look he slid over her was pure heat and need. "What can I do to convince you how much I want to be your friend?"

The blood began to pound in her temples, her stomach, and her womb. Her nipples budded, eager for his hands. He had barely touched her, and she didn't plan for him to get any closer.

He had dazzled and overwhelmed her senses and emotions the first time. Now she had memories to remind her that all the heat and lust in the world wasn't enough to sustain a relationship. She needed much more. He needed to understand that.

She unbuckled her seat belt, arched her back in invitation, and leaned in to whisper against his lips as she dipped a hand between his thighs. "What do you want, Scott? This? Is this enough for you?"

He didn't answer directly. He slid across the seat and took her in his arms.

He kissed her soft and slow, as if pressure wasn't about to leave permanent imprints in his erection from his zipper. She tasted of the orange she'd eaten for breakfast as they drove in to meet Lattimore, and her own unique taste.

When he lifted his head, his voice was almost strangled by his full arousal. "I want everything you got!"

"I feel it, too." And she did, literally. She had moved her hand over the bulge in his jeans. "But we can't just screw around like a couple of rabbits. We're adults with a job to complete. So, for now, you must understand how there can't be any more of this." She squeezed. "Or this." She reached up with her free hand and began unbuttoning his button-down shirt. "And especially not this." She took his lower lip between her teeth and tugged.

His lips parted with a little pop. Mercy. She knew how to turn him on.

She slid into him, her hands moving over the contours of his bare chest. "We need to behave like professionals."

Scott had the wild thought that he shouldn't be trying to guess what kind of professional she was thinking of because she had just climbed into his lap. He reached down and backed his seat up to give her as much space as possible between him and the wheel.

His eyeballs seemed to sweat because his vision was blurring as he gazed at her. To hold on, his hands went to her waist.

She pushed his shirt back off his shoulders. "You were about to say something?"

Maybe. If he could remember. Screw that! There was nothing he wanted to add because she had thrown her leg over him and fitted her lower body to his until the seat of her panties was pressed against his crotch.

She kissed a corner of his mouth. "This kind of thing must stop immediately."

A husky little laugh escaped him. "Uh-huh. This is the worst. Oh yes, the very worst. Torture me some more."

She kissed him again, long and sweet kisses with lots of tongue and stroking until they were both shivering and sweaty with desire. He could feel her melting into him, her full breasts dancing across his chest. He just needed to get her out of that little scrap of a cami and then . . .

It was over as suddenly as it began. Her sensual assault swiftly deserted his arms and his lips. He opened his eyes to find her moving away, back to her side of the truck.

He reached out and snagged her shoulder. "Whoa. Wait. You can't just stop."

She looked back at him, her eyes so smoked by desire they were almost black. "We have to live up to the trust Lattimore's put in us."

"Trust? Shit. This is about us."

"No. That's my point. There's no possibility of us until Noel and Sam are out of the picture. This was Noel and Sam acting like young lovers in the first blush of love."

"So? Clearly Noel and Sam are part of us. What's wrong with that?"

She bit her lip and shook her head. "It's make-believe. I don't want to wake up in two weeks, back in Montgomery County and you in D.C., and realize this was all a daydream."

His fingers tightened on her shoulder. "It doesn't have to be."

She brushed her mussed hair back from her face, shaking her head at the same time. "You're ready for a full-on relationship?"

He frowned at her, remembering that not only the task force, but X stood between him and his future. "I see what you mean. It's complicated."

"No, it's not. Because let me tell you what I want. I want a full-time man in my life. Eventually, I want a little house with a yard. For kids. I want children and a regular paycheck. And nights out. And evenings in. I want to grow a garden and maybe raise Bouviers. I want summer weekends at the shore and autumn weekends in the mountains. I want to come home to someone every day who thinks I'm the greatest thing ever. And I want to feel a smile in my chest when I catch sight of him across the room, before he even knows I'm watching him. I want to know when he looks at me he's seeing home."

She paused, all out of breath, and turned to stare straight ahead.

"That's a lot," Scott conceded after a few heartbeats.

She nodded, locking her seat belt into place. "So much it scares me to even say the words. But that's my list. I don't expect you to share it. But if you don't, I don't want you to spoil it for me."

She looked at him. Her eyes were so wide it was as if he was looking straight into the most secret, intimate place inside her. "Because you could ruin me."

The confession rocked him to his core.

He knew better than to answer her with some easy promise. Or even try to put her off. She'd given him an ultimatum, and issued a challenge. At the moment, he wasn't in a position to respond.

When he didn't say anything, just kept stroking her cheek with the back of his hand, she took a deep breath. "So, except in public, we're going to live like brother and sister."

He shook his head, trying to get his thoughts out of his pants. "I don't think so. Not unless you lock your door and put Hugo on guard. And even then, well, I'll think of something."

She half smiled at him. "You could lock your door."

"I'd have to Super Glue it shut."

"And the windows."

He sneaked a smile at her. "I was hoping you'd forget about the windows."

She shimmied her skirt back down her thighs. "We've got issues."

"Oh yeah." He buttoned his shirt. "Lucky for us we're professionals. We can handle the pressure."

She reached out and touched his thigh. Light as it was, the touch wrung a groan from him. "Cole. You need to take your hands off me right now or I won't be responsible. Shit. I can't even believe those words came out of my mouth."

"Sorry." Cole removed her hand. She had pushed him really far, farther than she had any right to do. And she was paying the price, trembling with frustrated desire. She definitely felt singed. But she had been honest, stood up for herself. That felt good.

"One more thing." He turned to her and slid across the seat until he had backed her against the passenger side door. He took her face in his hands, smoothing her frown away with his fingers. "I never meant to hurt you." His gaze hung doggedly on to hers. "You believe that?"

Cole nodded. But a spurt of pain arrowed its way through her heart as he kissed her softly.

Maybe there was something wrong with her that she couldn't completely trust him. Some righteous little demon kept her thinking that maybe, just maybe, he hadn't been all that faithful in the first place.

Or, maybe she just needed an excuse to run away, as she had the first time. Maybe she, not he, was the coward.

CHAPTER TWENTY-FIVE

Cole paced in the living room of their small apartment. Izzy and Hugo, stretched out on the floor side by side with chins in paws, watched her every step.

"What I don't understand is why you haven't heard from X. You called him out in public a week ago. Don't bikers always retaliate when challenged?"

Scott sprawled in the room's only comfortable chair with his long legs stretched out before him. "My guess is he is playing with me. That's been his strategy all along. He strikes then goes back into hiding and waits to see how rattled I get. The first two times, I gave him nothing."

"Because you didn't connect the vandalism to your parents' home to him. And I didn't tell you about my run-in on Richards's motorcycle."

Scott scowled at the mention of that near-miss. "I suspected about my parents' home but couldn't prove it. I sure as hell would have come down on him like a ton of bricks if I'd known about you."

"That could have gotten you arrested."

He shrugged.

"Why is he after you? What did you do to him?"

"If I had to guess it's because I was an undercover narc who infiltrated his gang. When things went sideways, he went to jail behind that."

"How did he find you?"

"Remember how I called you on our anniversary? Later that same night X and I ran into each other in the parking lot of the place I'd called from. I didn't think he'd made me. I look so different now. But after you found the hog's head in my parents' fridge I knew he was behind the destruction, and was using it to send me a message. Pig. Cop. Draw a straight line."

"So this is payback?" Cole looked worried. "He'll come at you again. And he won't do it directly."

Scott nodded. "More likely he's planning to come after someone close to me." He eyed her from beneath his lowered brows. "That's why you don't go anywhere without me."

She paused to plant a fist on each hip. "Fat chance, Lucca. I'm a cop. I'm armed. I go where I want."

He grinned at her. "Ooh, I like it when you act tough. Want to play cops and robbers? I'll let you catch and frisk me. You can even search all my secret places."

"Dream on." She resumed pacing.

They had spent four tense days in each other's company. The fact she even could joke about it helped make him feel better.

"I've got someone in law enforcement tracking down every scrap of information he can gather on X, past and present. We're going to find him before he acts again."

Cole paused before his chair. "You're just saying that to make me feel better."

Scott noticed her foot was wiggling. She was getting worked up. Time to change the subject. "You're just bummed because Shajuanna took the girls to the Bahamas so you've had nothing to do this week."

Cole conceded that point. She had really enjoying coaching Leila. Not that it could have continued for much longer.

She rubbed her brow. "How do you decompress after an undercover mission?"

"You make plans while you're still undercover. You decide what you're going to do first. And then second and third. You need to have some things to look forward to. Things you can't do now."

"Like patrol duty?"

"See, I would have gone with a short vacation. Time away is helpful. Lets you put a period between now and what comes next."

Cole gave herself a moment to think about bright waves breaking on warm sand. Sun heating her sunscreened skin. Lazy half-awake thoughts drifting in the shade of an umbrella. She could almost taste the salt water on her lips. "I haven't been to the shore this year."

"There you go. A week at the shore. You'll come back all tanned and rested and looking hot. These last weeks will be a dim memory."

Cole didn't bother to contradict him. The truth was, she was never going to forget the last weeks. She wasn't yet at all certain whether that was a good or bad thing.

But that wasn't her main concern at the moment. Her mind kept circling back to X. "How would you classify X's behavior?"

Scott frowned. "Intimidation. Mind games. He's a prick."

"Yeah, but it's like he's got a plan of escalation that is covert. Why not just shoot you? Or stab you, if he wants revenge. Instead, he's been coming at you through your friends and family. He's back-dooring you."

"What did you just say?"

"He's using covert action."

"Cop behavior." Scott sat up and reached for his cell phone. "You may have bought us a winning lottery ticket, Officer Jamieson." He punched his speed dial.

"Hear me out, Dave. What if X is one of us? Ex-law enforcement. SWAT or SOG. Probably got into undercover, loved the thrill of it, and went deep blue and stayed."

Scott had punched "speaker" so Cole could hear Dave's reply. "Wouldn't be the first time. No department wants to advertise their bad apples. Usually the guy is just written off and dismissed."

"We've got something else. That birth date he mentioned to his parole officer the other night. Want to bet it's different than the one on his paperwork?"

"How did I miss that? Wish we had a year to go with it, for investigatory purposes."

"A wild guess puts him in his early forties. He's lived hard a long time. Even if everything else on his prison forms is lies, you've got his face and fingerprints to run through law-enforcement channels."

"Called himself Dos Equis when you met, correct? Sounds like he's not from the East Coast. I've had to move carefully locally so as not to draw attention of the wrong sort. But I can be more straightforward in the Southwestern states, Texas to southern California, I'm thinking. I'll check with major internal affairs departments. Turn over a few rocks and see what crawls out."

"Thanks, Dave. I owe you."

"Only always."

When he'd hung up there was a smile on Scott's face. "You done good, babe. I've been thinking like a Pagan where X is concerned. I should have been thinking like a cop."

Cole shrugged, basking in the glow of his praise.

Her phone chimed with a text. She read the message and her smile deepened. Maybe their luck was changing.

"It's Shajuanna. She says she didn't make it to the Bahamas after all. She's enrolled Shujaa in an Agility competition near Philadelphia tomorrow and wants to know if I can meet her there. What do you think?"

"Let me check with Lattimore." Scott made the call. After he explained the situation, he scribbled something down on his pad. "Yes, sir. I've got it."

He looked at her with a smile. "We're good. You like Philly cheese steak sandwiches?"

"Sorry I overslept." Cole slid into the passenger seat of Scott's truck where he'd waited for her to dress. One motel room was too small for two people and two dogs. "I'm usually up half the night running obstacles in my mind. Not competing today removed the pressure."

"Take your time." He passed her one of the cups of coffee he held. "Shajuanna never shows up early."

Except that Shajuanna's motor coach was already parked in the lot next to the exposition building when they arrived thirty minutes later. Next to her coach was one marked WQQR. She had brought her TV crew with her.

Scott nudged Cole. "Looks like we're in for a show."

Cole nodded. "Wonder what sort of manufactured drama she's come up with this time?"

This event was much more than an Agility event. There were booths and rides, and other dog competitions set up on the fairgrounds. It was more like a festival with dog competitions as part of it. The indoor air-conditioned hall was packed with spectators as well as competitors. The Agility ring had been laid out under arena lighting with Astroturf flooring. The competition was well under way, with small dogs running first.

When they had walked through, not recognizing anyone from a previous meet, Cole and Scott, along with Izzy and Hugo on leashes, moved out onto the midway area.

Cole waved when she caught sight of Shajuanna among the crowd. Not that it was difficult. She was surrounded by her entourage and curiosity seekers, and spotlights on poles had been set up to light her effectively.

Scott nodded but said out of the corner of his mouth, "You go make nice. She's already told you I'm not her favorite person. I'm going to walk through to the dog competition staging area with Izzy and hope we get lucky."

Shajuanna greeted her with a big hug. "Hey, Noel. That is your name? Noel Jenkins?"

Cole felt the cool current of unease touch her. "That's right."

"Then, sweetie, can you explain this to me?" She pointed to an enormous video screen that had been set up next to the TV van. It burst to life with a grainy picture of Cole in her K-9 uniform and Hugo on a leash.

Cole felt as if a sinkhole had suddenly opened under her feet. The sensation of falling was so strong she reached out to clutch Hugo's collar for balance as she stared at the screen.

It was a picture from a six-month-old newspaper article from the *Gazette*. Beneath it the caption read, *Montgomery County Police Officer Jamieson and her K-9 partner Hugo on patrol.* At the bottom edge of the torn-out article a large *X* had been made with a felt-tip marker.

Shajuanna poked her shoulder. "Explain that, Noel. Or Officer Jamieson. Or whoever the hell you are."

Cole glanced around, feeling a trap snap closed around her. There were two cameras trained on her face. Embarrassment burned in her throat, all but strangling her words. "Where did you get that?"

"It came by mail earlier in the week."

Cole's gaze homed in on the scrawled *X*. "I need to know exactly who sent it, and the envelope it came in."

"Excuse me. Who are you, Noel Jenkins? Or is it Officer Jamieson? And I know that's your dog in that picture. So first you tell me, and everyone here, exactly why you've been lying about who you are."

Cole recoiled as the implication of the cameras trained on her fully impacted her. She needed to get away from them. "If you'll excuse me."

"The hell I will." Shajuanna reached out and snagged her by the arm. "Don't you dare run away from me until I get some answers. Why are you targeting me? I've done nothing. Is this a case of police harassment? Eye-C's got a record now, so we're fair game for any and all kinds of entrapment schemes."

Onlookers had pulled out their cell phones. With a sickening lurch of her stomach Cole realized that whatever was said now would be all over the Internet in a matter of seconds. "I don't know what you're talking about."

Shajuanna stepped in close to her, her gorgeous face hard with anger. "And here I was worried about Boyfriend. You are one cold customer. You played me, bitch. Worse, you played my children."

"No I didn't." Cole's gaze moved sideways, right and left. She lowered her voice. "Leila and I have a legitimate friendship."

Shajuanna recoiled as if she'd been slapped. "Don't you bring her into this. Don't you even say her name. I don't want to hear it in your mouth. That's why I had to send her away. You were using Leila. To get to me."

She turned a little toward the camera, her voice angry but trembling under emotion. "As a mother I try to protect my girls in every way. I tell them every day: don't trust anybody. Take nothing at face value. Be smart. Don't get hurt." She faced Cole again, one long polished fingernail waving back and forth. "But you, you played me in front of my girls. That's some cold shit, bitch."

Cole stiffened. "I'm really sorry if you think—"

Shajuanna held up her hand, her palm inches from Cole's face. "Don't speak to me. If somebody throws shit on me I will get even."

Cole felt her middle hollow out with guilt. Shajuanna was acting her butt off for the benefit of the camera and their audience, but the pain in her gaze was real. She had every right to feel betrayed. Cole had lied and cheated and wormed her way into her family. But Cole hardened her heart. There was nothing to do now but tough it out. She was still a law-enforcement officer taught to control a situation and never back down.

Cole held her ground, her voice firm. "I've done nothing to you or yours. You need to take a step back. Now."

"Or what?" Shajuanna took a step back, flung her hair back from her face with a toss of her head, and placed a hand on a hip and gazed down at Hugo, who growled in response to her stare. "You're going to sic your dog on me? Is that what you plan to do?"

Cole watched her carefully, willing her heart out of overdrive. Shajuanna was furious but she wasn't in meltdown stage. Hugo was simply alerting on the woman he knew. If she kept her own head, nothing worse could happen.

Cole turned to the cameras. "Turn those off. You're in violation of my civil rights."

"Your what?" Again, Shajuanna moved into Cole's space. "Your rights? What about mine? You going to arrest me for calling you out for the lying-ass double-dealing bitch you are?"

Cole stood her ground and locked gazes with the taller woman. "I would like to walk away, Shajuanna. Do you really want to test me?" She lowered her voice to a whisper and leaned in close. "You don't want your daughters to see their mother cuffed and taken away for accosting a police officer. You have more class than that."

Shajuanna blinked at her. For a moment, her expression crumbled, her voice choking her. "How could you? I trusted you. Had you in my home. Let you train my child."

Cole swallowed and the guilt felt like shards of glass going down. "I'm sorry."

"Sorry." Shajuanna's gaze hardened to black-diamond brilliance as she straightened up and struck a pose. "We're not done. First I'm going to run this tape on my show for all the world to see how the police treat people like me. Then I'm going to sue you. Sue your superiors. Sue your dog. Sue people who just know you by your first name."

With that she spun on a heel and walked away, trailed by cameras and onlookers.

It seemed like an hour. Cole moved toward the exit on legs so tight with tension it felt as if her feet had turned to wood. Sweat ran out from under her bangs to sting her eyes but she didn't wipe it away for fear the most persistent of the curiosity seekers would mistake her action for wiping tears.

Where was Scott? How far could he have gone? She kept walking but she couldn't see anything. It was as if she was deaf and blind. There was only the thundering of her heart and the deep-down soul burn of humiliation. She had been outed in public. The task force operation was blown to hell. All because she'd walked right into a trap without any plan at all.

"Noel. Noel!" Scott's sharp voice brought her to a sudden halt.

She looked up at him. She was shuddering so hard she couldn't focus.

"Jesus. What's wrong?" He raised his hands to frame her shoulders but she flinched away.

"Don't touch me. Just don't."

He dropped his hands but continued to study her face. She was showing all the signs of shock, pale lips, shivering, a hundred-yard stare. He couldn't guess what had happened. He glanced down at Hugo who seemed fine but on full alert as he stared full focus at his handler. He needed to get her out of there, and fast.

"Can you walk?" She nodded. "Then start moving. Parade march, Officer. Now."

Cole wasn't at all certain how she made it back to the truck. She wasn't aware of anything until the engine started. Finally she glanced at Scott, who was staring at her with worried eyes. Still he said nothing.

She swallowed hard. "I've been called a bitch many times in my career as a cop. This is the first time I felt someone was right."

CHAPTER TWENTY-SIX

"Way to go, Lucca. Flame out, much?"

"Go stuff yourself, Hadley."

The FBI advisor snickered as he passed Scott and Cole in the hallway of the DEA Baltimore offices. It was Monday morning and there was about to be a full meeting of the task force to decide how to proceed.

The story of the "outed" undercover policewoman had been all over the weekend news. Everyone from *Extra* to *Huffington Post* was vying for a chance to interview Cole and her "unidentified accomplice" who went by the name Sam Lott.

Most of the speculation centered around rumors that Cole was part of a sting operation meant to snare Eye-C in illegal activities that ranged from tax evasion to his re-entry into the world of illegal dogfighting. None of them came close to the real reason, which meant the puppy mule drug-smuggling operation could possibly continue.

One thing was certain. It was going to happen without the services of K-9 Officer Nicole Jamieson and Special Agent Scott Lucca.

Shajuanna was everywhere in the news and entertainment media, proclaiming loudly about the "police state" tactics of local and federal authorities. And promoting the late summer edition of her show, where she promised to reveal the "entire explosive footage" of her confrontation with the "heartless b-i-zitch who wormed her way into my innocent children's lives."

"The thing is, Shajuanna's right. Her family's done nothing wrong. That's all we proved, that she's innocent."

Scott kept silent when Cole spoke those words on their drive into Baltimore. They were the only words she'd spoken on the subject since they left Philly two days ago.

He was worried about her, deeply worried. Few undercover agents ever had their covers blow up so spectacularly in their faces. When an agent was outed, it was often in private, and sometimes just before a bullet ended their lives. While he felt for her, felt deeply, he knew she was going to be okay. She was alive and safe. But he also knew that was of little comfort at the moment. She still had to face Lattimore and the other task force members.

When they were shown into his office, Lattimore looked as if he had aged five years over the weekend. His expression was flat, his complexion paler than usual. "I've read your initial reports. Is there anything either of you want to say before we begin the debriefing process?"

"Yes. I'm sorry, sir." Cole's voice was calm, distant. "I should have been more wary. Especially after Shajuanna told me she'd made Agent Lucca."

"Are you referring to her claim to have some special 'sight' that allows her to so-called 'read' people?"

"Yes, sir."

"I'd have been more concerned if you had taken her seriously. I saw your report last week. That didn't concern me. Your explanation to her for Agent Lucca's attitude made more than enough sense to be believed.

"I'm more interested in the person who mailed that newspaper article to Ms. Collier. You were outed by a third party, Officer Jamieson. We need to know how compromised we are." His gaze strayed from one to the other. "Do either of you have any information on who and what is behind that?"

"That would be me, sir." Scott met the director's inquiring gaze. "I have recently been targeted by a Pagan gang member, a man who calls himself X. He went to prison after an undercover operation I participated in two years ago. He's out and looking to hurt me. I thought it had nothing to do with Officer Jamieson. Or this task force."

Lattimore's expression gave nothing away. "Why am I just hearing about this?"

Scott sat back. "My problem. I was handling it."

Lattimore snorted, the first emotional response Cole had ever witnessed from him. "Your way of handling things could be the reason Officer Jamieson's cover was blown."

Scott's jaw worked for a second. "Actually, sir, I'm certain it was. There's an *X* on the lower right-hand corner of the newspaper article Ms. Collier was sent. It was a message meant for me."

"But Scott, if he's after you, why not out you instead of me?"

Scott didn't look at Cole, afraid his fear for her would show. He spoke to Lattimore. "X won't try to take me down until he's wrecked everything important to me. But I'm not waiting for that to happen. I've been working with my former handler to get to X first. I should have told you sooner."

"Can you be certain he has no direct interest in our present U/C operation?"

"Not certain. But since it's not about him, my best guess is he doesn't give a shit. X just wanted to humiliate me, through my partner."

"Sir?" Cole waited until Lattimore's attention shifted to

her. "Shajuanna was only interested in the fact that I'm a law officer who befriended her under false pretenses. Even she didn't ask why. Every interview she's given stresses the fact that she thinks I was sent in to trip up her husband for crimes concerning his prior conviction. Puppy drug smuggling isn't on her radar."

Lattimore sat still for a long time, not looking at anything in particular. Finally he slipped his fingers under his glasses to rub his eyes. "We have a lot of resources and manpower involved in this task force. More than you know about. It was possible we had a leak here, on the back end. I needed to be sure that wasn't the case."

Cole let that sink in. Scott had warned her there were warring political factions at work for a man in Lattimore's position with fierce internal defenders and enemies, pro and con. The fact that the director thought it was possible they'd been betrayed by someone in-house was positively chilling.

Lattimore adjusted his glasses and gave the pair before him a tight smile. "Thank you for your candid answers. We've had worse outcomes, and more spectacular failures. Believe me. If we can verify that the task force's purpose remains unknown, our efforts will continue unabated on a different front."

Cole was grateful he didn't actually say the words "without you."

He stood up and offered Cole his hand. "Thank you for your work and dedication, Officer Jamieson. DEA depends on officers like you to do difficult work." He paused, looking at Cole with a very serious expression. "I know you are in a very difficult situation at the moment. But all of this will pass. You're a fine officer. You were able to infiltrate our target with remarkable ease. It's been good serving with you. Now if you will follow my assistant to the appropriate room, we can begin the debriefing." He glanced at Scott. "Agent Lucca, a private word."

Cole glanced back at Scott before she left. He looked tough, unapologetic, and ready for anything.

When she was gone, Lattimore turned to Scott. His eyes were silver behind his glasses and a vein had popped out on his forehead. "What the hell is all this about a man called X? I want details. Names, dates, everything that's happened."

"Screw that." Scott clicked off the TV and tossed the remote away. He'd watched five innings of a ballgame before deciding it was the slowest-ass game on the planet.

Scott and Cole had spent three grueling hours answering and reanswering questions from various task force members. They had been cross-checked against each other's statements separately, and then cross-referenced against the reports they had turned in weekly while undercover. It was necessary but it was an antagonistic process and sometimes just short of insulting. Once or twice it had crossed that line. But they had each stuck to their stories, omitting only certain previously agreed-upon events of that night in the alley.

He and Cole had returned to their rented apartment to pack. But neither of them had much energy for that at the moment.

In fact, Scott hadn't heard a sound coming from Cole's bedroom in over an hour. He thought she must be asleep. Now, he wondered if she wasn't just hiding.

He got up and crossed to her open doorway.

She was at the window, staring off into the middle distance as if the parking lot beyond was the most interesting sight she'd ever seen. But he knew she wasn't examining the parking lot, or anything else beyond the glass. She was all inside herself. Sadness was coming off her in waves he could feel. Hugo was at her feet, splayed out so flat it seemed as if he'd been run over. He was hurting because she was.

He didn't know what to say. He just knew he needed to get her out of here. "You ready?"

She didn't look back. "I didn't think . . . I didn't think." Her second sentence was a complete thought.

Scott leaned a shoulder against the doorjamb and waited. Even if it took her another hour to get out the next sentence, he'd wait. She needed to say things. The least he could do was bear witness to her pain, even if it tore at his gut.

"I should have been prepared." She traced a finger over the glass before her. "You told me what might happen. Still, I thought . . ."

"You could be a hero."

He saw a corner of her mouth jerk up for a second. She liked it that he'd called her a hero, without adding the *-ine*. Good. Something he'd done right today.

He left the jamb and moved toward her slowly. "Are we going to talk about it now?"

After a moment she nodded but she didn't look back at him.

He came up behind her and lifted his hands to frame her shoulders. But she flinched before he even made contact, just as before, so he let his hands fall to his sides.

"You can't ever know how these assignments will end, Cole. You think you know how you'll feel and how you'll handle it. But the truth is, whether it goes right or terribly wrong, you can't know ahead how you'll handle it."

"How did you handle it?" Her voice was so small he almost missed the question. The question was a kick in the stomach. He never really had talked about it. Not with his parents. Not directly with his anger management group. But he owed her the truth. He'd dragged her into this. He owed her a pound of his flesh.

"When my undercover operation blew up in my face, it just about did me in."

She glanced at him, surprise in her expression. "What happened that night?"

Jesus. What didn't happen?

He set a shoulder on the wall nearest her, angling his body toward her. "You really want to know?"

She nodded.

"That night—" He paused to see if she would flinch at the mention of the night that tore them apart. She didn't even shift her feet. But her focus remained on the window.

"That night was a Pagan initiation. Orgy or public sex. Those were my choices. I chose the latter. Thought at least that way I could control what I would be forced to do." He ran the back of a hand over his mouth. "Look, you don't want to hear this."

"I do." She didn't turn to him.

Maybe it was better that way. If she was looking at him he doubted he could utter the words she wanted to hear. Yet he needed to tell it in context. Then maybe she'd understand, at least a little.

"I won't burden you with everything that happened during the year I was trying to earn my way into the bastards' organization. I did some things, and saw a lot more bad shit that I still have nightmares about. You're warned about it, but still." He paused a beat to let that anguished wave of guilt roll through him.

"Now that you've been undercover you have a sense of how it is when you hang out with suspects. After a while they go from being scumbags you want behind bars to being ordinary human beings. Most of them."

Sociopathic personalities like X weren't exactly human to his way of thinking. At least, they weren't knowable. Even within the Pagans men like X stood a little apart. X was something he was still going to have to deal with.

She frowned. "So you became friends with the Pagans."

"Not exactly. There were almost daily experiences to remind me that I wasn't dealing with people who honor the normal social contract."

She glanced at him, her expression unreadable. "Are you going to tell me what happened that night?"

He didn't have to ask which night. Bad-shit night. The worst.

"I was being initiated into a chapter of the Pagans. We were about to do a drug deal with a Russian cartel out of Philly and they needed a full complement. Actually, we were to provide the muscle, be the enforcers. This was the kind of hookup my work was about. I was getting in at the beginning, and then." He shrugged. "It's the little things that can trip you up. Someone called the cops."

"The bartender of the place whose parking lot you had commandeered called my precinct."

He glanced at her. "I swear I didn't know we were in your precinct. We'd been riding and drinking all day. I'm not sure I could have told you what day it was by the time I had my pants around my ankles and that woman was— handling my junk."

She hunched her shoulders but her voice was determined. "Go on."

"You know the next part. Arrests were made. There were drugs on the premises. Folks went to prison after that. X did time. My extraction 'cover' was that I was wanted in another state and that I was extradited west for outstanding warrants. End of undercover operation. End of my career. End of our marriage."

She shrugged. "At least you got bad guys off the street."

"No, you and your precinct pals got bad guys off the street. I lost my U/C operation and offed my marriage. For nothing."

"What did you do after I left you?"

Died inside. But she didn't need to hear self-pity loser shit from him now. "Higher-ups said I had to be off the streets for a while, until things settled. So, I mostly stayed at home and went to hell."

He had never seen her chew her nails before but her thumb edged between her teeth. "Did you get into drugs?"

Complete honesty, Lucca. "Undercover, I snorted a few times. I tried to stay clear but there were moments."

He leaned in until she was forced to glance at him. "I didn't get hooked. It was the alcohol and guilt that did me in for a time. I just tipped the bottle back and tried to drown out everything else."

"Including me?"

"Especially you."

"What changed us?" Cole dipped her head. "Was it me?"

"God, no. Gabe happened."

Cole nodded. "You were close, like me and Becca. It really hurt you when he died. I understood that."

"Not even close." Scott raked a hand through his hair. "Sure, I loved my brother. Everybody *loooo*ved Gabe." The emotion in his voice pushed him away from the wall. "But the truth is, more than half the time I hated his guts."

Cole turned around, her face animated with surprise.

Scott's face was tight with cold, hard emotion. "That's right. I hated him."

CHAPTER TWENTY-SEVEN

"Didn't expect that, did you?"

Scott moved away from her shocked expression.

"You have no idea what it was like to grow up with Gabe for an older brother. Dad never spoke about him without a catch of pride in his throat. Gabe went to military school and won wrestling championships. He aced the ASVAB and got into the Naval Academy. He was chosen for Navy SEALS as a freshman. It was like living with fucking Captain America. Nothing I ever did could equal anything Gabe did."

Cole didn't say a word. Instead, she sat down on the bed, and waited.

Scott paced as he talked. "I tried to be like Gabe but I didn't have his endurance or his daring. Dad could see that early. By the time I was twelve, he was discouraging me from following in Gabe's footsteps. Said I was more academic. I'd make a good lawyer or doctor. I finished college in prelaw to please my dad, but then I enlisted in the army. I made Ranger but Gabe never let me forget that, as far as a SEAL was concerned, it was second-best."

Scott paused and stared at the wall. That was a hard admission for him, harder than facing his father's disappointment when he left the service to join law enforcement.

He shook off that memory with a physical roll of his shoulders.

"When we met, I was a D.C. SWAT. You were right. I loved that shit, the power and status and the knowing that not just the bad guys but the general public took a respectful approach when we SWAT guys were around. Even Gabe was impressed. It was the only time I'd ever felt good about myself." He glanced at her. "Until you."

Cole sighed. "The night we met, I was surprised you even noticed me."

"I couldn't *not* look at you. Your eyes were wide open and they were full of me. Not my badge or my status. You didn't know what I was. You weren't a badge bunny or a woman on the prowl. You were this serious cute chick, and you wanted me. I was flattered as hell."

Cole smiled for the first time. "I was impressed as anything."

"After we married I thought I didn't care anymore what any of my family thought. Not even Gabe. Let him have the glory. I had my own family. My own place. The best part was you were Blue, too. You knew and understood my life. We were a team."

"You never told me any of this before."

He hunched a shoulder. "That's because I knew how it would sound. I wasn't as good as Gabe. Everyone walking knew that. Why would I point it out to the one person who thought I was—" He stopped short. He no longer had the right to own that.

"The person who thought you were everything?" A flicker of humor brightened her gaze.

He nodded, his chest burning with emotion he dare not release.

"Scott, do you want to know my opinion of Gabe?"

"I'm sure I can guess."

"I thought he was a gorgeous self-absorbed prick."

It was Scott's turn to register complete surprise.

"Oh, Gabe was charming, when he wanted to be. But he could be ruthless, too. He never let an opportunity to belittle or embarrass you slide. He went out of his way when I was around to show you up." She shrugged. "I wanted to slug him that day he broke your thumb. He cheated to win at arm wrestling."

Scott let her words circle until they found landing sites in his thoughts. "You never said any of this before."

"How could I? You and your parents were so in love with Gabe's image of himself. I couldn't come in, an outsider, and start trashing your family's attitudes. I wasn't even sure they liked me all that much, in the beginning."

"They liked you from the beginning."

She smiled finally and stood up. "I liked them, too. But we were so raw and new to each other, I just wanted to fit in."

He moved in close to her, wanting to savor every inch of her smile. "So you didn't think Gabe was Mr. Studly?"

"Oh, from a distance, he was a total alpha-male-god-babe-magnet."

Scott felt a smile tugging at his mouth. "Up close?"

"He struck me as a bit of a jerk."

She moved in, too, and laid a hand on his cheek. "I'm not saying I really disliked him. He was funny and really good at telling stories. You loved him and he loved you. I get that now. Growing up with a sister, I didn't have any experience with how brothers show love. All that testosterone-filled competition. But being a SEAL was Gabe's only defini-tion of a life worth living. It was clear you worshiped him and he loved being worshiped. I was just immune. I'd been with you."

Scott didn't answer that, didn't have the words to explain how it made him feel, like the sun was shining on him from the inside.

He reached for her, half expecting to be stopped. Instead her hand landed on his chest as she reached up on tiptoe to meet his kiss.

It was the most tender moment they had ever shared. It felt good, yet new, as if they had totally missed out on some ways of being together and had not realized it until this very second.

When they were done, she broke away from him and moved back to the window where Hugo sat watching them. "Why did you shut me out?"

"I saw my father's face the day the navy brought the news about Gabe. The golden son, the one he bragged about to everyone, was gone. It was as if the light had been turned off in my parents' world. I knew the day of the memorial service that I needed to stop being a selfish prick. I'd been so happy in my own little world." He slanted a glance at her. "It was my turn to step up. That's why I applied to go U/C. I wanted to do something that would make my dad proud, even if he couldn't talk about it at the time I was doing it."

"You could have told me. You just came home one day and it was a fact."

"I was a dick about it but I didn't want to be talked out of it. I thought I could fill that hole in my dad's heart. Pitiful, right?"

She digested this. "What kept you from drinking yourself to death after we broke up?"

He shrugged. "I got tired of wallowing in a ditch, so to speak. First I got up and went to the gym to peel off some of the fat. Then I went to get back the only job I was ever good at, police work."

"Was it that easy?"

"Hell no. They wouldn't give me my position back. Said

I was too angry. They sent me to anger-fucking-management class." He cracked a smile. "Joke, maybe?"

Her smile flickered. "But not the class."

"No, the class was real. Dave Wilson, who had been my first partner, and then my handler undercover, helped get me back on my feet. When I had done that, he said I would be wasted on patrol or God forbid behind a desk. He recommended me to the DEA. I had experience as a narc and at the time they needed a K-9 officer. I went to sign up. I said yes because I get to be in on SWAT team take-downs but I also work solo with Izzy."

"Best of all worlds."

"Professionally, yes."

He stopped before her and, reaching out, pulled her in against him. He touched her face, tracing her features with his fingers as if he had never really seen them before. The wonder of her being here, in his arms, with him rocked his world. She had taken it all in, every bitter sad bit of his anguished, angry, humiliating confession. And she hadn't turned away in scorn or disgust. No, she was looking at him as if he was possibly the best man she'd ever known. He knew it wasn't true. But he wanted to be that man, this time. For her.

"I know I'm the worst thing that ever happened to you." He traced a finger down her lips. "But you are absolutely the best thing that ever happened or will ever happen to me."

She shook her head. "You aren't the worst, Scott. Walking out on our marriage was the worst. And I did that."

"You had cause."

"I certainly thought so." The sadness in her gaze added weight to his guilt.

"We can't get back what we lost. I know that. I'm not asking for that. Only . . ." He let the thought trail as his hand came back up to cup her face.

He leaned his body into hers until their lips met. The kiss was so tender tears pushed in behind Cole's closed lids.

When he lifted his head she scooped a hand behind his head to hold him close. "Maybe we don't need to go back. Maybe we can just go on."

"Seriously?"

Cole had never seen hope in Scott's face before. The wonder of it nearly stopped her heart. Suddenly she was afraid. She was promising, no, they were both promising each other huge things. It was more momentous than the first mad rave of love that consumed them body and soul. They now knew the risks.

As if he read her thoughts he pulled a little away.

She grabbed his neck. "Wait. I'm not saying no. We just need time. This is huge." She smiled. "We need ordinary days."

He nodded. "Yeah. We have a way of complicating our lives to the max."

She let her fingers curl more tightly into the column of his neck. "But we can share now."

His smile was slow to catch fire. The dimples hollowed out in glacial timing. But, finally, they came into view. "Yeah. We've got now."

"There's even a bed here that's never been used." She leaned into him, bringing them nose to nose. "So don't waste it, Lucca."

His confident male grin made craters in his cheeks as he pulled her close. "I never need to be asked twice."

She took his hand and led him to her bed and sat down. "We have yet to make love in a bed."

He followed her down, pushing her back onto the bedding as he covered her with his body. "The missionary position. Sounds kinky."

An hour later, Scott was still thinking. Mostly because his brain was the only part of him that was not thoroughly sated and exhausted. Something, maybe something huge, had just occurred to him.

"Cole? What kind of mileage would you say a motor home gets?"

"Very little, down to next to nothing." Her voice came from under her pillow.

"How much do you think it would cost to drive a motor home up from Florida to Maine?"

Groaning in reluctance, Cole leaned up on an elbow and reached for her phone. She punched a few things into it. "Okay, quick and dirty. It's seventeen hundred miles from Miami to Bangor, Maine." She punched in a few more words. "The average motor home gets six to eight miles per gallon. Split the difference. That comes to . . . about eight hundred dollars, one way."

Scott sat up. "No shit. Where do two retirees get sixteen hundred dollars, give or take, plus meals and entrance fees and so forth, to drive a Winnebago up the coast and back? Lorene's got medical bills and is buying medical marijuana, or so she says."

"How do you know that?"

"Jennifer told me after Izzy signed on Lorene vaping. It comes in vials."

Cole yawned. "That stuff's not legal in every state. Could be they are buying when and where they can, legal or not."

"True." Scott was silent for several moments. "How much does a fairly new but used Winnebago Sightseer cost?"

Cole made an unhappy noise but punched a few more words into her cell phone. "The first one that pops up, used, is a 35J for $82,500 or best offer. Here's one for $57,000 but it's smaller and has got lots of mileage. New ones begin well over a hundred thousand."

Scott whistled. "Do you see a disconnect here?"

"Maybe." Cole rolled over and climbed up and onto him, wiggling her naked hips against his equally naked groin. "But it's not our problem anymore, is it?"

He took her face between his hands even though his body was reacting predictably to her very intimate stimulation. "I know you've been through a lot of shit lately. But isn't that even more of a reason to want to be the ones who catch the bad guys?"

Cole shook her head. "I don't think I'm cut out for detective work. Can't we just have this night to ourselves? Nothing is going to change before morning."

The wistfulness in the tone reminded him of how desperately she wanted normal days with him. Now here he was pushing her. "You're right. We've got the night and each other." He leaned up and kissed her softly. "Tomorrow can take care of itself until we get there."

CHAPTER TWENTY-EIGHT

"Are you sure we're in the right place?" Scott peered through the rain of the sudden summer downpour that had turned Gambrill Park Road near Frederick, Maryland, into a flowing stream.

"Yes. There should be a trailer park sign coming up soon."

Cole glanced up from studying her GPS. After a few days of planning, they had decided to pursue Scott's hunch about Jennifer and Lorene. "I still can't believe you remembered that Jennifer said something about coming back to Maryland for the CPE Agility trials in Frederick tomorrow."

"It's only because Frederick is in the county next to Montgomery, where you're a police officer. I remember thinking at the time that that was one competition we should skip. The way police departments advertise themselves to the public these days someone at the competition might have recognized you or Hugo. That would have given away our U/C operation."

Cole sighed. "That worry is long gone."

She was still smarting from the public humiliation. She was staying with Scott in D.C. to hide from the media. She avoided all calls except from her sister, Becca, and her parents. Her boss, too, thought it was a good idea for her to lie low. "Until the shit blows through." How could she have thought U/C would be easy?

"How are we going to explain our being here?"

Scott grinned at her. "I don't have to explain myself. You're the one with a cred problem. You and Hugo can sit this one out."

"I don't think so." Cole shifted in the seat to look back at the covered kennels where Hugo and Izzy rode in back of the truck. "If we're right, you'll need backup. That's me."

He grinned at her. "I like it when you go all badass."

She shrugged and checked her GPS. "So far, all we've got is speculation."

"Don't underestimate the intuition of a shrewd and seasoned DEA officer." He winked at her, enjoying the edge his adrenaline surge in anticipation of a confrontation was giving him. "Jennifer and Lorene make ideal puppy smugglers when you think about it. They have mobility. They attend Agility competitions in different locations each week, which gives them access to lots of breeders and other dog people. No one is surprised to see them with dogs, or not. Jennifer as good as admitted not all their marijuana buys are legal. Maybe they set out to buy a little illegal weed and got sucked into something bigger."

Cole frowned. "Remember what Lattimore told us about hoofbeats and horses."

Scott laughed. "Yeah. But you said from the first that the task force's focus was wrong. Lorene and Jennifer just may be the zebras no one is looking for."

"Turn here." Cole leaned forward, straining to see through the rain. "The RV section of the park should be up ahead."

Scott drove past the turnoff to the RV park and then made a Y-turn to bring them back on the opposite side of the road, where he pulled over. "Izzy and I'll walk from here. It'll give us time to snoop around and pick up a scent. If she signs on something I'll move in."

"How can you be so certain the women will just let you into their RV?"

"Animal magnetism." Scott's dimples were on full display. "Jennifer's got a thing for good-looking men. She'll let me in."

"Ego, maybe?"

He leaned and kissed her hard. "Lucky for me, you fill up my whole worldview."

"And I'm just supposed to sit here while it all goes down?"

Scott thought of about a dozen flippant things he might say in answer to her hurt. But something stopped him. It was the thing that would have stopped him from trying to pretend a shitstorm was an April shower to a male partner. Sometimes it was enough to hunker down and ride it out together. They had done that. Now it was time to act. "I'll call you. Be prepared to move quickly, and bring Batman."

To his surprise, Cole reached out, latched a hand behind his head and hauled him in for a kiss. It wasn't just a good-luck smooch, but a long, slow, thorough kiss that left them both breathing a little hard. When he looked at her, her gaze was full of him.

"Be careful." Her voice was so low he felt more than heard the words because she spoke them against his mouth.

He brushed away a strand of hair clinging to her cheek with a finger then pulled the hoodie of her Montgomery County Police slicker up over her hair. "Let's go kick some outlaw grandma butt."

Jennifer opened the Winnebago door and blinked. "Why, what are you doing here, gorgeous?"

"You invited me to drop by sometime." Scott tugged on his partner's leash and Izzy came forward, her fur slick with rain. "I brought Izzy for a visit."

"Well, isn't that nice." Jennifer's expression wasn't as welcoming as her tone. "I'm sorry, gorgeous, but now's not such a good time."

Scott put his foot on the step well. "We won't take long. Is Mimi with you?"

"Uh, not this trip."

As Scott stepped up onto the RV Jennifer automatically backed up but balked. "Say, you're pretty wet."

"Sorry about that." Scott was inside with Izzy, who was already straining on the leash. They had done a preliminary walk around the vehicle and Izzy was signing. But he had to know for certain. And then wanted to see their faces when he confronted them.

The sound of yelping puppies was coming from a closed-off area in the back. He ignored that for the moment, pretending to look around. "Wow. This is really nice. I've never been inside one of these with the slide-out space. Must have cost a fortune."

"We're leasing." Lorene sat in the lounge chair behind the vehicle's passenger seat.

Scott nodded. "Still, for two ladies on retirement, must set you back a bit."

"We manage." Jennifer planted herself in front of him. "Look here. We're busy."

"So I hear." Scott nodded toward the rear of the RV. "You whelp a litter since last week?"

"We're just making a delivery for friends." Jennifer's eyes cut to Lorene. "Well, it's the truth, Lorene. No need to lie about that."

Scott reached down and unleashed Izzy.

Izzy took off like a rain-slicked bullet. When she reached the closed door, she sniffed and then barked brightly and bounced repeatedly against the frame. Finally, she dropped into a full prone position. Drugs, definitely drugs behind the door.

Scott turned to the women and pushed the edge of his open parka back so that they could see his holstered weapon. Then flashed his ID. "I'm DEA agent Scott Lucca. I need both of you to move over to the sofa and sit side by side while you answer a few questions."

Jennifer's lips twisted. "We heard about your girlfriend being a cop. You, too, hot buns?"

"All day long. Now sit down." When he was satisfied he had the situation under control, Scott punched a number into his cell to alert Cole. "They're dirty. Bring it."

"We wouldn't do anything to hurt dogs. We love them."

"You have a strange way of showing it." Cole and Hugo had joined Scott. She stood with her back to the door while Hugo watched the women from his heel position.

Scott came back down the hallway, carrying a frisky bundle that was a three-month-old boxer puppy. His face was grim as he flipped the little fellow over. There was a long sutured incision there.

Jennifer stood up. "That's just a neutering incision. They all have them."

Scott looked at Jennifer. "Why would you think I might think it was anything else?"

"Well, I—" Jennifer clamped her mouth shut but anger narrowed her eyes.

"Sit down, Mrs. Lutz." Cole pointed with her finger.

The woman subsided onto the sofa and crossed her arms. "I don't know what you think you're doing here but you have no right to break into our home like this. You're already in trouble, young woman."

"Not as much as you two are about to be." Scott gently

squeezed the boxer's tummy. "Feels like something's in there. Want to tell me what it is, Lorene?"

Lorene didn't make eye contact. "I don't know what you're talking about. He's a healthy fat puppy."

"We think it's something else. We think it's drugs. In fact, we know you've got an RV full of puppy drug mules."

"That's a goddamn lie!" Jennifer jumped to her feet with surprising agility for a woman her age. "Just because we're trying to save some puppies from being destroyed is no reason to call us dirty names. We sure as hell aren't drug smugglers."

"Izzy says different. She's a trained drug detection dog. She picked out your trailer on scent alone."

Jennifer eyed the chocolate Lab. "She could be wrong. You're all wrong. Now I want you out of my RV this minute. Lorene, call the real police."

"If you do that, you're going to lose an opportunity the local police won't have to offer you." Cole moved from her position by the door and pulled a manila envelope from under her parka. Scott recognized it was the one he'd given her weeks ago. Out came the photos of the dead and mutilated pups.

Cole handed a few of them to each woman. "This is what is happening to those puppies. We're willing to bet there's up to a pound of heroin stuffed into each of the dogs you have back there. No one will be looking out for their welfare, believe me."

The women gazed in horror at the photos and then at each other.

"I don't know anything about this." Jennifer dumped them on the floor. "That's disgusting."

"*Utterly,*" Lorene agreed with a shudder as she tossed them aside. "We would never have anything to do with something like that."

"Want to explain where the puppies came from?"

"We picked them up in Philly." Lorene sniffed and touched her friend's arm. "Go on, Jennifer. Tell 'em the rest."

Jennifer shifted her weight, as if trying to get comfortable, and then mopped her face with a tissue she pulled from her pocket. "We don't know anything about that ugly business." She toed a photo with her jelly sandal. "We're part of a secret animal rescue group. They rescue purebred pups that aren't up to national breed confirmation standards from puppy mills and we get them to safe shelters."

"Do you know what happens to pups that aren't up to standard?" Lorene's eyes again brimmed with tears. "They're drowned, or their necks are broken. Thousands a year. If that's not animal abuse, I don't know."

Cole pointed to the floor. "That is."

Scott followed up with another question. "Who runs this organization?"

"We don't know the leader, if that's what you mean." Jennifer's gaze slipped sideways toward Lorene, who shook her head. "They said it was safer that way."

Scott didn't doubt that. If caught, low-level runners like these women couldn't point back to the smugglers who hired them. "Who recruited you?"

"We were at an event in Fort Lauderdale back in the winter. A real friendly woman was admiring our daughter's dogs and said it was a shame all dogs couldn't be taken care of. We told her we would have a hundred dogs if we had the money and place to keep them. That's when she told us about this organization that was saving puppies from destruction and asked if we would like to help."

Jennifer nodded. "The woman said they stole pups marked for destruction and were looking for people willing to drive the pups to other states where they would be funneled into no-kill shelters."

"So you two said 'sign me up'?"

Jennifer's lips knotted at Scott's tone. "You don't have to sound so high-and-mighty. We thought we were doing a charitable thing."

"For which you were paid how much?" The two women turned in surprise at the sound of Cole's voice. "Besides the Winnebago, what have they paid you?"

Jennifer's gaze fell. "Ten thousand each, per round trip."

Scott and Cole exchanged glances. "Start at the beginning."

Their story tumbled out in fits and starts as each woman spoke over the other until the gist of the setup was told.

Jennifer, who had been sniffing on and off, wiped her nose. "We weren't doing anything wrong. Leastways, we didn't know it. Are we under arrest?"

"Not yet." Cole reached for her phone. "The Frederick County police will have that honor."

"There is another way." All three women turned to look at Scott, who waited a beat before he said, "The DEA is trying to shut down this drug-puppy smuggling operation. If you surrender to federal authorities and agree to help us, you might be eligible for federal protection."

"How can we do that? We don't know anything."

"You know more than you think." Scott sketched a smile. "Where are you delivering this shipment of puppies?"

Jennifer glanced at Lorene, who nodded. "If we tell you, can you see to it we don't go to jail?"

Lorene nodded. "We've been watching that *Orange Is the New Black* show and we're too old for that bisexual stuff."

CHAPTER TWENTY-NINE

They entered slowly into the gloom of an abandoned building in east Baltimore smelling of summer-baked trash, animal feces, and human piss.

Once past the entry the dark became so consuming that the muzzle of a pistol held two inches from a nose would not have penetrated one's senses. That awareness put all other senses into overdrive. Hairs stood at full attention along arms and the backs of necks. The rancid smothering smell caused the men to suck in careful breaths, as if they might choke on that tarlike blackness if they breathed too deeply.

Yet there were people here. The sound of a boom box blasting annihilation made the building quiver. And the yelping of puppies keened out over the percussive bass. Somewhere, up the next turn in the stairwell, people were living.

Scott felt a hand on his shoulder and flipped his night goggles down. The darkness suddenly jumped into eerie green-vapor focus. They were moving into a hallway with closed doors on either side. There were stumbling blocks ahead. An empty crate on the right. A tin can farther down on the left. A careless kick would send it careening noisily down the corridor, alerting all creatures of the night, harmless and lethal, that their lair was about to be disturbed.

The adrenaline push felt familiar, almost welcome. It had been a while. They had come to bust a dealer's hide.

Scott watched with a twinge of envy as the Baltimore DEA SWAT team fanned out down the hall. Once he would have been in there in the lead. Now he was second tier. But that was fine by him.

He reached down in the dark and petted his partner, Izzy. She shivered with excitement to match that of the men in the hallway. Yet she would not bark until and if given the signal.

There was light coming from under a door on the far end. Their target was here. The taste of success was tempered by the metallic burn of anxiety. No way of telling what lay beyond the door.

The SWAT leader signaled to his men to line up, chest to back. The point man with his weapon at the ready took up a position on one side while the second man moved to force the door. Night goggles no longer necessary, they flipped them up and entered.

It was pretty much chaos after that as the team rushed through, shouting orders and knocking over people and things until it was clear that they had total command of the interior.

A signal sent Scott and Izzy through the door. Izzy's attention went in turn to each of the two men and one woman lying prone on the floor, hands cuffed behind their backs. Her job was to detect weapons, money, cell phones, and drugs.

Izzy signed first on the woman. She was searched and a weapon missed in the initial discovery was found.

"Gute Hund!" Scott patted Izzy. Screaming and kicking, the woman tried to get at Izzy, who, safely out of reach, watched her with the detached interest she would have shown in a cavorting puppy.

One of the men was found to be concealing a cell phone in his shoe.

Once the suspects were locked down, Izzy's main job began.

"Izzy. *Such*." Scott took off behind Izzy, who went with methodical efficiency over every inch of the hellhole.

She signed on the sofa, which was missing its cushions. And on a spot behind a TV. Both places yielded a few one-pound packets of heroin. In the kitchen Izzy gave sign at an unplugged refrigerator that had twenty thousand dollars in cash taped to the underside.

Finally, Scott and Izzy moved into the bedroom, where two dozen puppies, two to four months old by the look of them, were corralled inside a large wooden crate.

Izzy put her paws up on the edge of the crate and began howling, so strong was the scent of drugs in her sensitive nostrils.

Scott scooped up what looked like a poodle and turned him belly up. A long bloody sutured seam lined his belly.

He held the puppy up for the SWAT team captain to see. "And that, gentlemen, is how it's done."

The group around him smiled and slapped him on the back. Mission accomplished.

Scott gave Izzy a treat as they stepped back out into the fresh night air. There had always been the possibility that the information Jennifer and Lorene had given the DEA would be wrong or out-of-date. But they had lucked out. After the women delivered their puppies to the assigned place in Baltimore, DEA agents had followed the drug puppies to this location. Jennifer and Lorene would be happy. Lattimore would be even happier.

* * *

"The women are retirees, living on small pensions, who say they were recruited with a story of animal abuse."

Scott took a moment to click up the next photo in his presentation to the DEA task force he and Cole had been dismissed from only a week earlier. A picture of Jennifer Lutz and Lorene Doggett in matching floral tops and white walking shorts appeared on the screen.

"Their job was to pick up a litter of pups in one state and deliver them to people in another state who, they were told, would then take them to no-kill shelters where they could be adopted."

"Regular Robin Hoods of the dog world," one task force member commented.

The table of participants snickered over the possibility of their do-gooder status.

"You believe them?" asked another.

Scott didn't take a position. "The pups were stuffed with drugs. The women must have had their suspicions. But, like many civilians recruited to be carriers, they didn't want to know. The initial urge to do good plus the lure of untaxable cash probably made it easy for them to look the other way."

Cole, who sat in the back of the room, finally felt compelled to speak. "After Agent Lucca and I approached them, it was a simple matter to persuade the women that they might mitigate their crime by cooperating with the authorities. As a good-faith gesture, they gave us their next drop-off point. And, as you are aware, the raid over the weekend was successful."

Scott brought up the shot of the puppies and bags of heroin taken in the raid. "In a show of good faith, the women have offered to continue their puppy deliveries and feed us leads until DEA can work our way back to the source."

"So we'd be using a geriatric Thelma and Louise of the

canine drug world as informants." Lattimore rubbed his chin. "Our liability and reputations will take a big hit if anything goes wrong."

Scott nodded. "Above my pay scale. Good luck with that. That's all I've got."

"Shit to Sherlock within a week. Nice going, Lucca." FBI Agent Hadley glanced at Cole. "You, too, Officer Jamieson."

When they broke up a few minutes later, Scott and Cole hurried to leave but Lattimore stepped into their path. "That was really fine detective work the pair of you did. It will go in your jackets."

Cole warmed with the praise. "Thank you, sir."

Scott was more reserved. "All in a day's work."

Lattimore's genial expression resolved into its usual neutral. "Now, about this other matter of X. Agent Lucca and Officer Jamieson, would you follow me? I have someone I want you to meet."

CHAPTER THIRTY

Cole made her mind a blank as she dressed. She put on a sports bra, tee, and cargo pants, under which she'd strapped her snub-nose pistol to her calf with nylon webbing. Then she put on her heaviest all-terrain boots with steel toes and stuffed her cuffs inside.

She blocked all other thoughts from her mind as she checked the equipment on her belt. *Be methodical. Be thorough.* Responding to a crisis required using muscle-memory skills and daily mental focus to get into the right frame of mind.

Her weapon was loaded and holstered, with an extra magazine attached. She checked her Taser, flashlight, pepper spray, handcuffs, and remote-control button that would allow her to release Hugo from the rear of her patrol vehicle even if she was out of sight. She looked at it a moment and then took the button off her belt and shoved it into her bra.

She was a police K-9 officer. She was ready to answer a call for help. Search and rescue. Hugo was part of her definition of herself as a K-9 police officer. They were a unit: one.

She refused to second-guess herself as she strapped her belt on. When she was certain she had everything she needed, she grabbed her Kevlar vest and windbreaker with MONTGOMERY COUNTY POLICE stenciled in block letters on the back.

She strapped Hugo's K-9 police collar on.

They'd been inactive for two long boring weeks, while she was a desk jockey for her unit. It wasn't punishment, her sergeant assured her. But it felt like punishment. The department was trying to wait out the notoriety that had put her face all over the media.

The latest episode of Shajuanna's reality show, the one showing Cole's cover being blown, had garnered the highest ratings of any cable show that week. She had a hit show on her hands. Moreover, Shajuanna was now an A-list celebrity, making all the major network talk shows, morning and evening, giving her a forum for her once maligned fighting-dogs rehabilitation efforts. And a new platform, one that promised that a portion of the proceeds from Eye-C's new album would go to start a legal fund for people who had been falsely profiled for crimes they didn't commit. According to entertainment media, the response was overwhelmingly positive.

Cole certainly didn't expect a note from Shajuanna, thanking Cole for her part in making her show a hit, but Cole felt a little better knowing that the worst day of her life was balanced by Shajuanna's new success. After all, Shajuanna was a wronged party in all this. So far, the threats about lawsuits hadn't been followed through. Maybe they were even.

Cole blew out her breath. Even so, she could do with a little peace and quiet.

There'd been a lot of teasing to face on the job. Hard, merciless teasing. But behind it she eventually noticed a grudging admiration that she had been tapped for a federal task force when none of them had been. The more she smiled or ignored the taunts of the jealous, the more a kind of respect grew around her. It would wear off. Such things did. But for now, she wrapped it around her like a life jacket. The experience had isolated her and she wasn't sure when and if she would ever feel completely part of her department again.

She couldn't talk about the ongoing investigation, couldn't even indicate where and what she'd been doing, even though she and Scott had broken the case after they were officially relieved of their duties. The main culprits behind the puppy-mule trade had not yet been identified but things were in motion for that to happen.

As she faced her fourth and final night of her first weekly patrol after more than a month off the streets, she tried to look on the bright side. At least while doing night patrol she wouldn't have to deal with the jokers or tolerate the curious stares of the envious. She was still too raw to put any of what had happened into perspective. She just needed to get through the night.

So, maybe she wasn't cut out to be a badass after all. Not everyone was. That didn't mean she couldn't do her job, and do it well.

Finally she reached for her cell phone. Scott had left her a text. It said GOOD LUCK. He, too, was officially back on duty after two weeks of riding a desk. Tonight, they were both going back to work.

"So then I said, 'Not if you want to keep both of your hands.' Taser must have read my mind because he lunged, barking and showing every scary tooth in his head. That's when the suspect decided that being arrested was going to be the better choice." Sandra Martin's laughter was as strong as the paper cup of coffee she held.

"At least you've seen some action." Cole anchored a hip on the edge of Sandra's cruiser. "My patrol so far this week has been quiet as a grave."

Sandra was the other female K-9 officer in the Montgomery County Police Department. Her partner was a golden-pelted Malinois named Taser. She'd met Sandra coming out of an all-night convenience store located where their patrols intersected. Cole was there to take a bathroom break and catch her own cup of coffee.

The radio crackled on Sheila's shoulder. After a brief exchange she shoved her braids back up under her hat and picked up her to-go cup from the hood of her cruiser. "I'm out. Some of us got a job to do."

Cole nodded. "See you this weekend for softball practice?"

"You know it." Sandra slid into the seat. "We gotta get our props back from PGCPD."

Cole walked toward the front of the store. She really didn't want any three A.M. coffee, often so thick it tasted like fuel oil. Nor did she need any Slim Jims or Little Debbie anything but it was not the best hour for shopping for anything wholesome. Even the bananas in a basket at checkout, she knew from experience, would be oily black by this hour.

At the corner of her eye she saw a van pull in to pump gas. She had parked her cruiser near the front door but off to one side. Hugo was in the front seat watching her. He always did that, watched her every move from the driver's seat when she left the vehicle. Otherwise he was content to ride in back where he was more protected. She waved on her way past, thinking she should walk him when she returned. Sometimes she just sat in the parking lot of this place on her break and ate a small bag of whatever seemed

the most harmless to her health as she watched the wee
hours of Rockville crawl by.

Once inside, she went quickly to the ladies', then the
drink cases, found a bottle of latte and grabbed a package
of almonds and headed for the counter.

The young man behind the counter looked less interested in her paying than in the game on the small TV behind the counter. She could probably have walked out and
he wouldn't have cared. She plunked her items down.

He glanced at her in surprise. "Oh hey, didn't see you
come in."

Cole looked at him. "You really want to pay more attention to who comes in here and when they leave. It's the
right time of night to be robbed."

"Uh-huh." He nodded, rubbernecking over his shoulder as he rang up her purchase. "Sure thing, Officer."

Cole waved off the offer of a bag and collected her items.
"Good night."

She saw a man coming toward the door as she pushed
through it. She paused and allowed him to enter. He was
big, ponytailed, with a tattooed neck and arms exposed
by his T-shirt. She skimmed the vulgar threat printed across
his chest and met his eyes. He jerked his head in greeting
under his cap as he moved through the door. She waited
until he was several steps past her before she exited.

The van was now pulled up before the store with a space
between it and her cruiser on her driver's side. No one in
the front seat. She surveyed the service station area. No
one else in sight. A single car drove up, slowed, spotted
her cruiser, and sped away. Hugo was watching her as she
juggled bottle and nuts to release her weapon in its holster.
Her heart was banging yet there was no clear reason.

The man exited the store and moved toward the driver's side of the van. She watched until he opened the driv-

er's side door. Relaxing a fraction, she set her goodies on the hood of her cruiser and with one hand on the butt of her weapon reached to open her door.

The front passenger door of the van swung open behind her.

She spun around, drawing her weapon, but it was too late. A man emerged from the van and grabbed her. He twisted her arm viciously to make her drop the gun. The van's driver had rounded the van and joined them, forcing a cloth with a chemical smell over her nose and mouth, choking her and preventing her from screaming. The first man caught her arms and pulled them behind her so quickly that she couldn't reach the button to release Hugo, who was barking and scratching, trying to get through the glass.

She fought hard, kicking and biting and trying to reach the Taser on her belt, but they had come prepared to eliminate her options. She connected with thigh and gut more than once before they simply picked her up bodily. Twisting and kicking, she tried every move she'd ever been taught but her arms and legs were losing coordination. No, she was losing consciousness.

The thought so enraged her she kicked out wildly when she was lifted up, her steel-toed boot connecting with muscled flesh.

Blinded by the cloth, she didn't see it coming. The blow of a fist jerked her head back. Through a burst of stunning pain brilliant comets shot across her vision. She tasted blood as she was dumped in the back of the van. And then she was sliding down into a suffocating slack-limbed blankness.

The coordinates the county police dispatcher had just given Cole's backup team were for an area of Montgomery County Scott didn't know well. That didn't stop him from driving like a street racer as his GPS locked onto the location.

He looked back over his shoulder. Hugo and Izzy were with him, in the back of his truck. That was little comfort. No one yet had eyes on the target.

Ever since they'd been alerted to Cole's abandoned cruiser in the convenience store parking lot he had been going nuts behind his calm exterior.

Locked inside the cruiser, Hugo had been beside himself, barking and whining and tearing at the upholstery.

No one had wanted to go near the distraught K-9. But Scott knew exactly what the Bouvier was feeling. The same adrenaline-pumped rage and sense of helplessness was running through his veins like burning jet fuel. Cole had been taken, and neither he nor Hugo had been there to help and protect her.

When released, Hugo had jumped out of the vehicle and into Scott's truck without any coaching.

The guy behind the counter at the convenience store barely remembered Cole's presence, until reminded that she'd bought the bottle of coffee and package of nuts the police had found dropped by her driver's side door.

Scott had questioned the cashier himself.

"I only called 911 because that big scary dog was barking and acting crazy, and scaring my customers. I seen the lady cop. Only I didn't see nothing after she left. Dude came in, arguing about the gas pump not being honest. How he was being cheated of pennies per gallon. By the time he stomped out, nothing else was going on in the parking lot. Dude, I have no idea where the lady cop went. I swear."

Scott had a few ideas, and each of them a worse scenario than the one before it.

If not for the wire on Cole, the police wouldn't have a clue where to look for her. As it was, they'd lost precious time. Surveillance be damned.

He tightened his fingers on the steering wheel, tearing through the dark well above the posted speed limit.

For the past four days, Cole had been under constant, if distant, surveillance by him. He couldn't be spotted shadowing her. For a change, the authorities agreed: X wasn't going to back off. He was just waiting for his next opportunity. Though there was no obvious gain in his need to hurt, humiliate, and harass Scott, they doubted X would cease until he was once again locked up.

Cole's night duty made her the likely target. Alone, after dark, patrolling lonely areas with Hugo. X wouldn't be able to resist.

Cole was more than happy to be their bait.

Scott had had his doubts. But DEA and the Montgomery County Police Department were in agreement to let her try. Scott fought for and won a spot on the surveillance team. He was the only agent assigned to devote full-time to surveillance. He had to be in on the takedown. This time, he wouldn't let Cole down.

Hugo pushed his muzzle through the opening, whining as he gazed at Scott. "I know how you feel, big fella. We'll get our chance. I promise you."

To keep himself focused, Scott went over in his mind what he knew. Cole was a professional law-enforcement officer and should have been able to hold her own against X until backup arrived.

She was supposed to signal for help the moment she spotted him. Why hadn't she signaled them as planned? And why had Hugo not been released?

The van. X wasn't working alone this time.

Scott shoved aside all thoughts about what that might mean. His gaze went to the GPS. Her signal was still moving. He would find her. He and Hugo would save her. That was the only scenario he could allow his mind to entertain.

And when he got his hands on X . . .

* * *

Cole didn't know how long she was out. Her head pounded. Her stomach heaved with every jolt and buck of the van flooring beneath her. Her arms were tied behind her, allowing her to bounce helplessly as the vehicle suddenly swerved when someone up front shouted, "Turn here."

She bit back a moan as she rolled over, not wanting anyone to know she was conscious. She ignored the taste of blood in her mouth and tested her bonds. They had used plastic handcuffs, pulled so tight her fingers tingled. She opened her eyes a slit as she tried to assess her situation. Think and assess.

She was no longer wearing her tactical belt. She lay flat on her stomach. No way to tell if they had taken the gun strapped to her ankle. Probably. They were efficient. She rolled a little to the right and left as the van left smooth paved road for rough gravel. Nothing in her pockets. No cell. No badge.

She shivered, chilled by sweat from the fight. But she fought the fear threatening to close over her head. She wasn't alone. She was under surveillance. The police, and Scott, would arrive soon. Meantime, she had to stay alive.

What did she know? She heard two men's voices. She didn't get a good look at them, but she knew neither of them was X. And they weren't amateurs. She'd been attacked and disarmed by men familiar with police and military tactics.

The van slowed. She lifted her head to try to see out but it was a panel van, no windows.

"Fuck it. He said there was a park here somewhere."

"Turn off there. Yeah. There's his hog."

The van rolled to a stop but Cole continued to bounce in rhythm to shocks badly in need of replacement. She choked on the irony. As if it mattered whether or not the shocks in the van that snatched her were safe. *She* was not safe.

"She's coming round." Someone reached back and grabbed her ankle. A whimper escaped her as she kicked out in fear.

"Shit!" She was released.

Maybe she was making things worse for herself. How could it be worse?

She swallowed as the doors up front opened and slammed, and then the panel door was sliding back.

There was a click and light flooded the interior from a high-beam flashlight probably taken from her belt. "Out, bitch."

Two pairs of hands reached for her. She cowered back in spite of herself. Then redoubled back on anger. She needed to stay angry. Fear was the enemy. Help was on the way. She had to think her way through the next minutes. Stay alive. That was all that was required.

They hauled her to her feet on grass and stepped back, two male silhouettes no more detailed than bulky shadows behind the high beam. They were taking no chances on being identified, if caught.

"Well, look who we got. Rhino's bitch."

Cole's gaze jerked left. X stood several few feet away. Easier to see because he wasn't behind the beam of light aimed at her. Confirmation of target. This was good.

What else? They were in a parklike area with grass and distant trees, and the sound of running water, and road traffic. They couldn't have taken her far.

"You've abducted a police officer. This isn't going to end well for you. You should let me go."

X moved in on her quickly and grabbed her chin in a hard hand, jerking her face up to his. "You don't get to talk until I say so. Open your mouth again and I'll stuff it until you choke."

Cole met his gaze. Straight-up bat-shit crazy. Nothing there to negotiate with.

He released her. "You get her gear?"

"What we could before we rolled her up."

X looked back at her, a grin pressing back the rows of wrinkles in his cheeks until he looked like a Joker mask. "She's a cop. She'll be carrying concealed. Cut her hands loose but hold her."

The plastic around her wrists came free as the two men each grabbed a wrist and hooked a foot behind each of hers, forcing her to a wide stance.

Cole gritted her teeth, not wanting to give X the satisfaction of her fear. But the men holding her had to feel the shivers rocking her.

Then she stood taut between them as X moved in to frisk her. He found her ankle holster and removed it. She didn't fight that. Even when his hand slid up between her thighs she looked straight ahead, giving away none of the revulsion she felt. His hand moved to the apex of her thighs. He cupped her mons and squeezed, hard. "I'm going to do a cavity check next. You know what that means."

Cole bit her broken lip, tasted more blood. Her heart beat in strokes so heavy she shook with each one.

Help was coming. Stay alive. Lots of variations on what "alive" meant. Sooner would be better than later.

She thought she heard a siren in the distance. That wouldn't be surprising. The men around her didn't seem to think so, either.

"Bring her along."

They half carried, half dragged her farther into the clearing of the deserted park. In the distance the hiss of traffic could be heard but the streetlights didn't penetrate very far. Only the yellowish glow of the sky overhead reassured her that they were still in a suburban environment. Yet they were enveloped in darkness so dense no idle passersby would notice them.

They pulled her into the ring of light made by the head-lights of the van.

X moved to within six feet of her. "Free up the bitch."

After they had stripped her of her belt and Kevlar vest worn under her uniform shirt, Cole was let go so quickly she stumbled and had to catch herself.

"Let's party, bitch."

She looked up at X. He held a wicked-looking knife in his hands.

She backed up instinctively but the two other men were behind her. One shoved her back toward X, careful to stay out of range of a kick or fist.

X moved in closer, the Ka-Bar blade reflecting silver-blue light off its edge. "The Pagans have a ritual. When a bitch becomes the property of a gang member she becomes gang property. You been banging Rhino, and he hasn't shared. Tonight you get to pay his debt. Here's how it's done."

Cole looked away and tried not to hear what he was saying because the words were too ugly. She knew they were going to give her nightmares even if she really didn't listen hard.

He beckoned her with the edge of his blade. "Step over here and take off your clothes."

"No." Her response was pure instinct.

He stalked over to her and made a slashing movement. Cole didn't feel a thing but her tee ribboned open from neck to waistline. "Take off your clothes."

Cole's teeth were chattering so hard she could barely make her mouth work as she gathered up her shirt. "Come over here and take them off."

The smile that spread across X's face changed him from a run-of-the-mill lunatic into a cold-blooded killer. "You just bought yourself a world of trouble."

She took another backward step, preferring her odds with his friends. They laughed but gave her space. Wolves around a wounded prey, they smelled blood and were eager for more. Except she wasn't prey. She wasn't a sheep.

She looked up at him, using her will to survive to steady her nerves. "You kill a police officer, they will hunt you down." This much, she knew was true.

"I ain't gonna kill you." X moved his blade back and forth in slow figure eights, like a magician trying to hypnotize a volunteer. "You'll just wish you were dead."

The push from behind sent her stumbling headfirst into X's embrace, a grip that held a knife. She scrambled desperately to right herself before she reached him.

The blade passed over her shoulder and down, this time slicing through her sports bra. She refused to register the hit. Fisting a hand over his shirtfront, she brought her knee up as fast and hard as she could.

She pushed herself away from him as he doubled over in pain, knife slashing out wildly. The momentum sent her sprawling. The air went out of her in a hard push. Her eyes filled with dust and began to tear even as she tried to get to her knees.

She didn't know which of them heard it first. Engines gunning through the night, and then the bounce of headlights through the trees as vehicles tore up the gravel road toward them.

The blip on the GPS had stopped moving five minutes ago, just about the time Scott's spit dried up.

He was in southern Montgomery County, in a parkland, if one could call the wooded stretch between the main road and the embankment of the Potomac River a park.

As he swung around a curve in the unpaved road, the woods opened up into a broad stretch of grass. His headlights lit up a van. Beyond it, in the vehicle's headlights, he saw a figure slumped on the ground with the letters MCPD on her back. Three men surrounded her, one holding a knife.

Scott sprang from the truck, leaving the door open, weapon drawn. "DEA! Drop your weapons! And get down on your knees!"

"Fuck this!" One man broke and ran back toward the van. The second man hesitated only a few seconds more before heading off in the darkness toward the trees. Neither of them interested Scott. He concentrated on X.

X grabbed Cole by the back of her shirt and pulled her up against his chest. He held a knife, oily with blood, to her throat.

Scott could see she was bleeding from her nose and mouth, and there was blood on her shirtfront. He swallowed down his emotion. None of that was important until the scene was secured. He steadied his gun as he moved slowly forward. He might get only one shot off. "Let her go, X. You got what you wanted. I'm here."

"Shit. You want me to do her first then deal with you? I'll do it. I will do it."

"I'm not going to give up my gun. You know why. You were Blue, too, Officer Harney."

"Fuck you! I was SOG. And now Pagan. You weren't ever one of us."

Scott glanced back as the van spun out behind him. If he were going to be run over— No, flashing police lights were spinning through the trees. Sirens erupted, splitting the silence.

X swung Cole around, fisted one edge of her shirt and brought his knife up to within inches of her face. "Ever wonder why they call me X?"

The deep guttural barking of an enraged canine coming at him full force jerked his gaze from her face.

Cole ducked, screaming, "Hugo! *Fass! Schnell!*"

The force of Hugo's attack knocked both of them off their feet. She heard X cry out as Hugo's powerful jaws closed over his arm. She grabbed for his knife hand but he threw her off. And then the awful sound of Hugo yelping in pain.

The knife. Cole scrambled to her feet as Scott reached her. "Oh God. Hugo!"

X had regained his feet and sprinted toward his bike.

Scott lifted his weapon but Hugo had regained his footing and was tearing after the biker. He didn't doubt Hugo's ability to close the distance.

He looked down at Cole. "How badly are you hurt?"

She shook her head though her hand was clamped over her arm. "Help Hugo."

"Stay here." Scott took off on foot after man and dog.

X swung a leg over his bike and rolled the throttle. As he began to move Scott cursed. But Hugo moved into overdrive.

As X came around, intending to head for cover in the trees, Hugo launched his heavy black body at the driver. The weight and momentum dropped the bike.

Scott heard a scream as the bike came down on X's leg and then another as Hugo clamped down on his arm, growling and tugging and swinging as he held on for all he was worth.

When he reached them Scott stepped on X's knife hand and pointed his gun at his head. "Don't give me a reason."

CHAPTER THIRTY-ONE

"He's going to be fine. The knife just scraped along his ribs. His heavy coat probably confused his attacker. He missed the gut."

Cole clutched Hugo to her as the vet examined him. "Will he need stitches?"

"A few. And antibotics. Leave him with me overnight."

"Only if you promise to take the best care of him. Anything he needs. He saved my life tonight."

"He'll have everything he needs, Officer Jamieson." The vet patted her shoulder. "Now I insist you see about yourself, young lady." He offered Scott a significant look over her head. "You're bleeding all over my examining room."

Scott had stood grimly to one side of Cole, arms folded, as Hugo was examined. Cole had insisted on bringing Hugo to the vet before she would even think about going to the hospital to be examined. But now that the vet had lifted Hugo out of her arms Scott saw with a surge of alarm that the front of her tee was soaked with blood that couldn't be all Hugo's.

"Damn, Jamieson. You're hurt."

He jerked off his windbreaker and wrapped it around her before picking her up in his arms and carrying her out to his truck.

Cole, released from worry about Hugo, snuggled in against him. "I like it when you get all angry alpha male."

"Shut up. You're woozy with blood loss. I can't take advantage." His voice was light but his expression was grim.

Scott drove to the emergency room with the same urgency he had driven to her rescue, one arm holding Cole tight against him while his cherry top flashed red through the night.

"Superficial wounds." The ER doctor held Cole's chart in his hand. "Officer Jamieson has lost blood and is in mild shock. We're keeping her overnight but she'll be fine."

Scott nodded, his eyes hooded and expression nonactive. "What else?"

"We did a bit of suturing. Luckily we were able to pull in a plastics doc to do her cheek and the nose. It isn't broken but she may want to see him again if it doesn't heal to her liking."

Scott swallowed. "Did he . . . are any of the wounds X's?"

"Excuse me?"

Scott made two crossing slash marks with a finger.

"No, nothing like that. There's a superficial cut down her sternum and one on her . . ." He paused. "Are you family?"

"Yes. Husband." Scott doubted any of Cole's colleagues standing nearby, who had rushed to hospital for moral support, would contradict him.

"Very well." The doctor pulled him aside from the others before extracting a photo from the file he carried. "It looks worse than it is."

Scott saw with the professional, detached part of his mind that the cuts on Cole's exposed chest were superficial. Her battered face had been cleaned up. He knew the bruising and swelling would subside. But the primitive, protect-my-mate instinct was harder to convince. "Was the suspect also brought here?"

"Yes. The police brought him in first, about an hour ago. He's suffering from a crushed leg, exhaust-pipe burns, and two serious dog bites."

"That's too bad. I was hoping he was really hurt."

Scott turned and walked away from the gaping gaze of the dedicated caregiver.

"I'll look like Frankenstein in a bikini."

Scott's eyes lit up. "A bikini. There's an image."

Cole rolled her head on the pillow away from him, toward the window of her hospital room. After a moment, a sound suspiciously like a sob broke the silence.

"You're not crying?" Scott's stomach hit the floor. He came around on the other side of the bed. "Cole?"

She shut her eyes so she wouldn't have to look at him.

"Cole!" Her eyes opened.

He was standing over her, still wearing his clothes from the night before. He wore a navy T-shirt stained with her blood, a weary expression, wary gaze, and a heavy stubble. He scrubbed his face with a hand. "I'm not good at this sort of thing. But, dammit, I don't care if you look like you've been trussed up like a Thanksgiving turkey. I didn't fall for a few unblemished inches of skin."

"I'm not being vain." Cole sucked in her lower lip and winced. It was twice its normal size.

Scott moved in beside her bed and took her hand. "You're the most unvain person I know. Undies choice aside." His heart did a flip when that drew a small smile from her. "So, you'll have a few scars. Tiny scars," he amended when she frowned. "The doctor said a plastics guy did your face. No scarring there." He crossed his fingers out of her line of sight. "You brought down a bad guy. Helped catch puppy-mule drug smugglers. You deserve to have some proof of your courage. Would you rather have a tattoo?"

Cole watched with quiet eyes that intensified as he held her gaze. He knew she was seeing him as she first had, like he was the best man in the whole world. It scared him to see that. It was something he couldn't live up to. But he was going to try. So help him God, he was going to try.

"You're a good man, Agent Lucca."

He shook his head and took her hand and leaned over to kiss her forehead. "I'm an ass. An idiot. You deserve better but you're stuck with me."

She gazed up at him, seeing weariness and worry in every line of his face. "If I'm so wonderful, why do you look so awful?"

Laughter sputtered out of Scott, the first carefree laughter he could remember for a long time. And then he took her face very carefully in his hands and kissed her even more gently.

She looked at him through wet eyes. "You really don't mind?" She made a gesture toward her face and torso.

He reached out and ran his hand over the contours of her body until he could cup a breast beneath her hospital gown. "You'll have proof to go with the story you tell our kids of what a badass their mama is."

Her eyes got bigger than he'd ever seen them. "Our kids?"

Scott smiled but sat down in the chair he'd not slept in as he sat by her side. He'd said enough. Probably too much. And he had nothing left, for now.

The Nikki he'd met was long gone. Yardley had been right about that. This woman, Cole, was stronger, more assured. And the miracle of it was, she was still with him. She reached for his hand, confirming that.

CHAPTER THIRTY-TWO

"It's a jurisdiction fight. The feds want X, formerly known as Agent Alphonso Harney of the LAPD, brought up on charges for having divulged information about an ongoing investigation. Your department is protesting that they have first dibs because he assaulted a police officer in their jurisdiction. Then there are the state police in Virginia, New Jersey, and Maryland who want their pound of flesh for violations, too. Meanwhile, X violated his parole in so many ways that he's back finishing his time while he awaits two or more trials on these new charges."

Scott looked over at Cole, who sat with her legs tucked up under her on her sofa. Hugo sat on the sofa beside her, providing her with a very unnecessary woolly blanket on this Labor Day weekend. He was reporting information to her on the disposition of X's case that he'd brought back from D.C. this afternoon.

"He'd been a cop." She shook her head. "I still don't get it. How could he switch sides like that?"

Scott was silent for a moment. "He was in Special Operations when he went undercover to infiltrate a gang.

The usual scenario is you step over the line so many times you stop seeing it, and start resenting anyone who points that out. In Harney's case, he killed a man while under-cover. Tried to make it look like a clean hit. But there were too many rumors of revenge. The department did what most do. They covered it up. No one talked. He was retired. So he came East, where he wasn't known, and exchanged the blue code for gang code where he was already accepted."

Cole sighed, stroking Hugo absently. In their concern for each other, they were hardly ever more than arm's reach away.

Hugo was fine. Except for the shaved place on his belly where stitches went in, no one would ever have known anything was wrong. Scott had proof of that every day when he took him out for exercise.

Cole was getting better, too. During the past ten days her face had healed nicely. The nose was not broken. And the discoloration had subsided enough for makeup to perform miracles. She was on medical leave, however, for a few more weeks. Her department agreed. She'd been through a lot and needed to recoup and reassess.

But Cole was bored beyond belief by the restrictions placed on her. Scott had been sitting on her like an egg that needed to be hatched. He worked most days by computer from her home. When he did go into D.C., like this morning, he was back like a boomerang before dark.

Worst of all, he'd become a monk.

Cole fidgeted with the remains of a sandwich he'd brought her for dinner. All those weeks they'd lived together undercover, there'd always been this red-hot current running between them, even when, no, especially when they were resisting touching each other. She had only to enter a room to feel his eyes on her with a hunger that kept her humming with awareness.

Now. Since X was taken down. Nothing.

Cole stole a glance at him. He looked at ease, slouched down in that chair with Izzy sleeping with her head propped on one of his shoes. But she knew better. He had that edgy vibe going on. His dimples were nowhere to be seen. He was a cop on guard duty, even though she no longer needed surveillance.

Guilt. He felt guilty. And unworthy. And, so like a man, he was doing the exact opposite of what he wanted to do, to punish himself. Hence Agent Celibate, while he looked after her.

Cole tried not to, but it was getting really hard not to resent the loss of the badass man she'd fallen in love with, twice.

A nursemaid she hadn't needed after day two. Housemate, she didn't have any use for, either. Except it was nice he exercised Hugo in ways her stitches hadn't allowed.

What she needed was a lover, and a friend. And she had just formed an idea of how to get what she wanted.

She slanted a glance at Scott. "About your parents' bar-becue and open house this weekend."

Scott grunted. "I told them not to expect us."

"I'd like to go."

He glanced at her with sudden wariness. "Why?"

"I want to see the house renovation. Will you take me?"

He groaned so low Hugo lifted his head in curiosity. "Sure."

They arrived early enough to help with the preparations. While delighted to see *her* again—Scott's father went so far as to kiss her cheek—Scott and his father shook hands like prize fighters and then retreated to their corners: Scott to watch a ballgame while his father begged off to finish working on his office files.

"The house is gorgeous." Cole reached for a head of lettuce. She'd offered to make a green salad. "And finished so quickly."

"Yes, it's very nice to have a fresh coat of paint everywhere. Of course there are things lost that can't be replaced." She paused and, very much like her son, shook her head to toss off the emotion that threatened her. "We are blessed to be alive and whole."

She perked up. "Scott's father is doing remarkably well. His doctor said it was a wakeup call. Now my husband lets me feed him more vegetables and we've taken all red meat off the menu."

"I'm glad. We were so worried."

She glanced at Cole. "I'm not prying but I have to ask, how are you and Scott doing?"

Cole smiled. "We're well. We have some things to work out. It's a cliché. We were young and both made mistakes. This time we know what the potholes look like."

She reached out and squeezed Cole's arm. "I'm so very happy to hear that. I knew the very first time I saw you together that you were the best thing that had ever happened to him. He just glowed around you."

"Thank you for telling me that." Cole put her rinsed lettuce in a colander to drain. "May I ask you a sensitive question?"

"About what, dear?"

"Gabe. We met once but I know almost nothing about him."

Again, Cathy Lucca's eyes lost their brilliance but she nodded. "What would you like to know?

Cole dried her hands and turned toward Scott's mom. "Tell me about him. What was he like?"

Cathy continued peeling potatoes for boiling. "He was a beautiful child. Smart and curious about the world. There was a fire in his eyes practically from the day he was born.

He loved adventure. 'No' was a dare to him. Scared me to pieces."

She smiled at some memory. "He crawled out over the top of his crib before he could walk and never stopped moving. He was strong, so much energy. By three years old he'd tackle older boys on the playground just for an excuse to wrestle. He was physically fearless." Mrs. Lucca shook her head again as more memories spooled out behind her thoughts. "I told his father we'd need to channel that lust for a thrill, or he'd get into trouble we couldn't handle."

"Scott never mentioned Gabe being in trouble."

Cathy set her paring knife down to give Cole her full attention. "That's because we shielded Scott from most of his older brother's antics. Scott thought the sun rose and set on Gabe. And Gabe loved Scott, and his adoration. Scott was probably the only person Gabe never tested growing up. But Gabe was driven, loved the thrill of testing his limits. When he couldn't find a challenge, he went looking for it. Finally, we couldn't keep him from getting into trouble."

Cole licked her lips, wondering if she was pushing too hard, but she had to know, for Scott's sake. "What kind of trouble?

Cathy looked away from Cole and returned to peeling. "There were a few minor things at first, stealing a beer from the fridge, smoking with some friends in the boys' restroom at school. Most of it was typical kid stuff but the summer he was fifteen he was arrested for boosting a car."

"He stole a car?" Cole couldn't control her surprise.

She sighed. "Gabe said he didn't know the car was stolen. That he just went joyriding with friends. The police let them go with a warning to the parents. But, a few days later, two of Gabe's so-called friends robbed the house of the man whose car had been stolen. It seems they had found the owner's house keys in the glove compartment when they stole the car. The police came and arrested all the boys involved in the car theft with breaking and entering and burglary, as well as grand theft auto."

"Why didn't I know any of this?"

Both women looked up guiltily to find Scott standing in the doorway to the family room.

His mother's cheeks pinked. "Scott, how long have you been standing there?"

He leaned a shoulder against the jamb. "Keep talking, Mom."

She straightened up, putting on her family-court judge face. "You should understand your father and I were trying to protect Gabe, and you. You were just ten years old."

Scott was silent.

Cole looked from mother to son, wanting to break the stalemate. "What happened. Gabe didn't go to jail?"

"No." John Lucca had appeared in the doorway opposite, coming in from the living room side of the kitchen. "Let me tell him, Cathy." He looked at Scott. "The D.A. was one of those hotshots, trying to make a name for himself by being hard on crime. He wanted to try the boys as adults. But your mother had clout because of her position on the court bench. Gabe's lawyer worked a deal for Gabe by promising the judge that if she gave him probation, we'd send him to a military academy for his four years of high school."

Cathy Lucca nodded. "It broke my heart to send Gabe away. But we were afraid for him. So we made the sacrifice to send him away."

John came over to put his arm around his wife's

shoulders but he spoke to Scott. "Your mother and I were trying to preserve Gabe's future, give him something to aim for."

Scott's face was stiff with emotions held in check as he looked at his father. "You should have told me. *Gabe* should have told me."

"I think he was ashamed. He didn't want to spoil your view of him as big brother."

Scott snorted. "So, instead, you rode me so hard. Made me believe I was less than because I wasn't like Gabe."

"I hoped to hell you wouldn't be like Gabe." His father's voice carried in the kitchen. "Son, I watched you day after day growing up, trying to be like your brother. Coming home bloodied after some school-yard fight where you'd tried some moves Gabe had taught you, so sad you couldn't even cry. It scared your mother and me to see you trying to imitate him. Gabe seemed to have been born with nine lives. Not like the rest of us. You were—"

"Weak?" Scott's expression was one of challenge.

His father sighed. "No, normal. Maybe we were too harsh. We didn't mean it like that. We just wanted different things for you."

"I'm different."

A corner of his father's mouth lifted. "And I'm grateful." He hugged his wife closer. "Gabe was great at a lot of things. He found his destiny in a love of country and duty. That became his reason for living. It served him better than we could ever have hoped.

"But we were always afraid he would go too far. I could see it in his eyes. He'd risk too much. Do more than anyone could reasonably expect. Eventually something got the best of him."

For several moments the only sound in the kitchen was the ticking of the clock on the wall as the sadness of the loss of a much-loved son and brother moved like a living thing among them.

Finally Cole moved to stand beside Scott but she didn't touch him. "I know I'm not part of this family. But, Mr. Lucca, you talk only about Gabe. What did you want for Scott?"

Her question seemed to surprise him. "Scott knows."

Scott gave his head a quick tight shake as grief and anger seemed to war within him. "I don't know. You never bothered to tell me."

The two men looked at each other across the width of a kitchen and a lifetime of misunderstanding. Cole held her breath, realizing she might just have asked the question that would tear them apart forever.

John seemed to tremble and then he spoke. "I wanted you to be the son I could do normal things with. Fish, talk sports and politics." He paused to draw in a long breath, as if every word was costing him. "We wanted you to marry, be a family man. One who'd give us grandchildren." His gaze flicked toward Cole but didn't stay. "I wanted you to be the kind of man who shoulders responsibility and doesn't walk away when the demands get rough."

Scott stared at his father a long time. "You could have just told me."

"We did." His mother came up to him and put her hand on Scott's cheek. "Over and over, we told you, you're not your brother. You needed to live your own life. Find your own way."

Scott glanced over her head at his father. "I thought that was your way of telling me I wasn't good enough. That I could never match up to Gabe so I should stop embarrassing myself, and you, with my failures."

John's mouth twisted, as if in pain. "Maybe I did a

crappy job. Your mother says I preach instead of teach."
He lifted his head and squared his shoulders, as if daring
anyone to contradict him. "I could have done better. I see
how you avoid us these days. You've moved on in your
life, without us. But I did what I thought was right at the
time."

Something flickered in Scott's face. "And now?"

His father scowled at him. "Fine. Have your pound of
flesh. I was wrong."

"An apology?" A corner of Scott's mouth sketched up
as he reached to check his pulse. "No, still ticking. Thought
I'd died and gone to heaven."

His father's scowl deepened but his eyes brightened.
"Don't get cocky with me, son."

And then he and Scott were moving toward each other.

Cole's heart contracted with emotion as she turned
quickly and walked away, leaving the Luccas with their privacy.

Maybe she had made things better. At least the truth was
out, and it was a truth Scott had needed to know for more
than half his life.

Two hours later, wandering past picnic tables filled with
enough food for three times the twenty guests at the barbecue, Cole thought she found the answer.

Scott and his dad were arguing, and laughing, about the
best way to marinate chicken for the barbecue.

It was at this moment she realized that in all their time
together she had seldom heard Scott laugh. Oh, he could
be silly and found things funny. But there was most often
a bit held back, even in his laughter. It was as if he thought
he didn't deserve full-on soul-shaking happiness.

Too bad. Because she was about to deliver it in daily
doses from now on.

She waited until he passed her, then snagged his arm

and drew him inside and up the stairs to the bedrooms on the second floor. Once there, she realized yet another surprise. She had never spent a night under this roof.

"Which room is yours?"

Scott pointed to the last door on the left.

Cole moved toward it, pulling him by the hand. When they were both through the entry, she shut the door and looked around.

It was a teenage boys' room. And, amazingly, it hadn't been touched during the vandalism. It was like a time capsule of the Lucca boys. She could almost smell the long absent locker-room dirty-sock ambiance. It was full of evidence of growing-boy stuff, from *Star Wars* to *The Sopranos*. An *Independence Day* poster hung beside one for *Tomb Raider* and another for *Call of Duty*. A PlayStation sat on the desk between twin beds. Cole moved over and tapped the poster of Lara Croft. "Impressive rack."

Scott grinned at her. "I was more in lust with her hardware."

After a perusal of a room that time forgot she wandered back to the door and punched the lock. She turned and leaned her back against it.

Scott shook his head. "What are you doing?"

"Making sure you can't get away."

"Why would I want to do that?"

"Because we are going to have wild monkey sex in your old bedroom right now while your parents are entertaining downstairs."

The look on his face was comical. "Ah, Cole, that's probably not a good—"

"That's the point. Live on the edge. Feel fully alive."

He smirked. "Come over here and I'll let you feel how fully alive I'm getting."

Cole shook her finger at him. "Not just yet. Show me what you got."

He ducked in his chin. "Listen, Cole—"

"Take it off, Agent Lucca. Take it all off."

A slow grin pushed those sexy dimples into his cheeks as he reached for his T-shirt and pulled it over his head.

Cole sighed in appreciation of the view of all that smooth and ripped muscle. Abs for fingers to climb. Delts worth licking. And obliques to grip as she slid down his body. Nothing was really flat. His torso rippled and tucked and bulged just enough in all the right places. Yet he was no caricature of male beauty. He was real. Hair on his chest, a few scars that suddenly made her feel better about her new imperfection. He was not perfect, and all hers.

When her gaze met his again she felt her whole body become aroused.

"Keep going." Where had her breath gone?

Those damn dimples deepened. "Anybody ever tell you you're a nasty girl?"

"You're a bad influence."

"God, I hope so." He shucked off his boots and reached for his zipper. Camo pants hit the floor along with his briefs in quick shucking movements.

Cole smiled. Oh yes. They were going to have fun in the narrow confines of his bed. "Looks like you're happy to see me."

He made a little pumping action with his hips that surprised and delighted her, his erection dancing happily along. "Come and get it."

She watched him with a rapt fascination he'd never seen on any woman's face but hers. For him. All for him.

He sighed despite his assurance of what she had in mind, when she reached for her top. As she undressed before him he didn't see the thin lines of fading red or the bruises or anything but the lovely wonderful body of the woman he loved more than life.

When she reached for him, hand closing over his ready-to-go erection, he pulled her in and kissed her with everything he had to give.

And then he slid a hand between her legs and felt the glistening proof of her readiness for him.

He pulled her down on the bed beside him and kissed her until she was shivering. Then he lay back in what had once been a lonely boy's bed and pulled her astride.

He watched her face as she raised herself up and then slid her body down over his. He watched her mouth open in pleasure at the filling that almost stopped his heart.

When she began moving on him, he thought he might not last. But then she looked down at him, a hard little frown on her lovely face.

"Don't you dare. I've waited weeks."

He grinned back, grabbed her by the waist and gave her the ride of her life.

He filled his mouth with her breast and his mind with her cries of pleasure and let the world as he had known it slide off and drift away.

The sound of a woman's footsteps in the hallway, along with thumps and scampering that could only be Izzy and Hugo, startled them. Scott looked at Cole, tucked in the curve of his arm, and whispered in alarm, "Mom."

A knock sounded on the door. "No hurry in there. Just wanted to let you kids know the dogs are hungry. Oh, and dinner's ready when you are."

As the sound of Cathy's footsteps retreated back down the hall, Cole scrambled from the bed to unlock and open the door.

Ninety-five pounds of shaggy black Bouvier and sixty-four pounds of silky-smooth dark chocolate Lab bounded through the door and ran full-tilt toward Scott, who still lay in bed. They pounced on him together, barking in excitement as if let in on some game.

Smothering giggles with her hand, Cole approached the bed and looked down at Scott. "Are we ready?"

Scott sat up and reached for her, cupping her sweet naked ass in his palms. "For anything."

DON'T MISS THE NEXT BOOK IN D.D. AYRES'S
K-9 RESCUE SERIES!

PRIMAL FORCE

COMING OCTOBER 2015